LAURIE GRAHAM is a former *D*
and contributing editor of *She* magazine. She now lives
in Italy, writing fiction and radio drama scripts. *Gone
With the Windsors* is her ninth novel. Visit her website at
www.lauriegraham.com.

Visit www.AuthorTracker.co.uk for exclusive
information on your favourite HarperCollins authors.

From the reviews of *Gone with the Windsors*:

'Graham succeeds in crystallising the lives of a social set
whose *raison d'être* was the next poolside gin-fizz. Alongside
le tout Baltimore, we await to see how far Wallis will jeopar-
dise her hard-won security with Ernest for the title of "Queen
of Nowhere". It's a testament to Graham's pitch-perfect story-
telling that we care'   *Independent*

'Graham's sunny control makes the abdication crisis sound as
fresh and tangy as Wally's favourite dinner party dessert,
strawberry sherbet. Maybell Brumby is a wonderful, sassy
creation: not exactly one of your heart-of-gold heroines, but,
more entertainingly, one with a heart of gilt'   *Sunday Times*

'With an enviable sleight of hand, Laurie Graham
affectionately impales her hilariously oblivious heroine. I ate
this book right up'
                    MARY GUTERSON, author of *We Are All Fine Here*

'[An] absolute pleasure to read from start to finish … Wryly
observed secondary characters are also a joy … By infusing

her sharp satire and meticulous social observation with a certain sweetness, Laurie Graham proves herself a master of showing without ever needing to tell' *Time Out*

'Laugh-out-loud funny' *Daily Telegraph*

'Refreshing, honest and very funny ... enjoyable without being thoughtless, smart without being superficial' *Scotsman*

'Maybell Brumby is a marvellous comic creation'
Scotland on Sunday

'Laurie Graham is such a vivid, creative storyteller' *TLS*

By the same author

FICTION
The Man for the Job
The Ten O'Clock Horses
Perfect Meringues
The Dress Circle
Dog Days, Glenn Miller Nights
The Future Homemakers of America
The Unfortunates
Mr Starlight

NON-FICTION
The Parents' Survival Guide
The Marriage Survival Guide
Teenagers

LAURIE GRAHAM

Gone With the Windsors

HARPER PERENNIAL
London, New York, Toronto and Sydney

Harper Perennial
An imprint of HarperCollins*Publishers*
77–85 Fulham Palace Road
Hammersmith
London W6 8JB

www.harperperennial.co.uk
www.lauriegraham.com

This edition published by Harper Perennial 2006
1

First published by Fourth Estate 2005

A catalogue record for this book is
available from the British Library

ISBN-13 978-0-00-714676-5
ISBN-10 0-00-714676-0

Printed and bound in Great Britain
by Clays Ltd, St Ives plc.

To Howard

Gone with
the Windsors

10th March 1932, Sweet Air, Baltimore

Six months since Danforth Brumby surrendered to the first hint of kidney failure and left me a widow. It always was the risk in marrying an older man. Yesterday his headstone was raised, so now it's time to look to the future. I still have my youth and my looks. Men are already flocking to my side and women are pursuing me as always for my advice and my vivacious presence at their dinner tables. *Le tout* Baltimore is impatient for my return to society, so tomorrow I shall drive into town, place my chinchilla in cold storage, and order a selection of spring outfits from Madame Lucille. A new chapter opens.

13th March 1932

A letter from sister Violet. *Why not come to London, Maybell?* she begs. *It will lift you out of yourself. It's impossible to remain sad for long in a house full of children.*

Well, that is a matter of opinion.

Pips Waldo is here, she writes. *You always liked Pips. And Judson Erlanger. Remember him? He's married to one of the Chandos girls.*

I'll say I remember him! Judson Erlanger took me to the Princeton Ball.

It's getting to be a real Little Baltimore over here, she concludes. *And who knows, we may even find you another husband. Melhuish knows quite everyone.*

I have already endured thirteen years of Violet's condescension, brought on by her marriage to Donald Melhuish—*Lord* Melhuish as she reminds me with tedious regularity. The truth is, I could have snagged Melhuish for myself, had my tastes run to cold castles and men in skirts, but I allowed Violet to have him and I've said nothing since to disturb her smug satisfaction in her title and her connections and her lumpen Melhuish offspring. To some, it is given to tread the wilder track, to risk the ravine in order to conquer more majestic peaks, and I have always had a head for heights.

PS, she adds. *You might think of spending some time with Doopie. She has missed you dreadfully.*

So there we have it. Violet doesn't want me in London for the zest I would undoubtedly bring to her life, nor does she particularly intend to find me a lord to marry. Tired of playing the angel of mercy, she hopes simply to saddle me with the retard.

What a trial Doopie has been to us all, a regrettable afterthought in a family already perfectly adorned by myself and Violet. If people must have children, two is certainly enough. But our misguided parents would have her, and they would allow her to arrive on my birthday, too.

"Maybell," Father said, "you have the best birthday gift a girl could ask for."

I had hoped for a new donkey cart, not an attention-seeking brat of a sister.

They named her Eveline and doted on every smile she smiled and every mew she mewed, but Sister Eveline didn't impress me. Over and over, she'd allow a person to take away her pacifier, then look injured and start her sobbing. She never learned to say "No." Then, after she caught inflammation of the brain, there could be no doubt about it. The child was a vegetable.

"Slow" was the word Mother used. "Slow, but special."

The fact is, Eveline is stupid. Always was, always will be. I renamed her Stupid, but she's so dumb she can't even say it. "Doopie" is the best she has ever managed.

They tried her at Elementary School, but she was an embarrassment to us all, and it was soon decided that she would do just as well at home. She's handy with a needle, I suppose. She can knit and crochet. And she's quite the green-thumb, which used to endear her to Father.

"I had given up that *Ficus* for lost," he'd say, "but Eveline has raised it from the dead."

He claimed she knew every plant in the conservatory and talked to them like friends. Well, that says it all about Doopie's powers of communication.

"Bayba," she used to call me. And "Vite" was the best she ever managed for Violet.

"She does love you so," Mother used to tell me. "Her eyes don't leave you for an instant when you come into the room."

There has never been any question of Doopie marrying, though I believe I am the only one who ever took the trouble to inform her of this. In 1914, when Violet was coming out, it was decided that because of the threat of war I had better come out, too. Just as well, because the Prussians quite ruined the 1915 season. Doopie helped with the trimming of our gowns.

"We're invited to the Bachelor's Club Cotillion," I explained to her, "which is something that will never happen to you."

She just smiled. How much of what one says penetrates her brain one never can tell, but she always seems contented enough. The only question was what would become of her. Father seemed to think that two sisters and a Trust Fund answered the case, but I was never consulted. And when Danforth Brumby asked for my hand, nobody asked him if he'd mind having a half-wit in the attic someday.

Violet thought she'd made her escape, I guess, settling overseas. I suppose she thought an idiot couldn't be sent on a sea voyage. But when the time came, after Father passed over and Mother had to be placed in the care of a full-time nurse, it so happened that Brumby and I were much burdened with the renovations at Sweet Air. It would have been most unsuitable for Doopie to move in with us. She might have bumped into a marble pillar awaiting installation and brought it tumbling on top of her, or wandered into the path of some falling beam. It was safer by far to send her to Violet. We provided her with a chaperone, and they traveled first class, and everything has worked out for the best. From their army of peasant retainers, Violet and Melhuish have been able to furnish her with the simple companionship she requires and then, with the arrival of the babies, she has gained a nursery full of playmates.

So, I will not fall for Violet's sly attempt at luring me to England. I see her little game. She hopes to catch me while I'm weakened by grief, and change the arrangements for Doopie. Well, they seem perfectly satisfactory to me. I shall stay where I am and reign over Baltimore.

20th March 1932

Stepsons are sent to try us. The earth has barely settled on his father's grave, and Junior is demanding to know my plans for Sweet Air. Do I expect to stay on, alone in such a large and isolated house? And if I were to think of selling, he knows his father would have wanted the place kept in the family. Junior has never liked me. He's never forgiven me for replacing his sainted mother and making Danforth smile again. He obviously hopes to spook me out of the place and then pick it up at a knockdown price. He'll probably come around tapping on windows and making hooty owl noises. Well, he'll find Maybell Brumby is made of sterner stuff than that.

24th March 1932

Randolph Putnam pressed me to join him for luncheon today, but I declined. I find him too eager, and anyway I'd already agreed to take tea with Nora Sedley Cordle. One social obligation a day is enough for anyone, especially where Nora is involved. She sat behind her Gorham teapot, pretending friendship, but I read her like a book. She's hoping I'll give up Sweet Air, too. I always was a challenge to her social ambitions and now I suppose she's hoping I'll get me to a nunnery. Well, one thing I can tell her. She may be a Daughter of the American Revolution, but she had better learn to leave the ruffled neckline to those of us who can carry it off.

1st April 1932

The telephone keeps ringing and no one speaks. Today a package arrived, *The World's Most Chilling Ghost Stories.* Junior must take me for a fool.

3rd April 1932

Not sleeping well. I've instructed Missie not to answer the telephone after ten p.m.

7th April 1932

Randolph Putnam crossed the street to tell me how strained I look and recommend I take myself off to Palm Beach for a while. And leave Nora Sedley Cordle to consolidate the gains she made while I was in mourning? I think not!

10th April 1932

A quantity of horse manure was deposited on the front steps during the night. Missie says she was wakened by the sound of unearthly laughter and didn't close her eyes again till morning. Much theatrical yawning when she brought in my breakfast tray. Just what one needs at a time like this: the help falling asleep on their feet.

12th April 1932

Another letter from Violet. *The most extraordinary thing,* she wrote. *You'll never guess who has appeared on the scene.* She then digresses, recounting in unnecessary detail various antics of the brood. Ulick won a trophy for shooting. Flora wet her drawers at Lady Londonderry's. Rory fell off his new pony and knocked out two teeth. On and on it went without at all getting to the point. Violet's meanderings are so fatiguing. I had to turn two pages before I learned who it was who had so extraordinarily appeared on the scene. Minnehaha, no less. Wally Warfield! Well!

I ran into Pips Waldo, she writes, *who told me all she knew. Apparently, she's married to someone who was in the Guards but is now in business. They have a little place somewhere north of Marble Arch, and from what Pips has heard, she's quite on the make.*

I can imagine. Her mother didn't have a dime, but Wally never allowed that to hold her back. She had sharp elbows and a calculating mind, and she didn't miss a trick. Great fun though. School was much more interesting once Wally was around.

She came to Oldfields in 1911 and only because an uncle was paying for her. One didn't expect a new girl to start throwing her weight around, especially a girl who was a charity case, but on her first day she warned everyone that although her given name was Bessie Wallis, she only answered to Wallis or Wally. I could see her point. Bessie's more a name for a cow or a mammy.

But more often than not, we called her Minnehaha, because of her cheekbones and the way she braided her hair, and she quite liked it. She reckoned she was descended from Pocahontas, but then so do a lot of people. Pips Waldo and Mary Kirk and I were her main friends. Lucie Mallett was a hanger-on, but she never invited Wally to her home, because Mrs. Mallett knew all the dirt about Wally's mother taking in boarders and wearing lip rouge, and the Malletts had very closed minds. But we Pattersons were raised differently.

"Let me not judge my brother," Father always said.

Anyway, it was Lucie Mallett's loss. Wally and I used to have such fun. Inventing pains so we could stay in and read fashion tips instead of playing basketball. Drinking ginger ale and eating butter cookies after lights out. I was always sorry we drifted out of touch. So, now she's in London. Perhaps I'll reconsider. It would be nice to see Pips. It might be interesting to pick up the threads with Judson Erlanger. And with Wally around livening things up, I think I could even endure a few weeks of dull old Violet.

15th April 1932

Dead crows nailed to the gate posts this morning and yesterday. I leave for England next week. And if Randolph Putnam is so anxious to be of service to me, he can arrange for the locks to be changed. I don't want to come back and find Junior has taken possession of Sweet Air.

11th May 1932, Carlton Gardens, London

A whole month since I found the energy for my diary. Can there be anything more prostrating than travel. And my recovery is being made a thousand times harder by the chaos in Violet's establishment. She and Melhuish had been in the country, so, when I arrived, the house in Carlton Gardens wasn't properly aired and my bed was distinctly damp. I threatened to move to Claridge's. Violet eventually asked a rebellious-looking domestic if she might find the time to fill a rubber bottle with hot water and rub it between my sheets, and seemed to think that addressed the problem. Said rubber bottle was finally delivered, with heavy sighs, an hour after I had fallen exhausted into my bed. If this house is anything to go by, England is on the very edge of revolution.

The good news is that the location seems to be the very best. Melhuish is handy for his clubs and the House of Lords, Buckingham Palace is practically in our backyard, so very convenient for Violet, who is thick as thieves with Their Majesties, and the shops of Bond Street are no great distance away. If I can only get my rooms heated, I think I'll be suited.

Violet has grown stouter and probably hasn't had her hair attended to since the day she left Baltimore. She clips it up, and she's no sooner clipped it than it escapes. Melhuish's hair, on the other hand, is now in the final stages of retreat. One thing I will say for Danforth Brumby, he kept a fine head of hair till the very last.

Of the children I have so far met only Flora. She is eight years old and has occasional lessons from a spinster who comes to the house whenever she can be spared by her sick relations. Otherwise the child seems to tag along with whatever Doopie is doing, which cannot be very much. They take each other for walks in St. James's Park and make tiny coverlets for a dolls' house. My arrival caused great excitement, and the child immediately showed signs of wishing to attach herself to me, so today I was forced to establish some rules. She is not to visit my room. She is not to lurk in doorways spying on me. She is not to play her drum within a country mile of me. One must start as one intends to go on.

As for Doopie, she never seems to age. She stared and stared at my face, then smiled and said, "Ids Bayba!" but I'm not convinced anything really registered with her. Violet credits her with understanding, but a person may smile in an aimless way without at all understanding whether there's anything to smile about. Nora Sedley Cordle springs to mind.

I haven't yet sighted the two boys. They are normally kept at a school called Pilgrims but are being allowed out tomorrow night for something called an *exeat*. Not on my account, I hope.

A sweet note of welcome waiting for me from Pips Waldo, now Crosbie. She and her husband, Freddie, are in Halkin Street, just off Belgrave Square. We lunch on Monday.

14th May 1932

Besieged. The house is filled with boys wearing hobnailed boots. They were brought down to the drawing room to meet me last evening. All Violet's children have Melhuish's carroty hair and freckled skin. Ulick is tall, I'd say, for twelve; Rory is like a skinned rabbit. According to Violet, he suffers from night terrors. According to one of the housemaids, who offers unsought opinions on everything while dust gathers in drifts inches deep, he sees "imaginings." Well, all children are prone to imaginings, and the less intelligence they have the more susceptible they are. I remember I used only to have to snake my arm out of bed and set a rocking chair in unexplained motion for Violet to start howling, followed rapidly by Doopie.

Anyway, both boys shook me nicely by the hand and Ulick asked me how many acres I have at Sweet Air. Rory was gazing at me with his mouth open, Ulick nudged him in the ribs, and when he still stood catching flies, Ulick said, "And how was the crossing? Agreeable, I hope."

Rory said, "You beast! I was going to ask that. You know I was. Now what shall I ask?" Quite droll.

But they've all been tramping overhead since the crack of nine and now, just as I thought I'd found peace in the morning room, Violet has appeared with her book of lists, and the child Flora has bounded in, draped in a tartan traveling rug. She says they're playing Highland Clearances and she is It.

This evening, Violet and Melhuish are dining with the Bertie Yorks. He's a brother of the Prince of Wales. Violet said, "I'll have cook prepare you a tray. I hope you understand. It's not the kind of dinner where one can arrive with an extra."

Extra indeed! As if I've come to London to beg dinners from junior Royalties! I shall go to a movie theater with a box of candy.

15th May 1932

The boys Ulick and Rory were driven back to their school after luncheon, Rory sobbing pitifully when the moment came to leave, begging to be allowed to have lessons at home like Flora. Ulick was in a fury with him. He kept saying, "Stop it at once. Melhuishes don't blub."

Violet busied herself in the library with committee papers while he was being bundled into the car. She says he always cries, but once he's back with his friends he soon cheers up. She said, "He'll toughen up. And someday he'll thank us for it. Imagine if a boy went into Officer Training still soft from home life."

16th May 1932

Lunch with Pips Crosbie. She now has a red tint and bangs and looks adorably modern. She goes to Monsieur Jules in Bruton Street and is going to introduce me. Her husband, whom she can't wait for me to meet, is in Parliament, a kind of congressman, I gather, but not in the same House as Melhuish. Freddie Crosbie had to get elected to his seat, whereas Melhuish has one simply because he's Lord Melhuish. It has been warmed by Melhuish b-t-ms through the centuries.

Pips and Freddie seem to see quite a bit of Judson Erlanger. She said, "As I recall, you had quite a pash for him."

Pips is misremembering. Judson was the one who pursued me.

Another name from the past. Ida Coote is in town, living some kind of artistic life in a rooming house full of White Russians. Extraordinary. I hadn't realized Russians came in any other color.

I don't believe I've seen Ida since Gunpowder River Summer Camp. It must be twenty years. She was another unusual girl. I can't wait.

Wally is now married to someone called Simpson, and I have her address from Pips. George Street. All I've been able to discover is that it's in some kind of backwater north of Marble Arch and absolutely *nobody* lives there. Poor Wally.

Pips says they've seen each other in passing at several receptions, but so far they haven't managed to get together for lunch. I sense Pips dragging her heels. She said, "I don't know. Maybe the years have improved her, but didn't you always find her rather mouthy?"

Actually, I liked that in her. I had the face and the figure, but Wally had the patter. We'd take a slow walk down to the Chesapeake tea rooms on a Sunday and collect ourselves quite an escort of good-looking Navy boys, in from Annapolis for the afternoon. We made a good team. Perhaps we will again. Me, Wally, Pips, Ida. At this rate, we belles of Baltimore will be taking over London.

Violet says Ida's address is in West Kensington, which hardly counts as London. Also that she'd hesitate to classify Wally Warfield as a belle.

Tomorrow to Swan & Edgar for woolen camisoles.

18th May 1932

Swan & Edgar's store knows nothing of customer service. They told me there was no demand for woolen camisoles at this time of year, when only two minutes earlier *I* had demanded them. They advised me that their next supply will arrive toward the end of August and asked would I care to leave my name and number. I said, "I see no point. I shall be dead of the cold."

A long wait while Ida was fetched to the telephone by one of her Russians. She screamed for joy when she heard my voice. Lunch tomorrow.

19th May 1932

Treated Ida to the Dorchester. She has dyed her hair black and wears costume jewelry, having lost everything in the Crash, but seems very gay. She said, "Money's a curse, Maybell. I'm a free spirit these days."

Of course, I don't know that Ida ever had *that* much money.

She's taking me to the Argentine Embassy on Monday. She says attendance at one cocktail party begets invitations to ten more, so there's no faster way to meet people and canapés also solve the question of dinner.

No call from Wally.

21st May 1932

To the Crosbies. Freddie Crosbie is very sweet in that dithering English way. He has no chin and makes only four hundred a year as Member of Parliament, but Pips obviously adores him. They must be very glad of her money.

The house is all beige and cream, what Pips calls "neutrals," and is run in the modern style. There's no withdrawing after dinner, which I very much applaud. I've never liked all that sitting around drinking tea, waiting for the men to finish their cigars.

The great shock of the evening was seeing Judson Erlanger after all these years. He never had what one could call chiseled features, but he did once have a certain amount of dash. Now he looks like a big, pink man in the moon and is married to Hattie, formerly Chandos, who has crooked teeth and a permanent wave and dukes in the family. Pips says Hattie's people go back years. But surely everybody's people go back years?

Still nothing from Wally. I begin to wonder whether Pips copied down the address correctly.

24th May 1932

How I missed Danforth Brumby last evening. Ida and I had no sooner arrived at the Argentines than she set off across the room in search of potato chips and left me at the mercy of a Latin with shiny hair and built-up shoes. What is one supposed to say to these people? Brumby would have struck up a conversation about silver mines or the price of beef, but I felt quite at a loss. Was finally rescued by an American press attaché called Whitlow Trilling, also married to an English girl. He knows Judson and Pips, but Wally's name meant nothing to him. Perhaps this whole Wally business is a red herring.

Violet came in before I was dressed, wanting to discuss something called Royal Ascot. Ascot is a race track, and there's a week of races there next month. I wouldn't mind going. Brumby and I went to Saratoga once and it was quite fun.

Violet said, "Oh I'm afraid it's not that simple, Maybell. Melhuish and I will be in the Royal party, you see? And I'm just not sure what best to do with you."

I said, "You make me sound like a surplus chair. It's very simple. I'll join the Royal party, too."

But she says that's out of the question. That one cannot invite oneself along, nor even propose that one's dearest sister, recently bereaved and newly arrived in a foreign land, be added to the invitation list.

She said, "Let me have a word with Lady Desborough. She's always very sweet about accommodating an extra."

That word "extra" again.

I said, "As a matter of fact, now I reconsider. I expect to be rather busy that week, so don't give it another thought."

She said, "Will you? Nobody'll be in town, you know? But it'll be a great weight off my mind. Their Majesties absolutely depend on us for Ascot, you see. Well, Melhuish has known them all his life."

Violet never tires of displaying her tired old stock of claims to grandeur. How she met Melhuish when he was traveling with the Prince of Wales. How Melhuish's father was equerry to two Kings, which as I understand it amounts to nothing more than being a royal errand boy. How Melhuish has known the Duchess of York since she was a baby in her bassinet.

She forgets how differently things might have turned out. If I hadn't stayed home to represent us at Lucie Mallett's wedding shower, I'd have been at Sulphur Springs myself. Who knows, I might have caught the Royal eye, never mind Donald Melhuish's. Not that I'd have wanted either of them. They say that crowns are unbearably heavy to wear.

I notice anyway that the Prince of Wales seems to have dropped Melhuish. Violet says it's not a question of "dropping." She says friends grow apart when one of them becomes a family man and the other continues to run with a fast set.

I said, "I assume you'll leave me with a cook at least, and a maid while you're being indispensable to Their Majesties?"

She said, "I'll leave you with everything but a driver. And you'll have Flora and Doopie for company."

So there it is. It doesn't bother me. I'm sure Royalties must be death to the natural gaiety of friendship. Better to stay at home and be one's true self, even if it does mean being left with a child to supervise, and an imbecile, and a staff of Bolshevik insurgents.

25th May 1932

Minnehaha at last! She said, "Maybell, you must think me such a slouch, but I've been sick. This is my first good day for a week."

Stomach ulcers, apparently. I didn't think she looked too bad, though. Still skinny, still parting her hair in the middle, still as tidy as a tinker. Little gray suit, white shirtwaist, good shoes. Her skin isn't brilliant but then it never was.

Lunch was a riot, we had so much to talk about. She's been married to Simpson for four years, his name is Ernest, and she's never been happier. Of course, she said that when she married the aviator, but it was all far too hasty.

The first summer we were "out," 1915, she got an invitation to visit a cousin who was stationed at Pensacola, Florida, and she was off like a shot. Wally always adored a uniform. The next thing we knew, she was back with a diamond on her finger, engaged to a lieutenant in the Aviation Corps. That was Win Spencer.

The wedding was at Christ Church, and I was supposed to be a bridesmaid, along with Mary Kirk, but then Grandma Patterson died and I had to go to the burying, so Lucie Mallett stepped in at short notice. I wasn't altogether sorry. The gowns were yellow, which has never been my color, and our bouquets were snapdragons. Somehow whenever I see a snapdragon, I think of Wally.

We lost touch after that. I said, "You could have written."

"Well," she said, "it wouldn't have made an edifying read. I knew the first week I'd made a mistake."

I think the honeymoon comes as a shock to every bride. It was years before I felt able to enjoy the Pocono Mountains again. But with Win Spencer, there was the additional problem of drink. They went to a resort in West Virginia, which was dry, but apparently he'd thought to bring along his own supplies.

She said it was the stress of flying that had turned him to alcohol. It was the usual thing to toast the flag before anyone went up in one of those crates, but Win would always have a couple more shots, to settle the first one.

She sounds to have had a pretty good war though. He was posted to California and they say the beaches at Coronado are divine. Then he was sent to China, and she thought it'd be more fun to tag along than sit it out on Soapsuds Row with all the other

Navy wives, so she followed him. There was never any stopping Wally. In fact, advising her against something only made her all the more set on doing it. Like the time she borrowed Nugent Wilson's suit and crashed a Bachelors' Club ball dressed as a buck.

She says China was a real adventure. Hong Kong, Shanghai. There was a war going on, people getting shot in the streets, heads appearing on pikes, and there was typhoid. She ended up in Peking, had an affair that didn't work out, and then decided to call it a day with Win. He was drinking more than ever. She went back to the States, got a divorce, and was staying with Mary Kirk for a while, getting back on her feet, when she met Ernest, who has business interests in London. So here she is.

I said, "You never looked up Violet? She's Lady Melhuish, you know, in Carlton Gardens?"

"Yes," she said, "I know. But I don't think Violet ever really approved of me, and these days she's so grand. Frankly, I'm looking to create a livelier circle. I'm more interested in what people *are* than who their grandfathers were."

I'm invited for Saturday. She says I'll find Ernest very knowledgeable on wine and literature.

Loelia and Bendor Westminster to dinner at Carlton Gardens. She's his third duchess and very young. They say she married him for his money. Poached salmon again. Violet might take time off from her committees one of these days to review her recipe book.

26th May 1932

Flora fell crossing the Mall, and came in crying. Even Doopie couldn't soothe her. "Mummy, I crazed my knee," she kept sobbing, but there was cold comfort to be had from Violet.

"Did you, darling?" she said. "Jolly good. Now off you skip. I have Fishermen's Orphans this afternoon."

Every day there's something. Consumptives, Highland Crafts, Unmarried Mothers.

A note pushed under my door when I woke from my nap. HULO written in wax crayon. The poor child spends too much time around Doopie.

28th May 1932

Wally's apartment is in Bryanston Court. A dull building in a dull street. Wally's on the second floor with a cook, one live-in maid, a daily, and a driver for Ernest. A claustrophobic entrance hall filled with white flowers and ivory elephants. A modest drawing room, mahogany and striped silk mainly, but one glorious lacquered Chinese screen and a table full of gorgeous little jade doodads. All bought for a song, I'm sure. Her China years may be glossed over whenever Ernest is around, but she doesn't make any effort to hide the booty.

Ernest came home at seven and presided over the drinks' tray. He's pleasant enough, dapper, a little too fat in the face to be handsome and he almost certainly dyes his mustache. To hear him speak, you'd take him for an Englishman. He showed me some of his first editions while Wally interfered in the kitchen. She always did love to cook. After her mother remarried, she'd often come home with me during vacation, and one time she took over our kitchen and made terrapin stew, because she heard Father saying it was his favorite dish in the whole world and nobody ever cooked it for him.

I reminded her about that. She laughed.

"Nineteen-twelve," she said. "I can tell you exactly. After Mama moved to Atlantic City with that four-flusher."

Her stepfather was a drinker and an idler called Rasin. Goodness knows what Mrs. Warfield saw in him. Wally used to say she prayed he was a seedless Rasin, because she was in no mood for any baby sisters and brothers. He was dead within two years anyway.

Ernest said, "You two certainly do go back a long way."

Indeed we do. Back as far as her mother's sad little boardinghouse, though I'd never dream of bringing up that kind of embarrassment now.

29th May 1932

Decided it was time to pick the brains of someone from the old crowd, so I placed a call to Lucie Mallett. Violet fretting in the background about expense, quite unable to understand why a letter wouldn't do just as well. She knows I always pay my way. I just wanted to find out if Lucie knew anything about Ernest.

She said, "All I know is, Wally came back from China with her insides in some kind of disarray, crossed the state line to get a divorce, and wasted no time in helping herself to someone else's husband. She met him at Mary Kirk's."

I said, "I know that. But who is he?"

"A nobody," she said. "And he left a child and an invalid wife, just because Wally Warfield snapped her fingers. Scandalous."

I said, "I'll tell her you said hello."

"Please don't," she said.

Another note under my door. HULO ARNT.

30th May 1932

Lunched with Pips and Wally at the Criterion restaurant in Piccadilly. I do feel a light touch is called for with mosaics, unless you're decorating a temple of worship.

The girls were a little stiff with each other at first, but a bottle of hock wine soon got them talking about past times. Pips remembered something I'd quite forgotten: how Wally talked Homer Chute into masquerading as her cousin and picking her up from Oldfields in his Lagonda one Sunday. They were gone all day at the pleasure beach and Wally came back with a tintype portrait of herself sitting on Homer's knee. Not that Pips was backward with the boys. She had more fraternity pins than any of us.

Wally says she doesn't know how long she and Ernest will be in London but she'd really like to liven things up while she's here, and leave her mark. Pips suggested costume parties, but she hasn't seen Bryanston Court. It's far too small for a crush. Anyway, Wally says unlimited drink is death to conversation. She prefers elegant little dinners where she can draw people out.

Wally believes the secret of success as a hostess is to mix important people with a sprinkling of interesting types from lower levels. Also, in the matter of food and presentation and entertainment to have the courage to season the expected with the unexpected. She says the King of England would be happy to come to dinner if he thought he might meet Mahatma Gandhi and be served a good, tasty hamburger on a Minton plate. Pips says Mahatma Gandhi doesn't eat hamburger.

After lunch, Wally took us to see an adorable gramophone she'd found in Wigmore Street, completely portable, in a lizard-skin case. I couldn't resist. But I've entrusted it to Wally, because if I bring it to Carlton Gardens, Flora will expect to play with it and it will soon be broken.

Pips was on the telephone the instant I got home. She said, "Minnehaha's as slow as ever to pick up a check, I see. And I hope you're not going to buy her every toy in the store. You're too generous, Maybell. Always were."

Well, what's a little money between friends? And I'm only *lending* her my gramophone.

2nd June 1932

Shopping with Wally. Ernest seems to keep her on a very strict allowance and goes through the account books at the end of each month. Thank heavens Brumby was never so particular.

Flora sitting on the stairs watching for my return. She announced that she'd been making "gakes" and had one saved for me up in the nursery, but I was too exhausted to climb more stairs. I said, "I'll come tomorrow."

A hammering on my door five minutes later, and there she stood, with a lump of warm gray dough in a paper case.

Tonight dinner with Violet and Melhuish's friends, the Belchesters, who can't wait to know me.

3rd June 1932

Anne Belchester's busybodying and charitable works make Violet look like a positive lady of leisure. She wanted to know about my Baltimore committees, but I told her, it isn't everyone who's suited to committees. There are talkers and there are doers, and I'm a doer. All that time spent shuffling papers and drinking tea. I'd sooner sign a check.

Billy Belchester said, "Careful now, Maybell. You'll have writer's cramp by the time Anne's finished with you!"

Melhuish said, "Violet gives her time, that's the thing, and her expertise. All the money in the world is no use if it's not wisely marshaled, and the thing about Vee is, she's terribly good with lists."

Anne Belchester said, "She is. She sometimes mislays them, but when they come to hand, they're absolutely first-rate."

Oh well, glory in the highest to Violet and her lists. I do my bit. I sort through my closets every fall and give to Christmas Goodwill. Quality woolens, shoes hardly worn, hats that aren't keepers. I just don't make a fuss about it.

Pips is getting up a party to go to Ciro's tomorrow night. So far the Judson Erlangers and Wally and Ernest. Ida is an unknown.

5th June 1932

We closed Ciro's last night. There was a wonderfully droll ensemble playing with homemade banjos. The Moses Jackson Coon Band! Judson and Hattie brought along the press attaché, Whitlow Trilling, and his wife, Gladys. Ida turned up with an

Argentine who smelled of brilliantine. Ernest had business papers to peruse, so cried off at the last minute. No great loss. He's so serious. People don't always want to be discussing Pluto's *Republic*.

According to Whitlow, a new First Secretary just arrived, and it's someone Wally knows from her Navy days in San Diego. Benny Thaw.

Pips said, "Is he an old flame?"

Wally says absolutely not, but she's going to look him up.

The birds were singing as I arrived home, so I looked forward to a restful day in bed, but Wally was on the telephone at ten, slave-driving me to go shopping for lingerie, and then a military parade started up. Violet says it was the Major General's Review. Men and horses tramping across Horse Guards' Parade. Drums, bugles, shouting, all bad enough in themselves, but Doopie and Flora came back from watching and proceeded to reenact it in the corridor outside my room. Doopie always did get overexcited by military bands.

Violet is walking around with a furrowed brow, because the Rutlands are dining tonight, all the way from their castle in the country, also the terrifically *von* Bismarcks, but someone has chucked, leaving her with thirteen, and I'm far too tired to make up the numbers. I don't have the strength to lift a soup spoon.

Caught my heel in the hem of my charcoal silk getting out of the car this morning, and there is apparently no girl among the overfed rabble of servants in this house who knows how to mend. Not one.

Light rain.

6th June 1932

I am completely recovered. Dr. Collis Browne's soothing nerve linctus certainly lives up to its promises.

Now I've tried it I shall never be without it. And while I slept, Doopie has quite expertly repaired my ripped hem. I shall buy her a box of candy.

Wally on the phone first thing. She sent a message of welcome to Benny Thaw and he replied immediately with an invitation for drinks. She seemed particularly excited about his being married to Connie Morgan.

I said, "Do you know her?"

"No," she said, "but I soon will. This should get the American scene here fizzing. Those Morgan girls all have money and style."

Lunched with Pips, who says she doesn't know anything about Connie Morgan, but what her sisters have is money and reputations. Gloria Morgan was married to Reggie Vanderbilt until he drank himself to death, and Thelma Morgan was Mrs. Bell Telephone but is now Lady Furness.

She said, "And we all know about her!" Then Ida turned up, raving about a miraculous new oxygenated face cream, and we somehow never got back to the subject of Thelma Furness and what it is we're all supposed to know.

Took a tray of fruit fondants for Doopie.

Violet was out at her Distressed Pit Ponies. Flora knows the days of the week by her mother's committees.

"Bunday, Pit Ponies, Doosday, Blood, Wesday, Falling Women and Not Forgottens."

She was stuck for a minute with Thursday but Doopie helped her out. Something called "Lebbers."

They seem to be great friends and have a most amusing sign-language they use from time to time. How simple their lives are! I have to dine with Lord and Lady Anglesey and Violet's gruesome in-laws, while they can play with their dolls and have sugar sandwiches for tea. There is something enviable about the life of an imbecile.

Of course, Flora will never learn to speak clearly listening to Doopie's version of things. I may take her in hand.

Violet finally came home at six.

I said, "Don't you think Flora's rather backward with her speaking? She just copies Doopie, you know?"

"Oh," she said, "they'll sort that out when she goes to school. They did Rory."

I said, "Well, I feel sorry for her. She never goes anywhere."

Violet said, "What nonsense. Doopie takes her across to St. James's Park. They walk to Duck Island almost every day. And she was invited to the Yorks for tea yesterday but would she get dressed?"

I said, "That's because no one has taught her properly. She sees you running out to committee meetings, hair uncombed, egg yolk on your blouse. It's no wonder she thinks she can go to tea parties in bloomers and a liberty bodice."

"Maybell," she said, "will you please go and bathe. Salty and Elspeth are coming at seven."

I said, "First tell me if you ever heard of Thelma Furness and if so, what's her scandalous story?"

She made a great business of closing the door to the drawing room, then said,

"Lady Furness is a friend of the Prince of Wales, but not the kind we mention in front of the children. Why do you ask?"

I said, "No reason. Wally knows the husband of one of her sisters. She probably thinks this is going to be her entrée to royal circles. She's as ambitious as ever. She keeps quizzing me about our connections with the throne."

"Well," she said, "first of all, *you* have no connections. Secondly, those who do have them never speak of them. And thirdly, I would say it's a very steep climb from acquaintance with the husband of a certain person's sister to meeting Royalties, too steep even for Minnehaha."

Violet has always taken herself far too seriously.

She said, "I hope it goes without saying, Lady F. is never to be mentioned in this house. And Maybell, hot water costs money. Please don't have your bath too deep."

Chance would be a fine thing.

7th June 1932

Flora has renamed one of her dolls "Lady Furness" and has banished it to the back stairs. I grow fonder of the child.

9th June 1932

All the talk is of Race Week. Violet said someone called Lightfoot might be willing to escort me to the Guards' luncheon tent, but I recognize crumbs when I see them falling from my sister's table. Three times today she's asked, "Are you sure you won't let Ettie Desborough squeeze you in?" Guilt.

Wally says, without a white badge, Royal Ascot isn't royal at all, so why bother? The white badge is the Open Sesame to the inner sanctum, the Royal Enclosure, but seemingly impossible to get unless one is on intimate terms with the Prince of Wales. So we may just ignore Ascot. We'll borrow Ernest's driver and go shopping for *bibelots* in forgotten backwaters.

12th June 1932

Wally and Ernest went to drinks with the Benny Thaws and met the unmentionable Thelma F. Wally says Connie and Thelma are both adorable and she's meeting them for lunch on Monday. Pips says if they're lunching with Wally, someone had better warn them to take along a fistful of their Morgan dollars.

Violet and Melhuish's luggage has been taken to Windsor, not a great amount of it for three days of banquets and royal carriage rides. Wally says fashion is everything at Ascot, but I'm certain Violet hasn't bought a single new gown. We might have had such fun shopping together, but no. She didn't even ask my advice about hats. Wally would have been much more fun as a sister.

13th June 1932

Violet and Melhuish left after lunch for Windsor. Ida Coote has been angling to stay with me while they're out of town. She seems to have become some kind of nomad since she lost her money, always offering to air people's villas or walk their dogs. She said, "You won't want to be alone in that great big house, all those empty rooms, all those portraits with eyes that follow you." But I'm not going to be alone. I shall have Violet's staff to lick into shape. Anyway, Ida has only two topics of conversation: Ida and men. It's all right for the occasional lunch, but a slumber party would be unendurable.

More rain. To Gamages for overshoes, then home for a nursery tea. Jello, grilled cheese, and gingerbread. Afterwards, we played at Royal Ascot, with dolls strapped to Ulick's spaniel and Melhuish's little ratting dog.

Gave Flora an almost, almost empty scent bottle. She wanted to know if I was going to live with them forever!

14th June 1932

I'm a great hit with my niece, not least because I've decreed no fish will be served as long as I'm in command. I told her she could choose her favorite dinner, and she came down in her nightgown to deliver her demands: LAB SHOPS. SIRUB TART. GUSTARD.

I said, "Flora, wouldn't you like to go to school?"

"No thank you," she said.

I said, "Other little girls do."

She said, "Lilibet York doesn't."

But Lilibet York is a princess. She'll never need to use her brain the way we ordinary girls have to. At the very most, she might get called upon to be Queen, but only if they ran out of Kings. All highly unlikely.

A lot of huffing and puffing from the housekeeper over my menus. Flora's choice tonight, then tomorrow a rib roast and ice cream.

She said, "I don't know, madam. Her Ladyship didn't say anything about specials. This kind of thing isn't customary."

I said, "I know it isn't customary. That's precisely why I'm ordering it."

Such a fuss. All she has to do is telephone Harrold's. They have everything.

"Carry on like this," she said, half out of the door, "Her Ladyship won't know the place when she gets back. We shall be all upside down with bilious attacks and overspending."

I'll deem it a failure if Violet *doesn't* see a difference. I've already put a stop to the maid Trotman's discussions. She now understands that if I say the tea is too strong I'm not inviting her to pour herself a cup to see whether she agrees. Give me a little longer and I'll break that footman of breathing through his mouth.

Tomorrow with Wally to the rolling hills of Cotswoldshire and all those darling cottages with hairy roofs.

15th June 1932

A profitable day in Chipping Norton, a most *characteristic* town, pretty little stone row houses with windows you can look right into from the sidewalk, ancient hostelries, all haunted, I'm sure, and such sweet, simple country folk. They seemed to find us quite fascinating.

We got Wally a set of silver-plated vanity boxes, quite good enough for a guest room. Also a bone china compote dish, with the tiniest hairline crack, and a very pretty set of Victorian creamers. Bryanston Court is the kind of apartment that needs all the help it can get. It has no features. Wally's done the best she can with her Chinese pieces, but the place still looks half-dressed. I suppose when Ernest got his divorce, the invalid wife was awarded all his good things.

Wally's going to give a dinner for the Benny Thaws and invite Thelma Furness, too.

I can't wait.

Doopie was in good form last evening, chatting away in that funny, snuffly style of hers. Flora seems to understand all of it. We looked through Doopie's albums, pictures I'd quite forgotten. Mother and Father with baby Violet, posed beside a potted palm. Me in a little cotton pinafore, with Doopie in her crib. That would have been before she lost her mind. Several photographs of our Season, too. Pips and Violet setting off for Mary Kirk's tea dance. Me, Pips, Violet, and Wally in our finery before the Bachelors' Cotillion. What a production that was. Wally and I used to practice our one-step together. "I'll be the man," she'd say. Homer Chute had taught her the tango, too, but that was far too racy for the Baltimore Bachelors'.

It looked at first as though Wally wouldn't be able to attend, because her uncle refused to help her out. He said it wasn't seemly to be giving balls when young men were laying down their lives in Flanders. But then he relented and gave her a gown allowance, and she spent it all on one fabulous white satin. She reckoned she'd rather star at one important ball than blend with the masses at half a dozen.

Flora wanted to know why there were no pictures of Doopie going to a ball. I told her there was a war, and left it at that. I supposed having been cooped up with Doopie in that nursery all her life, she thinks of her as normal. I must say though, they both sat up so nicely and ate so daintily I've ordered dinner served in the dining room tonight.

16th June 1932

Unexpected company last evening. We were about to go into dinner when Melhuish's friend, George Lightfoot, called in on his way back from Windsor.

He said, "I thought I'd look in on my favorite girls." Flora clambered onto his knee immediately, so I offered him a sherry wine and he stayed to carve the beef. He's a tall drink of water, rosy cheeks, tangled hair. He had a brother who was in the Grenadiers with Melhuish, lost at Passchendaele.

He said, "I would never have taken you and Violet for sisters, but you and Doopie, yes. I see a definite resemblance." I don't think so.

He said it was a criminal waste to eat such a fine-looking roast without a drop of wine, raced off to his cellars in South Audley Street, and came back with a bottle he described as "toothsome but sincere." I don't know that it was advisable to allow Doopie a glass, but afterwards she kept us quite entertained with her impersonations of Theda Bara and poor Fatty Arbuckle.

17th June 1932

Violet and Melhuish got back just as I was leaving to meet Pips for lunch. Flora came thundering down the stairs to greet them. "Mummy!" she said, "I've had a splendid time with Aunt Bayba. We had lab shops and ice cream and Doopie had red drink. Cook says she's never seen such garryings-on in her life."

"Not now, darling," Violet said. "I have to talk to Lady Habberley about raffle tickets."

Pips thinks Wally's only inviting Thelma Furness to dinner in the hope she'll bring the Prince of Wales, but I'm sure Wally knows that's out of the question. Theirs is a very private affair.

Pips said, "I suppose having the Prince's sweetie to dinner is still more than a little Cinderella like Wally ever dreamed of."

Poor Wally, tarred for life, even by a friend like Pips. It's not that there was anything particularly inferior about the Warfields. Her Uncle Sol had a very good house on Preston Street, and her Aunt Bessie is still well thought of. It was her mother who lowered the tone of things with one foolish marriage after another. Too many husbands and too much rouge. No wonder Wally's so determined to start over and make something of herself.

Tonight to the Embassy Club with the Benny Thaws.

18th June 1932

Violet says what I had Smith spend on meat for two days would feed an African for a year. Ridiculous. I don't believe Violet knows any Africans.

Interesting people at the Benny Thaws' party last night. Boss and Ethel Croker from Michigan. Ethel was a Navy wife before she met Boss. She knew Wally from China. Somehow Ethel seemed more pleased to see Wally than Wally did to see Ethel.

20th June 1932

Wally's birthday. I gave her a calfskin guest book and lunch at the Dorch. Ernest gave her a fountain pen. What a dull old stick he is.

We've been worked off our feet all afternoon planning her dinner party. There's so much to do. The menu to be decided and the *placement,* new table linens and stemware to be purchased, conversational topics to be studied. Wally reads the newspapers cover to cover every day, and she's skimmed through centuries of history and philosophy while having her hair done. She says one hardly ever needs to plod through an entire book.

21st June 1932

Lunch with Pips, who had invited along Ethel Croker, as she put it, "to help us join up a few more dots in Minnehaha's Chinese period."

Ethel's nice. Overdressed and hair an unhappy shade of brass, but very sweet and chatty. Ethel was in Panama, waiting for a transport to Hong Kong. When she joined the ship, they berthed her with Wally, and they became friends.

She said, "God knows, you needed a friend. It was hell in a sardine can. Heat and storms and doughboys fighting with knives. Five weeks of it."

She and Wally both got Navy quarters on Kowloon when they arrived.

She said, "She did try with Win Spencer, you know? She really did. I don't know why, because he was a bastard. If I'd been her, I'd have left him. But then he left her, added insult to injury. She went off the deep end a bit after that. Man crazy. And travel crazy. I went with her on a trip to Shanghai, to take her mind off Win, but I couldn't keep pace with her. I was a married woman, you know? There was a lot of talk about Wally. Still, it's all a long time ago now."

Ethel's made a good marriage with Boss Croker. They say he's Mr. Frozen Fish.

She said, "It'd be nice to catch up with Wally again. He seems all right, the new husband? A bit serious, but he doesn't look like a drinker. I'll bet he doesn't hit her."

Poor Wally. No wonder she grabbed Ernest when he came along.

She's still a man short for Tuesday's dinner. Pips says the obvious solution is to drop a lone woman, the prime candidate being me. She predicts Wally will ask me to fall on my sword, but I shall absolutely refuse. Given my outlay on guest towels from Liberty, the very least I'm owed is dinner with the fabled Lady Furness. If the situation is desperate, I'll suggest George Lightfoot. He seemed to me the kind of man who could fit in anywhere.

23rd June 1932

Pips was quite wrong. Wally couldn't care less about odd numbers.

She said, "This may be London, but aren't we Americans, Maybell? Don't we do things our own way? More women than men, so what? Anyhow, Nada Milford Haven is coming, and to all intents and purposes, she's a man. It's going to give my table a rather avant-garde complexion."

One thing about Wally, she's always made necessity the mother of invention.

The menu is now decided. We're to have caviar, followed by grilled squab, iced camembert, and then strawberry sherbet. It remains to be seen though whether Ernest will cough up for caviar. He seems to keep Wally very short.

I said, "Well, if it doesn't run to caviar, you can always serve soup."

"Never," she said. "Take it from me, Maybell, soup is the ruin of a good dinner."

I'm quite agog to meet this Milford Haven person. I wonder whether she wears pants!

26th June 1932

Violet's put out because she assumed I'd be free on Tuesday evening and now finds I'm engaged. The Nicholases of Greece and the Harewoods are dining. She said, "Now who am I going to pair with Lightfoot? I was depending on you. Surely, if it's only Minnehaha, you can chuck?"

I have agreed to stay for one drink, provided Melhuish has his driver at the ready, engine ticking over, to whisk me to Bryanston Court. It's like Baltimore all over again. Everyone wants me.

27th June 1932

A working lunch with Wally, putting the final touches. We'll be eleven. An interesting number. She's placing me between a decorator called MacMullen and a German commercial attaché. She promises me he speaks English.

Ernest telephoned while I was there. I heard her say, "Of course we must. First impressions! There's nothing worse than being offered caviar and then needing a magnifying glass to see it on your plate."

I must say, when it came to paying, I was rather shocked at her lavishness. Beluga, sevruga, *and* ossetra! She calls it an overture of caviars, but I could hear Ernest worrying away at the other end.

"Ernest," she barked, "think of it as an investment in our future. Do you want to meet the Prince of Wales or not?"

Pips says she doesn't eat caviar anyway, so there's one economy that could have been made.

29th June 1932

Flora came hammering on my door at some unearthly hour, found me prostrated by migraine, and fetched Doopie to minister to me. Cold compresses and a draught of something pleasantly medicinal. Flora said it's called Dog Hair.

Whatever it was, it made me sleep, and I woke restored. I think my headache must have been brought on by an unhappy mixture of beverages. A whiskey and soda with Violet and her guests, and then two deceptively strong Russian cocktails at Wally's.

The dinner was a qualified success. I found the squab a little dry, but the sherbet was delicious and my linens and crystal looked superb. The German did speak English but seemed to find Thelma Furness so fascinating he omitted to turn between courses, and Freddie Crosbie became engrossed in conversation with Benny Thaw, which left me easy prey for Nada Milford Haven who was seated across the table. Wally says she's not only a marchioness but also a Romanov. I can well believe it. She may have been wearing a gown but that didn't prevent her foot from romanoving up and down between my knees.

Thelma Furness and her sister both have pale, pale complexions and wild black eyebrows. They're exotic rather than pretty. The Prince of Wales can surely take his pick of the most beautiful women in the world, so he obviously has a taste for the unusual. They're both very sweet though, and Thelma doesn't at all trade on her special position. She has a child apparently. I wonder whose it is? Pips says Lord Furness stays in the south of France with a toot-sie, so as to leave the field clear for the Prince.

Flora has been tiptoeing in and out, waiting for me to be awake enough to inspect a little story she wrote this morning. It was about a good aunt who buys candy and ice cream but then gets sent away by the bad aunts.

She said, "Daddy said you were a loose cannon. Why did he?"

That's because I uttered the forbidden F word in the drawing room last evening.

Henry Harewood asked where I was off to in such a hurry, and I told him I was dining with Lady Furness. I only said it to provoke Violet. How was I to know Mary Harewood is the Prince of Wales's sister? The Royalties can be so confusing with their multitude of names. She, being the daughter, the one and only, of the King and Queen, is the Princess Royal, but she married Lord Harewood and likes to use his name. Odd. I'm sure if I were the Princess Royal, *nothing* would part me from my title. She's a homely little creature, too. Not my idea of a princess at all.

Rory and Ulick will be home from school on Friday.

30th June 1932

To Fortnum's, for a postmortem with Wally. She's already had a warm note of thanks from Thelma, so she feels she's established another useful friendship.

I said, "You're very keen to meet the Prince of Wales."

"Not especially," she said. "I already met him. But Ernest would be very thrilled, and anyway, who ever knows where these things may lead?"

She claims she met His Royal Highness at a reception in Coronado in 1920, when he was on his way to Australia and his battleship refueled at San Diego. Strange she never mentioned it before. And she doesn't remember what he said to her. I'll bet she didn't actually *meet* him at all.

I said, "So, what happens next?"

She said, "We wait and see. But I'll be very surprised if we don't get an invitation to Thelma's country house in the fall."

That's where the royal *affaire* takes place, apparently.

I said, "Why the fall? That's months away."

"Well," she said, "after the middle of July, nothing important happens till September. We're going to the Tyrol."

Pips wasn't impressed by Thelma Furness. She found her doe-eyed and vapid.

I said, "What else would she need to be? The Prince of Wales is heir to the throne. He's used to giving out edicts and laying down the law. He'd hardly choose a sweetie who answered back."

She said, "Oh, I don't know. I've heard he's pretty vapid himself."

She and Freddie are going to Italy for the month of August.

1st July 1932

Even Ida seems to be fixed up for summer, care-taking someone's house in Gloucestershire. When I asked Violet if she planned to remain in London, she looked at me as though I'd asked whether she intended jumping into the Thames.

"Maybell," she said, "*no one* stays in London in August. We go to Drumcanna, of course, and this year you'll come with us."

We'll see about that. It's so typical of Melhuish's family to have their castle practically at the North Pole. All that way, and for what? To catch a few fish when one could so easily have them delivered by a good fishmonger? To crawl across Scottish moors in pursuit of some kind of elk? Knowing Violet's culinary repertoire, we'll be dining on poached elk till Thanksgiving. No. I shall make other arrangements.

Wally and Ernest are dining with Boss and Ethel Croker before they leave London.

I said, "You and Ethel must have so much to catch up on."

"Not really," she said. "We were never close. But Ernest and Boss will find lots to talk about. They have a house on Long Island, you know? And they travel all over, first class. Ethel's certainly landed on her feet. Traded in a midshipman for a multimillionaire."

Hardly "traded in." Ethel's husband was killed in Canton, friendly fire.

3rd July 1932

Ulick and Rory are home. Doopie has been flapping around all morning, unpacking trunks and examining socks for holes and shirt collars for turning. After the summer, Ulick will be going to Melhuish's old school, Eton College, and so has to have his name stitched into dozens of new garments. A simple, repetitive task that would drive a normal person insane, but Doopie is clearly in her element.

Violet says the entertainments at Drumcanna will be simple, outdoor pursuits. Fishing, deerstalking, shooting. She says they don't keep late nights, because of making an early start, but they do play parlor games after dinner and they always give a ball, where the help and the guests mingle and dance. I told her I didn't think it was for me.

"Nonsense," she said. "You'll have a wonderful time. The mountain air will do you good, and you'll strike up new friendships. Jane Habberley is coming, and Penelope Blythe. Anyway, you can't stay here. Smith and the maids go to their families for August."

The butler and the driver go north with them, apparently, but Drumcanna is otherwise run by a staff of locals, even more wayward than the London tribe, no doubt, left to their own Scottish devices for months at a time.

I said, "Then I'll go to a hotel."

"You'll come to Drumcanna, Maybell!" she said, "and do what normal people do."

A note under my door at bedtime.

> *Dear Aunt Maybell,*
>
> *Please come to Scotland. Flora and I will be very sad if you do not.*
>
> *Yours truly,*
> *Rory Melhuish.*

4th July 1932

To the U.S. Legation for luncheon. The "Star-Spangled Banner" brought a tear to my eye and made me think of going home. But to what? Sweet Air will seem so quiet after the mad house at Carlton Gardens. To be alone in Baltimore or alone in London? Everyone is paired off, making their gay plans. No one considers you when you're a widow.

5th July 1932

Violet says I've relieved her of a great worry by agreeing to go to Drumcanna, and she promises me I won't regret my decision.

She said, "We'll go for lovely walks. It'll lift your spirits. And I think I can promise you you'll get to meet Bertie and Elizabeth York. They'll be at Birkhall and may very well invite you over. It's even possible you'll be presented to Their Majesties!"

Bertie is the second Royal brother. There's Edward, the eldest, except everyone calls him "David" or "Wales" when they disapprove of something he's done. He'll be the next King. Then comes Bertie, who's the Duke of York, married to Elizabeth, followed by Harry and George and, of course, the sister, who doesn't really count.

I asked if the Prince of Wales is likely to be there. That'd be one in the eye for Wally! But Violet thinks it unlikely.

She said, "Wales comes and goes. He's like a flea at a fair. Never settles to anything for long."

I said, "Thelma Furness calls him 'David.' "

Pursed lips. "Does she indeed?" she said. "Well, in the unlikely event of your being in his company, don't think of imitating her.

Be on your guard, Maybell. Don't let Wally and her set lead you into regrettable habits."

I'm going to retrieve my gramophone and my tango record from Wally before she leaves for the Tyrol. It sounds as though it may be the saving of those Drumcanna evenings, and Violet thinks a guest called Tommy Minskip might enjoy the novelty of it. He's a viscount, unattached, and prefers indoor diversions to the hearty outdoor activities Melhuish's other friends seem to enjoy.

Violet said, "Who knows, perhaps you'll hit it off!"

I do believe she's matchmaking.

Less than three weeks till we leave for Scotland, which allows very little time for purchasing mountain wear. Violet has offered me a green waterproof cloak she keeps for rainy days at Ascot, but I have no intention of meeting Viscount Minskip dressed as a cucumber.

7th July 1932

To Peter Jones department store for cardigan sets, warm nightgowns, and bed socks. Violet says we're not going to the North Pole. Life here may have thickened her blood, but so far it hasn't affected mine. In addition to Viscount Minskip, the guests at Drumcanna will be the Habberleys, the Blythes, the Anstruther-Brodies, George Lightfoot, and ex-Queen Ena of Spain. Melhuish's sisters and their encumbrances will be at Birkhall, staying with the Bertie Yorks.

Next Tuesday is Rory's eleventh birthday. I'm granting him his dearest wish and taking him to a cafeteria for poached eggs on toast. I said he could invite a friend, too, but he says he'll just bring Flora. Ulick has declined, and Doopie gets anxious in tearooms.

8th July 1932

With Wally to collect her vacation outfits. What she does is buy one good thing each season and then have it copied. She has a little woman in Cromwell Road, who does it for a song and also remodels gowns, if they still have wear in them but have been seen rather too often. Wally's accustomed to this kind of thing, of course. All her life she's had to make a little go a long way, but still, how depressing! I felt compelled to take her to Derry and Toms and treat her to a new day dress.

She says it's not that Ernest's poor, but he's in the family shipping business, which went through shaky times when his father was in charge, so even though it's now quite successful, Ernest has a fear of financial reversals.

I said, "Did you know this when you agreed to marry him?"

She said she didn't know very much about him at all except that he had nice manners and good taste. Also, he offered to divorce his wife, so he seemed like a better prospect than working as a stenographer and living in a walk-up, which was the bleak future she faced after she'd dumped Win Spencer. I still think she rushed into things. I made Brumby wait two years for my answer.

She insists they're well suited though. She says that apart from being a stickler over the accounts, Ernest is very quiet and undemanding. He's quite happy to smoke his pipe and read his books and leave the decisions to her.

10th July 1932

Last evening to Pips and Freddie Crosbies. Came: Judson and Hattie Erlanger, Whitlow and Gladys Trilling, and an English couple, Prosper and Daphne Frith. Prosper is in Parliament with Freddie. Much talk about vicious street fighting in Germany. The Communists are behind it, of course, picking on the National Socialists. Prosper Frith says the situation is particularly tense in Hamburg, which is precisely Wally and Ernest's first port of call. Ernest has an office there. I must warn her.

11th July 1932

Wally says Germany is a wonderful, law-abiding country, and she isn't the least bit nervous about her trip. After Hamburg, they'll be motoring south to stay with an American friend called Lily. She has a small castle.

12th July 1932

Rory's birthday. My success as an aunt knows no bounds. It was such a hot afternoon we went first to the Serpentine Lido, where Rory and Flora took off their shoes and stockings and paddled, then to Oxford Street to Lyon's Corner House for tea. Flora wanted to know whether we have Red Indians at Sweet Air. Rory quizzed me about Wally. So much for Violet's whispering. Children don't miss a trick.

I said, "She's a friend who went to school with your mummy and me, and she's had a rather hard life. Her people didn't have any money."

"Gracious," he said, "that must have been jolly hard. Couldn't they have sold one of their houses or something?"

I said, "There wasn't anything to sell. Imagine. But your grandma and grandpa Patterson were always kind to her. She used to come to our house all the time in school vacation. She was like an extra sister. And now she's in London and so am I, so we can be friends again."

He wanted to know if she's still poor. I said, "Well, she's certainly not rich."

He said, "I expect Mummy hasn't invited her to tea because she wears raggedy clothes."

Flora said, "That's not why. It's because she's vast. I heard Mummy say so."

I said, "No she's not. She's small and slender."

"Well," she said, "Mummy told Aunt Elspeth The Wally was as vast and bushy as ever."

Extraordinary.

I pumped Rory for information about this Viscount Minskip Violet has lined up for me.

He said, "I don't know really. He always comes to Drumcanna, but he never asks me or Ulick to play with him. Uncle George Lightfoot says he doesn't have both oars in the water."

I'm surprised to hear he rows. Violet gave me the impression he's more of a drawing-room man.

18th July 1932

Wally gave up my portable gramophone very reluctantly, but she and Ernest leave tomorrow, so she can't have any possible use for it. I also had to ask for my tango record, and she wouldn't let me borrow the two she bought. She said Ernest is very particular about lending things.

21st July 1932

The car, the luggage, and the butler have left for the long drive north, and what remains of the staff seems to be in premature holiday mood. Bells go unanswered, baths are run late, and dinner has been pared down to soup, an entrée, and a dessert composed from stale cake and canned fruits. Violet says we'll be glutted with good food once we get to Drumcanna. I suppose that means more salmon.

27th July 1932, Drumcanna, Aberdeenshire

We are at Melhuish's Scottish seat, by some miracle. Now I know how our great pioneers lived as they forged west. We had to change trains at Edinburgh and again at Aberdeen, into ever more spartan carriages, so that we arrived at Aboyne with every tooth shaken loose. There we were met by cars for another bone-rattling ride. Fifteen miles on rutted tracks and in unaccountably sweltering heat.

Drumcanna towers above the Burn of Skelpie, a big granite house with towers at the two front corners, complete with battlements and arrow holes. The chair covers are worn, the drapes are faded, and the principal decorative motif is animal parts. Ink wells, coat hooks, *objets d'art,* all seem once to have gamboled across Drumcanna Moor.

I've been put in a turret room below the nursery, pleasantly furnished but one can only reach it by way of a perilous staircase, one narrow, winding climb for everyone, people and servants alike. In the mornings, when the night potties are being taken down and the breakfast trays are being brought up, it must be like Oxford Street.

Melhuish is in a jovial mood and has been very attentive to me, teaching me a dance called the strathspey and savoring those moments when the lurching of the train threw us into each other's arms. I wonder if he has regrets about Violet? She's become so stout and plain.

The first guests arrive tomorrow, Ralph and Jane Habberley and Fergus and Penelope Blythe. The shooting doesn't start till August 12th, but they're coming to fish for brown trout. George Lightfoot is expected at the weekend, and Queen Ena on Monday. There'll also be some local people, the Anstruther-Brodies, but they only come for the start of the shooting. Violet says it's impossible to predict when Tommy Minskip may arrive, as he's a law unto himself. I begin to like him already.

28th July 1932

No breakfast trays allowed. Violet says it's too much for the help when they have to get luncheon ready, and anyway it's nicer if everyone comes down and starts the day sociably over a kippered herring. But nobody's here yet, and anyway, what is help for if not to help? We'll be expected to carry up our own hot water next.

I hardly slept. When Violet enthused about the cornucopia of wildlife in the Highlands, she omitted to mention the miniature mosquitoes that have eaten me to the bone.

Rory says they're called midges. He and Flora have been running wild all morning, building a camp in a coppice beyond the vegetable garden. I'm to be invited to view it the moment it's fixed up. Violet doesn't seem to care what they drag outside—pillows, tea cups, a meat safe.

I said, "Do you realize Doopie's allowed them to take a good coverlet?"

"Not now, Maybell," she said. "I must catch our Consumptives secretary before she leaves for Glendochrie."

The Habberleys and the Blythes have just arrived. Lady Habberley dresses like a stablehand, but the Hon. Mrs. Blythe, much to Violet's disgust, is wearing nail polish. Flora's eyes lit up. She adores nail polish. She always rushes to see what color I've chosen when I come home from a manicure.

29th July 1932

The men and Ulick went out to fish at five, banging doors, crunching on the gravel, and generally wakening the dead. I ventured down at nine, hoping to organize a little tea and toast and tiptoe back to my room, but Doopie saw me pass the door and cried out "Bayba!" so I had no choice but to go in and join the ladies.

Jane Habberley is a drab creature. Violet described her as "the backbone of our Highland Crafts Association" and certainly, everything she wears appears to be hand-knitted. Penelope Blythe is definitely more promising. She'd already spotted my gramophone and suggested to Violet that we have dancing after dinner this evening.

Violet said she had no objection, but we might find ourselves short of men. She said Melhuish doesn't do *that* kind of dancing. We'll see about that.

Penelope said, "Who's at Balmoral? If Prince George is there, I'm sure he'd adore to come over and dance."

Violet says Prince George isn't there, nor the Prince of Wales. Only Prince Harry, and Bertie York and his little family at Birkhall.

Penelope said, "Well, neither of them is any use. They only

dance reels. Do you know them, Maybell? Violet won't like my saying it, but they're *such* a dull bunch."

I said, "No, I don't. But I do know Lady Furness."

"Do you!" she said. "How thrilling! Well, of course, Thelma Furness is the *plat du jour,* but she's only the latest in a long line, and Wales still keeps up with some of his old sweethearts, you know? He visits Freda Dudley Ward all the time."

Violet sliced the top off her egg with a fearsome swipe.

She said, "I hope you're coming out for a walk this morning, Maybell? I very much hope you're not going to sit around gossiping."

She knows darned well I don't go for walks. One of my conditions of coming here was that I be left in peace to write my diary and peruse the great works of Sir Walter Scott and Rabbi Burns.

Penelope Blythe describes Viscount Minskip as *chetif.* Unfortunately, the library here is not equipped with foreign dictionaries.

30th July 1932

George Lightfoot arrived at tea time and was pleased to find I'd set up my gramophone in the Long Gallery. Penelope and I took turns with him, then Ralph Habberley appeared, drawn by the sound of the music, as did Doopie, Rory, Flora, and several spaniels. I think we've managed to give them all the rudiments, except for Flora, who won't apply herself to anything and made up her own wild Scottish steps. Ralph has more enthusiasm than ability, but George moves rather well, for an Englishman. The help were so fascinated, peering around the door at us, that the dinner bell was late.

31st July 1932

Jane Habberley stood on my tango record and destroyed it.

1st August 1932

There is no store in either Aboyne or Ballater that sells gramophone records.

2nd August 1932

I now know the meaning of *chetif.* Tommy Minskip is insane. He drives himself in a Bentley motor car, and travels without even a valet. He arrived yesterday with one small valise and a trunk containing dozens of toy soldiers which he has now laid out in the Smoking Room, ready to re-enact the Battle of Waterloo. George Lightfoot has explained it all to me. Every afternoon, as close to two p.m. as social obligations allow, the Royal Scots Greys charge the French infantry, with sound effects, Minskip captures the enemy's eagle standard and then falls, mortally wounded.

"Still a boy at heart," was George's explanation. I think he's too generous. If he were still a boy at heart, he wouldn't have disappointed Rory and Flora by omitting to visit their sodden camp.

3rd August 1932

Penelope and I have taken up watercolor painting. We find we can run off half a dozen before luncheon and smudges don't at all matter; indeed, they add to a picture's talking points. Rain kept us indoors today, but one doesn't need to be looking at a moor in order to paint an "impression" of it. Penelope tosses hers away at the end of the day, but mine might make interesting gifts for Christmas.

George Lightfoot is very amiable, playing at Dolls' Shooting Lunches with Rory and Flora in their hideaway and holding Doopie's skeins of knitting yarn while she winds them into balls.

He's been teasing Melhuish about his stags, keeps asking when he's going to "do a Sassoon" on them? Sir Philip Sassoon, apparently, has had his stags' antlers gilded so they catch the sun. Shudders from Melhuish. I think it a rather wonderful idea.

I said, "I think I'd like to know Sir Philip Sassoon."

George said, "You mean you haven't met him? Violet, what are you thinking of?"

She said, "But we never see him. I see Sybil, of course. She's on my Blood Bank committee, but Philip, almost never."

George said, "Well, *I* shall introduce you, directly we get back to London."

I said, "And where do Sir Philip and Lady Sybil live?"

"Oh no," he said, "Syb's not his wife. She's his sister. She's the Marchioness of Chumley, spelled *Cholmondeley,* nota bene Maybell. She's married to Rocksavage, but Philip's not married to anyone."

So much the better. Sir Philip sounds much more to my taste than Viscount Minskip. Penelope says Minskip owns practically half of Yorkshire, but I don't care. He's welcome to it.

5th August 1932

Ena of Spain has arrived, wheezing and perspiring but all smiles. She has perfect English, being an actual granddaughter of Queen Victoria and almost raised by her. She's an ex-queen though, so there's no need for those time-consuming deep curtsies. A sincere bob is quite sufficient. The ex-King isn't with her. They take separate vacations.

More thunder. More insects. Tonight's much-trumpeted treat for dinner was sea trout caught by Melhuish and Ulick. "How wonderful," Violet kept saying. "Only an hour out of the water!" Still a fish though, when all's said and done. I long for a filet mignon.

Ena took my hand and said she hoped we'd be friends. She said, "Violet has been my rock and Doopie's almost like a daughter to me, so I'm going to claim you, too. Then I'll have the full set!"

6th August 1932

Ena Spain is quite gay, considering the circumstances of her life. Her children are all sickly, her husband goes with actresses, and last year, when the rebels drove them out of Spain, he left without her. Ran off to Paris and left her to take her chances and follow with the youngest of the brood once they were healthy enough to travel. She says there were rioters ramming the palace doors with trucks, and if it hadn't been for two footmen helping them slip out the back way, they'd have been murdered in their beds. I wonder whether she lost her jewels. No one dresses here, so it's impossible to know whether she's been reduced to paste copies.

She's especially attached to Doopie, because by an extraordinary coincidence, one of her sons is the same kind of dullard. His name is Hymie, but they spell it with a J in Spain. She said, "Hymie and Doopie get along so well. They understand each other perfectly. It's a pity they're not closer in age, because I think they'd have made a very happy couple."

The very idea. I told her, they must never be allowed to breed.

She said, "I don't see why. It's not an inherited kind of deafness. And in every other respect, they're just like you and me. The Greeces have an aunt with exactly the same problem and she's led a very full life."

Penelope Blythe agrees with me that Doopie doesn't seem all there. George Lightfoot says she's sharp as a tack but deaf as a post. I'm beginning to think information has been kept from me.

7th August 1932

It's official. Doopie is deaf. I had it out with Violet while she was dressing.

I said, "Someone might have thought to mention it to me."

She said, "Mother told you. I know she did. You just never listen. And anyway, it couldn't matter less. Doopie manages very well and she's perfectly happy."

I'd just like to know when it was decided she's not an idiot.

She said, "You're the only one who ever said she was. Things take her longer, that's all. Some things."

I suppose now I'll be expected to apologize. Violet says there's nothing can be done about her ears. Apparently, Prince Hymie with a J tried a hearing aid, an electrical box that hung around his neck and plugged into his ears, for when he had to go to receptions, but it didn't help him at all. I'm not surprised. No one at receptions can hear anything. The only thing to do is nod intelligently and move swiftly along.

Rory says Thomas Edison, inventor of the light bulb, was also deaf. Greek aunts, ex-Prince Hymie, Thomas Edison. Suddenly deafness is all the rage.

8th August 1932

Flora is wearing an Atora suet carton hung on a string and is playing at Hearing Aids. George Lightfoot said there was no need to apologize to Doopie for thinking her an idiot all these years, because there have been many times when she's thought the same of me. But I *did* apologize, because even deaf people may have feelings.

Doopie said, "Aw ride, Bayba. No needa shoud. Dudn't mayg any divrent."

She has such a cheerful disposition. Of course, being handicapped, she has never been subjected to the stresses and strains of life as we normal people are.

10th August 1932

Melhuish's sisters motored over from Birkhall for luncheon. Jinty is even sourer than Elspeth, but she lives in the far, far north, so I'm unlikely to be troubled by her company again. Elspeth may be reconciled to the idea of a foreign sister-in-law; in fact, I think she's rather fond of Violet, but Jinty doesn't even approve of the English, so what hope for a patriotic American. The only time she addressed me was to ask me when I'd be returning to the United States. Worried I might stick around and bag one of those spare Scottish lords, I suppose. And she looked at the jug of iced water I requested as though I'd asked for a doggie woops to be brought to the table.

I said, "September. I'll be going back in September."

I hadn't realized I'd decided until I'd said it.

Tears from Flora. She fled from the table, Doopie followed her, and Rory followed Doopie.

Penelope said, "Oh Maybell, don't go. I rather thought we might be chums. You'll find things much livelier after the summer. Balls, parties. Do stay. Violet has room for you."

But I didn't say I was going back for good. Not at all. I'll simply settle my affairs, let it be known to provincialites like Nora Sedley Cordle that Maybell Brumby has gone international, and then return. And Violet's having room or not won't enter into it, because I shall take a house anyway. Somewhere I can have my bath run as deep and as hot as I please. And I won't have to lose sleep over the price of a good rib roast.

I'll be one of the Baltimore belles who are making their mark on London.

11th August 1932

A boot boy has gone by bicycle down to Aboyne with a wire to Fishbone and Strong. I've instructed them to find a good tenant for Sweet Air. Flora is happy. She's been dancing up and down the Long Gallery, singing, "Aunt Bayba's staying forever!"

Penelope seems very pleased, too. She says there's a house that may be coming up across from them in Cadogan Square. I don't know. I'll have to see if it's my kind of neighborhood.

The Anstruther-Brodies have arrived, which signals the start of the shooting party.

The quarry is a small bird called grice.

12th August 1932

The guns went out early, Ailsa Anstruther-Brodie among them. It was all too obvious at dinner last night that Melhuish is very smitten. He kept gushing about her being a first-rate shot, and bounding across the room to light her cigarette. It all seems to sail over Violet's head.

Everything now revolves around the shooting, even luncheon, so one has the choice of piling into motors and joining the guns, or going hungry. Even Viscount Minskip has been forced to reschedule his daily battle. Two long tables had been taken up to the moor and set with china and flatware kept especially for these occasions. Shooting lunches, they're called. The whole thing must be an enormous strain on Violet's struggling staff, and it would be altogether simpler if sandwiches were sent up in a shooting brake and the rest of us were left in peace, but no. Ladies, children, and Minskip at one table; men, loaders, beaters, and Ailsa Anstruther-Brodie at the other. Stag pie and salad and a cake decorated with flaked almonds, which Rory calls Toenail Cake.

Jane Habberley is now sucking up to me, asking my advice about watercolor painting—feeling pangs of guilt about my tango record, I hope.

13th August 1932

I now know everything there is to know about shooting parties. The guns come in at five and talk of nothing but the day's bag. More than sixty birds were taken today, which means we shall be eating them till kingdom come, but at least it will make a change from fish. The guns also dash away after one whiskey, help themselves to all the hot water, then commandeer the conversation at dinner. Weather prospects, heather bugs, gamekeepers droller than Beatrice Lillie, dogs smarter than Alfred Einstein.

Next year, I shall summer with my own kind of people. The raspberries here are delicious, however.

Weather close and thundery. Poor Ena Spain is suffering. She perspires even on a cold day. Her age, I suppose. She'll be moving on to Balmoral on Tuesday, to visit with Their Majesties. George Lightfoot says Balmoral is like Drumcanna with extra tartan. "Home from home," Ena calls it. She's been there just about every summer of her life.

She said, "Well, no one ever dared question it. Grandmama loved Balmoral, and wherever she went we followed. She never let Mama out of her sight. Even visited her on her honeymoon! But Mama doesn't come anymore. She had her fill of it, and she doesn't care for travel. She prefers to stay put."

Ena's mother is Princess Baby, still going strong, with an apartment at Kensington Palace and a house on the Isle of Wight.

Violet said, "And is she still beavering away at her diaries?"

Ena said, "She is. Almost finished, I think."

I told her I keep a diary.

"Well," she said, "these aren't Mama's own diaries. They're Grandmama's."

Princess Baby is apparently going through Queen Victoria's diaries, taking out anything that might cause offense and rewriting them in fresh notebooks. It's called editing.

I said, "No one had better change *my* diaries after I'm gone. I'll be very cross."

Violet said, "Maybell, rest assured, nobody will be interested in your diary."

14th August 1932

Rain beating against the windows all night, heavy snoring from Anstruther-Brodie, who is in the room below mine, and then, just as I'd dropped off to sleep, doors banging as the early birds went down to breakfast. When the party breaks up on Tuesday, I may try the room Jane Habberley's been occupying. She claims she sleeps like the dead when she's at Drumcanna, and I believe I can live with wall-to-wall tartan—for a few nights, at any rate.

An extraordinary question from Penelope. Have I managed to enjoy a little romance while I've been here? Romance!

I said, "I already told you what I think of Tommy Minskip."

"Well, not Minskip, obviously," she said. "But Habberley perhaps, or Lightfoot? You seem quite 'in' with him."

Well, Ralph Habberley has bad breath, not to mention a wife. George Lightfoot is certainly the best of the bunch, but a little too young for me. He never brushes his hair and he will sit sideways, swinging his long, gangling legs over the arm of the chair. If I were in a hurry to find a beau, which I am not, I'd be looking for a man with a little silver at his temples.

I said, "No. I haven't had a romance. Have you?"

"No," she said. "I put it down to the quality of the shooting. Last year they were coming in with very small bags, and I found Anstruther-Brodie quite in the mood for an adventure. But this year, not a nibble. Maybe I'll make a play for Lightfoot this evening, if you're sure I won't be trespassing."

How desperate and how dangerous. A person could so easily fall and break their neck, tiptoeing up and down those turret stairs in a state of ardor.

16th August 1932

Penelope winked at me over the kedgeree, signaling she made a conquest last night.

She said, "Maybell, why don't I stay and keep you company when Violet and Melhuish go to Birkhall? Fergus won't mind going on to Glendochrie without me."

I thanked her but pointed out that everyone else is moving on today. Including George Lightfoot. More winks. Then a lot of giggling in the morning room while she had me guess who she's seduced. Not Lightfoot, because he played billiards all evening and didn't tango with her once. Not Anstruther-Brodie, because that would be like reading yesterday's newspaper. And not Ralph Habberley, because he's a drip and the last man on earth. So who? Angus.

I said, "Who is Angus?"

"Shh," she said. "One of the housemaids is his sister. He's the underghillie. Isn't it a lark?"

An underghillie! That's nothing more than a junior fishing assistant. It would be like having an assignation with a boot boy.

She says she found him in the rod room.

Ena Spain, George Lightfoot, the Anstruther-Brodies, and Doopie, whom the Majesties appear to dote on, just left for Balmoral. The Blythes and the Habberleys are meant to be going south to Perthshire to another shooting party, but a major row blew up between Penelope and Fergus as to whether she should remain here instead. I'm afraid she got no support from me.

She said, "Oh but Maybell, what about Minskip? What if he makes a play for you? Shouldn't you like a chaperone?"

But Minskip is on his way home and anyway, I believe I'd have been safe in his company. The only way to get Tommy Minskip's attention is to disarrange his cavalry. And as for Penelope, I want nothing of her complications. I think a little of Penelope Blythe goes a long way.

17th August 1932

Violet, Melhuish, and Ulick have gone to stay with Bertie and Elizabeth York for three days at Birkhall, on the Balmoral estate. Which leaves me in charge at Drumcanna.

I've explained to the help how to make French toast, and it will now be served instead of oatmeal in the morning. Rory requested sausages for dinner, and Flora has asked for "gake with lots of jam" and varnish on her stubby little fingernails. It's so easy to make them happy. They're now skipping up and down the gravel sweep, crying "Hurrah! Hurrah!"

A wire from Fishbone and Strong. They have people from Kentucky keen to take Sweet Air but they'd want it by October. Can I have it ready so soon? I most certainly can. As soon as ever I'm released from duties as Favorite Aunt, I shall go to London and book my passage.

18th August 1932

A little girl called Ellen MacNab, daughter of the head-keeper, overcame her shyness and ventured up the drive to play with Flora. They are much of an age. We've had great fun, dancing tangos and reels and strathspeys, all without the benefit of phonograph music.

Rory asked to speak to me privately when it was time for Ellen to leave.

He said, "Should I walk her home?"

I said, "Would you like to?"

"Oh yes," he said, "but it's rather tricky. Daddy says one should always take care of ladies, but MacNab works for us, and Daddy also says one should be mindful of familiarity with servants."

I said, "We could get one of the maids to take her."

But he did it himself, with Flora tagging along.

He said, "I think it was the right thing, Aunt Maybell. I was very mindful."

20th August 1932

Violet returned from Birkhall, bringing with her Duchess Bertie York and her elder daughter. They stayed to tea. Princess Lilibet is two years younger than Flora, but very pink-and-white and refined. She sat neatly beside her mother for the entire visit and ate her scone without dropping a crumb. Flora, wearing Rory's kilt and an ecru lace runner from the dining-room sideboard, and for whose benefit I'm sure the call was made, glowered at her little playmate and then hid behind a curtain. The Duchess and Violet are great friends and I can see why. They're both so homely.

21st August 1932

Tomorrow to London and a midge-free suite at Claridge's. Violet is raising objections right and left. Why the haste? Why spend money on accommodations when I could wait only two more weeks and travel back with her to Carlton Gardens? Isn't it a rash move, giving up my home and plunging into the unknown?

It says everything about the differences between us. She clings to her lists and timetables and routines, whereas I'm not afraid to seize the moment. Why the haste? Because prospective tenants with good references and no children don't grow on trees, and the *Lancastria* sails on August 30th. And a rash move? Well, a two-year lease hardly amounts to burning my boats, and Belgravia isn't exactly darkest Africa.

I've reminded her it was her idea I should come to London in the first place. Gay diversions and eligible beaux were the inducements, as I remember it, neither of which Violet is in any position to provide, I now realize. She thought I'd be one of those wallflower widows, eager to meet a titled simpleton, grateful to be squeezed into Lady Desborough's guest attic. Now she knows better. I shall have my own coterie before Violet can say "agenda."

"Well, if you're absolutely sure it's what you want, Maybell," she keeps saying.

I am.

25th August 1932, Claridge's Hotel, London

Violet was right about one thing. London is dead. I woke a realtor from his August slumbers and have appointments to view three houses tomorrow, one of them catty-corner from Penelope and Fergus Blythe. What a surprise Pips and Wally are going to get when they come back and find me with my own establishment.

26th August 1932

I am taking a house on Wilton Place. It's light and very prettily done out in the palest greens and blues. More important, the owners are Americans, so it has a good, efficient furnace and a Kelvinator icebox. I didn't like the aspect of the Cadogan Square property. It was convenient for Harrold's department store, but the drawing room was full west, which can be very bothersome on summer evenings, and the house in Eaton Mews was too close for comfort to Melhuish's sister Elspeth and her husband. The last thing I need is her training the Rear-Admiral's telescope on my front door.

Wilton Place is exactly right for me. Pips and I will be neighbors almost, and when Doopie and Flora tire of feeding the ducks in St. James's Park, they can come and visit Hyde Park instead.

2nd September 1932, RMS *Lancastria*

The ocean is as calm as a soup dish, and I have unexpected company. Judson and Hattie Erlanger came on board at the very last moment. I bumped into Hattie as I was taking a turn on deck this morning. She had a friend with her, Daisy Fellowes, and they were on their way to the gymnasium. They begged me to join them, but I preferred to sit with a cup of bouillon and my own thoughts. They said they were going to bicycle all the way to New York, and went off shrieking with laughter. It seemed too early in the day for them to be tight.

3rd September 1932

Judson tells me Hattie's friend Daisy Fellowes is immensely rich. From what I saw of her at dinner last evening, she's certainly made inroads into the world's supply of pink diamonds. He's in a nice, gossipy mood. He thinks Wally must have stampeded Ernest into marriage, because he has the look of a man who's not quite sure where he is or what he's doing there.

I said, "I think the appeal of Ernest was he was effectively a free ticket to London and a fresh start."

He said, "Yes, that makes sense. She'd fouled the nest too much to stay in Baltimore."

Judson does rather go on about what a great girl Hattie is. I wonder if he feels under some kind of obligation to try making love to me again? I pray not. Our paths diverged in 1917, and if he has made a happy match with Hattie, I can only be pleased for him. Personally, I find her gratingly tall.

8th September 1932, Sweet Air, Baltimore

Sweet Air was bathed in sunlight as I arrived, and it feels so roomy and bright after those London houses with their rooms stacked higgledy-piggledy four and five floors high. I almost picked up the telephone and told Fishbone to call everything off.

But it is too big for me in my present circumstances. Too big, too quiet, too remote from invigorating company. I've grown accustomed to nightlife and the rattle of London trams. Also, Missie says Junior's wife stops her car outside every day and peers through the gates up to my pleasure porch. If I stayed, she and Junior would surely rob me of my peace of mind and destroy my health.

19th September 1932

The last of my boxes has gone, and the ticker-tape machine has been removed, my final reminder of Brumby. Whatever Junior may say, we were contented. I didn't bother him and he didn't bother me, at least not in recent times.

I've put Nora Sedley Cordle out of her misery. She's been making hay in my absence, hosting musical soirees and raising funds for the veterans' hospital, and must have been anxious about my returning home, worried I'd confiscate her new little empire. By a great stroke of luck, she arrived at Klein's just as my furs were being loaded into the car. A face like an anaemic chipmunk.

I said, "Hello Nora and good-bye. You know, I find Baltimore so narrow now I live in London. I wonder if we shall ever meet again."

I've always made good exits, though I do say so myself.

24th September 1932, RMS *Rex*

Junior and that grasping creature he calls a wife had the nerve to send a basket of fruit to my stateroom. All poisoned, I'm sure. I've donated it to the stewards' mess.

A squall is forecast for tonight.

25th September 1932

More than a squall. The girl from the infirmary ministered to me like an angel, but there are no hair appointments until tomorrow afternoon.

26th September 1932

Thelma Furness's sister Connie is on board. She claimed me in the Palm Court as I was trying to regain my sea legs. We shared a pot of tea, and when she heard of my difficulties, she made a call and immediately, miraculously, a hair appointment opened up.

She told me Thelma and her Prince have been summering secretly at Biarritz. No wonder he didn't put in an appearance at Balmoral.

A wire from Violet. Melhuish is sending his car to meet me when we dock, and she insists on my going to Carlton Gardens until my own house is aired. How kind everyone is.

30th September 1932, Carlton Gardens, London

Ulick and Rory have returned to their schools, and the pace of London life is quickening again. Violet already has a number of invitations on her mantel. I predict that by this time next year, mine will make hers look sadly bare.

She said, "Well, now you're here, what do you plan to do?"

My feet have hardly touched dry land. I said, "I'm going to make telephone calls, to see who's back in town, and tomorrow night I'm going to Ciro's with Pips and Freddie and the Whitlow Trillings."

"No," she said, "I mean what are you going to *do*? There are more important things in life than going to niteries."

She underestimates me. I'm perfectly aware I have to hire a cook and a driver. I also have to pick out new drapes for my dining room, something more confident than pastel stripes, something that says "Maybell Brumby lives here now." But one can't be slaving every hour of the day. Lunch with Ida.

1st October 1932

Ida has a new beau, acquired in a lecture hall in Tewkesbury. He's an Acolyte of the Seventh Ray, drinks only chamomile tea and is showing her the path to inner vitality. The people one meets in Gloucestershire!

Wally's back. Shopping on Monday. Her friend with the castle, Lily Drax-Pfaffenhof, is coming to stay, so she's splashing out on a new rug for the guest bedroom.

3rd October 1932

Heal's had a selection of perfectly adequate rugs, but Wally insisted on going to a little Persian in Sackville Street, and once those people have you in their clutches, they won't let go until you've seen their entire stock. Wally, of course, went to his most expensive item like a homing pigeon. "Oh," he said, "a most discerning choice. A most unique rug made in a mountain village to a pattern known only to one old man." They always say that, but

Wally's impossible to turn once she's decided on a thing. She's promised to get a check sent round to me first thing tomorrow. Another jolt to Ernest's careful budget.

She said, "Ernest will be fine about it. He'd rather stretch himself to buy something good than settle for mediocrity. We're of one mind on that. And I won't have Lily stepping out of bed onto the kind of thing a grocer's wife might buy. Lily's a landgravine, you know?"

A landgravine! Further complications. No doubt there will be the expense of special dietary requirements in addition to outlay on hand-knotted rugs.

4th October 1932

I've engaged a butler, a cook, and two housemaids, but still no driver and no satisfactory lady's maid. Penelope Blythe says there may be servants becoming available at the Orr-Tweedies' since Mrs. O-T passed away. She's going to inquire.

Ructions in the nursery. It's Melhuish's birthday on Thursday, and Flora had the idea of giving him a party. She said, "We can make a gake and Daddy can blow out the gandles."

Violet said it was a sweet idea but out of the question, because he's speaking on the Pheasant Bill that afternoon and then going on to a January Club dinner.

Doopie said, "Bedvus dime?"

Violet said, "No, Doopie. Mornings are far too hectic, especially when he's working on a speech. Don't pout, Flora. You can have a little party without him. I'll ask Smith to find you something special. Now off you skip. Mummy has to look for some papers for Lady Strathnaver."

Doopie looked at me, but there was really nothing I could do. The poor child was clearly disappointed, and I'd have taken her out to Harrold's and bought her a new dolly, but I was already committed to lunch with Pips and then a manicure. By the time I got back, it was too late to save Flora from herself. She'd gone into the writing room and created a snowstorm of papers, from Violet's desk and from Melhuish's, scrambling them up with her grubby little hands and tossing them in the air. The floor was still covered when I looked in, Fishermen's Orphans mixed up with Unmarried Mothers and the Hedgerows Bill. Trotman had hauled her upstairs, and she'd been sent to bed without any tea.

This must surely strengthen the case for sending her to school.

5th October 1932

Penelope Blythe has come up trumps. I've taken on Padmore, formerly lady's maid to Mrs. Orr-Tweedie, and also Kettle, who was her driver for nineteen years.

He drove me along Piccadilly and the Haymarket and then back by Pall Mall to Carlton Gardens, and he has a pleasingly smooth technique. He also carries a kind of Boy Scout emergency box, which he showed me before he stowed it in the trunk: flashlight, bandages, medicinal brandy, magnesia tablets, and a miniature sewing kit. He said, "In case of a loose button, madam, or laddered hosiery."

There'll be no need for that. If I ladder my stocking, I shall just have him drive me home so I can change it. Still, it does show he has the right attitude.

6th October 1932

Wilton Place is ready for me. On Saturday, I shall sleep my first night there. A fresh start, and how fitting. It will be a year to the day since I lost Brumby.

George Lightfoot was in the nursery when I returned from Monsieur Jules, helping Doopie and Flora fete the absent Melhuish with a rather dry marble cake.

"Ah," he said, "the very girl I was hoping to see. Come with me Monday next to Philip Sassoon's. He's asked me to Park Lane to see his new majolica urns."

Over drinks, I heard Melhuish say he didn't think Sir Philip was "quite the thing."

Lightfoot said, "What can you mean?"

Melhuish said, "I don't know. He strikes me as a bit of a Johnny-come-lately. Belchester told me he has a footman serve tea. Can you imagine!"

Violet said, "But dearest, he does raise a great deal of money for hospitals. And we're very fond of Sybil."

Melhuish said, "Oh, quite so. Sybil's one hundred percent. I used to play polo with her husband. Never see him nowadays, of course. Seems to spend most of his time in the south of France."

All I said was, "Like Thelma Furness's husband."

Violet said, "No, Maybell. Not at all like that. Rock plays in tennis tournaments."

That, of course, would be Rock Chumley, spelled *Cholmondeley*, nota bene.

Well, tennis, tootsies, whatever the excuse, it sounds to me as though the south of France is teeming with restless English husbands.

7th October 1932

To the Café de Paris with Pips and Freddie, the Erlangers, and the Simpsons for steak Diane and a Dixieland band. Wally and Ernest brought along Lily Drax-Pfaffenhof, who turns out to be much more fun than she sounds. Her first husband was in Manchester cotton and left her stony broke but fortunately, she made a good second marriage to a landgrave called Willi, which makes her a landgravine. Somewhere between a countess and a duchess, according to Ernest. Anyhow, she wears it very lightly. I think we shall become friends.

Wally believes she may know the Sassoons. When she was in Hong Kong, there was a family of that name, and she's almost certain she went to a party at their house, but Hattie Erlanger says it must be a different lot, because Philip and Sybil are Jews from Baghdad.

Freddie said, "Yes, Hattie, but not recently. Sassoon's been in the Commons twenty years at least."

According to Freddie, he's something important at the Air Ministry, entertains lavishly, and has a reputation as a firecracker, always sparkling and fizzing and dashing between his various wonderful homes. Sir Philip Firecracker Sassoon! I can't wait.

8th October 1932, Wilton Place

My first year without Brumby. It seems longer, so much has happened. Well, I think I've conducted my period of mourning in a decorous manner. Violet may make her disparaging remarks about niteries, but even widows have to while away their evenings somehow, and I'm sure Danforth Brumby would prefer me looking radiant in claret rather than haggard in black.

9th October 1932

I've suggested to Padmore that we dispense with the customary black dress for her, too. We can get her something more modern. Dark blue, perhaps, or dove gray, with a little white apron. "Whatever you think, madam," she said. That's the kind of attitude I like!

10th October 1932

I am in love! Philip Sassoon is delicious. He's the same age as Melhuish, but you'd never think it, he's so svelte and so vibrant. Also, he has exquisite taste. Blood-red roses arranged against a panel of black glass. Twinned pewter buckets filled with white ox-eye daisies.

He dashed around, showing us everything. The drawing room—*one* of the drawing rooms—all pink and gilt and tapestries. The dining room azure and silver. Everything done with a very sure touch. Only the ballroom was too hectic for my taste, no surface left unpainted. Camel trains, palm trees, sheikhs of Araby.

"The problem with owning a ballroom," he said, "is that one feels an obligation to use it."

Lightfoot sang my praises as a dancer, but, sadly, Sir Philip doesn't dance.

He said, "One always feels obliged to buzzz around like a bumble bee, pollinating one's guests with gaiety, and then, when the evening's over, the room looks horrrribly like the Battle of Culloden Moor."

A location from his Baghdad period, I suppose.

I said, "What you need is a woman to hold your balls for you."

"Maybell!" he said, "I think I may thrrrreaten you with an invitation to Trrrrent Park."

I said, "Invite away! You don't frrrrighten me." How we laughed.

A small point of accuracy for Melhuish. Sir Philip does *not* have a footman serve tea. He has foot*men*. And why not!

11th October 1932

Wally was infuriatingly vague about her plans for the day, and then, when I walked into the Ivy to meet Pips, there she was, tête-à-tête with Thelma Furness. They waved but made no move to invite us over to join them.

Pips says she finds it horribly entertaining to watch Wally at work. "Spinning her web," she called it.

She said, "Look at her. I mean, Thelma's nice in her own sappy way, but Wally can't possibly find her *that* interesting. She's just cultivating her so she can get her foot in Wales's door."

I said, "There are worse projects. I wouldn't mind meeting him myself. They say he's a nifty dancer."

Pips said, "Well, I think it's all rather desperate and sad. It reminds me of the trouble she went to to snag a dance with Chevy Auburn. Remember? Cozying up to his sister. Memorizing all his sprint times. And men are so dumb. They fall for it every time. I'll bet she worked the same old business with Ernest. I'll bet she pumped Mary Kirk for useful tidbits, filed them under 'Ernest,' and then fed them right back to him."

I think Wally just uses what little God gave her. She has a very plain face, no figure, and no fortune. It stands to reason she's had to develop her wits.

Pips could have shown more interest in my tea with Philip Sassoon. All she said was, "But isn't he a fruit?"

12th October 1932

Penelope Blythe says a fruit is a very useful, unmarried type of man friend, and she's often thought of getting one herself.

To Carlton Gardens for drinks. The Billy Belchesters were there, and Leo von Hoesch popped along from the German Embassy. *So* charming, and never married. I wonder if he's a fruit, too. Violet says he's the civilized face of Germany and quite abhors Mr. Hitler and his new ideas.

A note had arrived for me from young Rory, to remind me he'll soon be coming home on his midterm vacation. He writes, *I should very much like to take you to a Tea Room but I'm rather out of funds.*

No matter. What are aunts for if not the occasional piece of pie?

I've pinned down Violet and Melhuish to come to me this week. I want to throw a little party while the Crokers are still in town.

Violet said, "Just drinks, Maybell. Melhuish will never manage your jazzed-up food. And please, no gangsters."

I said, "Boss Croker is *not* a gangster."

She said, "Well, he sounds like one."

I've a good mind to invite Thelma Furness.

20th October 1932

I am launched, and to great applause! Just champagne, whiskey, and salted almonds, but Padmore served them very nicely. I believe she's thrilled with her new livery.

Came: the Crosbies, the Erlangers, George Lightfoot, the Benny Thaws, the Whitlow Trillings, the Crokers, the Fergus Blythes (who brought along with them a sweet creature called Cimmie Mosley, married to a mad revolutionary), Violet and Melhuish, and Wally and Ernest. Thelma sent regrets, as did Philip Sassoon, who was unable to get away from the Ministry, and Leo von Hoesch, who had to give a little reception for some Hohenzollerns.

I omitted to invite Ida. I didn't want her arriving with a bag full of pamphlets, or worse still, with Mr. Acolyte on her arm.

Much talk about Mr. Mussolini. Ernest has read that he's a great all-rounder. He plays the violin and governs his country, and yet he's not above rolling up his sleeves and helping with the corn harvest. A Renaissance man, Ernest called him. Also, he's electrificating the railroads. Freddie said that will be all very fine for the Italians but not so good for the Welsh miners, whose coal the Italians will stop buying. Well, I'm behind Mr. Mussolini on this. One has to look out for one's own.

Melhuish allowed Wally to flirt with him wickedly on the subject of trout fishing. He was quite pink by the time he and Violet had to leave for the Londonderries. He said, "Come to Sunday luncheon, Maybell. Bring your Simpson chums with you."

Violet was on the telephone first thing, putting paid to that.

She said, "I really don't want Wally here on Sunday. I'm sure her husband is perfectly pleasant, but she's as raucous as ever. We'll have the Habberleys and anyway, Wally's just not the kind of guest we'd want Flora to meet. Melhuish only suggested it because you'd given him far too much whiskey."

I said, "Don't worry. Wally and Ernest can't come anyway. They're going to a polo tournament. But I don't see why you have to be so against her. It was you who wrote excitedly to tell me she was in London."

Violet said, "I did *not* write excitedly. I mentioned her as one might report the arrival of a new dancing bear at the zoo. But I didn't mean you should pay to watch it day after day, and I certainly didn't mean you should bring it home."

23rd October 1932

Wally's in a state of great excitement. She and Ernest are invited to the Thelma Furness's country house for a weekend. Leicestershire. This will undoubtedly involve a long, cold train journey, because everything in this country does. It's a pity Mr. Mussolini isn't an Englishman.

I said, "And will the Prince of Wales be there?"

She said, "I don't know. I could hardly ask. But we're going to be quite prepared for it."

Ernest has a book on etiquette, and Wally's practicing her curtsies, but the main thing on her mind is clothes. She's talking about empire-line georgette with capped sleeves, but my advice was to buy every item of warm underwear Gamages have on sale, and fur-lined boots, too. Crazy. Wherever Leicestershire is, you may be sure it's nowhere near the frontiers of fashion.

Hattie Erlanger says Wally and Ernest will be expected to ride. She says it's inconceivable to go to Leicestershire without a hacking jacket at the very least. Wally says that's the trouble with people like Hattie. Their minds run along narrow, muddy ruts, and they fail to notice that thousands of civilized people go their whole lives without ever sitting on a horse.

25th October 1932

Yesterday to Fuller's Tea Rooms with Rory and Flora. If you want to know what's being said on the back stairs, take your nephews and nieces out to tea. Prince George goes dancing with black girls. The Duke of Westminster shouts at his new wife. And Lady Furness is getting a divorce. Funny Wally never mentioned that.

I brought them back to see my new house before Kettle drove them home. Both chiefly interested in which bedrooms they would have if I were to invite them to stay the night. I don't know that I would invite them. Tea is one thing, but not the complications of bedtime stories and prayers and night-lights.

3rd November 1932

Found a dear little cashmere cardigan for Wally, edge-to-edge with a braid trim. If she follows my advice, *that's* what she'll wear to dinner in Leicestershire. As a matter of fact, I think she should avoid décolletage whenever possible. She has no bosom to speak of, and the skin on her back is poor.

Dinner at the Crosbies. Anne Belchester says she's heard Thelma Furness keeps her country house ruinously hot for good paintings. Prosper Frith said he didn't realize the Furnesses had any good paintings.

4th November 1932

To George Lightfoot's for a small supper party. Came: Penelope and Fergus Blythe, a House of Commons man called Bob Boothby, and old Lady Ribblesdale. She's the one who paid lawyers to get her a good divorce settlement from John Astor, when had she but known it, she could have waited a little longer, waved him aboard the *Titanic,* and inherited everything. They say it would be a curse to see into the future, but I don't imagine Ava Ribblesdale thinks so.

Mr. Boothby was just back from a visit with Mr. Hitler in Germany, and said the man is quite insane and we'd better start building battleships while we still have time. Fergus Blythe said Boothby was squawking like a parlor maid who'd seen a mouse. I do agree with Fergus that Mr. Hitler is Germany's business and no one else's.

Much talk, too, about whether Roosevelt is going to beat Hoover.

Penelope said, "He should. He seems full of bright ideas for getting men back to work."

Indeed. Full of ideas that people like me will have to pay for.

Lightfoot ran things rather effortlessly, for a single man. Duck terrine, tenderloin of pork, damson tart.

All evening my mind kept drifting to Wally and Ernest. I wonder whether they had dinner with the Prince of Wales.

8th November 1932

Wally is back from Leicestershire with bronchitis. She said she felt too ill to see anyone, but what are friends for if not comforting the sick? I hurried round with a bottle of Dr. Collis Browne's soothing chlorodyne and a jar of chicken essence.

She *did* meet the Prince of Wales. Also his brother, Prince George, the one who's reported to dance with black girls. The two princes were staying at a nearby house but motored over each day in time for luncheon and stayed till late.

She said Wales is short, boyish, and trim, and he calls Thelma "darling." He didn't hunt. No one did. Mainly they played Old Maid and watched Tom Mix movies on Thelma's personal projection screen.

The big question no one dared ask is whether things will change after Thelma's divorce. Connie Thaw told Wally the Prince leads a dog's life, bullied by the King, chastized by the Queen. She said his weekends with Thelma are the only thing he has to look forward to. It seems to me it's quite straightforward. Thelma will get her divorce, the Prince will marry her, and they'll live happily ever after.

I thought Wally seemed rather flat; aside from a hacking cough, she doesn't have anything to show for her trouble. All that fussing at the beauty parlor and studying newspapers for topical subjects of conversation. So she met a couple of princes? I doubt she exchanged more than two words with either of them. I think Wally's gone about as far as she can go. Perhaps I should offer to introduce her to Ena Spain. Better to be properly acquainted with an ex-queen than to have one's nose pressed hopelessly against the gates of Buckingham Palace.

10th November 1932

Franklin Roosevelt is the new President. Well, I'm glad Brumby didn't live to see it. He never cared for him. Brumby was a Hoover man, through and through.

"Never vote for a lawyer, Maybell," he advised me. "They'll have their hands in your pocket before you can say 'dollar.'"

Tea at Carlton Gardens. There was an unpleasant odor in Violet's drawing room. I do hope it wasn't dear Ena Spain. She was perspiring as usual, in spite of freezing fog. Went up to the nursery and found Flora playing Divorces with her dolls. She's such a stitch.

"Let me smell your scent, Aunt Bayba," she said. "You always smell nice. Like talgum bowder and jim tonics."

I'm going to have fun when it's her deb year. I'll just take charge. If it's left to Violet, the poor girl will come out smelling of Coal Tar soap.

15th November 1932

Lunch with Lightfoot. He dined at Carlton Gardens last evening and says there was an unaccountably awful smell in the drawing room. He said, "I thought you might bring it up with Violet. It would be better coming from you."

Ena Spain wasn't present, apparently, so at least she's not to blame.

16th November 1932

Carlton Gardens is in uproar. The smell is now so bad it greets you before you reach the drawing room. When I arrived, a housemaid was flicking the pelmets with a feather duster—as though something like that could be dusted away!

Melhuish was pacing the floor, and Violet had even canceled her meetings.

The exterminator hadn't been sent for, however. I'd have thought that was the very first thing to do.

Violet said, "To exterminate what? We don't have rats."

Trotman said, "Oh yes we do, Your Ladyship. I've seen 'em the size of cats outside the scullery."

Thank heavens I've moved out. Melhuish took umbrage at my suggestion that the prime suspects must be the dogs. He said, "My dogs do not smell."

Well, they most certainly do, but I didn't particularly mean the dogs themselves, rather some little gift-offering one of them might have left behind. My advice to them was to have the room stripped out, ceiling to floor. Dollars to doughnuts they'll find a doggie woops.

Violet says it couldn't be more inconvenient. They have the Yugoslavias coming for the weekend. Crown Prince Paul and his wife, Olga.

17th November 1932

To the Paradise Club for Hattie Erlanger's birthday. She and Judson are going to Jessie Woolworth's for Christmas, in Palm Beach. Wally and Ernest are going to Landgravine Lily's, Pips and Freddie are going to the Prosper Friths in Kent. Everyone seems fixed up except me, but no matter. Solitude holds no fears for me. I shall have delicious little meals served on a tray and immerse myself in the great thinkers of the day. I've been meaning to take up reading for quite some time. Wally swears that an informed mind improves the face.

More fog.

18th November 1932

Violet's smell has been run to earth. George Lightfoot called me with the news this morning. Seven pieces of kippered herring tucked into pillow covers and down the arms of chairs. The finger has been pointed at Flora, but she maintains a "purgler" must have done it.

Lunch with Wally. Connie Thaw told her that Thelma's divorce won't mean the Prince of Wales can marry her. Some day he'll be king, and there are rules about who he can marry. Well, surely the answer to that is for them to continue as they are until he becomes king. Then, once he's in charge, he'll be able to *unmake* inconvenient rules. I shall ask Violet.

20th November 1932

Violet says the Prince of Wales can never marry Thelma Furness, or any other divorced person. Neither can he change the rules when he becomes king. Only Parliament can do that. I begin to wonder if there are any advantages at all to being king.

I said, "Well, it seems hard cheese for Thelma when her husband has gone off on tiger shoots and left the door very obviously ajar."

Violet said Melhuish enjoys a good duck-hunt when he can get it, but they've never allowed his absences to lead to moral laxity.

Flora is to be tried at Hope House School as a weekly boarder after Christmas, to see if she's suited. She's not supposed to know till nearer the time, but she does know. It was the first thing she told me when I went up to the nursery.

She said, "I won't be suited. I'll kick someone and then they'll send me home."

Doopie trying to explain to me about the business with the smell in the drawing room. She kept saying, "Vora but a gibba unna share."

That's the thing about the deaf. Insist as Violet may that Doopie isn't backward, she certainly can't get the difference between "kipper" and "gibba," and, I'm afraid to say, it has rubbed off seriously on Flora.

School can only be a good idea.

Melhuish said, "Peculiar thing to do. Waste of a fine smokie, too. Damned if I understand it. Never had any of that kind of carry-on with the boys."

23rd November 1932

I am invited to Philip Sassoon's birthday luncheon at Trent Park. The question is, what to buy the man who has everything.

25th November 1932

George Lightfoot is also going to the Trent Park party. He always tries to find a bottle of some unusual and undrinkable liqueur by way of a gift, but he says Philip is very keen on ducks and suggests I think along those lines. No help at all. What does he propose I do? Go to St. James's Park and capture a pair?

28th November 1932

Lunch with Wally, Hattie Erlanger, and Gladys Trilling. When Gladys heard about my invitation to Trent Park, she said, "Oh, Sassoon! The Court Jew! They say he's fabulously generous, and if you admire something in one of his houses, he's more than likely to give it to you. They say Her Majesty's done terribly well out of him."

Wally said, "Then I think Maybell had better introduce us all."

I shall do no such thing.

To the Army & Navy. Bought a doorstop fashioned from a mallard duck decoy, very pretty.

5th December 1932

Trent Park is a dream. Acres of parkland, lakes, tree-lined avenues, and dozens of dusky servants who glide around silently and appear the very moment they're needed. His sister, Sybil, attended, minus husband who was away at a tennis tournament. She looks haughty, very straight-backed, with iron-gray hair and rather hooded eyes, but she's really very agreeable.

"Violet's sister!" she said. "Of course! How very naughty of Violet not to have brought you to tea."

The other guests were Mrs. Belloc Lowndes, a Polish piano player called Rubinstein plus wife, a Sassoon cousin from Paris, and two Italian airmen, with whom one could only gesticulate and offer the occasional "olé."

We had oysters, flown up from Kent, and roast Guinea fowl dressed with home-grown oranges. In Hertfordshire! Then a blue cheese made on Sibyl's estate in Norfolk and a plum pudding carried flaming and aloft by a six-foot Ethiopian in silk livery. Everything was perfect.

Lightfoot said, "Now will you please set the record straight. Maybell doesn't believe you have stags with gilded antlers."

Philip said, "Oh but I do, and if only it weren't such a gray day, you'd see for yourself. I've trained them to note the position of the sun and waggle their heads accordingly. Syb believes animals should be left *au naturel,* but my stags are all trrragedians *manqué.* They'd have been deeply unhappy left naked on a moor."

I'm sure he's right. And I may not have seen the stags this time, but I did see his black swans. Very chic! I asked him how they were kept still long enough to dye their feathers, but he refused to say.

He loved his mallard doorstop and intends to place it at the entrance to his dressing room. Lightfoot took him a bottle of something made from roasted melon seeds.

7th December 1932

To Harrold's Lending Library to select my Christmas reading: Ethelda Bedford, Maysie Grieg, George Bertram Shaw, Alma Sioux Scarberry. Kettle had just carried them into the house when Violet telephoned. She said, "What is this nonsense I hear about you spending Christmas alone?"

I believe George Lightfoot may have said something. He didn't at all like my plans for a solitary Christmas, I could tell. He's so attentive. I think he may have a little pash for me.

I said, "I shall be perfectly fine. I was alone last year, except for being frog-marched to church by Randolph Putnam and receiving an unsolicited visit from Junior, and no doubt I shall be alone in the future."

"Not as long as I draw breath," she said. "You'll come to Carlton Gardens and be taken out of yourself."

12th December 1932

The whole day in and out of the car and up and down in elevators, searching for gifts. I'm beginning to agree with Penelope Blythe: Christmas takes all the joy out of shopping and should really just be left to the lower classes.

For Ulick, a Tri-ang fort, for Rory an Erector Set, which I'm assured is the gift of choice for boys aged twelve, and for Flora, a Betty Boop tea service. Whiskey for Melhuish, a gay jacquard scarf for Violet, to help modernize her look, and for Doopie, a copy of *301 Things for a Bright Girl to Do*. She needs to be stretched.

To Bryanston Court for dinner. Came: Pips and Freddie Crosbie and the decorator Johnnie MacMullen, with a woman I took to be his mother, but who turned out to be the very unusual Lady Elsie Mendl. She was an actress but now does rooms for people like the Vanderbilts and the Fricks and is apparently ruthlessly strict with her clients. If Elsie Mendl dictates you must have tobacco-brown walls, there is no gainsaying her.

Also came friends of Ernest, the Rickatson Hatts. He runs a news agency, of all things. Wally certainly keeps her pledge to seat interesting mixes around her table.

Pips says Elsie Mendl is an invert and only married Charlie Mendl for his title. If it's true, I must say she hides her tendencies very well. She even paints her nails.

There were no hackney cabs to be had, so I gave Mr. and Mrs. Hatt a lift to Westbourne Terrace. They were shy about accepting, but as I told them, I'm aware of the punishing hours people in their business are obliged to keep. Melhuish's *Times* is always on the breakfast table by eight o'clock.

14th December 1932

Johnnie MacMullen is going to advise Wally on the remodeling of her apartment after Christmas. She says he's hugely talented and has done Elsie Mendl's homes from A to Z. Well, he'll need to be hugely talented to make anything of Bryanston Court. I'd love to see her move somewhere with scope, but Ernest is such a stick in the mud.

She agrees with me that Mrs. Hatt is dull, but says she endures her because the husband is always good for whiling away an evening with Ernest. They often have macaroni cheese and peruse the Greek ancients, leaving her free to come dancing. The Hatts' little shop is called Reuters, but Wally has no idea where it is.

17th December 1932

A festive evening at the Benny Thaws. They had an adorable little chorale of children to sing us carols around the Christmas tree, American children from the compound, with proud deportment and straight teeth. It caused me a flicker of nostalgia for Sweet Air. Just a flicker.

Rory and Ulick are home from school.

23rd December 1932

Violet says luncheon will be served at twelve-thirty sharp on Christmas Day so the kitchen maids can get away to visit their mothers. It's going to make for a very long afternoon, unless, of course, we're expected to take our tea at three so the rest of the help can go gallivanting to Essex. I don't know why I don't just take us all to Claridge's.

24th December 1932

Violet says they always do things this way, it suits them very well and this is how children learn about their responsibilities to servants. Before the family meal is served, Melhuish goes below stairs to say a few words and carve the first slice of the servants' goose, and this year Ulick will go with him, to see how it's done. She says we can have tea whenever we choose, because Doopie will have charge of it, so as to allow Smith the rest of the day off.

All the more reason to go to Claridge's.

A greeting card from Randolph Putnam. His mother passed away. And I am missed in Baltimore. Of course.

26th December 1932

The best-laid plans. Rory claimed Flora's tea service and performed a very clever trick with overturned cups and disappearing sugar lumps, Flora was only interested in Rory's Erector Set, and Ulick remained disappointingly aloof from his fort. It would have remained in its box if Lightfoot and Doopie hadn't begun playing with it.

Violet gave me a calendar.

"So you can organize your time," she said. "You'll see the weeks laid out before you and be able to think how best to fill your days productively."

Rory gave me a rough-hewn letter rack made in his handicrafts' class, Lightfoot gave me a coffret of candy, and Flora gave me a pink satin letter M, stitched quite nicely and filled with padding.

Violet said, "How clever. Is it a scented sachet?"

"No," said Flora, "it's an em. We made it out of old ploomers."

Melhuish's sister Elspeth and the Rear Admiral Salty Laird looked in during the afternoon. Elspeth said, "Now Flora, are ye looking forward to being a big girl and going to Hope House?"

Flora closed her eyes. She does that when you say something she doesn't want to hear. She gets that from Doopie.

Rory said, "You'll like it when you get there, Flora. You'll make friends. And have cocoa every night. I used not to want to go to school, but you get used to it, you see, and then it's really good fun."

She said, "Then I'll come to your school."

Ulick said, "You can't. You're a girl."

She said, "Well, I shan't stay at Hope House. I shall run away."

Elspeth said, "Do ye know what happens to girls who run away,

Flora? The bogeyman comes after them and they're never seen again."

Doopie and Lightfoot both got her with the peashooter cannons.

Ulick said, "I really wonder why we're bothering with all this. Why not have her taught at home until it's time for her to be finished? That's what they did with Pentlow's sister and she's now out and practically engaged to Gore-Cummings. Education seems to me to be quite wasted on girls."

1st January 1933

Gala night at the Savoy last night. Wore my aquamarine chiffon with the beaded shrug. Pips and Freddie came, also the Prosper Friths and Ida with an old Venezuelan flaneur. She said, "Oh Maybell, no date?" I said, "Oh Ida, no taste?" She was putting away Manhattans all night, so I guess she has tired of Mr. Acolyte and chamomile tea.

I may not have had a date but I danced Prosper Frith off his feet, not to mention a foxtrot with Billy Belchester and two rumbas with Benny Thaw whose party was at the next table, minus Connie. Apparently, she and Lady Thelma are at Lily Drax-Pfaffenhof's, so won't Wally be thrilled. I bet she'll have been cultivating Thelma Furness like crazy.

Freddie stood us all champagne for midnight, which I'm sure he couldn't really afford. I'd happily have paid for it.

7th January 1933

Wally and Ernest are back from the Alps. She's wearing a plummier lip color, in imitation of Lady Thelma, no doubt. Landgravine Lily's house party had been quiet. Canasta, a treasure hunt, a little light shopping. Just Connie and Lady Thelma, a couple called Rothschild, and Crown Princess Cecilie, a sad remnant of German royalty.

Ernest has a carbuncle on his neck. Wally needs dental work. She said, "Don't you hate January? Nothing ever happens."

Lunch tomorrow.

9th January 1933

I'd given up on Wally and was about to order, when she sauntered into the Fountain Room in that skimpy little mink of hers smiling like the cat that's had the cream. She said she was sorry to be late but had been delayed by an important telephone call from Connie Thaw. "You see," she said, taking forever to sit down and then starting to nibble on a celery stick in the most annoying way, "you see, Ernest and I are invited to Fort Belvedere for the weekend. By the Prince of Wales."

I'm very happy for her, of course. This is something she's worked for tirelessly. I just hope she understands that the invitation doesn't spring from any desire on the part of the Prince of Wales. I'm sure he doesn't even remember who they are. But I expect he allows Thelma a certain number of her own friends, and she and Wally seem to have hit it off. They're always screaming with laughter about something.

I said, "But Ernest always seems to spend his weekends shuffling business papers. Are you sure he'll be allowed to take time off?"

She said, "Of course he can. Ernest's a director, not an employee."

If that's the case, I wonder he doesn't open the safe and bring home a little more money. There are things she's going to need, but she said she'd better wait till tomorrow, till Ernest has agreed to a budget. It only leaves her Wednesday and Thursday for all that shopping, not to mention hair, facials, and nails. What an impossible way to live. I offered her Kettle, to take them down to Windsor and bring them back on Sunday. It seemed the least I could do.

She said, "Maybell, you're such a treasure. The thing about Ernest's car is, his driver doesn't like to work on Sundays."

The thing about Ernest's car is it isn't a Bentley.

11th January 1933

Dinner at the Crosbies. Whitlow and Gladys Trilling, Prosper and Daphne Frith, and young Freddie Birkenhead, who's an earl. Everyone very exercised about what Roosevelt may be planning to do with the gold standard. When I asked Earl Birkenhead if I had any cause for concern, he said, "It rather depends how many double eagles you have under your mattress," but gave no clue as to whether having them would be a good thing or bad. I may drop a line to Randolph Putnam.

Gladys Trilling said blizzards are forecast for tomorrow. Pips said, "Friends of ours are going to Fort Belvedere for the weekend. I hope they'll be able to get through."

Prosper said, "Fort Belvedere! They'd be better off staying at home. Wales invites all kinds of nonentities. Get snowed in there, one could be sorry. Mediocre little house, too. The kind of place someone who'd done well in trade might go for."

Birkenhead said, "Well, that's Wales really. Small and mediocre."

12th January 1933

Wally has borrowed a ruby choker from Pips. I'm not supposed to know. Cold, but no snow.

13th January 1933

To the Fergus Blythes. George Lightfoot came with a girl with a jutting jaw called Belinda, not at all pretty. Penelope Blythe says the Prince of Wales generally wears a kilt in the evening and keeps his cigarette case in his sporran. Lightfoot says he likes to embroider after dinner and could bore for England. Well, I'm sure that after a week of ceremonial splendor, all he craves is the quiet life. I just hope Wally remembers not to try too hard. She does so love to outshine everyone.

16th January 1933

Kettle had instructions to bring Wally and Ernest back here so I could hear all about their weekend, but he returned with an empty car, Ernest having business papers to attend to and Wally being in pain from her ulcers. That's what comes of starving yourself into new dinner gowns.

I caught Ernest on the telephone. Wally was in bed and not to be disturbed.

He said, "We've had a thoroughly enjoyable time, but it would be indiscreet of me to say more."

Pompous ass.

17th January 1933

Wally recovered enough to be lunching with Thelma Furness and Connie Thaw, but not to have called me, and not a word of thanks for the use of my car and driver. She said, "Well, of course we're grateful, Maybell, but we didn't *ask* for your car. You almost insisted on our taking it. But do stop sulking. I want to tell you all about our weekend."

Tea tomorrow.

18th January 1933

Wally says Fort Belvedere is comfortable, full of good furniture, and generously hung with Canalettos, but lacking a woman's touch, except in the love nest itself, where Thelma had been allowed a free hand with pink silk. Also that the Prince did wear a kilt to dinner and has good legs.

She said, "David's very informal. He even mixes his own drinks."

So already it's "David." She says she only *refers* to him as David. When she addresses him, she calls him "sir."

She said, "He is the future king, Maybell. Never forget that."

20th January 1933

Freddie Crosbie, Judson Erlanger, Fergus Blythe, and Whitlow Trilling have gone to Klosters, so Pips is giving a ski-widows lunch party. Do I think she should also invite Wally Simpson and Ida Coote? Well, ordinarily I'd say no, because Wally demands opinions of people and tries to belittle them with her grasp of current affairs, and the only thing Ida brings to the table is a love life peopled by freaks, but on this occasion, I think the case for two extra Americans is strong. Hattie Erlanger and Gladys Trilling can be so overbearing, braying on about people one neither knows nor cares about, ancient British families who've been lords of the manor since the Stone Age.

26th January 1933

Penelope Blythe and Ida Coote got along famously yesterday. They both have men on the brain. I ought to have thought of introducing them sooner. Wally sparred with Gladys, each trying to outdo the other with inside information about the domestic arrangements of Royalties.

Gladys says it's a well-known fact that Prince George is a drug fiend and Wales is only interested in clothes, so it would be as well for the country if Bertie York is the next king, being a family man and practically a saint. Wally says Bertie York is reputed to snap like a rabid dog.

What a pity Violet was too busy to attend. I'm sure she could have given us character references on all of them.

5th February 1933

Tea at Carlton Gardens, where I was most surprised to find Flora, sent home from Hope House. She had apparently taken to lying on the floor and holding her breath until blue in the face, so the school nurse advised withdrawing her before she damaged her brain. Too late for that, I fear. The situation is to be reviewed after Easter.

Mr. Adolf Hitler has been hired as the new Chancellor of Germany. Melhuish says this can only be a good thing, because a properly run Germany is all that stands between us and world Communism. How worrying.

A delicious new cranberry nail polish from Elizabeth Arden.

6th February 1933

Lunch with Pips. She thinks getting in with Thelma and the Prince has turned Wally's head. She said, "I can hear that brain of hers whirring away. I reckon she's out to scalp herself a duke at the very least."

I said, "What about Ernest?"

"Ernest?" she said. "Oh please!"

But Pips doesn't know Wally like I do. All she ever wanted was to rise above that awful mother of hers, to settle down, and have nice things, and in his modest way, Ernest has made that possible. Now she's making her contribution, using her wits and vivacity to carry them into higher circles. I find them a very well-suited couple. And as for snagging a duke! Wally has certain talents, but I feel entitled to say, as a friend who knows her better than any, beneath all that careful grooming she's still far too coarse to be a duchess.

8th February 1933

A crisis at Bryanston Court. Ernest has gone to New York on business and left Wally seriously short. She says it's all a silly mix-up, but her cook is threatening to quit and anyway, there's the humiliation of it. She's meant to be giving a dinner for Lily Drax-Pfaffenhof and her friends the Eugene Rothschilds, and what's she supposed to do? Offer them bread and water? If she didn't have me to turn to, she'd be in an impossible position. I've advanced her enough to pay the help and cover the butcher's bill.

Randolph Putnam writes that I have nothing to fear from Franklin Roosevelt. He says Brumby Steel and Chemical has weathered the worst of things and is in good health, thanks to our Burma operations. He says my adventurous attitude to life has made him think of visiting London himself sometime. I do hope not.

I haven't come all this way to see his shiny face beaming at me across a crowded Grill Room. I've written back immediately to warn him that London is wet and sooty.

Ten to dinner tonight. Philip Sassoon, Wally, Pips and Freddie Crosbie, Anne and Billy Belchester, Fergus and Penelope Blythe, George Lightfoot. As Wally will discover, she isn't the only Baltimore belle who can fill a good table in London.

9th February 1933

My dining room looked superb last evening. Ivory candles, Brussels lace laid over a gold undercloth. Mushrooms on toast, saddle of lamb, nougat parfait. I could see Wally noting every detail. Wore my moss-green crepe de chine and amber beads. Wally gave her russet shantung another airing.

All the talk was of Mr. Hitler. Freddie says he's the man to destroy the Communists, root and branch. George Lightfoot predicts the working man will rise up, but as Freddie says, with six million unemployed, the working man will do well to keep his nose to the grindstone. Wally said England has nothing to fear from German rearmament. It was the French and the Poles who appropriated all that German soil, so they're the ones who'd better watch out. I noticed a little twitch in dear Philip's cheek. He has tribes of French cousins. He said nothing, but I don't think he took to Wally. I must make sure not to mix them in the future.

Belchester said if Adolf Hitler wants to reduce the number of men out of work, he can advise him exactly how to do it. One million can be set to paint the Black Forest white, one million can be sent to lay linoleum along the Polish corridor, and another million can busy themselves building a one-way railroad to Jerusalem. Much hilarity over this, but by my reckoning, that would still leave three million.

Philip was very quiet all evening. He pleaded a sore throat and left early. I believe he may be the kind of man who only sparkles in his own milieu.

15th February 1933

Flora's birthday. Her ninth. Gave her a silver-mounted hair-brush with her initials. Now someone needs to get her into the habit of using it. To a matinee performance of *Giselle* with Lightfoot, Doopie, and Flora. He's Flora's godfather, and Doopie is one of her godmothers, so he takes them to a ballet every year. Of course, if Doopie's as deaf as they say she is, it seems rather a waste. Flora was in a very cheery mood and properly dressed, too, for a change, in a good wool dress and Mary Janes. There's talk of a day school after Easter, but it's to be sprung on her at the last moment.

She quite stuck to my side all afternoon, one hand in mine, the other clutching her hairbrush. She said, "I wish you could be my other gobmother instead of Aunt Elsbeth."

16th February 1933

Have loaned Wally my sable. She's going to Leicestershire, to Thelma Furness's, and will surely freeze without a decent fur.

To the Florida Club with Judson and Hattie Erlanger and Pips and Freddie. Pips is wearing her hair and her skirts noticeably shorter. Freddie has told her she has the best legs in London. Who am I to rain on her parade. I do like her bob, however.

She said, "This Leicestershire jaunt is so typically Wally. She hates the countryside, she hates horses, but she'll go and endure it because she just might meet someone useful. I'm telling you, she's on the prowl for someone with a title."

Hattie said, "The idea is beyond bizarre. She doesn't even ride. And why would any man look at her twice? She always looks so . . . corseted. And that frightful, grimacing mouth. I mean, she's quite fun, but really . . . Anyway, no one important ever *goes* to the Furness house. One simply sniggers about it."

20th February 1933

According to the maid, Wally and my sable have gone direct from the country to The Cedars, for mud baths and facials. She might have asked.

Tonight to the Yugoslavs. I shall have to wear my mink.

23rd February 1933

Wally says The Cedars wasn't her idea. She got dragged along by Thelma and Connie but is glad she went, because she feels greatly rejuvenated. She described the weekend as low-key and cozy. She'd met some new people, the Bernie Cavetts from New Jersey, Humphrey Butler, who equerries for fun-loving Prince George, and the Perry Brownlows, who have a house near Thelma's. And the Prince of Wales had joined her by the fireside and chatted to her for half an hour at least. She says she wasn't a bit nervous.

She said, "I didn't even think about it. I was just myself, Maybell. I just treated him like I would any other interesting man."

I bet she didn't.

She said, "Strictly between you and me, I think he finds Thelma rather limited. She's sweet, but she doesn't have any conversation, and His Royal Highness has a wide-ranging mind. He wants to know about the lives of ordinary people, and who better to enlighten him on that subject than me."

She'd even told him about her mother's boardinghouse.

She said, "He was fascinated. He's never met anyone like me before, not socially. He found it refreshing."

Perhaps so, but I don't think Ernest will thank her for making such a feature of her regrettable background.

Philip Sassoon's sister has invited me to a musical soiree.

26th February 1933

To tea at Carlton Gardens. Fish-paste sandwiches and seed cake. Bertie York's wife, Elizabeth, was there with Ena Spain and a couple of Greek princesses who never smile. Only Ena could perspire in February. Flora was allowed down briefly to say "good day." She doesn't appear to be using her new hairbrush.

27th February 1933

To Sibyl Chumley's, spelled *Cholmondeley*, nota bene. Her husband, Rock, was present, charming and dashingly handsome but impatient to get away, it seemed. He kept popping open his Hunter to check the time. And dear Philip wasn't able to attend, being horribly busy with something called Air Estimates. Lucky Philip. It was such a long program and then, as if we hadn't had quite enough, one of Sybil's cronies asked Mr. Rubinstein for an encore, as if he needed any further encouragement. It didn't seem to occur to them that some of us had had a strenuous day and still weren't finished. I had the Erlangers and the Trillings waiting for me at the Paradise Club.

28th February 1933

The German Parliament has been burned down by Red agitators. Boss and Ethel Croker are taking a house for Royal Ascot this year and I am invited, as are Wally and Ernest. I'll just keep the information up my sleeve until Violet starts talking about squeezing me into Lady Desborough's attic. Ernest is expected home at any moment, and the sooner the better. Wally's in a flap about ordering gowns. I'm thinking pale lavender and the softest camellia pink. Wally says hats are absolutely de rigueur, a great shame for a natural blonde like myself.

4th March 1933

Lunch with George Lightfoot. He was at the Century Club last night and saw Wally and Ernest at the Prince of Wales's table. Poor Ernest. He's not a night person at the best of times, and he's only been back on dry land for five minutes.

6th March 1933

Five hours of shopping. We've decided on midcalf bias-cut for summer, which we'll follow with a shorter, more tailored look for the fall. Wally is *so* particular. She examines linings and seams practically with a magnifying glass. She says if she had my money, she'd have everything hand-finished. Our needs are different, of course. Curves like mine may not be the height of fashion right now, but let's face it, I'd look good in a sugar sack, whereas Wally has to rely on good window dressing to cover all those bones and angles.

At any rate, Ernest is so thrilled by their growing closeness to the Prince of Wales that he's lifted the latch on his cash box and told Wally to buy whatever she needs.

We didn't even stop for lunch, and then she dashed away in a cab. She's suddenly very assiduous about being at home with a welcoming drinks' tray when Ernest comes in from business. That's the deal, I suppose. She's paying for her Ascot gowns with wifely attention.

Called in at Carlton Gardens. Violet was running out to a Soup Kitchen committee. She said, "You should come with me. Do something useful. This has been a hard winter, Maybell. People are cold and hungry."

Well, I was in no condition. I'd been on my feet since ten o'clock.

I said, "I'll write you a check. I'm going up to the nursery to have tea with Flora and Doopie."

She said, "Then be aware that Flora is being punished. She stuck out her tongue at Lady Londonderry, so be stern with her and please don't give her candy."

I must say, Flora seemed to have forgotten she was in disgrace. We found some chocolate in my purse and made chocolate sandwiches, and then she and Doopie danced *Giselle* for me in their bedroom slippers. I don't think chocolate counts as candy. Chocolate is chocolate.

10th March 1933

Dinner at Judson and Hattie Erlanger's. According to Pips, Hattie's family owns much of Eccleston Square. All the more regrettable then that she doesn't invest some of her wealth in getting her teeth straightened. And why don't the English keep their diamonds clean?

The talk turned to Wally. I only mentioned that she longs to be presented at Court, and Gladys Trilling practically leaped out of her seat. She said, "Oh but that can never happen. Surely Wally and Ernest are both divorced?"

According to Gloria and Hattie, divorce is death to any Court ambitions.

I said, "But what about Thelma Furness? She's about to get her second divorce, but that doesn't seem to deter the Prince of Wales."

Hattie said, "There's all the difference in the world between sharing Wales's bed and being brought into the presence of Their Majesties, and I'm sure Thelma Furness has always understood her position."

If that's the case, I'm surprised she hasn't explained it to Wally. They're such friends these days, they must surely commiserate with each other about the taint of divorce. How frustrating. A youthful error with Win Spencer and now Wally's greatest desire is forever beyond her reach. Well, *I'm* not going to be the one who tells her.

14th March 1933

Philip Sassoon has invited me to his house by the ocean for Easter. A *fête champêtre* at Port Lympne! Whatever it is, I can't wait.

16th March 1933

The most extraordinary thing. I was with Wally at Bryanston Court early last evening, when the door opened and in walked the Prince of Wales. He said, "You didn't invite me, but here I am anyway."

Wally didn't miss a beat. She said, "Why sir! I hope you know you're welcome anytime. We're very informal tonight, just an old school friend, Maybell Brumby."

She was pulling faces at me behind his back, reminding me to curtsy. She doesn't understand that when I was at Carlton Gardens, Violet had Royalties trooping through on an almost daily basis.

His Royal Highness has very blue eyes and a rather high-pitched voice.

"Brumby?" he said. "A big name in Baltimore, I seem to remember. Iron, was it?"

Iron, coal, nickel, cobalt, silver, bauxite. Wherever it was in the world, Danforth Brumby would find it and have it grubbed out of the ground and turned into dollars.

I said, "Yes sir, Brumby Steel and Chemical, founded by my late husband. And you may have heard of my late father, too. John Patterson was a legend for his worker housing."

"Is that so?" he said. "Well, you must tell me about it someday. I'm awfully keen on worker housing."

Wally didn't like that. She thinks she's the only one who knows how to draw people out. She thinks I'm just a pretty face.

The Prince made us all scotches and soda, very much at home. He'd obviously done it before. Wally's a sly one. He told us about his week. He'd been in the North, cheering up paupers. Wally was plying him with questions, but he really wanted to know about me, what brought me to London.

I said, "Well, funnily enough, sir, *you* did. I came last year, after my bereavement, to visit my sister Violet. And if it weren't for you, I very much doubt my sister would be here. If you hadn't gone to Sulphur Springs with Donald Melhuish all those years ago, Violet wouldn't have met him and married him and moved to London. So, in a roundabout way, you're entirely responsible."

He has a funny little laugh.

"Melhuish!" he said. "Of course! When was that?"

It was 1919.

He said, "And you're Violet Melhuish's sister? Remarkable! You look nothing like her. A fine soldier, Melhuish. We were together at Verdun, you know?"

When Ernest came home, he didn't seem particularly surprised to find the Prince of Wales sitting on his couch, so I wonder how long this has been going on? Great shows of affability, but I believe I noticed Ernest relax when the Prince said he couldn't stay to dinner.

He said, "No, Ernest. As comfortable as I am, I can't stay, not even for Wally's goulash. I have to dine with Their Majesties."

He kissed Wally on the cheek as he left.

She said, "Oh Maybell, your face when the Prince walked in! I wish I could have snapped it."

I said, "You might have warned me. You were obviously expecting him."

She said, "Not really. He's dropped by a few times but he never calls ahead."

I said, "But you didn't even tell me he'd been here. Why the big secret? You were shouting it from the rooftops when he invited you to Fort Belvedere."

Ernest said, "We certainly did not. We've always been discreet about our friendship, and so must you be. Please don't go telling all and sundry about this evening. His Royal Highness feels at home here, thanks to Wally. She has the right touch. Clever girl."

So that's why she's been shopping with such abandon. Ernest's paid her a good dividend for hauling in the Prince of Wales. Well, their secret is safe with me. Apart from Pips and Violet, I won't tell a soul.

17th March 1933

I made a point of speaking to Melhuish on the telephone this morning. He said, "You've missed Violet. She had a meeting at nine and then she's going directly to the Habberleys. We're there for the weekend."

I said, "It was you I wanted. I was with the Prince of Wales last evening and he most particularly asked to be remembered to you."

Stopped him in his tracks. "Wales?" he said. "Really? Were you at the Belchesters?"

I said, "No, at the Ernest Simpsons."

"Simpson, Simpson?" he said. "Know the name, but can't place him."

I said, "You met him at my soiree. He was in the Guards, and his wife is called Wally. She talked to you about salmon flies. She was a school friend, but these days Violet disapproves of her."

He said, "Does she? Well, Vee's a good judge of people. As for Wales, these days I'm not entirely sure how sound he is. There was a time. We had a good war together, but he doesn't appear to have done much since. From what I hear, all he does nowadays is plague his tailor and run his valets ragged. He's a bloody clotheshorse, Maybell. If you ask me, we're going to get a dandy for a king."

It says it all. The Prince is so modern and unstuffy, and Melhuish is so set in his ways. How left behind he must feel.

Stood Wally lunch at the Dorch. Penelope Blythe came to our table and said, "Oh Wally, I hear His Royal Highness is back from Northumberland. How is he?" I could have killed her. I'd sworn Pips and Hattie to absolute secrecy.

Wally doesn't seem as anxious about things as Ernest, though.

She said, "Well, of course, *nothing* the Prince of Wales does goes unnoticed. And why shouldn't he call in on friends at the cocktail hour?"

I said, "I suppose what's remarkable is that he comes to an address like Bryanston Court."

"Not at all," she said. "That's the kind of prince he is."

The Erlangers want me to dinner. The Trillings are begging me. Pips absolutely insists on having me. Wally's schedule may suddenly be full, but they know they can get the story from me, and without earnest Ernest sucking on his pipe and pontificating about discretion.

20th March 1933

To the Crosbies. The Prosper Friths were there, also the Erlangers and the Belchesters. Billy Belchester said it didn't surprise him to hear that the Prince of Wales had taken up with people in the suburbs. He said, "It'll be his latest fad. That's Wales all over. Picks things up and then drops them. I hope your Simpson friends are prepared for that."

Freddie said, "Still, I think it was very astute of Maybell to get him onto worker housing. He's not the easiest of conversationalists, but that is a subject dear to his heart. Golf, too."

Prosper Frith said it was all very well for Wales to be keen on worker housing when he didn't have to find the money for it. He said, "Ask me, he should attend to his own affairs. Cut ribbons. Settle down and produce an heir. Leave politicking to those who understand it."

Daphne Frith said, "Well, I'd hate to have Royalties suddenly proposing themselves for cockers. It'd be such a strain, always being prepared."

Not for Wally, of course. Being prepared is what she does best. I do wonder about Violet and Melhuish though. The Prince is so agreeable, I can't think why they allowed the friendship to wither. Tea parties with the Bertie Yorks are all very well, but Wales is the one who'll be king someday.

Freddie says His Royal Highness is a big campaigner for pit head baths.

21st March 1933

Harrold's Lending Library had nothing on pit head baths. Ida says they are facilities to allow coal miners to perform their *toilette* before going home to dine. All at the mine owner's expense, you can be sure.

22nd March 1933

Lunched with Wally. The Prince of Wales has asked after me!

She and Ernest had dinner with him last evening at the Benny Thaws.

She said, "He loves Americans, you know. He finds us much more in tune with his thinking than those English stuffed shirts. And he's often at a loose end in the evening, especially when Thelma's in the country. Really, if we want him, he's ours for the taking."

She's talking about offering him a dinner. Not a potluck with just her and Ernest, but a proper dinner, where he can meet lively Americans. With only a cook and two maids, it sounds overambitious to me. Wilton Place would be far more suitable, but she didn't like my saying so.

She said, "I can manage perfectly well at Bryanston Court, thank you, and the Prince feels at home there. Obviously, I'll get in extra help. But don't be disappointed, Maybell, if you're not invited. The guest list will be out of my hands. That's the protocol, you see? David will have to approve everything."

Minnehaha Warfield lecturing me on protocol!

27th March 1933

Lunch with George Lightfoot, who didn't seem at all interested in the Simpsons and the Prince. He said, "It's no great coup, Maybell. I could introduce you to any number of people who spend their lives avoiding Royalties. They're costly to maintain and have the habit of encouraging familiarity, then suddenly frowning on it. Befriending them is like venturing onto creaking ice."

Flora is in trouble again. Violet took her to an outfitters to buy her clothes for starting at Miss Hildred's Day School after Easter, and when they got home with their purchases, Flora hacked her new straw hat to pieces with Doopie's sewing scissors.

Lightfoot said, "I'm afraid it won't save her from Miss Hildred's, though. She's going, bonnet or no bonnet. It's a shame really. I shall miss her singular ways. It's not often a child reaches the age of nine without being tamed."

Disappointed to find he's not coming to Philip Sassoon's at Easter. We could have traveled together. He was invited but had already accepted for something in Gloucestershire. The girl named Belinda with the jutting jaw.

I said, "Are you in love with her?"

"No," he said, "not noticeably."

2nd April 1933

To Carlton Gardens. The boys are home from school. I'd promised Rory we'd go to a cartoon theater this vacation, but now we have the complication of Flora, who was supposed to come with us but is in the doghouse. He was pleading Flora's case with Violet, and Flora was doing nothing to help herself, sitting on the stairs, shouting, "I'm not going to Miss Dread's and I'm not wearing a banama hat."

Ulick said, "It seems very clear to me that she hasn't yet learned her lesson. It'll do her no good at all to be let off scot-free. Melhuishes know how to take their punishment like a man."

Rory said, "But she's a girl. And if she can't come to see *The Three Little Pigs,* I shan't feel decent about going."

To be resolved.

4th April 1933

Saw Lightfoot on my way to Monsieur Jules. He says Rory took his appeal to the House of Lords, but Melhuish told him he never overturns Violet's decisions.

He said, "The only thing I can suggest is that I play the Christian mercy card. I am her gobfather, after all. I'll see what I can do."

5th April 1933

Violet has agreed to a compromise. Flora will be allowed to come out with Rory for a high tea, but there will be no cartoons until she has behaved herself for a full term at school. Lightfoot said, "There are conditions, of course. We're not to indulge her too much, or in any way let her forget her misdemeanors. Doopie said, 'Bedda nod smile doo mudge, Dordie. Bedda pud on gumby vayzes.' "

I don't see why Doopie always has to tag along on these occasions. And I wish she could be trained to say "George" instead of "Dordie."

7th April 1933

To Ruddle's for a fried-fish supper. Flora behaved impeccably. I don't know why Violet has such problems with her.

Rory asked about Wally. There's obviously been talk in the drawing room at Carlton Gardens.

I said, "You may very well see her yourself at Easter. You'll be at Windsor, and she'll be just along the road, at Fort Belvedere with the Prince of Wales."

"Gosh," he said, "even though she's poor? Are you going, too?"

I said, "No, I'm going to Kent to stay with Sir Philip Sassoon."

"Oh," he said, "the gaudy Semite."

Lightfoot said, "I say, Rory! Where did that come from?"

"Ulick," he said, "after Aunt Maybell told us he gave her luncheon on a lapis lazuli table. Ulick said he's a gaudy Semite and not our kind of person."

Doopie not following things at all, looking perplexed, asking Lightfoot over and over, "Who Horty Zeemide?"

We should leave her at home really. She never does well in restaurants.

Flora said, "Gaudy Semite is a nice name."

8th April 1933

A wire from Randolph Putnam. Franklin Roosevelt has announced that in the future, only the government may own gold bullion, and those of us who thought to put our hard-earned dollars into gold are going to have to sell it to the Federal Reserve. At a very poor price, you may be sure. How sound Brumby's judgment was. Never trust a lawyer.

10th April 1933

Two days to reach Randolph by telephone, then, when I did get through, he did nothing to put my mind at rest. If I don't turn in my gold, I can be prosecuted for hoarding and, as if that isn't bad enough, he's coming to England in June. I said, "I shall be at Royal Ascot."

"So will I," he said. "I'll be staying in a town called Maidenhead. I have a Putnam cousin there, twice removed. Now Mother has passed over I'm going to start seeing the world and I'm holding you to dinner, Maybell. We have a lot to catch up on."

I doubt that anything of interest to me has ever happened to Randolph Putnam.

15th April 1933, Port Lympne, Kent

If Trent Park was a dream, Port Lympne is paradise. Terrace gives onto terrace, vista onto vista, and the lawns are carpeted with daffodils. Dickie and Edwina Mountbatten are here, he being a nephew of Ena Spain and brother-in-law of the betrousered Nada Milford Haven. Everyone in this tiny country is connected to somebody. Alex and Nelly Hardinge are also guests. He's the King's private secretary, but I don't suppose His Majesty dictates letters on a holiday weekend. So far I haven't found out who they're related to.

Others present: Tom Mitford, just back from Munich, Germany, where he and his sister Unity met Mr. Hitler and judge him to be the coming man, Sir Philip's cousin Hannah, a Frenchman called Hippolyte, who plays tennis, and Marthe Bibesco, who is personally acquainted with Mr. Mussolini. She says he has a magnificent, manly jaw. Arriving tomorrow, the Winston Churchills—he's something in politics—an actor called Gielgud, and a coal porter! Sir Philip certainly doesn't give a damn for class distinctions.

16th April 1933

This morning, a treasure hunt for eggs, each couple being provided with a list of clues written in aquamarine ink. I was paired with young Tom Mitford, who's just back from Heidelberg and speaks very highly of the German nation. Our clues led us to the orangerie, where, hanging from a tree, we found a perfect little egg-shaped crystal pendant for me and a tiny basket with a plover's egg for Tom.

A simple, rustic luncheon was served on the lawn: spit-roasted kid and pineapple ice. Then Philip took us up in his airplane, one at a time, for an aerial view of the estate. What an accomplished man! He makes one feel nothing is too much trouble, and he's tireless. Everything must be perfect. Last evening, he had the Union flag hauled down, because the red in it clashed so violently with the orange sunset.

Musical diversions after dinner. Philip's wonderful dusky servants brought in thimbles of coffee, which they somehow set ablaze, and then the coal porter, who, I must say, is very well-scrubbed considering his trade, claimed the piano and played and sang for quite an hour. He was really rather good. I've advised him to think of taking it up professionally. There must be a great many people in London who'd be willing to pay him, and it would surely be more agreeable than portering coal.

Philip said, "Maybell, you're a rrriot!" He's so easy to amuse. I think I could very happily be Lady Sassoon.

17th April 1933

Marthe Bibesco says the man who played for us last night was Mr. Cole Porter. Philip might have made it clearer.

18th April 1933

How drab Wilton Place seems after Port Lympne. I found the men rather standoffish, especially Johnnie Gielgud. And Alex Hardinge didn't smile, even when he was hunting for eggs. They say the King enjoys a joke, but I suppose servants only smile when given leave, and once a servant, always a servant. His wife was adorable though, and so was Clemmie Churchill, and I liked Philip's cousin once I grew accustomed to her swarthy appearance. She has very good emeralds and superb pearls, but without them, one could quite imagine her selling fish from a barrow in Lombard Street. I couldn't warm to Marthe Bibesco. She's one of those predatory types who fastens on to the most important man in the room and allows no one else to get a word in.

But an exquisite weekend. Rrrravishing, as dear Philip would say. I wonder why he never married. It may be Cousin Hannah and Sister Syb have stood guard over him too fiercely. Well, they don't deter me.

19th April 1933

Wally and Ernest are back from Fort Belvedere with the Prince's blessing to make him a dinner on May 2nd. We start work tomorrow.

Lunch with George Lightfoot. He says Marthe Bibesco is a *grande horizontale*.

Something else to look into at the Lending Library.

20th April 1933

Wally says a *grande horizontale* is a ceiling expert.

For his dinner, the Prince has requested a list of lively, interesting people, with a good sprinkling of Americans. She's told him she can accommodate fourteen, which is stretching Bryanston Court to its absolute limit. Pips and Freddie are already on the master plan, whereas I am scribbled in a margin along with the Judson Erlangers, the substitutes' bench. She said, "It's not that I don't want you there, Maybell. And you probably will be there. I just have to weigh every place very carefully. Pips and Freddie are a good combination. She's sparky, he's political."

I said, "Well, don't think I'm going to keep the date open indefinitely."

She said, "Go ahead. Fill it up if you must, but if His Royal Highness summons you to dinner, you'll have to drop everything.

One doesn't turn down Royalties. I'd have thought you'd know that."

Of course, if she'd only transfer the dinner to *my* dining room, there'd be seats for twenty.

21st April 1933

Lunched with Pips. Told her she and Freddie are on Wally's A list. She said, "Only because she owes me, I'm sure." Not just the loan of a ruby choker, apparently. There have been opera pearls. And a crocodile bag.

25th April 1933

Flora's first day at Miss Hildred's. Lightfoot had drinks with Melhuish this evening and says there were no reports of mayhem.

26th April 1933

Wally called me to tell me her plans: only three courses, and no wines, because she's going to serve curried chicken. There'll just be gin fizzes and then cold beer with dinner.

I said, "It's of no interest to me. I've made arrangements to go to an operetta in aid of Navy Widows."

She said, "Then you'd better unmake them. I've just finished the *placement,* and I've put you between Prince George and Prince Louis Ferdinand."

I knew she wouldn't be able to manage without me! And Prince George! Naughty, rebellious Prince George. We're sure to get along. Prince Louis Ferdinand is a German, but Wally says he speaks perfect English. His mother is Crown Princess Cecilie, a regular at Lily Drax-Pfaffenhof's house parties. Wally says it's quite on the cards that Mr. Hitler will restore the monarchy, and then Louis Ferdinand may reign some day.

I'm undecided between my magenta crepe and my copper silk.

28th April 1933

To Carlton Gardens for drinks. Chatted with dear Leo von Hoesch, told him I was dining with a future Kaiser on Tuesday. He said, "How astonishing. We don't have Kaisers anymore."

I said, "But surely the National Socialists say they'll bring them back?"

"Yes," he said, "they do say that, don't they."

I fear Ambassador von Hoesch is losing touch with things.

Violet says Wally mustn't feel too let down if the Princes don't appear. She says neither of them is known for their punctuality or reliability. Sour grapes, I'm sure.

Flora has apparently gone to school like a lamb every morning.

29th April 1933

Wally's guest list is finalized. No room for Judson and Hattie, because His Royal Highness wanted Thelma's friends, the Bernie Cavetts, and he's keen to meet Boss and Ethel Croker. Pips says she'd happily give up her seat. She thinks the idea of Ernest bowing and scraping all evening is excruciating.

I said, "Don't you want to know the Princes?"

She said, "Not particularly. They're not like real people. And anyway, I'll bet Wally's going to seat me way down the table. I hope so. I'll probably get the truck man."

Bernie Cavett made his fortune in road freight, apparently.

30th April 1933

To Bryanston Court, to help with the finishing touches. The menu is decided: avocado ice cream, curried chicken, apple fritters.

Ernest has cold sores. He's anxious about Wally's idea of serving beer and keeps bringing out bottles of his cherished claret to try and persuade her, but, as she says, the Prince of Wales has access to the finest cellars in the world and anyway, he's no great wine drinker. He'll much prefer the novelty of beer.

One thing Ernest doesn't need to worry about this time is the expense. Funny how an overture of caviars was deemed necessary to reel in Thelma Furness, but the Prince of Wales is getting something more akin to a porch brunch.

3rd May 1933

Last evening I danced with two princes, three if you count an exile, which I think I do. More, anyway, than Nora Sedley Cordle will do if she lives to be a hundred, and I shall make sure she hears about it from Randolph Putnam.

The two Princes are very different. Wales fidgets a lot and allows his gaze to wander when he's in conversation. Prince George seems more assured, much more attentive as a dinner partner, and an excellent dancer. Freddie Crosbie had described him as "lavender-toned," but he looked perfectly healthy to me.

And Prince Louis Ferdinand is delightful. He's been living in Michigan, helping out Mr. Ford at his automobile factory, and adores our American way of life, but he may soon have to give it all up, because his elder brother has chosen to marry a commoner, which places Louis next in line should the Germans bring back Royalties. His mother wants him to go home and find a suitable bride.

Zita Cavett said, "Why go home? Why not choose a gorgeous American girl?"

He said, "A wonderful idea, but your husband got there first."

They all pant after Zita. It's her legs. Bernie Cavett found her in the chorus at the Chicago Majestic. A showgirl at a dinner for the Prince of Wales, and with seats at a premium! Hattie Erlanger would be furious if she knew.

There was no withdrawing. Boss and Ernest lingered over their cigars. The rest of us rolled back the rugs and played Thelma's latest hoochie-koochie records on my gramophone. It was the greatest fun. The Royalties didn't leave till midnight and were effusive in their thanks. Ernest was quite pink with pleasure, but Wally was as composed as ever. All that dancing and not a hair out of place. The whole thing an undoubted success. I must hand it to her.

The trouble with such an exceptional evening is what to do the day after. Ida Coote is between men and wanted lunch, but I'm going to remain in bed, place a few telephone calls, and recover my strength.

4th May 1933

Wally got flowers from all three Royalties, and Ernest is overcome with pride.

I said, "Well, what next?"

"Nothing in particular," she said. "We're just very happy to have David's friendship."

Well, if a day comes when Minnehaha doesn't have a scheme, it'll be the first.

5th May 1933

Lunch with Pips. From what she saw at Wally's dinner, she thinks Prince George is the star of the royal Princes; funny, gossipy, good-looking. They say Bertie York and Prince Harry are both dull, and Pips doesn't rate Wales's looks at all.

She said, "He's like a schoolboy, only with lines on his face. Small fry. I don't think I could ever take him seriously as king. And he's not very bright. I heard him agree with two completely opposite opinions in the space of five minutes. But I know exactly what Wally's after. She's playing the long game, hoping to hang in there till King David and Queen Thelma are on the throne."

That could be a long wait. The King may look old, but he's only sixty-eight.

8th May 1933

Penelope Blythe says everyone is talking about Wally and Ernest as "the awful American couple who served the Prince of Wales beer in a bottle."

This can only have come from Hattie Erlanger, still aggrieved about not being invited. But how quickly the facts get distorted. Wally served the beer in lead-crystal chalices. I should know. I helped pay for them. But Pips must have given half a story to Hattie, who never listens anyway, and before you know it, Wally and Ernest's names are being dragged through the London mud.

Penelope said, "I find Wally Simpson rather direct, don't you? I hope she didn't ask the Royalties any impertinent questions."

Not at all. Wally just likes to draw people out, and I, for one, found it fascinating to hear that if Prince George didn't have to be a prince, what he'd most like in the world is to do something with fabrics.

Marthe Bibesco was seated a few tables away, face heavily powdered. We exchanged waves. Penelope said, "How do you know that old harridan?"

I said, "She was at Philip Sassoon's at Easter. I believe she's a connoisseur of ceilings."

"Maybell!" she said. "What a hoot! I've heard it called some things."

According to Penelope, Marthe Bibesco is a pensioned-off trollop who's made deposed royals her speciality.

"Willy Hohenzollern and Fonso Spain, to name two and omit hundreds," she said. "Connoisseur of ceilings! I shall repeat that."

13th May 1933

Flora has been removed from Miss Hildred's. When I called in at Carlton Gardens today, she was confined to the nursery and told me proudly, "I don't go to school anymore. Miss Hildred said I was a little wild animal."

Violet says she'll just have to stay at home now until September. She has two charity balls and then Royal Ascot, as well as her usual workload, so the last thing she has time for is trailing around, interviewing schools.

16th May 1933

Judson and Hattie Erlanger have been invited to Fort Belvedere for the weekend. Wally says Thelma's only done it because she knows how disappointed they were not to attend the dinner at Bryanston Court, but even so! I'd have thought I was a far worthier candidate. The problem is, people think only in terms of couples.

It takes a host of Philip Sassoon's imagination to think of inviting a lone woman. And now the summer is looming. I'm sure Violet's assuming I'll go to Drumcanna, but I absolutely cannot. A whole month of midges and Jane Habberley.

Wally and Ernest are going to Lily Drax-Pfaffenhof's. I know Lily would have me, too.

18th May 1933

Lunch with Ida. She has a vague offer of a villa at San Sebastian, but I've heard that kind of talk from Ida before. Dinner at the Crosbies.

20th May 1933

Freddie and Pips won't hear of me going to the Tyrol with the Simpsons. Pips says I spend far too much time around Wally as it is. "And not just time," she said. "Money, too. I've seen you. You're too generous, Maybell. You must come to Italy with us. We pay our own way."

The only drawback to this is Gladys Trilling, who I can take in small, lunch-sized doses, but a whole month? Hattie Erlanger is more bearable. She's careful around me, mindful that Judson and I have a history, but Gladys! Well, perhaps she and Gladys will stick together.

21st May 1933

Penelope Blythe's friend Cimmie Mosley has passed away. She was married to Tom Mosley, who some call Oswald and some call Kit in that confusing English way. Why not just call him Sir Mosley and be done with it? Anyway, Tom-Oswald-Kit and poor Cimmie were both in Parliament as Socialists until they visited with Mr. Mussolini and decided to get up their own party instead. Well, her politicking days are done. She died after having her appendix removed. So young. How fragile life is.

To Monsieur Jules for a tint.

25th May 1933

Thelma Furness has obtained her divorce. Wally says it merely frees Marmaduke Furness to marry his new sweetie and will make no difference to Thelma's end of things.

27th May 1933

According to Padmore's *Daily Sketch,* the Prince of Wales has been seen several times in the company of Mrs. Amelia Earhart, the aviatrix. Perhaps Thelma's days as Special Friend are numbered. That would be bad news for Wally and Ernest. Bad news for all of us really, just when everything is going along so nicely.

28th May 1933

To Carlton Gardens for tea. Lightfoot was there.

I mentioned the story about Wales and Mrs. Earhart. Lightfoot said, "Yes, everyone's talking about it."

Violet said, "No George, only silly people are talking about it, and it's of no consequence anyway, because he's about to announce his engagement."

Lightfoot said, "Who? Not Princess Ingrid? Don't tell me they've sold him Ingrid of Sweden!"

Violet was shaking her head, lips sealed, refusing to say more, but Doopie was nodding wildly.

Lightfoot said, "Ingrid of Sweden! I don't believe it. He won't marry her."

Violet said, "It's his duty to marry, therefore he will marry and soon. Even Wales understands that."

30th May 1933

Wally says the Amelia Earhart story is a spiteful fabrication and that HRH is as in love as ever with Thelma. She says when they're at the Fort, the King telephones all the time, wanting to know who he's got there and what they're up to that's so fascinating he can't spare a little time to go visit with his mother like Bertie York does. She says Bertie York is the blue-eyed boy in that family, and poor David Wales can't do anything right.

Wondering what to do about Philip Sassoon. He seems to need encouragement.

2nd June 1933

Lunch with George Lightfoot. He says Flora has made a bridal veil for Melhuish's terrier and renamed it Princess Ingrid. Advises me against making any claims on Philip Sassoon. He said, "He's a particular type, Maybell. Do you understand? A dynamo of a man and a superb host, but an elusive friend. And not cut out for romance. I think they missed that piece out when they were making him."

And Lightfoot still sees that Belinda, but isn't "seeing her," whatever that means. What is wrong with these Englishmen? Well, whatever, I'm going to have Sir Philip over for drinks. A little pre-Ascot cockers, as Hattie would call it. But not when Wally's around. She'd be sure to mug up on Chippendale porcelain and all kinds of subjects just to get her foot in his door.

5th June 1933

Lunch with Connie Thaw and Ethel Croker. They're planning a surprise birthday party for Wally, and my mission will be to waylay her and bring her to Quaglino's. Hattie Erlanger and Gladys Trilling saw us and invited themselves to join us for dessert.

Hattie said, "Ethel, tell us about Wally in China. We hear there was talk."

Ethel said, "There's always talk among expats. They've nothing better to do. She was young, that's all. Young and lonely and she liked gambling. She was good at it. Baccarat, blackjack. She used to make herself quite a bit of pin money."

Hattie said, "No, but something else. Connie, do you know? Something she told Thelma? Tricks she learned to do for men?"

Connie said, "Sort of. She knows this thing you can do, to slow a man down, if he's one of those hair-trigger operators. I don't know if that was China though, was it?"

Hattie said, "Hong Kong. Ask Thelma. I heard she learned it in a whorehouse. It's called Ching Chong or Fong Wing or something like that. Ethel, you must know."

Ethel said, "Well, I never went to any whorehouses and I don't think Wally did, either. There was a place at Repulse Bay she reckoned she went to once, a singsong house, but I didn't believe her. Even Wally wouldn't have been that crazy."

I agree with Ethel. And what on earth is a hair-trigger operator? Something else beyond the scope of Harrold's Lending Library, you may be sure.

6th June 1933

Philip Sassoon has accepted for drinks on Friday. Also George Lightfoot, Boss and Ethel Croker, and Pips and Freddie. I'm not inviting any person who refers to Philip as "the Babylonian," and Wally will be gone, so he'll be safe from *her* attentions. She and Ernest are going with Lady Thelma and HRH to the Perry Brownlows for the weekend. They have a grand pile in Lincolnshire and a thousand acres. More bracing walks for Wally. What a country girl she's become.

7th June 1933

A wire from Randolph Putnam, whose boat is about to dock. Dinner on Saturday? Does he think I'm sitting around with nothing in my appointment book? I shall go to Leake Priory and weekend with the Blythes. Penelope Blythe has been pestering me for long enough.

8th June 1933

Penelope can be so infuriating. She has begged me and begged me to go to their place in the country, and now, when it's convenient to me, she and Fergus are going to Hampshire for polo. Freddie and Pips have to go to his constituency on Saturday, to press the flesh of his voters and keep them sweet. Lightfoot is going to the Hon. Belinda's, and even Ida Coote has commitments. Dog-walking commitments, more than likely, or Buddhism. That's her latest thing. Well, I'm sure Buddha wouldn't mind her helping out a friend and having dinner on Saturday.

9th June 1933

Still at my breakfast tray, and I've received the inevitable call. Randolph Putnam. "Surprise, surprise!" Not really. I know far more than I need to of his movements while he's in London. I've agreed to dinner tomorrow. May as well get it over and done with. I suppose he's feeling rather lost and overwhelmed, his first time away from the United States. His feet kept him out of the war, or possibly his mother. When one has traveled and forged a new life, one easily forgets how limited some people's worlds are. Well, charity, Maybell. Christian charity.

This evening, an elegant little coterie from *my* new world. Daiquiris, shrimp toasts, prunes in bacon, knackwurst and pickles.

10th June 1933

Randolph Putnam pretty much ruined my party. Philip Sassoon was the last to arrive, and when he was shown in, he had Putnam at his side. He said, "I found your friend outside." Randolph, bright-eyed and annoying as ever, said, "Didn't intend crashing in, Maybell, but I couldn't wait to see you."

He fairly took over, yarning with Boss Croker as though he'd known him all his life, attempting to stroll down memory lane with Pips. After three daiquiris, Pips Crosbie misremembers *every* story about me. And to top it all, Randolph gave Philip the distinct impression that he has some kind of claim on me. I heard him say, "She's a wild one. I've had to chase her halfway across the world. But she looks younger and more darling every time I see her."

If it hadn't been my own party, I'd have fled. Ethel Croker squeezing my elbow.

George Lightfoot raising his eyebrow. Tonight Randolph Putnam has to be told, straight.

11th June 1933

Randolph Putnam is impossible. He proposed marriage and appeared not to notice the firmness of my refusal. He said, "I'm a patient man, Maybell."

He envisions us living out our days together at Sweet Air, me in a rocking chair, no doubt, while he goes around winding all his clocks.

I said, "My life's in London now."

"Yes," he said, "I see that. But times change, and they say wanderers eventually return to the place they started out."

I believe the end of the world would have to be nigh for me to think of going back to America. He wanted to know if I am seeing anyone.

I said, "I see lots of people. You were lucky to find me at home."

"Well," he said, "London's gain is Baltimore's loss."

He seemed to be under the impression that crayfish are an aphrodisiac. *Au contraire.* Butter on his chin.

14th June 1933

At the Shim-Sham till dawn. Hattie Erlanger turned her ankle trying to find the powder room in the dark. Whitlow Trilling got very tight on vermouth. Gladys was livid. Saw Marthe Bibesco smoking a cigar.

Shopping with Wally this afternoon. We need gay umbrellas for Ascot, and Wally is due a birthday gift.

15th June 1933

Wally chose a silver punch bowl. Pips says it was too much. She said, "You're a fool, Maybell. You should have ushered her toward the embroidered handkerchiefs. Well, I'm afraid all she's getting from us is a box of crystallized fruits."

We wonder whether she'll get something from Thelma and the Prince. Pips doubts he sends birthday cards. She thinks he'd get the Lord Chamberlain to do it. *I am commanded by His Royal Highness to send you hugs and kisses!*

She said, "Did Ethel say anything to you?"

I said, "What about?"

"Nothing," she said. "Absolutely nothing."

What can *that* be about? Ethel Croker had better not be about to bump me from their Ascot party.

19th June 1933

Wally had guessed something was afoot, but she allowed me to kidnap her and take her to Quag's, and she very obligingly feigned surprise. And she *did* get a birthday gift from Thelma and HRH. The Prince is at Windsor, but Thelma had brought along a twig in a terra-cotta pot. Ernest says it's a rare orchid.

He'd given Wally ear studs. Amber, supposedly, although they're so small it's not easy to see what they're made of.

It's the Prince's birthday this week, too, but according to Connie Thaw, they're born under very different signs. David Wales is Cancer the Crab. He clings to the things he loves and hates to leave his shell. Whereas Wally is an adventurous, quick-thinking Gemini. I'd have loved her to tell me what I am, but then the cabaret started.

I notice Wally's dropped a year from her age. It couldn't matter less to me, except that if she does it again, I shall be forced to do likewise.

To Sunninghills.

20th June 1933, Sunninghills, Berkshire

Sunninghills has neither sun nor hills, but the beds are comfortable and Ethel Croker has hired an excellent staff. Pips and Freddie rode down with me in the Bentley and told me all about our forthcoming vacation to Italy. They promise me black-eyed men and wine that tastes of sunshine!

The Trillings and the Erlangers were here ahead of us, also a Canadian couple called Bedaux. Tomorrow the cars take us to the racetrack at noon. The big race is the Prince of Wales Cup. *Our* Prince of Wales! Wally says Thelma is at Fort Belvedere, but it's all hush-hush, because Their Majesties expect the Prince to toe the line during Ascot Week. Ethel says she has a surprise for me tomorrow. So *that's* what Pips was hinting at. Philip Sassoon, I'll bet. I saw them in a huddle about something at my soiree.

The forecast warm but overcast.

21st June 1933

A mixed day. Ethel's surprise was Randolph Putnam. He arrived, creaking in new shoes, in a taxi cab. He's staying over.

She said, "I never can resist a little matchmaking."

I'd love to wipe that smirk off Pips Crosbie's face.

Wore my caramel polka dot with a black straw coolie hat. Wally was all in grapefruit. Pencil skirt, square neckline, and a bolero jacket.

Charlie Bedaux wore salt-and-pepper trousers with his morning coat, which scandalized Ernest but Fern Bedaux says that's

Charlie. Tell him the rules, and he won't rest till he's broken them. He's an ugly little man, like a prizefighter, but worth millions.

The royal parade was very pretty. Queen Mary was in shell pink, Elizabeth York in forget-me-not, and the Princess Royal in king-fisher. Melhuish was in the third carriage with Ena Spain, Bertie York, and the Duchess of Buccleuch. Violet was in carriage number four, with the Nicholases of Greece and Prince Harry.

No sign of Thelma. I expect she stayed at the Fort and read magazines.

Ethel got Wally reminiscing about China over dinner. She said, "Remember the smell, Wally, when we disembarked at Hong Kong?"

Wally said, "Oh yes! Cinnamon. And sandalwood."

Ethel said, "Was that what it was! I thought it was rotten fish and pee-pee. And Shanghai. What a shambles. Remember that hotel?"

Wally laughed. She said, "It was called the Astor House, but it wasn't like it sounded. Your shoes stuck to the rugs. And run by a madman. He was ex-Navy, and when dinner was served, he sounded 'Cook House' on an old bugle."

Ernest said, "But still, a great cultural experience."

Ethel said, "Oh yes. Definitely that."

Every time I look in Randolph Putnam's direction, he's smiling at me. I suppose I have to be thankful he hasn't tried to steal a kiss.

22nd June 1933

Ladies' Day at Royal Ascot. Wore my lilac-and-white geor-gette, with a white cabbage rose on the brim of my straw. Wally very severe in a beige turban. Ethel had a picnic catered by Fortnum's so we wouldn't miss the procession of Royalties along the racetrack. Dressed crab, tarragon chicken, and a strawberry mousse. Elizabeth York was in the first landau with the Majesties. She wore primrose, and Queen Mary was in ice blue. Freddie said she looked like the Jungfrau, whoever she is. The Princess Royal's hat was like a speckled hen.

Violet was promoted to second carriage today, but I believe I've seen that peppermint toque before. Several times.

Ernest left to go to his office immediately after they'd run the Gold Cup, as did Freddie, the Trillings, and Fern and Charlie

Bedaux. Fern is so gracious and Charlie is so florid and common-looking. They make an odd couple. I have an open invitation to visit them in any of their many lovely homes. Ethel says their French chateau is divine.

Randolph is staying on in Maidenhead for a further week and hopes we'll have time for another talk. Oh dear.

24th June 1933

Having begged a ride with me and Pips, Wally has now taken off to Fort Belvedere. There's a lunch party for the Prince's birthday.

26th June 1933, Wilton Place

Wally says Connie and Thelma are very concerned about their sister Gloria Vanderbilt, who stands to lose her only child. Gloria lives in Paris and always has a very hectic schedule, so she left the little girl with her sister-in-law in New York, for safekeeping. But now the sister-in-law is refusing to give the child back, and it may come to a court case. No faster way to beggar yourself. And I wonder why Gloria wants the child back all of a sudden. Better to leave her where she's settled, I'd have thought.

Daphne Frith on the telephone. She and Prosper want me at Hoxney Court for a weekend before everyone disperses for the summer. Pips and Freddie are also invited.

27th June 1933

Lunch with Randolph. He said, "I've so enjoyed seeing you in your new life, Maybell. I can quite see you're not ready to leave it just yet. But we Putnams know a good thing when we see it, and I'm prepared to wait."

My only consolation is that he's cheerful in his disappointment. He sails on Friday.

28th June 1933

Dinner at the Crosbies. Freddie says Hoxney Court will give me a true taste of rustic England. I already hear the clank and splutter of ancient plumbing.

1st July 1933, Hoxney Court, Kent

Hoxney Court is a great creaking hull of a place. Daphne says it's been in Prosper's family for more than three hundred years and still has many of its original features. Indeed, I believe the mattress on my bed may be one of them. A sultry night forced me to risk an open window until I heard a band of lunatics cackling out there in the dark. Prosper says it was only frogs, but my window will now remain locked.

Today we meet the natives. Pips and I are assisting Daphne in the judging of an embroidered-tablecloth competition. Freddie and Prosper have to crown the Carnival Queen.

We're only fifteen miles from Lympne. I put a call through to Philip, who was expected although no one seemed to know when.

2nd July 1933

Freddie is laid up with an ankle sprained during yesterday's sack race, and Daphne and Prosper had to put in an obligatory appearance at church, so Pips and I motored over to Port Lympne on the off-chance. Philip was at home and made us very welcome. He gave us champagne and took us down to watch the dragonflies dancing on his new pond. Not his usual bubbling self though. Her Majesty the Queen has proposed herself for tea this afternoon, so he'd been up till very late, painting modesty shorts on those saucy Egyptians in his dining-room frieze, in case she decides to tour the house.

What a chore. After all that, I hope she doesn't cancel.

Daphne has been quizzing me about Wally and Ernest, but never when Prosper's within earshot, I notice. She said, "How thrilling for two such ordinary people suddenly to find themselves whisked into the Prince of Wales's circle. And how odd that he should choose such people. He's certainly going to be a very different style of king than his father. If he ever becomes king."

I said, "Why wouldn't he?"

She said, "Because he may burn himself out with fast women and smokey niteries. Prosper believes, and he's not alone in this, that Bertie York should be our next King."

4th July 1933

To the U.S. compound for drinks. Ernest yawning constantly, because Thelma and the Prince kept them out until three last night. As Wally says, he has no pep. At thirty-six, a man should be good for a little dancing after dinner.

6th July 1933

To the Army & Navy store. Pips says silk beach pajamas are essential for Italy. Chose fuschia and oyster.

Padmore is *so* excited about the promise of foreign travel. When she worked for Mrs. Orr-Tweedie, they never ventured farther than the Suffolk coast.

Rory says he'd like to go to the circus for his birthday treat but doesn't think Flora will be allowed, and then there'll be a scene. He said, "We could pretend you're taking me to the dentist."

I don't think I'm inclined to tell a lie. Better to say nothing and proceed by stealth.

12th July 1933

To Bertram Mills's Circus and to a Corner House for high tea. I simply waited until Violet had left for her Fallen Women committee and then collected them all. Rory, Flora, and Doopie. It was the greatest fun. They had chimpanzees dressed in adorable little romper suits, and when they brought them out into the audience, one of them tried to climb onto Doopie's lap.

Flora kept saying, "Won't Mummy be surprised."

Rory was anxious though. He said, "Mummy might be surprised in a bad way, Flora. I think it'd be better if we didn't say too much about it."

That was what was agreed. Even Doopie understood. Then, when I dropped them off, Flora burst straight into the drawing room, crying, "Mummy! Aunt Bayba took us to the cirgus and then to the Gorner House but we're not going to say too much about it!"

Ulick said, "I thought she was gated until further notice?"

Rory said, "It was for my birthday."

Ulick said, "The whole point of a gating is to make one realize the error of one's ways, not to have exceptions made because it's someone's birthday."

Flora said, "Anyway, a bunkey sat on Doopie."

Violet said, "No more fibs please, Flora. Now run upstairs."

Rory said, "Aunt Maybell's going to the Venice Lido, Ulick. Don't you wish we could go?"

Ulick said, "No, I do not."

13th July 1933

George Lightfoot has gone to Yorkshire. He's visiting Viscount Minskip, then traveling with him to Drumcanna. Wally is taking a prevacation cure at The Cedars with Thelma and Connie. She and Ernest leave for the Tyrol on the 20th.

Thelma and her Prince will be apart through August. Thelma's going to Biarritz, and HRH has to go yachting with the King and then hurry up to Balmoral for the shooting. Penelope Blythe is pleased. She says if Wales is going to be around, there'll be a good chance of some proper dancing.

"And if not," she said, "next summer I shall tag along with you to foreign parts. I couldn't be more bored with Drumcanna."

15th July 1933

Lunch with Pips. She says Gladys has bought a very daring bathing suit. I'd say any style of bathing suit would be risky on Gladys. When a person has been delivered of two children, she'd do well to keep herself artfully draped.

17th July 1933

Gladys Trilling on the telephone. I seem to have drawn a shared berth with her in the *wagons-lits* to Nice. Whitlow can't get away for another week at least.

She said, "Isn't it a lark? We can get to know each other much better."

I said, "Do you snore?"

"Like an old sow," she said, "but don't worry. I'm sure we'll be too busy chatting to do much sleeping."

18th July 1933

The kitchen maid has revealed herself to be in the family way, put there by the outdoors boy. Just what I need on the eve of my departure. A major domestic crisis.

19th July 1933

The kitchen maid and the outdoors boy have been sent packing. They can argue about their nuptials in their own time. As

Padmore says, it's a saving. There'll be no fires needed and no entertaining, so we can make a fresh start with new help in September. What a sensible girl she is.

21st July 1933

Violet predicts that come September, I'll be looking for a new lady's maid, too.

She said, "Taking a girl like that to Italy. She's bound to fall into the clutches of some oily Romeo and that'll be the last you'll see of her. I don't know why you insist on keeping a lady's maid anyway. I've managed without one for years."

All too obviously. And a smoothing iron. And a clothes brush.

23rd July 1933

Zita and Bernie Cavett have taken a villa in San Remo. They've invited us all to visit on our way back from Venice. The Trillings won't be able to, of course. Gladys frets about the children.

28th July 1933, a train, approaching Genoa

No sleep. Pips and Hattie were in and out in their pajamas and face cream, tight on champagne, and then Gladys kept me awake with her latest notion about Wally. She thinks she's a man masquerading as a woman.

I said, "I was at school with her. She used to sleep over at our house. I've known her since she was fifteen."

She said, "Yes, but did you ever see her in the altogether?"

I don't need to have.

She said, "You must admit, she does look terribly manly. Those great big hands. And no bosom at all."

I said, "You seem to be forgetting she's had two husbands and quite a number of sweethearts."

She said, "That doesn't signify. Some men like that kind of thing."

Some men may, but not Ernest Simpson, I'm sure. I never met a more vanilla character.

She said, "Well, I shan't be convinced until I've seen what she's got inside her bloomers."

And they call Wally vulgar.

30th July 1933, Venice Lido

I adore Italy. Sunshine, smiling porters at the railroad station, and a sleek, shiny launch to whisk us to the Excelsior. The chandeliers are exquisite. The linens are sumptuous and the sands are kept immaculately raked. All I ask is to be left in peace beneath this perfect blue sky.

1st August 1933

Pips and Hattie are attacking the sights of Venice, and Freddie and Judson keep disappearing to the tennis courts, which leaves me with Gladys, who insists on reading aloud from an Italian phrase book. I wish Ambassador Bingham would hurry up and release Whitlow from his desk.

4th August 1933

Freddie had promised us drinks in a real Venetian palace, with an old college friend, Bobo Farinacci, but Bobo turns out to be in Switzerland. Pips says his palace is locked and shuttered. Gladys's monumental thighs have turned pink. She's convinced she has a poolside admirer. I hate to disappoint her.

Whitlow is rumored to be on a train heading toward Nice.

7th August 1933

Pips seems to have wrung the city dry of Tipolettos and Tintiolos and has now moved on to mosaics, but Hattie has had enough. She's offered to help me improve my game of tennis, which will certainly be preferable to listening to Gladys's fevered fantasies every time a pool boy lights her cigarette.

8th August 1933

I have sacked Hattie and hired a professional tennis instructor. She deliberately tried to befuddle me with technicalities: tram lines, backward forehands, lets, lets-not. Surely the main thing is that the ball travel back and forth over the net at an agreeable pace, without people yelling "out!" all the time.

10th August 1933

A very exciting development. The Prince of Wales arrived this morning. He's not yachting in the Solent, not shooting grice on Deeside, but right here on Venice Lido. And not with Thelma. The concierge told Padmore he's traveling alone, apart from two detectives and a valet and an equerry.

Hattie has sent him a note. When we reckoned up, she has known him longest.

11th August 1933

We heard nothing from HRH. So much for Hattie Erlanger's credentials as an acquaintance of many years' standing! Then, as I was going up to change for luncheon, I bumped into him coming out of an elevator. He greeted me very warmly. "How splendid," he kept saying. "How splendid!"

He's in Italy on a fact-finding tour, apparently. The conditions of the working man. He's proposed himself for dinner. Joey Legh is equerrying. Now there's a man who should be told that a smile costs nothing. Freddie says if I had to pick up after the Prince of Wales like the equerries do, I wouldn't find much to smile about.

Venice is a very strange resort. There are perfectly lovely beaches here, but everyone makes a beeline for the canals. Stinking little alleys with water the color of gasoline and everything needs fixing up. I refuse to be dragged over any more bridges or gaze at any more crumbling palaces. Palaces! I've told Pips she can come and find me at Quadri's café. I'll be there in time for my afternoon ice cream, observing the fashions and listening to the band.

12th August 1933

HRH looked for Wally and Ernest when he joined our table last evening. I think he was disappointed not to find them. And then Hattie and Gladys would gush so. Little wonder he became rather subdued. I've seen it happen before. It takes someone like Thelma or Wally to draw him out when he's in that mood. Sometimes I sense a very lonely man.

There had been talk of going to the casino, but he suddenly decided to turn in early. Freddie stayed down and had a nightcap with Joey Legh. Legh doesn't care for Italy. He told Freddie he couldn't understand why HRH couldn't just go to Balmoral, like a normal prince. Captain Legh has obviously never felt the prick of a Deeside midge.

This morning, they left without even saying good-bye. I suppose he's had to hurry on with his tour of working conditions. Next stop, Monte Carlo. A prince's work is never done.

17th August 1933

Barbara Hutton is in town, honeymooning with her Russian prince. She's throwing a little cocktail party on Saturday and has invited all of us on the basis of Judson's connections with her aunt Jessie Woolworth.

Pips said, "What a sad sack. Imagine inviting a bunch of strangers round when you're on your honeymoon."

It depends on the length of the honeymoon. When a husband is in business, as Brumby was, he gets back into harness before boredom sets in, but I suppose all Prince Mdivani has to do is count Barbara's money. Anyway, it's nice to meet new people, even on a honeymoon.

19th August 1933

The Hutton party was pleasant enough. We went over by motor launch and arrived in a thunderstorm. The sky was dull orange, and the Grand Canal looked rather as though it were coming to the boil. Barbara looked so young, so bewildered. I think she was grateful to those of us who braved the weather. Gladys wore a print day dress and no jewelry. Hattie with a run in her stockings and a sad little topaz brooch. These English girls!

The skies had cleared completely by the time we came home. We bumped back across the lagoon at quite a clip. The Lido lights looked like a diamond bracelet strung out.

Tuesday, to San Remo. It will be a relief to be around someone like Zita Cavett, someone else who has a sense of elegance. The Trillings are going straight back to London, and Freddie is going to Ireland to fish with Lord Templemore, so there'll be just me, Pips, Hattie, and Judson.

23rd August 1933, San Remo

The Cavetts' villa is heavenly. Corn lilies everywhere, and wild thyme and basil, and the sea is midnight blue. Zita and Pips went for a swim in the buff.

Another couple are arriving tomorrow. Kath and Herman Rogers, Americans, but they've made their home in France. And why not? If Randolph Putnam could see me now, relaxing beneath a fig tree, sipping a glass of pretty pink wine, he'd realize there'll be no luring me back to Baltimore.

25th August 1933

Herman and Kath Rogers are not only great company, they also know Wally Simpson, or perhaps *knew* is the word. They were in Peking in '24. Herman was attached to the U.S. Embassy. Kath said, "I'll say we knew her. We practically adopted her. Actually, I knew her slightly from San Diego, before I married Herm. But then she turned up in Peking, no husband, no chaperone, and it was such a dangerous time. Fighting in the streets, foreigners being kidnapped, and Wally was wandering around, like a kid at Luna Park. She didn't seem to have any sense of danger. In the end, we persuaded her to move in with us, inside the Legation compound."

I can see Kath taking someone under her wing like that. There's something motherly about her. I find her rather jolly.

She and Herman didn't know about Ernest. They haven't heard from Wally since she went back to the States.

Kath said, "I'm so glad she met someone. I hope he's nice. She was a mess when we knew her. Please tell her all the best from us."

Hattie said, "What I want to know is, did she really learn 'secret Chinese arts'?"

Pips said, "Yes, she did. The secret art of never picking up the check."

27th August 1933

The Rogerses left this morning. They have a house near Cannes, which Herman says "makes up with charm what it lacks in amenities," and they hope to see me there someday. I offered Kath Wally's London number, but she said she wasn't sure she wanted to get involved again. Apparently, after Wally moved in with them, she developed a crush on Herman. Well, he is a very attractive man. Yale, Phi Beta Kappa, but with muscles and a wicked smile.

Kath said, "I always felt with Wally it wasn't that she particularly wanted Herman or any of the other men she went after. She just seemed to want to prove she could get them."

I said, "Did she go after lots of men?"

"Several," she said. "I shouldn't gossip like this. Please don't tell her. She was young. She made a few mistakes."

I said, "One of our English friends has got it into her head that Wally's really a man. Can you imagine?"

Kath laughed. She said, "I don't think so. I remember at least two Italians she was involved with. I don't think they'd settle for a fake, do you?"

I can't wait to tell Gladys.

4th September 1933, Wilton Place

Flora was to have started at St. Audrey's this week, but has the chicken pox. Tomorrow to Fuller's with Rory. A boy needs a cream meringue to set him up for a new school year.

5th September 1933

I have all the Drumcanna news from Rory. Prince George came to tea and, more importantly for Rory, so did the head gillie's daughter, little Ellen MacNab.

Their Majesties were disappointed the Prince of Wales spent so little time at Balmoral. Flora caught her first fish. And Ailsa Anstruther-Brodie had a mishap and discharged her gun into George Lightfoot's shooting butt. No wonder I haven't heard from George. Apparently, Ulick has announced that when the moor belongs to him, he won't allow girls to shoot.

But the great *scandale* centers on Penelope Blythe, though Rory told it with such innocence.

He said, "Lord Habberley got confused in the dark and went into Mrs. Blythe's bedroom by mistake and kicked her potty and broke it. Mummy was furious because of the mess, but the maids thought it was jolly funny. I suggested to Lord Habberley that he could have my old night-light and then he wouldn't get confused anymore."

Penelope Blythe and Ralph Habberley! Well! I can't say I'm surprised about Ralph. I remember how stimulated he was by our tango sessions last August, and, of course, Jane Habberley has no allure. But for him to choose Penelope! Well, in my absence, she was the best of a dreary crowd, I guess.

6th September 1933

George Lightfoot says Ailsa Anstruther-Brodie didn't make a very good effort at killing him, but would only laugh when I asked him about Ralph Habberley and Penelope Blythe. He said, "When I go to bed, I go to sleep, Maybell. I don't lie awake waiting for the sound of breaking potties."

I think I'd better have lunch with Penelope.

He says Tommy Minskip has lost a few more spots off his dice.

We both received, in this morning's post, invitations from Ida Coote to a lecture on Reincarnation, and from Sir Philip to a charity ball at Park Lane, both on September 20th. Lightfoot says this affords us the opportunity to go from the ridiculous to the sublime all in one evening, though how he expects me to attend a lecture *and* have time to dress for a ball I can't imagine.

8th September 1933

Wally is back and filling up her schedule like a demon. She was in the chair next to mine at Monsieur Jules.

She said, "I need you to get Philip Sassoon to invite us to his ball."

I said, "He doesn't know you."

She said, "What rot. It's a charity ball. Does he want to raise money for this pet hospital of his or not?"

Well, I'm not asking. Philip is *my* friend. How would she feel if I elbowed my way into Fort Belvedere? Besides, what use can she be to a raiser of funds? She doesn't have a nickel.

I said, "I met some old friends of yours. Herman and Kath Rogers? They asked to be remembered to you."

"Oh yes?" she said. "Are they still together? I wonder he didn't tire of her long ago."

I said, "They seem devoted. I liked them both very much. And he's so good-looking."

"Is he?" she said. "That's not my recollection."

I guess he turned her down. How humiliating.

I said, "And while we're on the subject of China, what's this I hear about secret bedroom arts?"

The girls who were doing us were all ears.

She said, "We weren't on the subject of China. And there's only one bedroom art a woman needs. The art of keeping her husband otherwise occupied."

Of course, Ernest *always* brings home business papers.

11th September 1933

Lunch with Penelope Blythe. She says Ralph Habberley was just one of those things. More questions about Wally and her "secret power over men." Hattie Erlanger and Gladys Trilling have evidently been gossiping. It's too ridiculous.

I said, "If Wally acquired secret powers and the best she could do with them was seduce Ernest Simpson, she'd better go back and take the class again."

She said, "Oh, I don't know. I think Ernest is rather a darling."

Well, Penelope has already established her want of discrimination by allowing Ralph Habberley to enter her room and kick her potty.

13th September 1933

Wally called to thank me for getting her an invitation to the Sassoon ball.

I said, "I didn't. I haven't spoken to him since I got back from Italy."

"Oh Maybell!" she said. "Well, thank you anyway, for fixing it by telepathy!"

Lightfoot. It has to be.

14th September 1933

Lightfoot it was. He asked Sybil Chumley, unaccountably spelled *Cholmondeley*, if it was possible the Simpsons' invitation had gone astray in the mails. I do wish he hadn't.

I said, "If Philip's invalids in Clacton-on-Sea have to rely on the benefaction of Ernest and Wally, they'll be in a poor way."

He said, "Oh, what does it matter? Wally's happy, and I'm sure Philip Sassoon couldn't care less. Syb says Wales and Prince George may look in."

So *that's* what it's about.

To Shriner's for evening pumps. A pair of peep-toes in gold

pleated leather and a pair in silver satin with a rhinestone button on the ankle strap. Gorgeous.

15th September 1933

Lunch with Ida, who has learned that she was formerly a princess in 18th Dynasty Egypt. With the Friths to a reception at the Austrian Legation, then on to dinner at the Belchesters. Also came: the Dickie Mountbattens, the Perry Brownlows, and Anne Belchester's brother, Seb.

Game soup, boiled capon, mushroom savory. I was longing to leave, and the men sat for far too long. I feel a chill coming on.

17th September 1933

All day in bed and still feverish.

18th September 1933

No improvement. Canceled Wally. Canceled Monsieur Jules. All these days without eating, my ball gown is going to look even more divine.

19th September 1933

Chicken pox.

29th September 1933

Back from the grave's edge. I'm as weak as a kitten and must be at least ten pounds lighter. Padmore has been an angel. Darling Philip sent grapes from Lympne and a Jasmin de Coree pillow spray. Lightfoot says neither of the Princes put in an appearance at the ball. Violet brought an egg custard and books, which I made her take away again. I'm too frail to turn a page. Doopie has shingles.

30th September 1933

When Wally visits a sickbed, she certainly doesn't outstay her welcome. She stayed only long enough to tell me what a fabulous ball I missed. Dancing to a band from the Pig Ankle Club, shepherd's pie served by flunkeys in powdered wigs, and raffle prizes from Cartier—Ernest won gold sock-suspenders. Thank you so much for sparing me no details, Wally. Also, that Philip Sassoon is going to invite her to Trent to show her his collection of porringers. And she promised that in the next few days I may learn something to my advantage.

She said, "Now do buck up, Maybell. It's time we shopped for gloves."

2nd October 1933

Wally has produced the promised rabbit from the hat. I'm invited to Thelma Furness's for the weekend of the 13th. She said, "I can't guarantee that His Royal Highness will be there, but there's a very good chance."

Well anyway, I do like Thelma.

3rd October 1933

Monsieur Jules couldn't do a thing with my hair. He says it's the fever. I may go to The Cedars to recuperate.

8th October 1933

Violet said, "If you're going to a convalescent home, you might think of taking Doopie with you. She's still far from well."

I said, "It's not a convalescent home. It's a rest cure, with beauty treatments. There's nothing for Doopie there."

She said, "Why not? She enjoys a little lip rouge."

I said, "Okay, let her come. But I'm going with Wally and Lady Furness and her sister."

That was the end of that.

She said, "I do wish you wouldn't. Associating with those people may cost you the friendship of others, who are more worthy."

I said, "Surely, what's good enough for the Prince of Wales is good enough for Violet Melhuish?"

"Don't test me, Maybell," she said. "The Prince of Wales may think he can afford scandal, but that doesn't mean the rest of us should follow him like a herd of swine."

Poor Violet. She just doesn't know Thelma and the Prince as I do.

Two years today since Brumby passed over. May he rest in peace.

9th October 1933, The Cedars, Hertfordshire

Connie Thaw and I have been wrapped in steaming hay all afternoon and I certainly feel the better for it. Connie told me that Thelma didn't at all set out to seduce the Prince. It was he who pursued her, and he was seeing Freda Dudley Ward at the time, so it was all rather awkward. When it was clear how smitten the Prince was, Mrs. Dudley Ward offered to retire gracefully, but her children were terribly upset, because they'd grown very fond of the Prince and regarded him as a special kind of uncle.

Connie said, "There's only one reason David still keeps in touch with Freda Dudley Ward. Thelma insisted on it, for the sake of the children. She never monopolizes him, you know. You must have noticed. Thelma has a big heart."

She does. I think she'd make a very good Queen.

11th October 1933

Wally says Thelma has the very latest cartoon movies at Borough Court.

She said, "But I hope you're preparing conversational topics, Maybell. You don't always pull your weight, I've noticed."

The ginger of it!

I said, "And what kind of conversational topics do you recommend for Leicestershire?"

"Range widely," she said. "Be unexpected. Gertrude Stein, perhaps. Or *Ulysses*. Those are lively topics."

The names meant nothing to me or to Pips. I shall make World Affairs my subject.

Connie and Benny Thaw will be there, also Poots and Humphrey Butler and the Perry Brownlows.

13th October 1933, Melton Mowbray, Leicestershire

Wet leaves blown against the window panes, but Borough Court is warm and has every modern convenience. The Prince is staying nearby, at Craven Lodge, but motored over for dinner with an equerry called Oxer Bettenbrooke. Wore my oyster silk. Much talk about Germany leaving the League of Nations. I made a knowledgeable showing, though I do say so myself. Humphrey Butler agrees with me that the Germans simply feel they've been punished quite enough. The war has been over for fifteen years and all they're doing is standing up for themselves a little.

Brownlow said, "Well, I wonder whether Mr. Hitler's motives are quite as peaceable as he promises."

But as HRH reminded us, sometimes you have to prepare for war in order to keep the peace.

He said, "If there's another showdown, it'll be against the Communists, and if it comes to it, we'd better align ourselves with the Germans, because no one else seems willing to take on the Red Menace. Except possibly Mussolini."

Poots Butler said, "I don't know. Mr. Hitler. Mr. Mussolini. Mr. Stalin. Dictators seem to be all the rage."

Ernest, who has another carbuncle, which is making him feverish and disagreeable, said, "Yes, who knows, maybe we'll get one in England before long."

There was a deathly silence until Thelma picked up the gayer subject of Mediterranean cruises. Wally gave Ernest a look to chill the blood.

We adjourned to watch Mickey Mouse cartoons, but Wally went straight up to bed. Not really *comme il faut* when Royalties are present, but she pleaded a headache, brought on I'm sure by Ernest's gaffe. As Oxer Bettenbrooke pointed out, it was tantamount to treason. Ernest hurried away to the billiard room with Benny Thaw.

14th October 1933

The Perry Brownlows, Humphrey Butler, the Prince, and Oxer B are out, engaged in something called cubbing. It's to get the hunting dogs fit for the season and give the fox cubs foretaste of the need to run. I drove with Thelma and her little boy to watch the hunt meet at Kneilthorpe House. Hounds milling everywhere and horses rearing and frisking. Lady Merrick, who looks like a washerwoman, was shouting orders, and her sister, just as ruddy-cheeked, was thundering around with trays of something made from brandy and lemons and hot sugar water. A stirrup cup, delicious even for those of us not in the saddle. Thelma says there's an interesting American sister-in-law, one of the mustard Minkels, but all we saw of her was her dog, trotting up and down the terrace with a little Hermès scarf around his neck.

Thelma says she may give up country life now she's divorced. Her son likes the horses, but she says he could have all this and more in the Argentine.

I said, "But what about the Prince?"

"Oh," she said, "I won't run out on him. I'll wait till my time's up."

I said, "Has he found a princess? Is there a wedding on the cards?"

She said, "Oh, not *that*. I expect he will marry soon, but that won't make any difference to us. No, I mean when he finds someone new."

I said, "But he adores you."

"Yes," she said, "but he adored others before me, and I'm sure there'll be many after me. My Little Man has a restless soul."

I wonder what happens to his circle when he moves on. Wally won't be happy if the Thelma connection is severed, after all the hard work she's put in.

A scratch lunch. Thelma's resting, Benny's making heavy weather of a crossword puzzle, Ernest is dozing with a book. The dressing needs changing on his carbuncle. Wally ought to see to it, but she's in the morning room with Connie and Poots and causing great shrieks of laughter. Sharing advice on the secret bedroom art of Pang Chung, I suppose.

How slowly time passes in Leicestershire. Prince George is dining this evening.

I think my ox-blood crepe and an angora wrap.

15th October 1933

A narrowly averted disaster, for which I blame the Chinese, with their mischievously confusing language, and Hattie Erlanger, who sowed the seeds of a dangerous misconstruction. First, Thelma's boiler failed, and it being Sunday, nothing can be done to repair it. Then Poots Butler insisted we play bridge, but I left the table at the earliest opportunity. Bridge can bring out such unpleasantness in people. I'm sure anyone can mislay a silly card, especially when they're playing in gloves.

The Prince doesn't care for bridge, either, and was working on his needlepoint. He patted the seat beside him. "Maybell," he said, "I'm chilled to the bone. How about warming up with a spot of Ping Pong?"

I believe I blushed. One hears of *droit de seigneur,* but he was so matter-of-fact about it, and we were fully within earshot of Thelma, and thank goodness. She saved me from myself.

She said, "Darling, don't drag Maybell off to the games' room. It's like an icebox in there. I'm already worried she'll go home with pneumonia. I'll ring for tea. We can watch some more Mickey if you like."

Wally said, "Anyway sir, Maybell never hit a ball in her life."

He said, "I think you're mistaken, Wally. When we were at the Lido this summer, she was the talk of the tennis courts."

That silenced her!

He left after tea. He has to go to Birmingham tomorrow to visit a bicycle factory, then on to South Wales.

16th October 1933

Sad farewells to Thelma. She's leaving for the States on Wednesday, going to help her sister Gloria get back the child that's rightfully hers.

She said, "Maybell, I'm depending on you and Wally to take care of my Little Man while I'm gone. He's sure to be lonely."

17th October 1933, Wilton Place

With Wally to Asprey for an urgent belt. She said, "Thelma's going to be gone for months, so this is our chance to become indispensable. As soon as David gets back from visiting his coal mines, we're going to give him the most wonderful time. Cozy suppers. Lively people. It's a pity you don't have a country house, Maybell. If you were to get one, I could help you do wonderful house parties. Not like those dull little affairs at Borough Court. Thelma's sweet, but for an American, she really doesn't have much style."

I think HRH seems perfectly contented with Thelma's weekends. Anyway, I'm not interested in getting a country house. More staff to subdue. More cold corridors to heat. Violet is a perfect example of the dangers of spreading oneself too thin.

Rory is allowed home from school this weekend. It's called an *exeat*.

21st October 1933

To Lyons in the Strand for a Viennese Whirl. Flora was allowed to join us, because she's notched up a full week at St. Audrey's without any misdemeanors. She doesn't appear to have made any friends yet. Rory said, "You soon will. You should pick out a girl who looks nice and start chatting to her during recreation time."

She said, "I don't want to. I like torging to myself."

To the opera with the Friths and the Belchesters. *Elektra* by Strauss. Not one of his usual, hummable waltzes. Lightfoot was in a box with that girl Belinda.

25th October 1933

Zita and Bernie Cavett are taking a house on Mount Street till January. Zita says the first thing they're going to do is throw a costume party.

To the Century Club with the Crosbies and the Erlangers. The Simpsons promised but never showed up.

27th October 1933

Wally says the Prince has dined with them three evenings this week. I said, "We expected you on Monday evening. Why didn't you bring him to the Century?"

She said, "He was too comfortable to move."

I said, "And who have you invited to dine with him? Aren't your old friends good enough anymore?"

She says Benny Thaw came one evening, but otherwise they've just been a threesome. She said, "It's not at all that you aren't good enough, Maybell. But sometimes he likes to relax and not be with lots of people."

Surely, that's what a tray supper for one is for.

1st November 1933

Lily Drax-Pfaffenhof wants me for Christmas and won't take no for an answer. Wally and Ernest will be going, and Wally's keen to have me along. Once Ernest gets his head in a book, he's no company.

Lunch with Pips, who is very tense waiting to hear whether Freddie's got promoted to PPS. Whatever it is, I hope it means more money for them. Daphne Frith says they're living on their capital.

3rd November 1933

To Bryanston Court, where there are now *three* armchairs arranged around the fireplace. They never know if the Prince is coming until he appears, sometimes as early as five, sometimes as late as nine. Tonight we knew he definitely wouldn't come, because he's gone to Norfolk to shoot with Bertie York.

I said, "Don't you waste an awful lot of food?"

Ernest said, "We waste nothing. Wally's very thrifty in the kitchen."

I said, "But it must be so unsettling, waiting around for hours."

"Maybell," he said, "I can think of nothing more rewarding than entertaining the future King of England."

Some kind of stew, followed by crepes filled with the Prince of Wales's leftovers.

Ernest says a PPS is a parliamentary private secretary, which doesn't sound to me like a promotion. Freddie Crosbie as a stenographer!

7th November 1933

Freddie Crosbie didn't get the new job. Daphne Frith says the problem with Freddie is everyone likes him, which is all very well on the golf course but useless in the Commons. He completely lacks the killer instinct.

10th November 1933

George Lightfoot gave a small dinner at South Audley Street. Came: Fergus and Penelope Blythe and a couple called Metcalfe. Baba and Fruity. Baba is the sister of the poor departed Cimmie Mosley, and Fruity is just Fruity.

Penelope said, "What's happened to your friend Wally? I haven't seen her anywhere lately."

Baba Metcalfe said, "Wally who?"

Penelope said, "Simpson. A little American. Before the summer, she and her husband were all over London like a rash."

Lightfoot said, "It's true. Wherever two or three were gathered together and a small bottle of tonic wine was opened, Wally Simpson was guaranteed to appear, but not recently. What's she up to, Maybell?"

I said, "She's taking care of the Prince of Wales."

Uproar. Fruity Metcalfe said, "Bugger me. I thought Oxer Bettenbrooke was supposed to be doing that."

Much laughter. Apparently, Fruity also equerries from time to time.

Baba said, "But why should Wales need looking after?"

I said, "Because Thelma Furness is in America and she particularly asked Wally and me to make sure he wasn't lonely."

"I see," she said. I don't think she did though. According to Lightfoot, she's from a top-drawer family, the Curzons, but I never heard of her. He says she was reckoned to be a great beauty in her day. Fruity cuts a good figure, tall, commanding. I can see he was a catch.

Lightfoot suggests I go to the Cavetts' party as Little Bo-Beep. He's offered to accompany me as a pet lamb.

11th November 1933

Remembrance Sunday. Melhuish laid a wreath at the Cenotaph War Memorial. Lest we forget. I wonder how healthy it is to keep harping back. The world is surely a better place than it was, except for those Roosevelts and the Reds. We're all friends now. And if you start brooding over all the people who've gone to their rest, you can end up feeling too depressed even to face the breakfast tray.

To tea at Carlton Gardens. Flora didn't say a word. Just sat on a couch, swinging her legs and gazing vacantly.

Doopie said, "Vora's nod abby."

Violet said, "Flora's perfectly happy, thank you, Doopie. Please don't interfere. She's been a very good girl this week."

I went up to the nursery to see how Doopie's getting on with my shepherdess gown. She said, "Bayba, Vora's nod abby adall."

This was always likely to happen. Doopie's had the child to herself since the day she was born, and she doesn't like it now Flora's going to school and learning how to behave like a young lady. I'd say it's Doopie who's "nod abby."

My gown is looking very well indeed.

12th November 1933

Wally has asked to borrow my diamond stomacher for the Cavetts' party. She's going as the Snow Queen. Pips is undecided between the Little Match Seller or the Pied Piper of Hamelin. Lightfoot is being very perplexing about his costume. He said, "I shall be a wolf in sheep's clothing. Or is it the other way round?"

There also remains the problem of a shepherd's crook.

15th November 1933

Ernest is worried about insurance for my diamonds. He turned quite pale when I told him they were worth ten thousand at the last valuation, not to mention their sentimental value. He said, "In that case, I think they'd better remain in your bank. Wally can wear paste."

Wally was furious. She said, "Wally cannot wear paste. And I'm not ruining my costume because you lack nerve, Ernest. Maybell's diamonds will be quite safe with me."

Personally, I think she's overdoing things. It's only a party in a vacation home, after all. It's not as though she's going to Londonderry House.

16th November 1933

Monsieur Jules wants me to try a finger wave. Not sure.

Drinks at the Yugoslav Legation. Good champagne, but served with an extraordinary sour jam. Perhaps they can't afford caviar. Wally was touting Ernest's slight acquaintance with a commercial attaché. As I reminded her, *I've* taken afternoon tea with their Royalties on many occasions, Crown Princess Olga being practically *glued* to my sister Violet's side.

17th November 1933

I'm invited to a gala ball at Lancaster House, in aid of Anne Belchester's orphanages. Offered to make arrangements for Violet to get something done with her hair, but she declined. I bet she's going to turn up in that ancient *eau de nil,* too. Tired brocade and day shoes. No wonder people can't believe we're sisters.

19th November 1933

A wonderful party! Zita and Bernie spared no expense, and my Bo-Peep gown looked darling. Spotted white muslin over a full skirt in sky blue satin silk, and a ravishingly deep sweetheart neckline.

George Lightfoot seemed to have forgotten he was meant to be a Lost Sheep, and turned up as the Tin Man, but I forgave him, because he'd managed to borrow me a divine brass crozier from one of his bishop friends.

The Erlangers were Humpty Dumpty and Miss Muffet, Pips was the Pied Piper, because Freddie had told her she has good legs and should show them off to their full advantage. I don't think they're all *that* good, especially in harlequin-patterned hose. Freddie himself was in a yellow vest, making absurd noises all evening, supposed to be a motoring character called Mr. Toad. Ernest wore a muffler and carried a jar of honey. A feeble effort, I thought. He said he was Pooh Bear. Daisy Fellowes came as Tinkerbell.

Tinkerbag, Lightfoot kept calling her. Not sure who Bernie was meant to be. Some kind of gnome. But Zita looked very pretty as the Sugar Plum Fairy, in froths of pink net hung with candy. HRH looked in briefly and was asked to judge the best costume. I'm sure it was a close-run thing between me and Zita, but Wally pushed herself forward beneath a chandelier so my diamonds would sparkle to advantage on her white taffeta. Even her opera gloves had rows of tiny rhinestone buttons. Lightfoot said she wasn't so much the Snow Queen as the Walking Icicle.

I suppose after all those dinners she's made for him recently, HRH felt obliged to choose her. She got a magnum of champagne and a kiss on the cheek.

Zita said, "We hoped you'd come in costume yourself, sir."

He said, "Lord no, I spend enough of my life in fancy dress."

She said, "But if you had to, who would you be?"

"No idea," he said. "What do you suggest?"

She said, "Peter Pan."

Wally said, "Oh no, sir! I don't agree. I'd make you the King of Hearts."

Pips muttered, "Oh please! Take me somewhere I can throw up."

20th November 1933

Lunch with Penelope Blythe. She just had an "adventure" with a man who came to rehang her dining-room doors, and recommends the experience. "None of those boring preliminaries," she said. "You know? Drinks. Dinner. Phone calls. You should try it. It'd take you out of yourself."

I told her, I don't want to be out of myself. I'm quite happy where I am.

24th November 1933

Philip Sassoon will be celebrating his birthday at Park Lane this year. A Sunday afternoon tea party. Wally and Ernest have gone to Fort Belvedere for the weekend.

Pips said, "What are they doing? Keeping Thelma's place warm for the King of Hearts?"

Since Freddie failed to get that position he'd hoped for, I notice Pips has become very bitter about the success of others.

29th November 1933

Anne Belchester's ball. Violet wore full-length tartan and a limp white blouse. She said, "I know it's not quite the thing, but Trotman forgot to freshen up my *eau de nil.*"

Melhuish said, "Stop fretting, Vee. You look ravishing."

Ha!

I thought the flowers rather skimped. Violet said, "The idea is to raise money, not waste it on flowers that will be dead by midnight."

I'm sure the orphans wouldn't have begrudged us a few hundred carnations.

4th December 1933

Philip Sassoon's birthday. I gave him a walking stick with a cherrywood duck's head handle, Lightfoot brought him a bottle of something made from Polish liquorice.

Sybil was there, with two of her children. Also the dark-complexioned Cousin Hannah.

Philip said, "Maybell, your friend Wally Simpson bombards me rrrelentlessly with invitations. It's like being back in the Somme."

I said, "Yes, she's very keen to get you. She's taken charge of the social life of the Prince of Wales while Lady Furness is away. She wants to keep him entertained."

"Ach," he said, "Wales! As well try to entertain a pet rrrodent. Tell her to put him inside a little rrrrunning wheel."

Smoked haddock sandwiches, an original touch. And delicious chocolate cake all the way from Austria.

Philip wore a long velvet jacket and zebra-hide slippers. Such a pity he doesn't think of marrying.

5th December 1933

Lunch with Ida Coote. She's taken to blackening her eyes with a kohl pencil since learning of her Ancient Egyptian lineage.

6th December 1933

To the Adelphi Theatre with Lightfoot to see *Nymph Errant*.
He said he'll be relieved when school ends, because he doesn't
think St. Audrey's is suiting Flora at all.

I said, "But she's finally settled down. She hasn't done anything
naughty since she started there."

"Precisely," he said. "And she looks like a wan little candle. I
think she's depressed."

I said, "You mean Doopie thinks she's depressed."

"Yes," he said. "And I agree with her. We do know her rather
well. We are her gobparents, after all."

I see the start of a campaign. I shall warn Violet.

10th December 1933

Violet says St. Audrey's has been a great success and Flora has
never been more amenable. She said, "Lightfoot's a dear, but he's
something of a theorist on the raising of children. Well, he'll find
out someday."

I said, "Do you think he's going to marry that girl Belinda?"

"Very likely," she said. "It would be perfectly suitable. Her people have a very fine house in Gloucestershire, her uncle is Lord
Lieutenant, and her brother was at school with Lightfoot. I can't
think of a more perfect match."

15th December 1933

To Elspeth Laird's Bazaar in aid of Life Boats. An entire stall
filled with Doopie's handicrafts. Padded coat hangers, lavender
sachets, little knitted hats for soft-boiled eggs. Flora was assisting
her uncle Rear Admiral Salty on the Lucky Dip. Violet was with
Elspeth on the tea urn, Melhuish was selling prize draw tickets,
Rory and Ulick were circulating with Guess the Weight of the
Cake. A real family affair.

Lady Strathnaver won the cake.

18th December 1933

To Hamley's with Rory. Flora was obliged to go to a birthday
party for one of the Belchester children, but Rory picked out a
hand puppet he believes she'll like: a pig. He didn't know what to

suggest for Ulick, so I bought him a banjo. He has no interest in music, so it may be the very instrument for him.

Something from the Cusson's range for Doopie and for Padmore. They're both fond of scented bath salts and dusting powder, but there's no sense in going overboard. No one ever smells them. I noted which model battleship Rory most admired and sent Kettle back to purchase it while we went to the Star Grill for sausages and creamed potatoes.

He said, "I wish you were coming to our house at Christmas, like last year."

I said, "Well there'll be other Christmases. I'm going to the Tyrolean mountains with my friend Wally."

He said, "I know. Mummy said The Wally is a climber."

He got a good report card, except for geometry and gymnastics. I told him, math can be a puzzle to the best of brains, especially geometry, which is of no use to anyone, and gymnastics don't matter, either. They're an optional extra, like playing the violin or speaking French.

He said, "Oh, but I'll need geometry when I go into the Navy, so I can navigate. And I have to be able to climb up a rope. Uncle Salty told me."

Such nonsense. They have people to do the navigating for you, and I've been on many a boat and never seen any rope-climbing. There are staircases.

To the Cocoanut Grove. Came: Wally, Ernest, and the Prince, Zita and Bernie, Hattie and Judson.

19th December 1933

Drinks and Christmas caroling at the American compound. Benny Thaw says the news from Connie and Thelma about their sister Gloria isn't encouraging. Reggie Vanderbilt having drunk himself into an early grave and Gloria being so busy in Europe, it seemed like a sensible arrangement for Gloria Junior to stay with Reggie's sister Ger for a while. She has a garden and space for a pony, and nothing much to occupy her time. But Ger Whitney was only ever meant to be *borrowing* the child. Now she refuses to give her back, and they're worried her lawyers have something up their sleeves. As Benny says, it's all too easy for a misconstruction to be placed on a person living in Paris. He says the Prince of Wales is pining for Thelma. Well, he seemed cheerful enough last night.

Dinner at the Crosbies. Came: Anne and Billy Belchester, Benny and Connie Thaw, and young Lord Birkenhead. Everyone is agreed that Mr. Hitler is quite a phenomenon. He's pulled Germany out of its depression, and now has the whole nation behind him.

Freddie said, "What Hitler needs now is a nice English wife, to remind him who his friends are. Or an American. How about you, Maybell? Shall we send you on a special mission to woo Mr. H?"

I don't think so. Politics can be such a dangerous business, and anyway, they say he's very keen on women having babies.

Tomorrow to Paris, Thursday to Lily's.

23rd December 1933, Schloss Pfaffenhof, Bavaria

Lily's *schloss* is a real miniature castle, and much better arranged than Drumcanna. At Lily's, the help sleep in the turrets and the guests sleep in proper suites. Snow but blue skies. Dear Prince Louis Ferdinand is here with his mother, Crown Princess Cecilie. Ernest bows to her every time he sees her, but I'm sure it isn't necessary. Strictly speaking, she's in the same category as Ena Spain: dispensed with as a Royalty and dispensed with as a wife.

Arriving tonight, a couple from Milwaukee, the Gunters, and Baron and Baroness Rothschild.

24th December 1933

Christmas shopping in Innsbruck with Kitty Rothschild and Wally. Wally was drooling over the displays of crystal, but I bought scarves for all the girls and pocket silks for all the boys. Afterwards, to Café Katzung, where we sat in a snug little booth and thawed out with hot chocolate and whipped cream.

There's to be a Tyrolean ball on Friday, and Lily has persuaded us all to buy jacquard evening dirndls. Not my idea of a flattering garment, but no one can accuse me of not entering into the spirit of an occasion. Wally says I suit the look because I'm *zaftig*, which I certainly am not. Indeed, it's a rather juvenile fashion best suited to someone with no bosom, Wally being a perfect example.

The Gunters are tedious. They travel with photographs of their dogs and pass them around at every opportunity. The Rothschilds are nice, easygoing. Eugene kisses one's hand, just like Philip Sassoon. I suppose it's because they both have French blood mingled with the Oriental. Kitty is sporty-looking and plain-spoken in that refreshing American way. I don't think Wally likes her.

26th December 1933

Slipped on freezing snow on Christmas morning and am bruised black-and-blue.

Lily's doctor says there's nothing to do but rest. Of course, couch-bound one is easy prey for bores. Mrs. Gunter taxed me for a full hour with her own medical history.

27th December 1933

Everyone has gone to the casino in Garmisch, except for Cecilie Hohenzollern, who went to bed early, and Ernest, who has insisted on keeping me company. I think the truth is he prefers not to see Wally gambling. Ernest isn't a risk-taker, while according to Ethel Croker, when Wally sits at a table, she becomes a demon.

He roasted chestnuts and grew sentimental on pear schnapps.

He said, "I like nothing better than a cozy fireside. I'm afraid I hold Wally back sometimes. She has so much energy."

The only respect in which he holds Wally back is money but, of course, I couldn't say so.

I said, "Yes, she was always a live wire."

He said, "I have no complaints, you understand. Wally's drawn us into illustrious circles, and I'm very grateful to her. We don't broadcast it, but His Royal Highness has become quite one of the family. It's more than I could ever have dreamed of."

I got him talking about his people. English grandparents on his father's side, American on his mother's. He and his sister grew up in New York. They're not close. The business he's in now was started by his father, ship brokerage.

His first wife suffered from nerves. He said, "Our splitting up was nothing to do with Wally, you know. Dorie and I were on the brink of divorce anyway."

She took the child and went back to her family in Massachusetts.

He said, "I have a daughter, nearly ten. I hope someday to be a father to her again. Have her to visit. She'd like London."

I bet Wally hasn't been asked about that. I can't see her trailing around the zoological gardens with a child.

30th December 1933

Too sore to dance, but I made the effort and attended the Tyrolean ball. Actually, not so much a ball as a raucous evening of peasant-like simplicity. Enormous steins of beer, heaped platters of sausage, and an oompah band. But fun.

Lily, Wally, and Kitty polkaed all the men under the table.

The Gunters have moved on to another party, in Salzburg. As they were leaving, she said, "If ever you find yourself in Wisconsin, Maybell."

I hardly think so.

1st January 1934

Last evening we listened to Dr. Goebbels on the wireless. Lily translated. It was a very uplifting speech about how much has changed in Germany in one year. Despair and civil unrest have been replaced by optimism and stability, and the Bolshevik specter has been laid to rest. We all drank to that. My own private little wish is for a quiet year to come. Too much busyness is bad for the nerves.

8th January 1934, Wilton Place

To the Victoria Palace Theatre with Rory, Flora, Lightfoot, and Doopie, to see a children's show called *Goody Two Shoes*. We all joined in the singing and shouting and had great fun. Doopie's eyes never left the stage. I don't suppose she made much sense of what was going on, but she enjoyed herself in her own little way. Her life is so sadly narrow.

Wally is talking about going to Paris to order gowns. Ernest doesn't have that kind of money.

I said, "Can you really afford to?"

She said, "The question is, Maybell, how can I afford not to? This is going to be our year. David's promised to get us presented to the King and Queen, and I'm not going to do that wearing something from Derry and Toms."

I said, "But what about your divorces?"

She said, "David says they're irrelevant because they were in America. They only count if they happen here."

I must tell Violet.

10th January 1934

An emergency at Carlton Gardens. Flora climbed out of the nursery window onto a little roof rather than be sent back to St. Audrey's. She had on her topcoat and mittens, and took a bottle of milk and Pigster puppet, so it was all planned. The hook-and-ladder men were called out, but it was Lightfoot who persuaded her to climb back through the window. He promised he'd help find her another school, where she'd be happy, and she promised to do her lessons at home every day and try a new school when they find somewhere suitable.

All very well, but in the meanwhile, she's falling further and further behind with her math. Lightfoot said, "Mathematics doesn't concern me. She'll catch up. She's perfectly bright. Doesn't miss a trick. But she doesn't have any friends. *That's* what school's about. And, of course, she didn't make any friends at St. Audrey's, because she was only there for six weeks, which isn't long enough for anybody to take to an odd little soul like Flora. I don't know. It was too awful. Doopie was crying, Violet was shouting at Melhuish, Melhuish was screaming at the firemen, as though they were on a parade ground. She could have fallen and been killed."

I said, "I'll go and visit."

He said, "I wouldn't. Not yet. She's both in disgrace and being treasured like Lazarus back from the dead. It's a very strange atmosphere. I'd wait if I were you, till Violet returns to her committees and the normal chaos prevails."

11th January 1934

Benny Thaw was right: Connie and Thelma's sister does indeed have a battle on her hands. Gloria has been accused of washing her feet in champagne. Well, there's a hanging offense! Gertrude Whitney's argument is that the child is better off on Long Island with a nurse and regular hours than she is in Paris with a lively, popular mother, and, of course, the judge is sure to see things her way. The unnatural Nada Milford Haven's name has been whispered, which can never help anyone's cause. I shall never forget how her eyes lingered over my décolleté at Bryanston Court.

Anyway, the whole business about the little girl is a terrible worry to them, and Wally says Gloria stands to lose thousands per month in child support. Meanwhile, HRH is deprived of Thelma's company and doesn't seem to know what to do with himself. I suppose courtiers direct him in every particular of his official life, but when it comes to a spare hour or two, he has no idea how to fill it. That's why he allows Wally to monopolize him so.

12th January 1934

Called at Carlton Gardens. Flora has a chill, caught sitting out on rooftops in January. She said, "I wore my muvvler, Aunt Bayba, and so did Pigster. We were higher than the trees. It isn't hard. I can show you one day."

Doopie said, "You will nod. You gibben me nidemares."

Trotman says a man is coming to fit bars tomorrow.

16th January 1934

A bad start to the week. Ernest has put his foot down over Paris gowns, even though he and Wally are invited to the Duchess of Westminster's ball. For some unaccountable reason, I am not.

He said, "Women of much greater means manage to dress without spending that kind of money. Look at Maybell."

Wally said, "I aim higher than Maybell."

I agree with Ernest. Elegance is wasted here, and Paris gowns are not the way to endear yourself to London.

18th January 1934

Wally has asked to borrow Pips's sapphire bracelet.

Pips said, "It was such a sob story. Ernest's imposed such a cruel budget it sounds as though she'll be going to the Westminsters in rags."

Of course, Pips was never as close to Wally as I was. She didn't see how she struggled to have any kind of Season. Her uncle kept her on pins till the very last moment, about whether he'd loan her a car and a driver. She could never take anything for granted, as we could.

I said, "She just wants to shine."

Pips said, "And she will, in my sapphires. But honestly, what a fuss. I'll bet old Ernest had no idea he was marrying such a princess."

20th January 1934

Wally is getting a "Paris gown" without going to Paris. Ida Coote's little woman in South Kensington is making her a copy of a Vionnet gown. Sepia silk velvet with a halter neck, which saves her borrowing a necklace and will look very well with Connie Thaw's pageant tiara. If my shoulders were as beefy as Wally's, I believe I'd keep them covered, but she's satisfied, and Ernest is satisfied, so who am I to interfere.

She said, "What a pity the Westminsters didn't invite you. We could have shared a car." If that was a hint about my Bentley, I allowed it to pass unheeded.

More snow.

24th January 1934

The Germans have executed the Bolshevik who set fire to their Parliament. Mr. Hitler is certainly showing the world he'll stand for no nonsense. I think Brumby would have very much approved.

I'm going to give an impromptu dinner, but only for people who have topics of conversation other than balls.

3rd February 1934

If Loelia Westminster's ball was half as successful as my little dinner, she must be a happy woman this morning. Came: Bernie and Zita Cavett, Marthe Bibesco, Benny Thaw, and Ida Coote. Marthe said I should have invited the Stanley Baldwins. She said, "To create a salon is not so hard, Maybell. All you have to do is recognize nobodies who will one day be somebodies." She said she always wished she'd thought to cultivate Ramsay MacDonald while he was an undesirable, because since he's been Prime Minister, no one can get him.

My gamble on Ida paid off. Everyone enjoyed her reminiscences of Ancient Egypt, and Bernie confessed that for years he's been convinced he was formerly a Roman centurion on Hadrian's Wall.

6th February 1934

Sir Philip hasn't forgotten me, after all. I am invited to Trent to see the snowdrops.

He said, "Name your day, Maybell. One word from me, and they'll pop up their heads."

8th February 1934

A "little talk" from Violet. Why don't I find myself some useful work instead of lunching with drones every day? She can put me in touch with many worthy organizations. I defended myself. I'm sure I make more decisions over one lunch than her committees do after hours of discussion. And none of *my* friends drones. Well, Ida does, a bit.

12th February 1934

Philip's snowdrops had indeed popped up their heads. He manages to have his gardens worth touring when everyone else's are nothing but wet leaves and frozen earth. I thought he looked fatigued, but he dashed around, showing me his latest acquisitions. A scarlet-and-silver japanned mirror, an antique pole lantern from Venice, and a new pair of king penguins for the lake. He said he's been feeling too cross for parties.

I asked him what he thinks of Mr. Hitler. "Rrrraving," he said.

14th February 1934

Valentine flowers from a secret admirer. They are cellophane-wrapped, so must *not* be from Philip Sassoon. I fear I detect the clumsy hand of Randolph Putnam.

18th February 1934

The King of the Belgians is dead. We didn't know him.

19th February 1934

At last! I am invited to Fort Belvedere. The Prince of Wales bids me for the weekend of March 9th. Pips and Freddie are also invited, but that in no way diminishes the thrill. In fact, it will be fun to have someone to confer with about gowns.

Wally says she arranged it, but she can only arrange what she knows to be the Prince's wishes.

Violet tried to make light of my invitation. All she said was, "The ninth? Oh, we'll be at Royal Lodge with Bertie and Elizabeth the very same weekend."

I sense there must have been a big falling-out between Melhuish and the Prince. As young men, they went everywhere together, but now they never see one another.

Lunch with George Lightfoot. He says with Melhuish and the Prince, it's been more a drifting apart than a rupture. He said, "Wales still loves to do new things and meet new people, especially Americans, whereas Melhuish has become rather set in his ways. But Melhuish is loyalty itself, you know? If Wales asked for him, he'd be there like a shot."

23rd February 1934

To the Ham Bone Club with Wally, Ernest, HRH, and the Erlangers. A rather knowing little pansy sang at the piano. Wally and the Prince laughed loudly, but I can't say I found him so amusing. Gladys Trilling is expecting again. Poor Whitlow.

26th February 1934

Wally recommends knitted sweater suits for daywear at the Fort. I just nodded politely. They may flatter a mannish figure like hers, but they do nothing for us real women. I happen to know she's asked to borrow Hattie Erlanger's amethysts.

2nd March 1934

I have decided on a vine as my weekend gift to HRH. I know he's an avid gardener. The Crosbies are going to drive down with me on Friday afternoon. Boss and Ethel Croker are going to take Sunninghills again for Ascot week.

6th March 1934

Saw Benny Thaw at the Belchesters' cocktail party. The court case has been heard, and Ger Whitney has been granted custody of Gloria's child. He said it was a lost cause once they called the child's nurse to the stand, because she embroidered all kinds of exaggerations about Gloria's way of life. Drink, men, *women*. All very hard cheese for Gloria, because she'll now have to adjust to a lowered income. The good news is that Thelma and Connie will soon be on their way home. This weekend's party may turn out to be the last one Wally's asked to organize.

9th March 1934, Fort Belvedere

The Fort is a sweet little turreted house, convenient for Windsor town. A sort of miniature castle in the suburbs. Not at all grim and brooding like Drumcanna. It looked enchanting as we approached, lights streaming from the windows, liveried footmen waiting like statues on the gravel, and then HRH himself came out to the car to greet us. I am in bedroom No. 3, with a view of the swimming pool. Pink sheets, pink drapes, even pink soap, in a wonderful American bathroom with a wonderful American shower. There's every sign that when he becomes king, the Prince will do much to improve this country.

Also here: Fruity and Baba Metcalfe, Lord Templemore, and the Humphrey Butlers. He occasionally equerries for Prince George.

HRH is delighted with his vine. He asked me whether I cared for gardening.

I said "Sir, I adore gardening. At Sweet Air, I employed ten men."

He said, "Maybell, you must call me David."

I wonder whether Violet's ears caught that up at Royal Lodge.

Wore my beaded celadon to dinner. Pips was in biscuit satin, Poots Butler in lilac, Wally in black taffeta and diamonds borrowed from Pips. Excessive, I thought. The Fort isn't grand, and we were very informal. HRH himself carved the roast lamb and then, after the savory, he entertained us on the bagpipes. No withdrawing. Just lots of jolly chatter around the table and then dancing to gramophone records in the Octagon Room.

10th March 1934

By the time I came down this morning, HRH had organized a working party, and the men were all hacking at old shrubs, clearing an area he visualizes as a new rock garden. It was most amusing to see Freddie Crosbie armed with a machete. David and Fruity in ancient tweeds, having the greatest fun with billhooks. Ernest in a brand-new sweater, pecking at undergrowth as though it might peck back. He's not an outdoors person.

Wally and Poots Butler went to the kitchen and made club sandwiches for lunch. Baba Metcalfe says the chef and the majordomo were beside themselves, but HRH does love Wally's club sandwiches, so they daren't complain.

Tonight, I wore my peacock shantung. Wally was in forest green, with Hattie Erlanger's amethysts. Baba Metcalfe wears practically no jewels at all. Prince George joined us for dinner, and afterwards we played Assassin, spoiled for me by Ernest, who accused me of extraneous winking. As I explained, I have a slight chill in my tear gland. "Then you should disqualify yourself from playing," he said. "The rules of the game are clear."

He can be a puffed-up little know-all for a man who allows his wife to wear borrowed jewels.

HRH received a telephone call just before midnight. Thelma, from New York. She sails on Monday. Pips said, "There'll be rejoicing below stairs. No more club sandwiches. No more corn being popped at all hours. And as soon as the *Bremen* docks, Wally'll be back in the chorus line."

11th March 1934

There has been a turn of affairs. Wally and HRH were missing for nearly two hours this afternoon. Heavy rain was falling, so we knew they couldn't be inspecting the gardens. Ernest was asleep in an armchair, making annoying little whiffling noises, so he couldn't be questioned. Then Fruity found out that they'd taken a car and gone up to the Castle. Baba said, "I hope they haven't dropped in at Royal Lodge. The Yorks would have a fit."

People were just going up to dress when they reappeared, all jollity and dripping umbrellas. They'd been to a church service. Evensong in St. George's Chapel. Well! I can understand that the Prince feels an obligation to do these things. Someday he'll be king, and so must set an example to the lower classes. But Wally? She was enthusing about the spiritual uplift of the music, which was all embarrassing enough, but then she completely overstepped the mark.

She said, "Oh, look how muddy my shoes are. David, take them off for me, would you?" and HRH got down on his knees and undid her laces.

Fruity and Ernest both studied the floor, and the majordomo turned quite white.

Pips came along to my room the minute she was dressed.

She said, "There goes Wally's career as royal apple-polisher. Enjoy the evening, Maybell. I don't think any of us will be coming back in a hurry."

But HRH was all lightness and gaiety at dinner, and so was Wally.

Poots Butler says she may be forgiven a first offense, but someone should have a word with her before she goofs again. Well, it's not going to be me.

Anyway, perhaps princes get sick of people bowing and scraping.

14th March 1934, Wilton Place

Calls from Anne Belchester and Daphne Frith, who had it from Hattie that there'd been an incident at the Fort, with Wally screaming at the Prince of Wales to lick her boots. Hattie says she's only repeating what she heard at the hairdresser's.

15th March 1934

To the Dorch with Penelope Blythe. She says it's common knowledge in Cadogan Square that Wally was wrongly accused of trampling mud onto a priceless rug and Ernest, incensed, had demanded an apology from the Prince of Wales. How Wally must be enjoying all this.

16th March 1934

Treated Wally to Claridge's. She says Thelma has a rude shock awaiting her when she returns to London. While crossing the Atlantic, she's been accepting bouquets and playing shuffleboard with a certain Prince Aly Khan, and that word has reached the HRH.

I said, "How do you know? They must still be at sea."

"I'm not at liberty to say" was all I could get out of her.

19th March 1934

Penelope Blythe says Aly Khan is a swarthy-skinned prince whom women find irresistible. She says Wally must have the information from HRH himself. She says he probably has spies watching Thelma's every move. Pips thinks he probably does, but she doesn't believe Wally can be party to such sensitive secrets. Also, according to the *Times*, he's in Ayrshire at a Boy Scout Jamboree, so even if his snoops are keeping him *au courant* with events in the middle of the Atlantic, Wally has no way of hearing about it. I think she's just making the whole thing up.

20th March 1934

Dinner at Carlton Gardens. The Boddie-Fultons and the Salty Lairds. I happened to have bumped into Fiona Boddie-Fulton only this morning, when I was in Cramphorne Doggit with Wally, looking at silver epergnes. She said, "Did you find something to your liking?"

I said, "It wasn't for me. It was for my friend."

Violet said, "Not Minnehaha? An epergne?"

Hoots of laughter from Elspeth Laird. She said, "How very ostentatious! Violet, didn't you tell me that this person lives in Paddington?"

I hold no brief to defend Wally Simpson, but it seems to me *any* home would be improved by an epergne.

23rd March 1934

Drama at Bryanston Court. Wally and I had just started tea when Thelma Furness was announced and came in looking most distressed. She said she'd seen the Prince three times since her return from America, and he'd been noticeably cool toward her and now he won't even say what he's doing for the weekend.

Wally said, "He's going to Oliver Templemore's."

Thelma said, "Then why didn't he say? Has something happened while I've been gone? Has he found someone new?"

If it had been left to me, I'd have told her about those shipboard stories that have reached the Prince's ears, but Wally gave me one of her looks and cut right across me.

She said, "I'm sure you're imagining things. David's been lost without you. He's been throwing himself more into his work. He's looking into the question of Glaswegian slums at present. I expect he's just distracted."

Thelma said, "Slums never distracted him before."

I heard the telephone ring. Wally chatted on, about the Westminsters' ball and our Christmas in the Tyrol. No one touched the shortcake triangles. It was as if we were all waiting for some next thing to happen.

The new maid came in, and Wally tore her off such a strip. She said, "I told you I wasn't to be disturbed."

She said, "I know that's what you said, madam, but it's the Prince of Wales again and he's most insistent."

Wally didn't say a word. She just got up, left the room, and closed the door behind her. Thelma was leaning back in the chair with her eyes closed.

She said, "You knew. Wally's stolen him."

I said, "That's nonsense. Now tell me honestly, did you have a little adventure on the voyage home?"

She never did answer that. All she kept saying was, "I trusted her and she's stolen him."

I said, "On the contrary. There are some who think Wally may have worn out her welcome. She's been quite impertinent at times, and she's upset the kitchen staff at the Fort, scrambling eggs for David at all hours."

She said, "I didn't know he liked scrambled eggs."

It was a difficult moment.

I said, "How was New York?"

"Cold," she said, "and full of traitors. Just like here."

She's no great conversationalist. We sat in silence, waiting for Wally to reappear. I was about to ring for more hot water when the maid came in.

She said, "Madam makes her apologies. She's had to go out directly."

I said, "Where to?"

"Oh, to York House, madam," she said. "The Prince sent a car for her and she doesn't expect to be back for dinner. Will I fetch your coats?"

By the time I returned from powdering my nose, poor Thelma was gone. I went straight to the Crosbies, but Pips had already left for the constituency, and Hattie Erlanger was on her way to a sister in Gloucestershire. Friday afternoon is the worst possible time for sharing a bombshell. I had no choice but to take it to Violet, and all she said was, "Maybell! *Pas devant les enfants!*"

Flora dancing around the drawing room, singing, "I know what that means. I know what that means."

24th March 1934

I've gone over and over yesterday's events and can make no sense of them. Called Bryanston Court at nine and was told that

Mr. and Mrs. Simpson had left for Lincolnshire and will be gone till Monday.

25th March 1934

Benny Thaw called me. Connie has taken Thelma, most distraught, up to Leicestershire. Did I know anything? I told him what I'd heard about Mr. Aly Khan and the daily deliveries of roses to Thelma's stateroom. He said he didn't believe a word of it. All I can say is, before a girl starts playing shuffleboard with playboys, she had better think of the consequences.

He said, "Look, Maybell, I have to ask you. Have Wales and Wally become lovers?"

Benny can be such a dope. Thelma getting dropped in favor of scraggy old Wally! I said, "The idea's too crazy for words. How can you even suggest it?"

He said, "Because I remember how Wally operates. I know she's no beauty, but she acts sassy and takes the lead, and I have a feeling Wales is just the type to fall for it."

He's wrong, I'm sure, and Lightfoot agrees with me, though I thought he went on unnecessarily about Thelma's perfect skin and the dark smolder of her eyes.

I said, "If you're so taken with her, why don't you hie yourself up to Leicestershire. She may be back on the open market."

"Oh, Maybell!" he said. "Really!"

26th March 1934

Finally got through to Wally. She said, "We were at the Perry Brownlows. I know I told you we were going."

I said, "Well?"

"Well what?" she said.

I said, "Don't play games with me, Wally. Suddenly you're at the Prince's beck and call, suddenly you have cars being sent for you."

She said, "We're *all* at his beck and call, Maybell. That's what makes him a prince. He just wanted to talk about public housing."

Public housing! I said, "Thelma thinks you've betrayed her."

She said, "Well, Thelma has to realize men can tire of even the prettiest of faces. There are times when they prefer the company of a woman with a well-formed mind."

She and Ernest are invited to Fort Belvedere again for the weekend, so that's one in the eye for Baba Metcalfe. After the shoe incident, she was predicting years of ice-cold exclusion.

Lunched with Pips. She said, "Well, well! So now the question is, how long has David Wales been playing in Ernest's toy box?"

I said, "But Ernest always goes with her to the Fort."

She said, "So what? Ernest's a ten-o'clock man. He'll be too far gone in sleep to hear the boing of royal bedsprings."

It's unthinkable.

27th March 1934

George Lightfoot spoke with Perry Brownlow, who definitely has the impression Wally has moved into a position of special importance to the Prince. As Lightfoot put it, "She's promoted Queen Bee, and Thelma Furness is reduced to the ranks."

He buys Wally's line about the appeal of a lively mind. He said, "She's unusual. Not particularly original perhaps, but Brownlow says she remembers useful things and recycles them very cleverly. Wales is always impressed by that kind of thing, having absolutely nothing going on inside his own head."

Hattie Erlanger says there's nothing unusual about a married woman being asked to act as chatelaine for a public figure who has no consort. She said, "Thelma was too retiring. I always thought so. But I don't understand why HRH had to choose another colonial. It's just too galling."

Gladys Trilling is suddenly very warm toward Wally. She's thinking of asking her to be godmother to the unborn child. Judson says we'd all better start being especially nice to Wally. I think I've always been especially nice to Wally.

29th March 1934

Took Rory and Flora to Fortnum's Soda Fountain for ice cream sundaes. As we walked in, Wally was just leaving with an overrouged little woman in a fox stole. "Can't stop," she said. "Emerald's taking me to meet a new dressmaker."

Lady Cunard. Flora was open-mouthed. She kept asking, "But how did she get her hair so jellow?" With the help of a color-blind hairdresser, one can only suppose.

Rory was more interested in The Wally, as he calls her, having heard her mocked and slandered in his mother's drawing room. He said, "Mummy says she's a dangerous person we don't want to know. She doesn't look very dangerous."

I said, "She's not. I just don't think Mummy ever liked Wally very much, even when we were girls, and now she's cross because the Prince of Wales goes to Wally's house and he doesn't come to yours."

He said, "Oh, but we don't want him, too. Ulick says he's jolly unsound."

31st March 1934, Hoxney Court, Kent

Apart from the Crosbies, a dull group at the Prosper Friths, but I'm not sorry to get away from all that silly London jabbering about Wally. Daphne Frith hasn't even mentioned the subject. Lord and Lady Halifax are here, and Alex and Nellie Hardinge, so we're all seriousness and propriety. Pips says Hoxney Court is a place where men sleep with their wives and all's well with the world, but that may change tonight, when Penelope Blythe arrives.

2nd April 1934

Now even here the talk is of Wally. Penelope Blythe was the one to break the silence, and then Mrs. Hardinge couldn't wait to tell us that Ambassador von Hoesch has been placed in an impossible position by this new friendship. HRH had asked the Ambassador to put on a little dinner for him at the German Embassy, and now he's demanding that Wally be added to the invitation list, which, according to Nellie Hardinge, who is a walking encyclopedia of protocol, is absolutely not done.

She said, "Royal Highnesses do not *parade* other men's wives at official dinners."

I don't see the problem myself. Wally's good value at anyone's table.

Lady Halifax said she'd leave the room if there was any more talk about Wales and his dreadful friends. Daphne Frith covered with embarrassment. She said, "I'm sure Dorothy didn't mean you." I don't care if she did. Dorothy Halifax is one of those Englishwomen who say "dreadful" rather than utter the word "American."

Edward Halifax has only one hand. I suppose that eliminates golf.

3rd April 1934, Wilton Place

The Crokers have arrived for their season. Pips and I are having lunch with Ethel tomorrow. Pips has chosen a brand-new eatery in Beauchamp Place. Ethel hadn't heard the gossip about Wally and HRH. She said, "Are you kidding me? The Prince of Wales? Holy smoke! I mean, she always knew how to get men. But the actual *actual* Prince of Wales. Wait till Boss hears about this! And poor Ernest. It's not just his wife he's lost. What about those royal weekends he's so proud of?"

4th April 1934

Ida Coote had discovered Pips's new restaurant, too. She spotted us before we'd even ordered and hung around our table until Ethel said, "Why don't you pull up a chair, dear? Take the weight off your pins."

Pips said, "Okay, the question before us is, has the P of W bedded Wally Simpson? All those who say 'obviously,' raise their right hand."

I was the only one who disagreed, but then, none of them knows Wally as I do.

I said, "She once told me she never felt inclined to sleep with either of her husbands."

Pips said, "No need to get into technicalities. Even if they sit up all night talking soup kitchens, I say it counts."

Ethel said, "Me too."

Ida said, "And anyway, we're not talking about any old beau. We're talking about a *prince*. *The* Prince, actually. I'd sleep with him in a heartbeat."

That signifies nothing, though I was friend enough not to say so. Ida Coote would sleep with a corporal of the King's Horse.

Tomorrow to Bryanston Court for dinner. I'll soon get to the bottom of this.

5th April 1934

A tense evening at Bryanston Court. Judson and Hattie Erlanger and a rather bohemian Russian couple, the Dimitri Shapaleffs, he with an eye patch, she with a silk bandana tied around her head. Also an up-and-coming architect who has ideas about housing for the working classes. Wally's idea of introducing items of particular interest to the Prince.

Most unusually, Ernest wasn't late for his own party and arrived ahead of the Prince, but as soon as HRH did appear, *he* began handing around canapés and generally playing the host. Hattie raised an eyebrow.

Wally pushed the conversation along all evening, but it felt very brittle. Then Ernest made his excuses after half a cigar, pleading masses of paperwork before he leaves on a trip to Hamburg.

He said, "I'll leave Wally to take care of you, sir."

Another eyebrow from Hattie. I don't know. Violet always says it's unforgivable to retire before a Royalty.

As HRH was leaving, he said, "Maybell, come to the Fort this weekend. Wally, have Maybell brought to the Fort."

"Oh, sir!" she said. "You make it sound like an arrest!"

Now, do you really call a man "sir" after he's crossed a certain threshold? I don't think so.

6th April 1934

Pips had Hattie on the telephone first thing. She said, "See! Ernest leaves for Hamburg and Wally sets off for the Fort. It's in the bag. Jeepers, Maybell, you're going to have a ringside seat. Take notes now. I'm relying on you."

7th April 1934, Fort Belvedere

The Perry Brownlows are here, plus Judson and Hattie, Oliver Templemore, and Oxer Bettenbrooke. Wally has bedroom No. 1. The Erlangers are in Thelma's old quarters. Hattie invited me in to see. It's like the inside of a chocolate box.

8th April 1934

Hattie came in at seven, still in her wrap. She said, "I can't sleep. I'll absolutely burst if I don't tell someone. Judson went down to get a glass of milk at about midnight, and he saw the back of HRH trotting along the corridor to Wally's room. "So, it's definite. How thrilling."

Hattie says she isn't convinced Ernest really had to go to Hamburg. She thinks he knows when he's beaten and is probably at Bryanston Court quietly licking his wounds.

She's convening an emergency lunch for Tuesday. As she says, this is pretty momentous stuff.

9th April 1934, Wilton Place

Pips called first thing. She said, "Don't even think of coming to lunch without getting the facts from Wally. We want to know where it started, when he crossed the Mason-Dixon Line, and when she's going to meet his folks."

Wally wasn't playing. She said, "We've become close, yes, but I can't say more. I'm just running out the door. I'll see you later in the week."

Violet feigned indifference. She said she was expecting the Yugoslavias any minute.

I said, "He wants to settle down. He told me himself."

She said, "And he will settle down. It's not widely known, but Wales is giving very serious consideration to Frederika of Hanover. And Prince George is on the brink, too. This could very well turn out to be the year of two royal weddings. Their Majesties would be so happy."

Flora playing on the back stairs with Pigster wearing a wedding veil.

With George Lightfoot to the Gaiety Theatre. *Anything Goes.*

12th April 1934

Dinner at the Belchesters. Violet and Melhuish, Ambassador von Hoesch, Lady Desborough, and the Marquess of Graham. Mulligatawny soup, sweetbreads, baked apples. Billy Belchester was holding forth about HRH. He said, "He goes on these tours amongst the poor and makes sympathetic noises, and all it does is whip the working man into a fever of unrealistic hopes. Princes have no business expressing political opinions."

Ettie Desborough said, "But the little people feel they can speak to him, and hope costs nothing."

Jimmy Graham said, "Wales may be a small, loose cannon when he's leaning over hovel gates patting urchins on the head, but Adolf Hitler looks upon him as a staunch future ally against the Russkies, and that's a very important point."

Dear Leo von Hoesch, always discretion itself, just smiled.

Violet said, "Anyway, His Majesty is alive and well, so what Wales does or doesn't do hardly matters."

All said looking very squarely at me.

13th April 1934

Wally's dining at the Italian Embassy tonight. It's something in honor of HRH.

14th April 1934

Gladys Trilling says Wally's invitation to the Italians wasn't so very great a coup.

Whitlow was there, and according to him, Wally was seated tables away from HRH. Practically in the street, Gladys says.

Invited to the Fort again for the 21st. Me, the Crosbies, Crokers, and the Otto Bismarcks. Pips and Freddie already have something arranged in the constituency, but Wally says they'll have to chuck. You don't say no to the Prince of Wales.

21st April 1934, Fort Belvedere

HRH was delayed on his return from prince-ing in Wales, and barely made it here in time for cockers. He said, "Sorry, darling. Are you managing to hold the fort?"

She was, indeed! She already has the air of the lady of the house. There's been a little standoff between her and the butler over the stylish glass-and-chrome drinks' cart she had delivered. He's refusing to acknowledge its existence. Pips's money is on Wally.

After dinner, we played a wonderful new board game brought along by Boss Croker. It's called Finance. Otto Bismarck couldn't get the hang of it at all. He bought properties that earned peanuts in rent, and ended up ruined, Wally bought up all the railroad companies, and HRH spent most of his time in jail, but he seemed to enjoy himself. We didn't finish till two, and then he and Wally went downstairs and made us all bacon and eggs. "What fun!" he kept saying. "What jolly old fun!"

Ethel said he was like a boy who'd been allowed to stay up late with the grownups.

22nd April 1934

Found myself alone with HRH momentarily after breakfast. He said, "I hope you're quite comfortable, Maybell."

I said, "Sir, this is the most comfortable English house I've been in."

He said, "I wish I could be here all the time. I always dread going back to York House. It's nothing more than a place I have to sleep when I'm in town."

Wally told me it isn't palace-like at all. Just a warren of small rooms, quite unsuitable for entertaining. She says the whole place needs gutting.

I said, "Perhaps you could refurbish it. Wally's good at houses."

He said, "To tell you the truth, Maybell, I'm not interested in York House. I know Wally could do wonders with it. She has so much energy. But this is where I feel at home. I'm ready to put down roots, and this is where I'd like to do it. I'm going to be forty this year, you know? Hard to believe, but I am."

I don't find it so hard to believe. His skin is really quite wrinkled. I'd have thought the Palace beauticians could have done something for him.

26th April 1934

Dinner at the Prosper Friths. Came: the Belchesters, George Lightfoot, the Habberleys, Melhuish and Violet. Belchester said, "Well, Maybell, your Simpson friend has really shot her bolt this time. Dickie Mountbatten tells me Wales's York House butler has been fired and it's all her doing."

Melhuish turned quite purple. He said, "If it's true, then it's a bloody outrage. That butler was given to him when he was first out of the nursery. Been with him for years."

If that's the case, it's time he was pensioned off anyway.

Lightfoot said, "You know, for the past year, everyone's been saying Wally Simpson's a nobody. Extraordinary to think a nobody has that kind of power."

I said, "Yes, unless the Prince of Wales has no mind of his own."

Melhuish said, "Precisely. And there's the nub of it."

I can always tell when I've rattled Melhuish. He plays with his earlobe.

27th April 1934

Wally says the York House butler was obstructive and insubordinate, and as old as Methuselah. He refused to put ice in the drinks, for one thing. Ernest is back tomorrow. They're driving straight to the Perry Brownlows for the weekend. HRH is going to the royal estate at Sandringham to visit with the Majesties, so Ernest will have Wally all to himself.

To the Fergus Blythes for two nights, after much begging from Penelope. She says a host of interesting men are coming, and she's short of women.

29th April 1934, Leake Priory

A red-brick pile. It's been in Penelope's family since the seventeenth century. Walled gardens, a carp lake, and little outhouses where ice is stored. Surplus to requirement, in my opinion. Ice could be stored quite safely in the bedroom I've been allocated. The Mulberry Room. The drapes around the bed are my only hope of warmth tonight. Also, Penelope has very odd ideas as to "interesting" men. HRH's silly equerry Oxer Bettenbrooke is here, and a chinless wonder called Algy, who has a spread in Somersetshire. Tommy Minskip had also been invited but never replied. Small mercies.

Penelope has squeezed every last drop of juice out of Wally's story. She's cast HRH as the ardent lover and Ernest as the husband who will be expected to absent himself on long tiger shoots. As I explained to her, Ernest's account books keep him obligingly out of the way. There'll be no need for any tigers to pay the price.

I said, "But time is hardly on Wally's side. HRH is going to be forty. He has to hurry up and settle for one of these princesses. He has to produce an heir."

She said, "Of course he must, but that needn't affect Wally's position. I'm sure he'll be very glad of her advice. Just think of it, *our* friend will probably choose the next Queen of England! How exciting!"

Of course, it takes very little to excite Penelope. And I'd hardly describe Wally as *her* friend. "Acquaintance" would be more accurate.

Raining stair rods.

2nd May 1934, Wilton Place

To Bryanston Court. Wally wearing a new cocktail watch, pink gold accented with brilliants. She said she's had it for years, but I know the inside of Wally's jewelry case as well as I know my own. HRH didn't appear at his usual hour, and no one else had been invited. Ernest was home by seven.

I said, "What's this? Did they fire you?" He laughed. He said, "I made a particular effort, Maybell. I see so little of my wife these days."

An awkward moment. I said, "Then why don't I leave you to enjoy your evening together?"

Wally said, "You'll stay to dinner, Maybell, exactly as we agreed."

She must have known what was coming. We'd just refreshed our drinks when the maid announced that a car was outside, sent by the Prince. Wally showed no surprise and neither did Ernest. She was on her feet in a trice. She said, "In that case, you may serve Mr. Simpson and Mrs. Brumby their dinner on trays," and she left. I wished myself anywhere else in the world.

We were brought some kind of overpiquant macaroni, and a macedoine of fruits. I played with mine, but Ernest ate every scrap and didn't say a word until he'd put down his dessert spoon and lit his pipe. Then he said, "I expect you're wondering why only Wally was sent for?"

I said, "I know she's been advising him on refurbishments at York House."

"Yes," he said. "And His Royal Highness understands I have a business to attend to. Many evenings, I have papers to look through, and I can't expect Wally to stay at home on my account. She's a damned vivacious woman, after all."

He didn't strike me as a man who felt wronged. Just a little lonely, maybe. Perhaps he doesn't mind sharing Wally with HRH. Perhaps he really believes she's just an adviser on royal drapes. He didn't mention the Prince again all evening. He began fetching books from his library so I could admire their bindings. Then he was threatening to introduce me to the delights of Aeschylus, but fortunately, he was called to the telephone. Just as well. I was really in no mood for solemn music.

4th May 1934

Wally was tête-à-tête with Lady Cunard in the Grill Room this afternoon and barely gave me a flutter of her hand. She had better not forget who her friends were when she needed a silver fish-slice.

8th May 1934

Hattie Erlanger says it's all over town that Thelma Furness isn't the only one who's been consigned to history. Thelma's predecessor, Freda Dudley Ward, had still been fondly regarded even though retired with full honors, but as of this week, the switchboard at York House has refused to put her calls through.

Hattie said, "Wally really seems to be the one and only golden girl."

Wally may be the flavor of the month, but she's no *girl*. She tampers with her birth date. Her eyes are a pretty shade of mauve, and she has a retentive mind, but that's the best one can say for her. Her hands are very coarse, she laughs like a jackass, and she doesn't have a cent.

George Lightfoot says lack of money won't matter, because HRH will take care of her expenses. He predicts Ernest will be offered some kind of ennoblement or be encouraged to live overseas with a tootsie. Or both.

10th May 1934

Mr. Hitler's new special envoy is in town. Mr. Joachim Ribbentrop. Freddie met him and came away quite reassured about Germany's rearmament intentions. Pips says the wife looks like an accident in a lace shop. Leo von Hoesch is giving a little dinner on Friday so HRH can meet them. Melhuish and Violet are also invited. Rory has an *exeat* this weekend. We may go to the Zoological Gardens.

13th May 1934

Yesterday to the Gorilla House with Rory, Flora, and Doopie. Flora's pig puppet, formerly Pigster, has been renamed "Mrs. Simpson," but not within earshot of Violet.

Rory said, "Daddy went to dinner at the Germans and The Wally was there. He said it was a damned disgrace and it's a good thing Mummy has an abscess and couldn't go, because it would have been an insult to have to sit at the same table. Why would it?"

I said, "I have no idea. We were all at school together, you know. Would you cut an old school friend?"

He said, "Only if he were a complete bounder. But ladies can't be bounders."

I looked in on Violet when I dropped them off. Her face is still very swollen. Melhuish fussing over her. He kept saying, "You never get ill, Vee. I don't ever remember you getting ill."

He said he's not sure about Mr. Ribbentrop. "A second-rater, if you ask me," he said. "A bit of a buffoon, if I'm not mistaken."

I said, "And did Wally shine?"

"Wally!" he said. "Don't bring up that name. It was a bloody affront, and Wales should know better. Dragging his popsie here, there, and everywhere. In fact, I'm thinking of bringing it up with him. I think it's time someone gave him a friendly rocket over a spot of lunch."

Violet said, "Don't do that, dear. Much better if one of the Royalties pulls him back into line. Why don't I mention it to Elizabeth York when I see her? She could get Bertie to say something, or, better still, pass it on to someone with His Majesty's ear. Let it go through the usual channels."

He said, "Good idea! You are a clever girl. Even when you're ailing you know the best thing to do."

I called Wally to warn her. She just laughed. She said, "What do they imagine they can do? Send me to Australia? They're too late, Maybell. David can't manage without me, and there's not a damned thing any of them can do about it."

16th May 1934

To Ciro's with Wally, the Crokers, the Erlangers, Whitlow Trilling, and, at Wally's suggestion, the Ribbentrops, or the *von* Ribbentrops, as she now insists. He's fair, pale eyes, sounds more like a Canadian than a German. The wife smiles all the time and talks about her children. Wally says she's the one with the money. Her people are in champagne. He danced Wally off her feet, in the absence of both her husband and her Prince.

Ethel said, "Look at her! Did you ever see such a flirt? I'm going to keep Boss glued to my side."

Hattie said, "Relax, Ethel. I don't think anyone trumps the Prince of Wales. Not Mr. Hitler's envoy, and certainly not Boss."

The Crokers' entire Ascot party is invited to Fort Belvedere for Wally's birthday. Ernest finds he has to be in New York, however.

Ethel said, "How very obliging of him."

23rd May 1934

To Carlton Gardens for tea, which turned into a lecture.

Violet said, "I hear Minnehaha is running Wales's Ascot party, with her husband out of the country. Does she have any idea what an affront it is to Their Majesties?"

I said, "Why don't you ask her?"

She said, "The opportunity will never arise. I don't associate with kept women, and if you have any sense of how to behave, you'll distance yourself from her."

I said, "Even if I wanted to drop Wally, which I don't, it's not so simple. The Prince counts me as a friend, too."

She said, "In that case, you'd better use your friendship to discourage him in this folly. You, of all people, know Wally's background. Tell him. Remind him about her husbands. The Empire will thank you for it someday."

Flora was parading up and down the nursery corridor, draped in a counterpane, playing Queen Simpson. She seems to have regained her good spirits.

Doopie was out to a matinee with George Lightfoot. *The Chocolate Soldier.* They might have asked me.

26th May 1934

To Trent Park for lunch. Seated between Lord Birkenhead and Lord Duveen. Crab flown up from Lympne, truffled noodles, warm apricots.

Philip took me to one side. He said, "Your naughty friend is causing rrructions, I suppose you know? Syb says her name rrreverberates at Buck House."

Wally will be thrilled.

29th May 1934

Lunch with Ida. She's met a man who knew her thousands of years ago. They were walled up together alive in Babylon, apparently. How small the world is.

1st June 1934

Saw Benny Thaw on my way into the Savoy. He cut me stonedead. It made me very sad when I think how often we used to see him and Connie. We used to have such gay times. I appreciate he must feel a certain loyalty to Lady Thelma, but after all, it wasn't me who stole the Prince of Wales. These things don't seem to bother Wally. She and Ernest are going to a dinner for the Ribbentrops, given by Lady Cunard. The *von* Ribbentrops. Wally says omitting the *von* is a gross discourtesy.

4th June 1934

Lunch with George Lightfoot. He was at the Cunard dinner. He said "*von* Ribbentrop, my eye! The man's a complete phony. He bought his title. He married his money. And I'm not even sure he's so very bright. I think he's only here because he speaks English. He's Hitler's fake Englishman."

George heard from Nellie Hardinge that the King has ordered HRH to look very seriously into marrying Frederike of Hanover. He said, "I don't think he'll do it without a big fight. She's young enough to be his daughter. But frankly, he's brought it on himself. This Wally business is just the final straw for Their Majesties."

I asked him why he'd taken my idiot sister to a matinee. He said, "Because they're less crowded than the evenings."

I said, "You know what I mean. If you pay her attention, she'll develop a crush on you, and what a mess that'll be. You know she's not normal."

He said, "That hadn't occurred to me."

Precisely. People just don't think.

7th June 1934

Hurried off the telephone by my own sister. She said, "The Nicholases of Greece are here, and I have a thousand things to do. Call me after Ascot."

All I wanted to do was to deliver a little sisterly advice on the subject of Doopie, and verify Lightfoot's rumor about the German child bride.

8th June 1934

Anne Belchester's charity auction. Violet was in attendance, with Elizabeth York. She was about to present me to Princess Nicholas Greece and her girls, when she suddenly froze. She said, "A certain friend of yours has just walked through the door. Have the goodness to keep her away from Their Royal Highnesses." Spoken through clenched teeth.

As though Wally, whose bedside rug has been trodden by princely carpet slippers, could give a hoot about Duchess Bertie York and her poor Greek relations.

I bid for a very pretty musical box but let it go to Daphne Frith.

Ernest has sailed for New York. He has important business to attend to at his office there. HRH has arranged for Wally to watch Trooping the Color from a window in the Admiralty Building. Wait till the Salty Lairds hear about that!

11th June 1934

Wally's apartment is awash with flowers. Calla lilies and black iris from HRH. Red carnations from Mr. von Ribbentrop. With his wife in town, too. How blatant.

I said, "Why didn't you send them back?"

She said, "Why go to the trouble? They're only flowers. And anyway, he's all right. One never knows when a tame German may be useful."

I said, "Has the Prince seen them? Won't he be jealous?"

She said, "He doesn't come here anymore. I go to him. But anyway, a little jealousy in a man is never a bad thing."

I said, "Are you in love with him?"

She said, "Surely the question is, is he in love with me?"

Always joking, always avoiding the point.

I said, "George Lightfoot heard they might have found a princess for him. Frederike of Hanover."

She laughed. She said, "Frederike! That news is so old people have it laid underneath their rugs. David won't marry her. You can take it from me. They're going to have to come up with something better than that."

I said, "Well, everyone's saying he'd better hurry along and make up his mind before all the princesses are taken. He is obliged to marry, after all. And then where will that leave you?"

She said, "It'll leave me precisely where I am now. Even a prince is entitled to private happiness, and his marrying or not marrying doesn't come into the case."

Hattie Erlanger says Wally's not entirely wrong about this. She says, the longer HRH delays in choosing a wife the greater the risk of having an absolute horror foisted upon him, which would strengthen Wally's position as special friend and provider of extramural pleasures.

15th June 1934

Red carnations continue to arrive at Bryanston Court. From Ribbensnob, as George Lightfoot calls him. Wally swears she's done nothing to encourage him, but still. I said, "Just remember what happened to Thelma. An innocent shipboard friendship, and she was done for."

"Maybell," she said, "Thelma was finished before she even set foot on that ship. And don't presume to tell me my business. I'm no Thelma Furness. No one has ever meant what I do to David."

Of course, men *say* things like that. She's sleepless wondering what he's going to give her for her birthday. She's going to be so disappointed if it isn't the black-pearl bracelet she keeps visiting and viewing and sighing over at Van Cleef. Well, what are birthdays for if not surprises?

I think I may give her scented drawer liners. They are always useful. It's much harder to know what to give the heir to the throne for his birthday. He must have vaults full of cuff links and tie pins. I'm thinking of a cigar cutter. Wally is getting him a silver frame for her new photograph.

16th June 1934

Lunch with Penelope Blythe. She says the Ribbentrops will never amount to anything in London. According to Fergus, he doesn't even have a portfolio. Perhaps Wally should think of getting him one next time we're in Asprey.

18th June 1934, Sunninghills

To the Crokers with Pips and Freddie and Judson and Hattie. Charlie and Fern Bedaux are also here. The azaleas are a picture. Wally's at the Fort with the Fruity Metcalfes and the Perry Brownlows. HRH has to go up to the Castle each day for the landau procession.

Ethel has a girl coming up from the town to do our hair and nails before we go to the track tomorrow. We'll show those English frights.

19th June 1934

Ladies' Day. Wore my cerise. Violet was in the third carriage in a disaster of lime silk and marabou. She springs for new gowns so rarely, if only she'd come to me for guidance when she does.

Dinner at the Fort. HRH is giving Wally a dog for her birthday, but it's too young yet to leave the kennels, so she has a photograph of it for the time being. I thought it fell rather flat until he brought out a delicious little package from Cartier. A brooch. A Cairn terrier in white gold with yellow sapphire eyes. A stopgap until the real terrier is of an age to come home and begin the ruination of her rugs. "Oh sir!" she said. "You spoil me!"

He said, "Wally darling, I consider it my duty to spoil you."

Violet would have had a fit.

Champagne by the swimming pool. Shrimp appetizers, veal scallopine, and a kumquat parfait. After dinner, HRH played "Happy Birthday" on his ukulele, then we danced till late. We're all invited back for his birthday on Saturday.

Wally's showed the kitchens how to make Southern fried chicken and peaches in bourbon. The housekeeper is reportedly fit to be tied, but Wally knows what the Prince likes, and they'll do well to listen to her recommendations.

24th June 1934

HRH adored the cigar cutter I gave him, and added it to his watch chain immediately. Wally was in high spirits all day. She gave him her new photograph framed in silver and a rubber duck for his bathtub. Evidently some kind of private joke, because they spent a great deal of the evening replying to one another with quacking noises.

HRH has taken a villa in Biarritz for the month of August and particularly asked me along. "For *Einum Meinum*," he said. "A special holiday. She's worked tirelessly, reorganizing things for me at York House. She's been making an inventory, you know? And choosing new decorations. She really deserves a rest, but Ernest finds he can't be spared from business, so she'll need a companion. If you could join us, Maybell, I'd count it the greatest favor."

We leave on August 1st, which means barely six weeks for the purchase of villa-wear.

Freddie says *Einum Meinum* is Walesian German for "one's own most precious little chickywickywoo."

26th June 1934

HRH has asked the Crosbies and the Erlangers to Biarritz, too. Of course, he asked me first.

3rd July 1934

Bathing suits, kimono wraps, open-toe sandals, all picked up at bargain prices, because the woolen suits are about to come in. The sales clerk said the time to buy summer wear is February. Perhaps for people like Violet, who know they'll be spending every August of their life in Scotland.

6th July 1934, Fort Belvedere

Wally, Boss, and Ethel Croker, the Humphrey Butlers, Whitlow Trilling, and the hugely bloated Gladys. Why she doesn't just stay out of sight until this child has arrived I can't imagine, nor why people insist on having a third. Look at what a mistake Doopie was.

7th July 1934

Prince George drove over to dinner. He taught us a wonderful new dance called the Palais Glide. He learned it from a footman at Buckingham Palace.

Poots Butler says there's a great deal of maneuvering going on between the equerries. No one wants to be the one to go to Biarritz. She said, "Their Majesties are appalled that Wally's been invited without her husband."

I said, "But Ernest can't get away for a whole month. He's in business."

She said, "I know. It's frightful. And as far as the King's concerned, Ernest's first business should be to keep his wife in check."

It seems to me whatever he does, Ernest is bound to displease one Royalty or another.

12th July 1934, Wilton Place

Rory's thirteenth. Heavy rain, so we went to a cartoon show and then to Ganes's Tea Rooms. He had requested a place called Ye Little Tea Shoppe in Charing Cross Road. His friend Massingham had been taken there by an uncle during the Easter break, but Melhuish has forbidden Rory to go anywhere near it. He says it's the haunt of theatricals and showgirls. How does Melhuish know, is what I'd have liked to ask but I didn't, for the boy's sake. Actually, not such a boy anymore, although he's still on the short side. I don't think he'll ever make the Grenadier Guards.

He starts at Eton College in September, so will have Ulick overshadowing him again, but he doesn't seem concerned. He says he'll be in a different House, and they'll practically never see each other.

The Habberleys won't be shooting at Drumcanna this year, apparently.

He said, "I think Mummy's still cross about the broken potty."

13th July 1934

According to Penelope Blythe, the real reason the Habberleys are missing Drumcanna is that Ralph has become most erratic and has gone off, quite contrary to Jane Habberley's wishes, to Ceylon, to look into tea.

15th July 1934

Ernest is back from New York. HRH has left on a tour of Scotland. Hattie says they've become like those little weathermen on a barometer. When one's out, the other is in.

18th July 1934

Wally's dog has arrived. It is to be named Mr. Loo.

20th July 1934

To the Kit Kat. Saw no one we knew.

24th July 1934

Mr. Loo makes Ernest sneeze. Wally says it hardly matters, because he has to go to Sweden next week.

26th July 1934

A potluck at Wally's. Just me and the Crosbies. Pips said, "I'm not going if Ernest and Sir are both going to be there."

I said, "They won't be. David's away prince-ing."

She said, "I hope you're right. The sight of Ernest being cuck-olded at his own drinks' trolley would be too gruesome."

It turned out just a rather dull evening. Even Wally didn't seem able to jolly things along. Ernest was pink and wheezy, brought on by the dog, he says. Wally says he has a summer cold.

Pips said, "Poor Ernest. I reckon Wally only invited us so she didn't have to spend an evening alone with him."

29th July 1934

To the Palm Beach Club with Wally, the Erlangers, and Penelope Blythe. Fergus has already left to fish on Deeside. Wally asked to come and stay with me at Wilton Place till we leave for Biarritz, because Mr. Loo ate von Ribbentrop's predictable carna-tions and was so sick she had to get the cleaners in. It would have been just too inconvenient. The house is practically closed up, and I'm down to just Kettle, the cook, and one maid. Also Mr. Loo has not yet learned to ask for the restroom. She went to the Erlangers instead. They're as silly as she is about animals.

30th July 1934

Wally stayed at York House last night. The maid told me when I telephoned. That maid needs training in discretion. I might have been anyone.

2nd August 1934, Biarritz

Caught the afternoon boat train with Wally, the Crosbies, and Hattie Erlanger. Judson, HRH, and Jack Aird who is equerry-ing, flew to Le Bourget and joined us at the railroad station.

Castel Meretmont is adorable. Pink-and-white stucco, shady catalpas around the terrace, and matchless ocean views. I can hear the thunder of the surf from my bedroom. I find it perfect, but Wally started making changes the moment we arrived. Chairs moved, the whiskey changed, a large order placed for perfumed roses, the help sent searching for extra vases.

Hattie's already drawing up lists of activities. Today a display of folkloric dancing in Anglet, but Freddie was the only one she could persuade to go with her. He's so good-natured.

She said, "Let's motor into Spain at the weekend and see a bull-fight!"

Let's not! Her infernal busyness reminds me of Violet. Ida Coote says the urge to fill every minute with activity may be a reflection of unresolved turmoil from past lives. Anyway, Wally's not the only one who's had a busy year. I'm here to rest and take beautifying cures.

4th August 1934

Dinner in town and then baccarat. Several familiar London faces at the Casino. Marthe Bibesco, the Dimitri Shapaleffs, Daisy Fellowes.

5th August 1934

Pips and I have begun our seawater therapies. The Erlangers are only here for two weeks, and Judson was hoping to play some golf, but so far HRH won't budge from Wally's side. Jack Aird says Judson should regard this as no great loss, because HRH has a weak drive and a tendency to misremember his score.

Wally and HRH are being most unsociable, emerging late, taking long siestas. And when they are by the pool, there can be no sustained conversation, because he's always fidgeting around, rearranging her pillows, or preparing a towel for her while she's taking a dip.

7th August 1934

Judson still mooning around, playing imaginary golf strokes. Jack Aird asked to be released for the day so he could play with him, and Wally tore him off such a strip. She said, "You're not here to take a vacation. You're paid to take care of His Royal Highness."

Pips said, "I'll bet he *isn't* paid."

Boss and Ethel are coming over tomorrow. They're staying with Jessie Woolworth at Saint Jean de Luz.

9th August 1934

A fabulous poolside party given by Jessie Woolworth's friends, the Bajavidas, who have taken Chateau La Colline for a month. The gardens floodlit, a team of gleaming kitchen hands turning an ox on a roasting spit, and a gay Cuban band to entertain us. Daisy Fellowes swam in her diamonds.

11th August 1934

I have taken up watercolors again and have been teaching Hattie and Pips. We motored out to a picturesque harbor for a couple of hours. Hattie's getting the idea, but Pips is too fastidious. The secret is simply to splash on the colors. If it turns out not to look like fishermen mending their nets, then call it something else.

Jack Aird is very sour about being kept under house arrest with nothing to do except, as he said, "Police the functions of madam's dog and read day-old newspapers."

13th August 1934

I don't know that Biarritz is doing Wally much good. She's become very scratchy, threatening to fire the help, snapping at Jack Aird, and sneering at poor Judson at the tables last night. She said, "Hattie, does your husband have anything going on upstairs? Doesn't he know he should always bet on the bank?" Hattie was livid. She said she's glad they're leaving. Pips says she wants to leave with them, but Freddie said they must stay at least until the Perry Brownlows get here. He said, "We can't abandon poor Maybell. And anyway, it's absolutely not done to curtail a visit with a Royalty, unless there's some kind of emergency."

Pips said, "Then darling, please wire Mussolini and ask him to create one."

14th August 1934

Hattie and Judson left this morning. Wally sent her maid down to say she was still busy with her hairdresser and so couldn't come down for good-byes. She appeared just before luncheon and lay bronzing herself, HRH playing Itsy Spider on her arm. "David," she said, "why don't you go and play golf?"

Pips swears she heard Jack Aird whisper, "Off with her head!"

15th August 1934

Dinner in town with Marthe Bibesco, the Crokers, and the Dimitri Shapaleffs.

Marthe heavily laden with sapphires. Wally and HRH didn't join us. Wally had a sick headache and David refused to leave her.

Ethel said, "Has she had too much sun?"
Jack Aird said, "No. Too much heir."

16th August 1934

Wally is completely recovered. She came down sporting a pair of fire opal ear clips, which appeared on her breakfast tray this morning. HRH silent but attentive. He held her hand all through luncheon. The Perry Brownlows arrived, having motored all the way from Lincolnshire, and went straight onto the tennis court. HRH was called to the telephone twice this afternoon and then again during cockers. Something is going on.

Freddie thinks the King may have ordered David to cut short his vacation. He said, "The whole thing is pretty blatant, you must admit. Aird's scandalized and he's seen a few things in his time. He's probably fired off a complaint somewhere it was likely to reach the right ears."

No baccarat tonight. A storm blowing in.

17th August 1934

A thunderstorm woke me early. I came downstairs for a glass of milk and found HRH busy on his cycling machine. I said, "The telephone was very lively last night. Not bad news, I hope?"

"Not at all, Maybell," he said. "Actually rather exciting news. I'll let you in on a little secret."

Yesterday's calls were from Prince George. He's borrowing David's airplane to go and sound out Marina of Greece. If he's favorably received, he's going to pop the question. Marina of Greece! She's one of those plain janes Elizabeth York brought to Anne Belchester's charity auction. Violet's been promoting her cause for months. I must say I found her rather abrupt. She'll be very lucky to get Prince George. He's such a good dancer.

18th August 1934

More telephone calls from Prince George. We're not allowed to talk about it in case the help eavesdrop, but one senses that the news is encouraging.

Perry Brownlow says it'll be a great relief to the King and Queen if it comes off, because George has gotten himself into so many scrapes. Jazz singers, drug fiends, undesirables who've had to be paid off. Well, I'm sure Marina Greece will soon clip his wings.

19th August 1934

Pips and Freddie have left for Ireland. Pips said, "Come with us. Wally doesn't need you and she certainly doesn't deserve you." But I like it here. The villa is a dream, and anyway, I like being at the heart of things. It's worth putting up with Wally's tantrums to do calisthenics with the future King of England and hear news of royal marriages before the rest of the world does. I can just imagine Nora Sedley Cordle catching flies in her silly open mouth if she could only see me!

21st August 1934

Marina of Greece has said yes, and I was one of the first to know. David and I enjoy an early-morning chat most days since he introduced me to the benefits of calisthenics. He feels Marina is just the girl for George. Steady without being dull, royal without being grand. Kitsie Brownlow appears to know her pedigree by heart. Her father is a Schleswig-Holstein, her mother is a Russian Grand Duchess, and her sister is married to Paul Yugoslavia. All that said, they're as poor as Job. The Royalties have a very strange attitude toward money. Many of them don't have any, and the ones who do hold on to it like grim death. Like HRH. All the times I've been with him at Ciro's or the Kit Kat, I don't know that I've ever seen him with any jingle in his pocket.

Perry lured him onto the golf course this morning, so Wally has been in a better mood. She's decided to go to Paris at the end of the vacation. According to HRH, Prince George and Marina are likely to get married before Christmas, so Wally's in a hurry to order gowns for the occasion. Kitsie Brownlow said, "But Wally won't be invited, not even with Ernest at her side. Absolutely not."

I said, "But Prince George has eaten at their table many, many times."

She said, "Prince George has eaten at countless tables and slid beneath not a few, but that's beside the point. Wally's true position is no secret. She'll never be allowed to set foot anywhere near Their Majesties."

Time will tell. But nothing is going to persuade her against going to Paris.

23rd August 1934

Prince George's happy news has been announced officially from Balmoral. I expect they're *en fête* at Drumcanna. Violet may even have ordered cream to be served with the oatmeal this morning. Marina Greece's people seem to lead a vagrant existence, considering all the thrones they've occupied. They're now based mainly in Paris and don't keep a London house, so who knows, she may even be married from Carlton Gardens.

Walter Guinness, an old acquaintance of HRH, has turned up at the Hotel du Palais. He has his yacht here, presently being provisioned before he sets off on another voyage. He's a rugged man with startling green eyes and a strange line in conversation. Eskimos. Solomon Islanders. Prehistoric ferns. Mohammedans. One could feel sorry for the wife, but I suppose his enthusiasms leave her plenty of time for bridge.

24th August 1934

HRH announced a plan over luncheon. Prince George and Marina are going to be in Cannes briefly before going to London to be feted, so he's going to charter a plane and hop over to see them. He said, "It'll be great fun and give them such a jolly surprise."

Wally said, "Sir, you know I won't fly."

I saw a flicker from Jack Aird. I suppose because *he* daren't disobey a Royalty, he doesn't care to see anyone else do it. But I understand Wally, and so does the Prince. She saw too many planes fall out of the sky when she was a Navy wife. Nothing will get her into the air, not even a Royal Highness.

25th August 1934

There is now a revised plan. Since Wally won't fly and David won't be parted from her, we're going to borrow Walter Guinness's yacht and sail to Cannes. We're inviting the Crokers to join us.

26th August 1934

Boss Croker is being a spoilsport. He says the *Rosaura* is not so much a yacht as a leaking paddle steamer and he's not yet tired enough of life or Ethel for either of them to sail on it. Also, Walter Guinness is not as grateful as he might be to have the Prince of Wales charter his boat. He says the weather forecasts are worrying, with a strong likelihood of storms. Kitsie Brownlow says she adores rough seas. HRH said, "And after the storm, there'll be a delicious calm. We'll be able to swim off the yacht. What heaven!"

I had a horrid dream. Marina Greece was getting married to Melhuish on board a ship, and Wally and I were trying to carry her train, but the deck kept listing, and waves kept breaking over us and ruining our hair. Perhaps I should return to London, after all.

27th August 1934

Wally has begged me not to miss the cruise. She says seasickness is a state of mind. She says she trained herself out of it when she made the crossing to China, so I can certainly do the same for a little jaunt around Gibraltar.

She said, "Anyway, I need you, Maybell. You're my only friend here."

I said, "You've got Sir. And the Brownlows."

She said, "But you're my only true friend here. Aird hates me. Guinness is crazy. And I'm still not sure about the Brownlows. They may be Palace Guard disguised in Prince of Wales suiting."

We sail tomorrow.

28th August 1934, the *Rosaura,* at sea

Guinness says we have no chance of reaching Cannes in time to greet Prince George and Marina, because the *Rosaura* burns vast quantities of whatever it is that makes ships go and we'll be forced to call at many ports. I hoped we might be allowed to disembark, but HRH wasn't at all discouraged by the news. He said, "If I miss George, I miss him. It was just a fanciful idea anyhow. He'll understand. We'll visit as many ports as you deem necessary, Walter. I'm in no hurry, and I'm having an absolutely blissful time."

Our aim now is to reach Marseilles in time to see another brother, Prince Harry. He'll be calling there on his way to Australia to do some prince-ing.

29th August 1934

I am dying.

30th August 1934

No mercy.

1st September 1934

The storm has ended. I ventured far enough from my cabin to ascertain that we are in the hands of the insane. There is a monkey running free, owned by Walter Guinness in the way normal people might keep a cat, also two stewards who are never sober. Perry Brownlow told me dinner began with ice cream last night because the cutlets weren't ready. It matters little to me. I shall never eat again.

2nd September 1934

We have put in at Corunna. Kitsie Brownlow and Jack Aird have gone off with Wally and HRH to visit a cathedral. Perry gallantly stayed behind to protect me from the monkey and the crew. He believes this cruise is the Prince's last fling. He said, "Next year is Their Majesties' Silver Jubilee, and I predict its crowning glory will be David's marriage. This is his final self-indulgence, Maybell. His farewell to boyish pleasures."

I said, "But who will he marry?"

"Ah," he said, "there you have me. But she's out there."

Walter Guinness estimates it will take us nine days to reach Cannes, building in a little time for HRH's sightseeing whims.

3rd September 1934

Wally had her first encounter with the press yesterday. Word had leaked out that the Prince of Wales might be putting in to Corunna on an informal visit, and a crowd of well-wishers had gathered. A small child presented Wally with a bouquet of flowers and a doll dressed in national costume.

She said, "I felt rather like a queen."

HRH said, "Darling, you are my Queen."

Jack Aird almost choked on his brandy.

She's given me the doll. It will do nicely for Flora.

4th September 1934

We are moored off Vigo, where we heard the news that Ena Spain has lost a son, only twenty years old. He had a slight bump out motoring with his sister and sustained only a bruise, but Violet once told me none of the Spain children is strong. Kitsie Brownlow says they have a bleeding disease. The boys bleed and the girls pass it on to the next generation. Poor Ena. HRH and I both sent notes of sympathy.

5th September 1934

We have been abandoned. Wally and HRH went ashore this morning for sightseeing and have just sent word that they've met up with someone Wally knew during her China years and have gone with him to see his house and vineyards. Guinness's instructions are to send Jack Aird and Wally's maid in the tender with enough clothes for four days and then to put to sea. They are going to motor down to meet us at Gibraltar. Perry's furious and was all for getting off and going home, but Kitsie said, "Dearest, Maybell promised to stay and we can't leave her. No one ever said Royalties make easy friends."

The weather is set fair. We're staying on to Gibraltar.

8th September 1934

According to the Brownlows, Ralph Habberley is not in Ceylon visiting tea plantations but in Kenya with a cigarette girl. Also that Penelope Blythe's name has been linked with George Lightfoot. A lie if ever I heard one.

Kitsie has been pumping me about Wally. She said, "What are her intentions?"

I said, "Surely the question is what are David's intentions?"

She said, "His Royal Highness isn't at liberty to have any, as I'm sure Wally knows. But she seems a terribly well-organized person. I'm sure she has a plan. I'm sure she knows exactly what she wants to get out of all this. A good house, I suppose? And a title for Ernest?"

I don't know. Perhaps that is all she wants. She certainly doesn't seem very much in love. HRH is besotted with her, but Wally always did tire of novelties quickly. If he were anyone else, I'm sure she'd be moving on to new projects by now. But how do you follow the Prince of Wales?

9th September 1934

We have made Gibraltar in good time and glorious weather. Walter has been showing me his collection of seashells and has given me one for Rory. He has really led a most interesting life.

Wally looked ravishing when she came aboard, especially considering she's been living out of a valise for four days. White linen skirt, a hand-embroidered shirt she'd picked up for peanuts, blue glass beads.

She was bubbling with excitement about her little Portuguese diplomat, how he was as handsome as ever, what a divine house he has overlooking Viana, how wonderful it had been to reminisce about China, and the more she bubbled the tighter HRH held her hand.

He said, "I know, let's go to Majorca! I don't want this holiday ever to end."

11th September 1934

Majorca is enchanting. Sandy bays, pine groves, windmills, and such bargains to be had in the shops. Wally, Kitsie, and I spent the morning sampling orange blossom perfumes. Kitsie can be very forthright. She said, "Wally, I hope you're not losing your heart to our Prince."

Wally laughed. She said, "Not at all. I have no illusions. I'm just here to entertain. I'm the circus before the execution. He doesn't have much to look forward to, does he? Prince-ing. Marriage to some desperate Prussian wallflower. Babies. More prince-ing."

We spent the afternoon dipping in and out of clear, blue waters. HRH is as frisky as a lamb. Jack Aird is very tense. He says the Prince's dawdling has now caused them to miss two appointments. Prince George and Marina waited in Cannes as long as they could, then had to leave for London, and Prince Harry, whom he'd cabled most specifically to arrange a little farewell in Marseilles, has had to sail without seeing him.

The Brownlows are leaving us as soon as we get to Cannes. It'd be nice to see the Cavetts if they're still around, and those nice Rogerses.

13th September 1934, Cannes

The floors of the Miramar appear to be in constant motion. I've been far too long at sea.

A note from Kath Rogers, offering dinner. They have Zita and Bernie staying with them, so it's all worked out beautifully, although Wally doesn't agree.

She said, "You might have asked me before you wired them. The last thing I feel like is trailing up to someone's little villa."

HRH said, "I don't know, darling. I rather like the idea."

She said, "Well, don't expect much. The Rogerses won't run to your usual level of comfort."

I said, "I heard they made you very comfortable when you were in Peking."

She said, "Then you heard wrong, Maybell. Kath Rogers knows nothing about food."

Boss and Ethel's lovely friends the Bedaux are here. They sent champagne across to our lunch table.

14th September 1934

The Rogerses house is very pretty, especially the gardens. Hibiscus, frangipani, night jasmine, and we could look down and see the *Rosaura* at anchor in the bay, hung with lanterns.

HRH said, "I should like to hear all about your China days. It must have been fascinating."

Herman said, "Well, I guess 'fascinating' covers it. Kath thought she was in for a quiet life when she married me, but China was a tinderbox. Not one war, you understand? Lots of little ones. You never knew where things would erupt next. Amazing really how we managed to carry on with normal things like tennis parties and receptions."

HRH said, "And I'll bet Wally sparkled through it all."

Herman said, "Indeed. I'm sure she made as great an impact on Peking as Peking made on her."

Wally snorted. She said, "I think of my life as having begun when I arrived in London," and she gave Herman a very long, cool stare.

As we were leaving, HRH said, "Your house is adorable. I should love to stay here someday."

Herman said, "It's yours for the asking, sir. Anytime."

After the car door slammed, I heard Wally say, "Anytime after hell freezes."

15th September 1934

I am a wreck. Wally and I went straight up and left HRH having a nightcap with Charlie Bedaux. I was asleep when the telephone rang. "Maybell," he said, "it's David. I have to go shopping and I need your help. Meet me in the lobby."

It was one a.m.

I said, "Sir, everywhere's closed."

"No," he said, "it's all right. I'm having Cartier opened. The night manager is seeing to it now."

The man from Cartier was very obliging, although I noticed he hadn't combed his hair. He brought out tray after tray. Jack Aird sighing theatrically every few minutes. It was finally narrowed down to a large amethyst pendant or a canary diamond bracelet charm. HRH said, "You must make the final choice, Maybell. I turn to you in my hour of need."

Funny how little men understand about jewels, even royal princes. Whatever its size, a canary diamond beats an amethyst any day.

"Not a word now," he said when we were in the elevator. "I shall present this to her when we're back on board ship."

Aird groaned. He said, "Sir, shouldn't we be starting for home?"

David said, "Don't be such a killjoy. I don't have to be back till the twenty-fifth. We still have heaps of time. I'm going to tell Guinness to take us to Italy."

What a night. Padmore gets more sleep than I do.

16th September 1934

The Cavetts and the Bedaux are going to join us for our trip to Italy. I'm so happy. Wally's being a crosspatch. She scolded Jack Aird for yawning and HRH for handing out invitations without asking her.

He said, "But darling, Charlie Bedaux is a terrifically interesting man. He knows all about labor unions and working conditions. And he and Fern have homes everywhere. They might be terribly useful. Also, *Einum Meinum,* Fern and Zita will be company for Maybell. I'm afraid she must get very lonely when I'm monopolizing you."

Wally said, "Then don't monopolize me. You must go and play golf the very minute we put in to Genoa. I can't be at your side every minute."

17th September 1934, the *Rosaura* again

Wally is wearing her canary diamond and a smile. HRH set up a very seductive scene last night, and it seems to have paid off.

He took Wally up on deck after dessert and Jack Aird motioned to the rest of us to stay put.

He said, "His Royal Highness has exclusive use of the moonlight for the next hour, so I suggest we make ourselves comfortable down here."

I said, "Is she getting the diamond?"

He said, "The diamond, the stars. Perhaps even a bagpipe serenade."

Fern said, "How romantic! I don't know about you girls, but I always have to tell Charlie when it's time he went shopping, and what to buy. Really it's easier if I do it all myself."

Danforth was the same. He was a busy man.

"Pick yourself out a bauble, Maybell," he'd say. "I'll go to five hundred."

When Aird gave us the all-clear to go on deck, the lovebirds had already retired. What a bump down to earth London is going to seem to Wally. Just boring old Ernest and unlovely George Street.

18th September 1934, Grand Hotel des Iles Borromées, Stresa

We have said our final farewells to Walter Guinness and his lunatic crew. We put in to Genoa at eight this morning and were met by cars, which have brought us to a hotel on Lake Maggiore. Tomorrow we're going by motor launch to view some recommended gardens. Wally had been threatening to spend a day in Milan, buying pocketbooks, but that little Cartier diamond has improved her mood no end. Lady Cunard has arranged an appointment for her in Paris on the 21st. A designer called Main Bocher. She says he's fresh and American and will soon be in the vanguard.

Charlie Bedaux says he'd love to take HRH in hand for a year. He said, "I could really do something with him. There's a lot of potential in the boy, and I see it going to waste. I guess his old man's too busy chopping off heads."

19th September 1934

To the gardens at Isola Bella. Terraces covered with lemon trees, white peacocks, marble grottos. Nothing to touch what Philip Sassoon has done at Lympne, but still very lovely. Wally made copious jottings. I hadn't realized she was so interested in gardens.

I said, "Are you and Ernest thinking of getting a place in the country?" She said, "We already have a place in the country. It's called Fort Belvedere."

Fern says they have twenty gardeners at their chateau. Wally said, "Really? I'd like to see it sometime."

Fern said, "Then come. We don't stand on ceremony. And bring David."

Wally said, "Bring David? Fern, let me save you from future embarrassment. People don't *invite* His Royal Highness. They wait for him to propose himself."

Fern said, "Is that right? How quaint. Well, in the meanwhile, if ever you want to bring your husband, I guess that wouldn't be breaking any rules."

Wally stalked off.

20th September 1934

Our vacation is at an end, although HRH is dragging it out till Saturday. His usual chirpy chatter has subsided, and he's preoccupied with the busy weeks ahead. He said, "I have to go to Scotland, Maybell, to launch the new Cunarder. I'd give anything to take Wally with me. I'm going to miss her dreadfully."

I'll be glad to see London. Being surrounded by foreign jabber for weeks on end is very fatiguing. The Bedaux are off to Germany on business, Bernie and Zita are staying on for another week, and we leave tonight. Mr. Mussolini has kindly sent us his private railcar, and by tomorrow we will be in Paris.

21st September 1934, Meurice Hotel, Paris

Just called in to Ena Spain's suite to condole. She said Gonzalo's death had come as no surprise to them. They've known since he was a boy that he had the bleeding disease. Another of her boys has it, too. Poor dear. She seems so resigned.

Wally had gone out for some last-minute shopping with HRH, so the desk put Ernest's call through to my suite.

He said, "Where is she, Maybell? I absolutely insist on her being back here by next Wednesday. I have some important clients, and I need her to make a dinner for me. Two months is surely vacation enough for anyone."

They came back with hat boxes. I passed on Ernest's message stripped of its aggrieved tone.

David said, "But that works out perfectly, darling. I have to be in Clydeside, and now you have to feed Ernest's industrialists. Let no one say we don't attend to our duties!"

Wally doesn't feel it works out perfectly at all. She had hoped for at least a week in Paris. Prince George's wedding has been announced for November 29th, which, as Wally says, leaves no time at all for undoing fashion mistakes one has been rushed into.

22nd September 1934

David's plane collected him from Le Bourget aerodrome this afternoon. Wally and I went directly to see Mr. Main Bocher. His atelier is on Avenue Georges V, white walls, white tea roses, mirrors everywhere, and very witty zebra-hide armchairs. He's a Chicago boy, refined, beautifully manicured nails. He and Wally hit it off immediately. He told her she has the kind of figure that would look fabulous in a paper bag. Of course, Mr. Bocher has all the appearances of one of those men who never marry, so his ideas on the womanly form are bound to be bizarre.

He had his people running in and out with bolts of cloth, everyone wearing white cotton gloves to prevent soiling. Wally's chosen a very striking purple lamé for the ball and a soft blue velvet for the Abbey. I'm sure she has no idea how much any of it is going to cost. He said, "When you come back for your first fitting, you must bring with you the mink you're planning to wear and the tiara. I have to see the full picture."

She loves all that. She said, "He's a perfectionist, like me. We're going to show those Royalties a thing or two about elegance."

I said, "What are you going to do about a tiara? Will Ernest be willing to buy one?" She said, "He won't need to be. For a royal wedding, jewelers are going to be vying with one another to lend me one."

23rd September 1934

To Le Havre. Wally is in the kind of good humor that follows successful shopping, and quite expansive. She says she never intended for HRH to become so attached, but now he has, the advantages outweigh the drawbacks. She said, "He's sweet, in many ways, but what he really needs is to be properly employed. He has plenty of vim but it needs to be channeled."

Very much Charlie Bedaux's view of things.

She said, "No one ever helped him till I came along. He gets into such a state when the King sends for him. His father always gives him a row, and his mother sits tight-lipped, disapproving of everything. They sap his confidence. All they ever do is tell him what he *can't* do. Well, I'm fixing all that. I'm building him up, putting some backbone into him. I'm going to turn him into a king no one'll ever forget."

I said, "All very well, but what about Ernest? How can you run a prince and a husband?"

She said, "Ernest understands. He admires the monarchy. He completely sees the value of what I'm doing. And the association is very good for business. Practically the same as a Royal Warrant above the door. Anyway, I'm on my way home to him now. The vacation's over, and David has engagements enough to keep him occupied, so I shall be able to give Ernest my undivided attention. And Ernest isn't nearly as exhausting as Sir."

I said, "So you do still love Ernest?"

"Maybell," she said, "you're such a stitch! Love! I'm *married* to Ernest."

24th September 1934, Wilton Place

Just before we docked, we received a message that a car would be waiting for Mrs. Simpson outside the customs shed. She said, "If Ernest asks about Paris, don't blab about the gowns. I like to deal with these things in my own good time."

But from the rail, there was no sign of Ernest, only Kettle with my car and Ladbrook with HRH's Buick.

Wally said, "Sir's sent his car for me. See, Maybell? This is what happens when you have a royal connection. Queues disappear, cars become available, doors open." And doors certainly did open. There, sitting together in the back of the Buick, were Ernest and the Prince of Wales. Wally didn't miss a beat.

She said, "Sir! I thought you were in Scotland launching liners!"

He said, "I'm leaving directly, but I thought it'd be fun to surprise you and Maybell, and then when we arrived, I found Ernest had had the same idea. So here we both are. We've had time for a splendid chat."

Ernest was in a very affectionate mood, holding Wally's hand. The hand HRH has clung to these last seven weeks.

"Well, dearest," he said, "we mustn't delay. I have a car waiting outside, and His Royal Highness has a long journey ahead of him."

A mountain of correspondence waiting for me at Wilton Place. I shall be doing nothing for weeks except open envelopes.

25th September 1934

To Carlton Gardens. Violet was expected back from her Sanitarium committee momentarily, so I went up to the nursery to wait. Doopie loved her orange blossom soap, and Flora seemed pleased with her Spanish doll, although she removed all its clothes.

She said, "Uncle Prince George is getting married, and I'm going to be a flower baid."

Doopie is making her dress.

I said, "Well, you'll certainly have to have your hair combed before you can be a flower maid. And my friend Wally is going to the wedding, too. So I shall hear all about it."

Had a small sherry with Violet. She said, "You may tell me about places of interest you've visited, but I don't want to hear about anyone whose name begins with W."

Flora then appeared with the naked doll, piping, "Mummy, Aunt Bayba says The Wally is invited to Uncle Prince George's wedding, too. Isn't that a surprise!"

I noticed that funny little twitch Violet always gets in her cheek when something unsettles her.

"Now Flora," she said, "go downstairs and tell Smith we'll be two extra for dinner. Tell her Lady Habberley will have just an omelette."

Flora said, "Am I allowed gake?"

Violet said, "Yes, a small slice. Now kiss Aunt Maybell goodnight. She's just leaving."

The moment the door closed, she said, "How could you! Uttering *that* woman's name to an innocent child. How could you!"

I said, "It's not only me she hears it from. Everyone knows Wally is Wales's friend. I'm sure even your boot boy knows."

She said, "Knowing about it is one thing, speaking of it is quite another."

I said, "Well, pretend all you like, Violet, but London is going to be seeing a great deal more of Wally. She and David are inseparable."

She said, "Maybe so, but she certainly won't be invited to George and Marina's wedding, nor to any other occasion where she'll be in the presence of Their Majesties. Wally is a divorced person, and her so-called husband is a divorced person. This is England, Maybell, not a Hollywood movie lot."

I said, "You're so old-fashioned. The Prince of Wales doesn't care about people being divorced. Heavens, Wally even soaps him in his bathtub!"

She leapt to the door to check that no maids had been listening.

She said, "I never wished to quarrel with you, Maybell, but for the sake of my family, I must draw a line. Until you disassociate yourself from this scandal, you are not to see my children. People talk. Even boys of Rory's age. Imagine if it became known at school that his aunt is that woman's friend."

I said, "Are you banishing me? I'm your sister."

She said, "The remedy is yours. Walk away from Wally and the rest of Wales's silly set, and you'll be as welcome here as ever."

26th September 1934

Gladys and Whitlow Trilling have another daughter. I do hope they're not going to keep on till they get a boy.

27th September 1934

Lunch with George Lightfoot.

He said, "If it's a choice between patching things up with Violet and sticking by Wally, I'd drop Wally. She'd drop you."

But I don't think she would. She appreciates my friendship. She knows she can turn to me when she finds herself short, or HRH has forgotten his billfold. Anyway, I hate small-mindedness and that's the trouble with people like Violet. They can't see beyond the fence to the Royal Enclosure.

I said, "What about you? Are you going to 'draw a line'?"

He said, "Of course not. But I'm not in the same position as Violet and Melhuish. I don't have Their Majesties' good opinion to consider. Let's just hope this affair soon burns itself out. You must admit, they make a rather odd couple. The wee Princekin and Mrs. Pushy."

As I thought, the story about him and Penelope Blythe is untrue. He said, "I think she may have had a bit of a crush on me, but she's started seeing Billy Belchester. He keeps a little service flat on Portman Square.

Billy Belchester! There's desperation for you. He's jowly, he perspires, and he has the ever-smiling Anne and all the junior

Belchesters waiting for him with open arms. I'm sure he can't be a very attentive lover. But Penelope's never happy unless she's avoiding someone's wife or waiting by the telephone. I suppose that's why George Lightfoot soon lost his appeal, having no wife to betray and being scrupulously reliable about returning telephone calls.

He agrees with Violet that Wally's invitation to the wedding is sheer pie in the sky. He said, "Wales always opens his mouth before thinking. I'll tell you what'll happen. Ernest and Wally's names will appear on the guest list, the Lord Chamberlain will show the list to the King, and Ernest and Wally's names will disappear from the guest list."

1st October 1934

Lunch with Hattie and Pips. Hattie says their friends are more fascinated by Wally than scandalized, and certainly no one has dropped them.

I said, "Well I'm banned from Carlton Gardens, and Philip Sassoon hasn't returned either of my calls."

She said, "Well, I wouldn't lose any sleep over that. The Sassoons are only five minutes out of their desert tents. I'm sure they're completely untrustworthy."

Pips said, "Yes. Unlike Wally, who'd lay down her life for any one of us."

2nd October 1934

A letter from Rory. He writes that he won't be able to go to tea and the Planetarium as we'd planned at Long Leave, because he's invited to his friend Massingham's house in Gloucestershire. So Violet's gotten at him, too.

4th October 1934

I intercepted Doopie and Flora in St. James's Park. Flora spotted me and immediately began whooping, "Aunt Bayba, Aunt Bayba! We're not allowed to speak to you because of The Wally. But we can do zignals."

She and Doopie playacted a little scene. Nurses with bassinets turning to stare at them. I said, "What did that all mean?"

She said, "It meaned we'd still like to go to the National Mystery Museum and then for fidge and ships. It meaned we still like you."

Doopie said, "Nod vair, Bayba. Nod vair adall. Bud dode worry." She actually hugged me. What Doopie lacks in intellect, she makes up for with simple, honest affection.

8th October 1934

To Bryanston Court for drinks. Ernest was grumpy because Mr. Loo had destroyed his new carpet slippers, and Wally kept talking about tiaras. She's off to Paris tomorrow for fittings, and, I suppose, the whole money thing is making him anxious. Twice he said, "Remember to stay within your budget, Wally. Only a fool spends what he doesn't have."

HRH's name never cropped up.

I said, "I wonder when your wedding invitation will arrive?"

Wally said, "Plenty of time."

Well, I know for a fact the Belchesters have already received theirs.

11th October 1934

Lightfoot says Prince George and Marina are taking a house in Belgrave Square, just around the corner from the Crosbies. Pips says she expects Marina will be on the doorstep all the time, asking to borrow a cup of sugar.

Lightfoot got his invitation, too. All this money Wally's spending at Main Bocher. I hope she's not in for a disappointment.

16th October 1934

To Covent Garden for *Parsifal*. Came: the Humphrey Butlers and the Otto Bismarcks. No Ernest, but he is coming to the Fort this weekend. HRH fell asleep during Act I, and Wally slapped his hand. Much horrified rolling of eyes by Poots Butler, but my sympathies are entirely with the Prince. I'd have nodded off myself if my foundation hadn't become uncomfortably puckered. If someone thought to present an operatic show which dispensed with all the posturing and weeping and simply featured the best tunes, I believe they'd have a great success on their hands.

17th October 1934

Pips says she's lost all sympathy for Ernest if he's willing to crawl back under the Prince's roof. She said, "To keep up the pretense in public is one thing. You have to give him something for maintaining his dignity. But agreeing to spend a weekend at the love nest! That speaks volumes about Ernest. Basically, he's just a ridiculous little snob."

Pips can be very judgmental.

19th October 1934, Fort Belvedere

The Fruity Metcalfes are here, and the Perry Brownlows. HRH overheard Kitsie Brownlow telling Wally that those who are getting wedding invitations have already received them. He said, "Wally and Ernest don't need an invitation sent through the mails, because I put their names on a list and that's all there is to it."

Wally gave Kitsie such a triumphant smile.

HRH and Ernest pruned roses together this morning. I wonder what they talked about. Baba Metcalfe says Marina Greece is shy but adorable, and Prince George is deliriously happy, picking out rugs and drapes for their new house. Wally and Ernest are going to give them an inlaid cigarette box. It was a gift from the Benny Thaws and has hardly been used.

22nd October 1934, Wilton Place

Penelope Blythe says Prince George has a love child that was spirited out of the country and is being raised in obscurity. She says everyone knows about it. I'll bet shy but adorable Marina doesn't. Penelope says Billy Belchester is a surprisingly good lover.

25th October 1934

To Lady Strathnaver's gala for the Not Forgottens. At George Lightfoot's table, as were the Erlangers, the Crosbies, and the Belchesters, putting on a united front. Wally and Ernest were at the Metcalfes' table. HRH is at Sandringham.

I took care to bump into Violet in the powder room. She was cool but polite, so obviously knows nothing of my rendezvous in the park with Flora and Doopie.

5th November 1934

A brusque call from Hart Casey at First Maryland. He wonders when he may expect a reply to his letter of September 3rd. He obviously has no idea how much mail a person returns to find after a two-month vacation. I said, "I don't believe I've even seen your letter yet."

He said, "Mrs. Brumby, if you had seen it, you would remember. Your checking accounts are seriously overextended. We really have to do something about it."

Damned cheek. I reminded him that Danforth Brumby practically got him into that bank. He said, "He certainly did. And he always impressed on me the importance of knowing what you've got and where it is. I know he wouldn't want First Maryland to allow your accounts to fall into bad shape."

I said, "Well, why don't you just transfer money from accounts that aren't overextended? Do I have to teach you your job?"

He said, "That's the problem, Mrs. Brumby. There isn't really anything to transfer."

There's obviously been some kind of error.

I said, "I'll look into it when I have a moment."

He said, "And when do you estimate that might be?"

Landsakes, this is a very busy season in London, not to mention I have a friend going to a royal wedding. I'll get Randolph Putnam onto it.

To the Grill Room with Pips.

7th November 1934

Randolph says this is not a good time to sell Brumby stock. Pips says she knows nothing about money. She leaves all that to her trustees.

9th November 1934

George Lightfoot says he's the worst person to go to for advice. His family have been selling off castles for centuries and they still never make ends meet.

Hattie Erlanger said she has no trouble managing on her allowance, as is all too clear from the way she dresses.

10th November 1934

Ida Coote says wealth or poverty are of no importance. What matters is inner contentedness. How annoying friends can be in times of trouble.

13th November 1934

Saw Doopie and Flora in the park. Gave them an ounce of candy to share.

Flora says her flower maid's dress is pretty but her wedding shoes pinch. That's because she's allowed to go barefoot so much.

I wonder how much there is in Doopie's fund? She has absolutely no need of money.

14th November 1934

To Wally's, to see her Paris gowns. They are stunning. And exactly the style for someone who has no natural figure. This regime of lemon juice and hot water she's been following is doing nothing for her neck. After thirty-five, a woman needs a little avoirdupois beneath her skin.

16th November 1934

A voice I wished never to hear again. Junior. He said, "Greetings, Step-ma! I hear you're in difficulties. Now why don't I take Sweet Air off your hands? Free you up some walking-around money."

Over my dead body. It's thanks to his mismanagement that my dividends are down. Brumby must be spinning in his grave.

20th November 1934

I have decided to sell Sweet Air to Randolph Putnam. He always admired the place, and I've no use for it anymore. He was so thrilled. He said, "I'll give you a fair price, Maybell. And some day, when you come back where you belong, it can be yours again. My offer of a wedding band still stands."

I said, "Don't cloud the issue. If you want the house, buy it. And find a nice girl, because I won't be coming back."

He said, "Okay, Maybell. I hear you."

A good move all around. I've thwarted Junior and I'll be able to get Hart Casey and the First Maryland off my back without ending up as Randoph Putnam's sex slave.

21st November 1934

London is filling with minor royalties. The Yugoslavias, the Greeces, the Bulgarias, the Denmarks. I asked Wally if she wasn't the tiniest bit nervous about arriving at Buckingham Palace without a board invitation. "Not a bit," she said. "David is taking care of everything." He certainly seems to have pulled strings at Cartier. They've poked around in their vaults and found an old tiara for her to borrow.

22nd November 1934

To the German Legation. A little reception for the Hohenzollerns. Von Ribbentrop beaming and glad-handing everyone. He said, "Maybell! Where is our splendid Wally this evening?"

I said, "I believe she's engaged elsewhere."

"Ach!" he said. "I understand! Mummy is the word."

He was really behaving as though we were guests in *his* house, but Ambassador von Hoesch was far too polite to put him in his place. Violet pecked me on the cheek. Melhuish said, "I'm glad to see you don't have Wales's peg doll in tow."

Pips says she's suffering from Royal Wedding Fatigue. She's getting up a lunch for people who want to discuss other subjects.

26th November 1934

To the Ivy with Pips, Hattie, and Zita Cavett. Hattie couldn't wait to tell us what she'd heard from Poots Butler. Humphrey is equerrying for Prince George this month. Apparently, HM King noticed Wally and Ernest's names had been added to the list for the wedding ball and demanded to know who was responsible. Prince George said it was HRH's doing, and the King ordered them to be removed immediately. Then HRH was sent for and hauled over the coals about it in front of Humphrey.

27th November 1934

Pips called first thing. She said, "Freddie saw Ernest at the Guards' Club last night. He says he looked like the cat that'd been promised a lifetime supply of cream, so what are we to think? Will the Simpsons go to the ball or not? The world holds its breath."

Wally unreachable, of course. First she was resting, not to be disturbed. Then she was with her hairdresser and taking no more calls till tomorrow. I guess that means they're going.

28th November 1934

Wally and Ernest *did* go to the wedding ball. She called me at ten and said, "Come over, Maybell. I'll make us French toast and tell you all about it."

She was in her kimono, sipping milk and very happy to hear everyone is talking about her. Poots Butler was right about their names being removed from the guest list, but only temporarily. She said, "It was a mistake. David had it fixed as soon as he realized, and he came down personally to greet us, to make sure we didn't have trouble with any more mix-ups. It was such a scream. He whisked us through the vestibule, straight past Violet and her gang. You should have seen their faces. And I outshone the lot of them, Maybell. Especially the Royalties, all lined up in their prissy pastels, dressed like a herd of milkmaids."

I said, "And did you meet the King and Queen?"

"No," she said. "The stumbling block there is that Ernest and I have both been divorced. But we may be able to do something about that. I may be able to get Win Spencer annulled. In Ernest's case, it might be harder, because there was a child, but an annulment isn't out of the question. You just have to know the right people."

She wanted to hear all the gossip. Who's for her, who's against her, but I told no tales. I said, "All you need to know is *I* have always been for you."

She said, "I know, Maybell. You've been a treasure and I'll never forget it."

29th November 1934

Prince George is now styled the Duke of Kent, which sounds to me like a demotion. Better surely to be a prince than a duke.

The other disappointing news is that Wally and Ernest didn't go to the wedding, after all. Hattie says the King probably had Gurkhas posted everywhere to keep them out, but Wally says it was just that Ernest had an emergency at his office and she didn't feel she could face the cold of the Abbey.

Such a shame, after Main Bocher did such beautiful work on her gown.

She said, "Well, it was only a wedding. When you've seen one you've seen them all."

To the Whitlow Trillings for Thanksgiving turkey and fixings. The new child was handed around, very red and howling. They have named it Loelia, after the Duchess of Westminster. I hope they got a good gift.

30th November 1934

Carlton Gardens is still swarming with wedding guests. Trotman showed me into the morning room. The Melhuish sisters were there with Paul Yugoslavia's wife, and Violet looking at me through narrowed eyes, bracing herself for what she knew must come.

She said, "Were we expecting you?"

I said, "No, but I happened to be passing and I wanted to hear how you enjoyed the wedding ball."

She said, "It was charming."

I said, "Yes, Wally thought so, too. She had quite a triumph, by all accounts."

She said, "Is that what you call 'a triumph'? Crashing in uninvited, in fact, quite expressly *dis*invited. Dancing past Their Majesties dressed like a Christmas tree. A vulgar error is what I'd call it. A grotesque exhibition of bad manners."

That's Violet all over. She'll never back down.

Flora was on the stairs when I left, in her flower maid's dress and Wellington boots. She was soaping her Spanish doll, which she has named "Damned Wales." She said, "Hello, Aunt Bayba. Are you still banquished?"

4th December 1934

Two full days helping Wally pick out Christmas gifts for HRH's households. Penknives, neck ties, almanacs, figurines, all very bargain-basement and so fatiguing. I'm starting to agree with Lady Cunard. The whole business of Christmas is too boring for words and can only have been invented to entertain the lower classes.

Bernie and Zita Cavett have taken a house near Teddington and want me for the holidays. I don't know. The Crosbies are going to South Africa. Wally and Ernest are going to Devonshire with Ernest's newsagent friends.

Lunch with Lightfoot. He said, "Maybell, I think you're being treated somewhat shabbily by Violet. Your only crime seems to be loyalty to a friend, and I intend bringing it up with Melhuish. If moves aren't made to welcome you back into the bosom of your family, there'll be no pantomime for Flora and Rory this Christmas, gobfather or no. Doopie feels the same way. She's absolutely solid with me on this."

He is a dear.

10th December 1934

A visit from Violet. Lightfoot obviously issued his ultimatum. She said, "Maybell, don't let's quarrel."

I said, "I haven't quarreled."

She said, "No, well. It's upsetting Doopie dreadfully. Say you'll come to us for Christmas."

I said, "I'm afraid I can't. I already promised the Cavetts."

She said, "Who are they? I don't know them."

I said, "Bernie and Zita. They're friends of the Prince. Americans. They've taken a house in Middlesex."

She said, "Will you-know-who be there?"

I said, "If you mean Wally, she'll be in the West Country with her husband."

"Oh good," she said. "That's as it should be. Even better if she were to go back to the States. Well, let's hope."

We embraced when she left. She said, "You know I only do things for your own good, Maybell. When all's said and done, you're still my little sister."

15th December 1934, Fort Belvedere

Our last weekend before HRH leaves for Sandringham. The Erlangers are here, also Bernie and Zita, Oliver Templemore, and Fruity Metcalfe. No Baba. She spends a great deal of time with her brother-in-law since her sister Cimmie died. There are young children to be consoled.

Wally had had a tree brought into the Octagon Room and lit with tiny electric candles. The men all received cigars from HRH and the ladies engraved cigarette lighters, but I know Wally also got a pin with square-cut emeralds. I saw HRH claim his thank-you kiss while Ernest was playing billiards with Templemore.

16th December 1934

HRH wants us all to go with him to Kitzbuhel in January. The Erlangers and the Cavetts are up for it, but Ernest doesn't think he can get away.

Wally said, "Never mind. Maybell's going. She'll keep me company."

Ernest said, "Or you could make your excuses and decline."

She said, "Ernest, don't be such a fool. No one refuses Sir when his heart's set on something."

Fruity says it will fall to Oxer Bettenbrooke to equerry.

I think Fruity and I were the only ones to witness HRH's tears as Wally and Ernest drove away after tea.

"A whole month," he said. "A whole beastly month without her."

Fruity shook his head.

He said, "You'll be so occupied with the festivities, sir, a month will pass in no time."

HRH said, "No it won't. It'll drag, and it'll be bloody, and I'm going to hate every damned minute of it."

21st December 1934, Wilton Place

With Hattie to buy skiwear. Wally refuses. She says she's never skied in her life and she doesn't intend starting now. She says she'll just wear furs and take along lots of books.

Hattie said, "Wally had jolly well better learn to ski. And hunt. And play golf. David's going to get pretty bored with her if all she does is shop."

It's hard to imagine HRH ever growing bored with Wally. He seems enthralled by everything she says and does. He doesn't even mind watching her try on hats.

23rd December 1934

To the compound for hot cider and Christmas carols. Benny Thaw acknowledged me, but Connie turned her back. A card from Randolph Putnam. The Sweet Air papers will be ready for signing by the end of January.

28th December 1934

Zita Cavett thinks Wally should go to Reno, divorce Ernest, and snap up HRH while he's still a free man. I told her, it's a bit more complicated than that. He's the next King.

She said, "So? If they went off quietly to a little wedding chapel, what could anyone do about it?"

Maybe she's right.

30th December 1934

Wally says she's not interested in marrying HRH. She said, "Everything's just fine the way it is."

I said, "Even for Ernest?"

She said, "Especially for Ernest. He knows which side his bread's buttered."

1st January 1935

A new year, a new copybook.

Last night to the Florida Club. George Lightfoot wrapped his silk scarf around his head and looked into his crystal cufflink. His predictions: Ralph Habberley will turn up in Borneo with a lost memory, and Jane will forgive all. Whitlow and Gladys will produce another red-faced daughter. The Hohenzollerns will rediscover a princess they had mislaid in a turret room, and HRH will become engaged to her on the eve of Their Majesties' Silver Jubilee. Ernest will become Baron Simpson of Bryanston.

5th January 1935

To the Drury Lane Theatre with Lightfoot, Rory, Doopie, and Flora to see *Dick Whittington.*

An impromptu invitation from Philip Sassoon. Park Lane, for tea. I said, "I thought I'd become a persona ingrata."

He said, "What nonsense! I want you to see my new rrrococo paneling."

6th January 1935

I'm one up on Wally. *I* have been presented to HM the Queen.

She suddenly materialized at Philip Sassoon's and asked Violet to bring me to her.

Violet said, "Just make a short curtsy. It's only four o'clock. And wait for her to speak first."

She was in gray shot silk, sitting on a long, blue couch. It struck me that she looked rather like one of those round-prowed barges at anchor.

I believe she said, "They have the very best raspberries at Drumcanna," but her voice was too quiet for me to be sure. I simply smiled and inclined my head in an attitude of compliance, and it all went off smoothly. Violet was very happy.

She said, "Isn't she marvelous? So gracious. Twenty-five years and she's never made a false step, Maybell. You see how fortunate this country is."

Philip's new paneling looked very well. It had been brought all the way from Austria, as had the chocolate cake.

9th January 1935

Gave Wally lunch. Her number-one aim this year is to make a big splash at the Silver Jubilee. We're going to Paris on our way to Kitzbuhel so she can order gowns.

I said, "Can you afford it?"

She said, "I don't need to afford it. I'm a favored customer, Maybell. No one here had heard of Main Bocher till I wore him. Now he's the talk of London. Everything will be on the house."

Emerald Cunard stopped by our table, wearing an excessive amount of rouge, I thought, considering it was only one-thirty. She'd just had a vexing morning with her telephone out of order and the Postmaster General unable to do anything about it because he's shooting at the Perry Brownlows. She made a great fuss of Wally but practically ignored me. I did admire her hat, however. A natty little *faux* fur pillbox with a half-veil.

Drinks at the Prosper Friths. Much talk about brilliant speeches Tom Mosley has been making around the country. The Communists hate him, of course, and have been doing everything they can to disrupt his meetings, but he now has his own trusty band of stewards with smart black shirts, just like Mr. Mussolini's men. According to Daphne Frith, Mosley is completely bereft by the death of Cimmie, but Baba Metcalfe is going to exceptional lengths to comfort him in his widowhood. She has moved into his bed. Well, he is *very* dashing. Tall and distinguished, like Fruity, with the added spice of a bad leg and a gallant war story.

But I do hope Baba isn't creating some kind of precedent for sisters-in-law. Melhuish always had a soft spot for me, but it would be too awful if Violet went early to her reward and he expected me to warm his sheets.

12th January 1935

Randolph Putnam keeps trying to tie me down to a date for the closing, but I have no idea when we'll be back from Kitzbuhel.

I said, "This is a royal skiing party, not a railroad company. We don't go by timetables."

He said, "Doesn't Prince Wales have work to do?"

I said, "Traveling the world and being seen is a prince's work. My lawyer will wire yours as soon as I'm available to sign the papers."

He said, "You just better hope Junior doesn't have me murdered while you're gone. That wife of his keeps calling your tenants. If ever she gets her hands on a door key, you'll never get the place back, only in a court of law and maybe not even there. Well, it's up to you. Either I buy Sweet Air fair and square, or I walk away from it. I can't say more."

Randolph always did fuss. He lived too long with his mother.

18th January 1935

HRH is on his way to Austria with Oxer Bettenbrooke. Tomorrow to Paris. The Cavetts are already at Lily Drax-Pfaffenhof's and will meet up with us in Kitzbuhel.

21st January 1935, Meurice Hotel, Paris

Hattie spent the entire journey from London doom-mongering about Wally's prospects of going to a State Ball.

Wally refused to get riled.

She just said, "Hattie, better to have a gown and no invitation than an invitation and no gown."

24th January 1935

Wally has chosen full-skirted silk chiffon, one in silver and one in gold. There were a couple of accounts outstanding, for lingerie and shoes. I've made her a small loan to tide her over.

HRH has telephoned twice, urging us to set off before more avalanches prevent the trains from getting through, but Elsie

Mendl has invited us to dinner at Trianon, and Wally has run into an old Washington friend, Kenny Opdyke, who has a warehouse full of rugs and clocks and other lovely things, all for sale at advantageous prices, so Wednesday really seems to be the soonest we can leave.

27th January 1935

HRH is so fretful without Wally. He telephones constantly to see whether we're on our way, although he knows perfectly well when to expect us.

I said, "How will he manage when they marry him off?" She laughed. She said, "He'll probably keep me behind some secret door in a bookcase. No. I'll have been dropped by then. I won't be missed."

I said, "Is he going to drop you? He seems more ardent than ever."

She said, "That's just absence working its old magic. But of course he'll drop me. He drops everyone eventually. All I need is one more year. Give me another year, and I reckon I'll have secured my future."

After Kitzbuhel, HRH is going on to Vienna for a few days. Wally says we should go with him. She's heard the shops there are exquisite.

2nd February 1935, Kitzbuhel

We are installed at the Lindenhof and have the use of a commodious lodge with veranda views of the slopes. Lily is here with the Cavetts, the Eugene Rothschilds, and the Milwaukee Gunters, and the British Embassy in Vienna has sent HRH a junior attaché to do a little equerrying, as Bettenbrooke speaks no German. Our man from Vienna is Dudley Forwood, and Wally has already taken quite a shine to him. She says he plays a very good game of backgammon.

Hattie says she'd have liked a little more ice on the slopes, but that the snow is powdery and ideal for those who lack her expertise. I'll take her word for it. Wally, Zita, and I sunned ourselves on the veranda all morning, and HRH floundered past every so often, flanked by Forwood and a detective, waving his ski poles and shouting, "Are you watching me, darling? Aren't I doing splendidly!"

3rd February 1935

We quite took over the Klammer Stube last evening. Hattie, in drink, offered the opinion that skiing isn't the Prince's forte. Wally fairly froze the cherry brandy in her glass. The last thing she wants is for HRH to grow discouraged and start hanging around our veranda all day.

As nice as he is, I don't know why Forwood was sent for. The Prince gabbles away in German to the serving girls as though it were his mother tongue.

Kitty Rothschild says it *is* his mother tongue. I don't think she understands that this is the Prince of Wales we're talking about.

5th February 1935

Blizzards, but Hattie, Oxer, and HRH refuse to be defeated. They've gone out for a sleigh ride while we hug the fire. Dudley Forwood has been explaining the Austrian situation to us. The Austrians need Hitler's friendship, because they're in a bad way financially, but Hitler isn't interested in being just a friendly neighbor. Being an Austrian by birth himself, he sees Austria as family and wants Germany to adopt it. Then there's Mr. Mussolini. It's all so complicated, especially after a glass of glühwein. Wally was taking notes.

6th February 1935

HRH came in yesterday so enchanted by his sleigh ride Wally has agreed to give it a try. I believe she's slightly uneasy about the amount of time he's been spending in Hattie's company, though I don't know why. I don't think Hattie's apple-cheeked heartiness can hold any attraction for him.

Kitty Rothschild says HRH is like a twelve-year-old in an old man's skin.

7th February 1935

Wally has decided to make sleigh rides her winter sport. She said, "Ermine rugs, Maybell. Once you've snuggled beneath ermine rugs, nothing else will do. And they lit our path with flares. Such a wonderful, racy look. I'm going to see about copying that."

Not along George Street, I hope.

Tonight dancing to a Schrammel band. The Rothschilds are leaving in the morning, for their Austrian estate. HRH has proposed us for dinner with them while we're in Vienna.

8th February 1935

Three vigorous polkas with HRH last evening. He was in such a good mood.

9th February 1935

The Rothschilds left early. There's nothing like the promise of a royal visit to quicken the heartbeat. Forwood has also gone to make sure everything is in order for our arrival in Vienna. HRH and I were the only two down to wave them off. We shared a pot of chocolate and a plate of ham for breakfast.

He seemed rather flat after last night's high spirits. Only one more week, then he has to steel himself for a year of more-than-usually-hectic prince-ing. The Silver Jubilee celebrations, State luncheons, levees, tours around the country. It seems no boondock will be left un-princed.

He said, "What an enviable life Rothschild has. A *schloss* in Austria, a place in Paris, and a spread on Long Island. A little shooting, a little shopping, a little golf. I'd settle very happily for that."

10th February 1935, Hotel Bristol, Vienna

My suite has a view of the Ringstrasse, but there's no noise. Enormous snowflakes drifting down. I've ordered extra comforters. We sat for hours with the train moving forward in fits and starts as the drifts were cleared, and arrived hours late, but the British envoy was there with Forwood at his side, and there were warm cars waiting for us. I think I'm going to like Vienna.

11th February 1935

HRH was on the road early, looking at worker housing, but word has circulated that he's in residence. By the time Wally and I had finished breakfast and made hair appointments, quite a crowd had gathered outside. There are Socialists down there, who seem to be for him, because he's interested in the lot of the working man, but there's another group, Reds, who are against Germany and so are chanting slogans, because HRH has a lot of German cousins. Well, no one can help their cousins. One of the Woodhams on Mother's side was fond of naked swimming in public places, and Father always said there was a Patterson who was hanged in Dundee, Scotland, but in neither case did it cause us any inconvenience.

Wally is nervous about the rabble at the front door, so the hairdresser will now come to us.

12th February 1935

All ended well yesterday. HRH braved the crowd outside and engaged them in German chitchat. He charmed them into silence. Most of them, at any rate. Forwood says they'd been standing in the snow long enough for the fire to have gone out of their bellies. By the time we went out to the Wunder-Bar, only a few stragglers remained, and when they noticed we were wearing red corsages, they gave us a hearty cheer. A little tact and imagination goes such a long way. I think diplomacy is a field where I would have excelled, and perhaps still may.

Today shopping, then drinks with George Messersmith, our man in Vienna.

13th February 1935

At Ambassador Messersmith's insistence, Wally and I went to see a horse-riding circus. It was quite interesting, but horses smell like horses however well trained they are.

Also bought woolen suiting, winter silks, and embroidered cushions. HRH had a meeting with the Chancellor, but we're not supposed to talk about it, because it wouldn't be approved of in London. Not that it's any of London's business. They should be grateful to have a prince who takes an interest in international affairs.

HRH feels the Austrians have all the right instincts, remaining firm with Germany and at the same time friendly toward Italy. They told him there's even the possibility of bringing back Archduke Otto. Never a bad thing, as he says, for a country to temper the rough-and-tumble of politics with the nobler spirit of royalty.

To the Rascal Club. Men dressed as women, women dressed as men. What a very long way we've come from Baltimore.

14th February 1935

David has given Wally a Valentine pin, a pink beryl heart set in white gold. Tonight we drive up to Schloss Enzesfeld to have dinner with the Eugene Rothschilds. I wonder whether our path will be cleared of ice and lit by burning torches!

Tomorrow HRH flies back to his duties, and we begin our long trek home by train. I do wish Wally would take a pill so we could fly, too.

15th February 1935

Wally and HRH chucked the Rothschilds at the last minute so they could dine alone in their suite. I went with just Dudley Forwood and Oxer Bettenbrooke. Kitty R. was very gracious about it. She said, "Never mind. Perhaps we'll have a nicer time. I've always suspected Royalties might be bad for the digestion."

Forwood very wickedly agreed.

Kitty gave us her analysis of the Prince's personality. She said, "He reminds me of a dog. He sees a lamppost and becomes completely obsessed with it, until someone sticks another one under his nose. Then he completely forgets the first one."

Eugene said, "Darling, you're embarrassing our guests."

She said, "Nonsense. They know it's all said most affectionately. Now the puzzle is Wally. She's very bright, but does she really understand how he ticks? I've noticed how sharp she is with him when he hangs around, getting in her way, but that's not the way to deal with him. It seems to me the crosser she gets with him the more eagerly he wags his tail."

Well, he certainly wasn't wagging his tail this morning when he had to leave for the airfield. He just hates being separated from her.

19th February 1935, Wilton Place

Sweet Air, where Danforth Brumby took me as his bride, now belongs to Randolph Putnam, and my bank account is in glowingly good health. I put a call through to him immediately after I'd signed the papers.

I said, "Well, you finally got what you wanted."

"No, Maybell," he said. "I got part of what I want. The other part is sitting stiff-necked in the office of a London lawyer, if I'm not mistaken. Tell me, how's your Prince of Wales?"

I said, "In love. With Minnehaha Warfield. You'll be reading about it in the *Globe* before long, I'm sure."

He said, "Isn't that something! You mean we could have Queen Wally visiting with us at Sweet Air someday?"

That wasn't what I meant at all.

21st February 1935

Took Violet's Tyrolean tray cloth to Carlton Gardens, and a cuckoo clock for the nursery. Doopie was out, visiting Ena Spain at Kensington Palace.

Violet says Their Majesties are greatly invigorated from their Sandringham break and eager to begin their celebration year. I braced myself, but neither of the W words came up.

A brief note from Junior and his wife. May I rot in hell.

22nd February 1935

Aching and feverish. Perhaps Junior has had a curse put on me.

23rd February 1935

Canceled lunch with Pips and Ida. Padmore says I have influenza.

24th February 1935

A visit from Ida Coote who brought honey and canned spinach. She says we are what we eat. Well, I have eaten nothing since Monday.

Wally's pestering me to go look at a house on Eaton Square. HRH to foot the bill.

I said, "Will this be for you alone or for you and Ernest?"

She said, "That's up to Ernest, but it makes perfect sense to keep things the way they are."

I said, "Well, count me out. I'm as weak as a kitten."

6th March 1935

I feel like a new woman! Lunch with George Lightfoot who jestingly steered me away from all drain covers lest I slip through in my new svelte condition.

He was in a strange mood. He said, "Tell me your thoughts on marriage, Maybell. Do you recommend it?"

I said, "If you marry that Belinda, I'll be heartbroken. She has no warmth."

He said, "No, I'm not talking about Belinda, though she's much nicer than you say. I'm just asking about marriage in general. I'm thirty-six. A decent age to start thinking about it, don't you think?"

It is, indeed.

7th March 1935

Hattie has been looking at houses with Wally. Chesham Place, Lowndes Street. It's all supposed to be very hush-hush, but let Hattie Erlanger in on a secret and it will appear in tomorrow's *Times*.

To the Ham Bone Club. The Crosbies, von Ribbentrop without his smiling *hausfrau*, Wally without her husband or her Prince, and the Trillings. Gladys's reentry into the world. Her waistline is still looking pretty slack.

Von R. danced with Wally all evening. He knew every detail of our trip to Vienna.

10th March 1935

The Crokers have arrived. They've taken Sunninghills again. Ethel said, "I hope Wally is going to let us have you for Ascot Week."

14th March 1935

Lunch with Ethel and Pips. First thing Ethel said, "And? Has our Prince popped the question?"

Pips said, "That'd be a bit premature. There's the little matter of Ernest."

Anyway, that's not at all the plan. HRH has to marry someone who can be Queen.

Ethel said, "Okay. So, what happens to Wally if he wakes up King tomorrow?"

I said, "But he's not going to."

"No," she said, "but just say."

I said, "Then he'd hurry off and marry one of those Biedermeyer-Bechsteins. Keep her confined to the palace with a brood of babies and slip away as often as possible to see Wally."

"God!" she said. "Long live the King!"

Pips said, "Apart from anything else, Wally wouldn't be any use as a brood mare. She's too old and she has very irregular insides."

20th March 1935

Penelope Blythe has it from Kitsie Brownlow that the King sent for HRH and asked him straight out whether he and Wally are lovers and HRH swore absolutely not. She says it spread like wildfire from the Palace to York House and the Fort, and the servants can talk of nothing else, because they've seen what they've seen and they know what they know. But the King was apparently satisfied with David's answer, and as a show of cordiality, he's agreed to turn a blind eye to the fact that both Wally and Ernest have been divorced and allow them to attend one of the Jubilee balls.

Just as well, because Wally's in Paris having fittings, and they're hardly the kind of gowns she'd have occasion to wear in Marylebone.

I said, "What's going to happen when the King finds out the truth?"

Penelope said, "Oh, he already knows the truth. But having posed the question, it wouldn't do for him to disbelieve Wales's answer. And everyone now feels better for a slight clearing of the air. It's all quite understood."

Not by me.

24th March 1935

A call from Ernest. Would I share a simple supper with him tomorrow evening? He said, "Wally's still in Paris, as you know. But I'd very much like to talk to you, just we two. I'd count it a very great favor, Maybell."

I'm filled with dread. I do hope he doesn't cry.

25th March 1935

To Bryanston Court, full of trepidation. A fire lit. Cold cuts and baked potatoes served on trays. I was hardly through the door before Ernest showed me the invitation: A Court Ball on May 14th. He said, "The greatest honor of my life. Something undreamed of."

Small talk about Vienna while we ate, but then he grew wistful over coffee.

He said, "Well, Maybell, you see how things are. Thanks to Wally, the Prince of Wales has become a close personal friend. The next King of England. He gave me these very cigars. But to get to the point, he's fallen in love with my wife. I have to face facts. I can't keep her to myself."

He was very calm.

I said, "I expect this year will be different. David has a very full appointment book, with the Jubilee. Hardly a day off."

He said, "Yes. But, of course, there'll be another long vacation after the celebrations. Another cruise, I dare say. I can't be away from business for weeks on end, guarding my wife, and anyway, it's rather gone beyond that. I'd be *de trop.* I suppose you know they're lovers?"

I told him the truth when I said Wally has never admitted to any intimacy.

He said, "Still, there can be no doubt."

I said, "What will you do?"

He said, "I'm not sure. Wait, I suppose. See what happens. Do you think she wants me to leave her?"

I said, "Not at all. I think she expects to be dropped as suddenly as she was taken up."

"Yes," he said, "that's what she told me. She expects to be let go with a handsome pension. As though that makes it worthwhile. Are people laughing at me, Maybell?"

Again I spoke the truth when I said they were not. People hardly remember he exists. Ernest is one of those people who's forgotten the moment he leaves the room.

He said, "I have to go to Germany next week. That's one thing about being in business. It keeps one occupied."

He was still sucking on his royal cigar, but it had quite gone out.

4th April 1935

George and Marina Kent are back from their honeymoon. She's expecting. Doopie will be thrilled. I'll bet you can't hear yourself think at Carlton Gardens for the clacking of knitting pins.

10th April 1935

To the Shim Sham with Boss and Ethel, Judson and Hattie, Wally and HRH. Ernest is in Hamburg. Judson now calls him "The Invisible Man."

12th April 1935

A little ladies' luncheon. Soufflé omelettes, Florida salad.

HRH has gone to Leicestershire for the weekend, but didn't dare take Wally, because Their Majesties are staying nearby. Hattie said, "I wonder if he'll bump into Thelma," and Wally snapped, "Not if he knows what's good for him."

As Ethel said, one might almost have thought that was a flash of jealousy. She said, "You don't think she's fallen in love or anything, do you?"

Pips said, "Not Wally. She's just guarding her nest egg."

15th April 1935

Wally is timing her final gown fittings to coincide with Jubilee Day. She says she can't bear to be in London with everyone talking about processions and who wore what. She said, "All those carriages full of homely princesses, all that waving and nodding. It's nothing to do with the David I know."

I said, "Wally Warfield! Are you in love?"

She said, "No. Well. Maybe it's a kind of love. It's nice to be needed. I suppose that's why some people have babies. I don't think anyone would believe how much David needs me. That's why it's so awful to feel invisible when he's out there prince-ing."

For a moment, she looked quite forlorn.

18th April 1935

Ambassador von Hoesch has invited me to join Violet and the children at the German Legation to view the procession on Jubilee Day, so my reinstatement as a worthy aunt seems complete. What wonders time and an Austrian tray cloth can work! Melhuish will be in the procession, riding with the Prince Nicholases of Greece.

Violet says we may expect another royal wedding this year. Prince Harry is engaged to Alice Montagu-Douglas-Scott. Her father is the Duke of Buccleuch and an old friend of the King.

With Rory to Oxford Street to see the Jubilee decorations, and then to Selfridges for Welsh rarebit. He's becoming such a young gentleman, always takes my arm when we cross a street and walks on the outside.

He's been learning magic tricks from a boy in his House and wants magician's accessories for his birthday. I said, "I'll bet there's never been a magician in the Melhuish family."

He said, "Well, one can't do it for a living obviously, but it's rather good fun when there are guests. Uncle Prince George greatly enjoyed my rope trick, except Flora told him how it was done. Ulick says conjuring's for the lower classes."

Pips and Freddie have declined an invitation to the Fort for Easter.

I said, "You always reckoned it wasn't done to decline."

Freddie said, "I've also always thought it's completely not done to call a chap your friend while you're stealing his wife."

Wally says the Crosbies are no loss to them. The Perry Brownlows are coming, Boss and Ethel, Judson and Hattie.

21st April 1935, Fort Belvedere

HRH went up to the Castle for Easter church and came bouncing back. "Duty done!" he said. "Now I can relax with *my* kind of people."

He's looking into chartering a yacht for the summer. We'll cruise to Italy and Greece. I can't wait. I shall try out the new sun-kissed look and study the Ancients.

26th April 1935, Wilton Place

Wally believes she's being slandered at the Palace. Nellie Hardinge has been heard to say that she must have been very busy in China for so many people to have known her.

Wally said, "Someone's been poking around, looking into my past. Well, let them. If I'm still around when David's King, I'll make sure the lot of them are fired."

4th May 1935

Dinner at the Belchesters. Came: the Westminsters, the Crosbies, the Prosper Friths. Daphne Frith asked rather slyly after Wally. She said, "I must say, the Prince of Wales has never looked more handsome."

Anne Belchester said, "The whole family is on the crest of a wave. A Silver Jubilee for Their Majesties, the Kents radiant, the Yorks so greatly loved, and now even Harry has found a bride."

Daphne said, "Yes, all we need to make it a perfect year is for Wales to name his princess. Maybell, you're on the inside. Anyone in prospect?"

I said, "No. I don't think he's in any hurry."

She said, "Well, he shouldn't delay much longer. He's at that time of life when he'll suddenly lose his looks."

Pips said, "Of course, there's always Wally Simpson."

Billy Belchester said, "With the current mood of the country, Wales could get away with a great deal. Marry a Hottentot, almost. But not the dreadful Mrs. S. Never that."

6th May 1935

Jubilee Day. I've seen enough processing dignitaries to last me a lifetime. Prime ministers from distant lands, courtiers in wigs and silk stockings, minor foreign royalties, obscure British royalties unidentifiable to everyone except Violet and Ulick, who'd suddenly cry out, "There's Athlone!" or "Is that Tommy Lascelles?"

Dear Louis Ferdinand watched with us. His mother was in a carriage with the Denmarks.

There were marching bands, troopers on horseback, drums, bugles. Finally, we got to the meat of the matter. Prince Harry and the Princess Royal, then the Bertie Yorks, she in *eau de nil*. She looks quite pretty in a procession, whatever Wally may say.

Violet was calling, "Flora, come and wave to Lilibet and Margaret Rose," but to no avail. She was conducting her own imaginary procession at the back of the room. She's to be tried at a different style of school in September, in a remote backwater of Suffolkshire, but it's not to be mentioned until the day dawns.

After the Yorks came the Kents, she in cream and tan. Then HRH in a landau with two aunts, Toria and Maud. It felt very strange indeed to see him riding in state when I'm accustomed to seeing him on his exercise bicycle. Wally did right not to be there to watch. She would have found it unbearable listening to people who consider themselves insiders. After all, no one knows HRH as Wally does, and next to the Majesties, *he's* the most important person in the land.

More bands, and then the King and Queen, both with very tight little smiles, she in silver-and-white brocade, with her vast bosom covered in pearls. Hattie Erlanger says if you see the King close up, his beard is stained with tobacco.

Went back to Carlton Gardens afterwards for a late luncheon. Poached salmon, inevitably, and sherry trifle, and endless cups of tea as people drifted back from the service of thanksgiving. Melhuish reported that the King had been moved to tears by the warmth and gaiety of the crowds. Rory performed a card trick and made a penny appear and disappear, but it began to feel like a wedding breakfast after the bride and groom have left. We were only saved from complete anticlimax by Lightfoot who had the idea of taking Rory and Flora on an omnibus to see the fireworks and the bonfires burning in Hyde Park. Such an adventure. One has to climb a steep stairway to reach the top deck of the bus. Doopie pushing me from behind, shouting, "Ub ya go, Bayba! Ub ya go!"

I had the impression she'd done it before.

Goodness knows what she and Flora get up to, filling their empty days.

The park was entrancing. Shooting stars tumbling down over the bonfires, little children writing their names on the sky with magnesium sparklers, bands playing show tunes, booths selling delicious saveloys with fried onions. It was easily the best part of the day. And when Kettle drove me home, well after eleven, Piccadilly was as crowded as if it were the middle of the day. I don't think London is going to sleep tonight.

8th May 1935

Wally is back from Paris. She's decided to wear the gold gown to Buckingham Palace on the basis that everyone else, lacking imagination, will go to a Silver Jubilee Ball dressed in silver. I'm sworn to secrecy about her jewels. HRH has given her a parure of black sapphires. Ernest doesn't know about them yet.

She says the last thing she needs is for him to get worked up and develop another carbuncle on the eve of a State Ball.

A setback to our summer plans. The King has forbidden HRH to go take his vacation on a yacht, because of a grave situation in Abyssinia. It's so ridiculous. All we need to do is steer clear of the place. I've never heard of anyone putting in there anyway. Nothing worth buying, I'm sure.

15th May 1935

Last night to the Embassy Club with the Crokers and the Erlangers to wait for Wally and Ernest to come on from the ball and give us their report. They arrived just after midnight, Wally followed by HRH followed by Ernest, very self-conscious in knee breeches and silk stockings. Boss actually bowed to Wally. Hattie screamed, "Boss, what *are* you doing?"

He said, "I couldn't help myself. Those are some rocks you're wearing, Wally."

She was radiant. She told me in the powder room that the King studied her very closely each time she danced past him. She thinks the next thing will be an informal meeting, rather than the problematical business of being presented. She thinks it'll happen next time she's at the Fort and the Majesties are at Windsor.

16th May 1935

Violet says HRH caused great offense by dancing the second dance of the ball with Wally. She says after he'd danced with Her Majesty, he should have danced with his sister and his sisters-in-law, and only then with Wally, if at all.

She said, "And she gave Their Majesties such a cheeky look as they danced by. I was embarrassed ever to have known her. And as for the husband. What a buffoon. I suppose he'd never worn court dress before. It was really rather comical to see him sweating and concentrating so. He treated his sword like a third leg!"

Flora waltzing around the upper stairhall in a car rug and Christmas-tree tinsel. What a rude awakening the child has coming to her in September.

Doopie has had her hair bobbed.

18th May 1935, Belton House

At the Perry Brownlows with Wally and Ernest. The sunshine continues, but not from Wally. HRH is prince-ing in the West Country, and must have telephoned her five times at least. She grew quite exasperated with him. Kitsie B. remarked that the "sapphire dividend" seems to have worn off rather quickly.

25th May 1935, Wilton Place

There's a story going around that Ralph Habberley has been sighted in Bolivia. I saw Jane H. in Derry and Toms only yesterday. We didn't speak.

With Pips and Freddie to a Jubilee garden fete in the constituency. Torrential rain, but I won a bottle of egg flip in the prize draw. Bought glass necklaces for Flora and Doopie and marmalade for Violet.

27th May 1935

Wally invited herself to lunch. She said she couldn't face going to the Dorch and wanted only bread and soup, because of her ulcers. She does look haggard.

She says things have grown very tense between herself and Ernest since the Jubilee Ball, and she's afraid he may make some kind of scene next time he sees HRH. I said, "Is it the jewels?"

She said, "No. He thinks he's being talked about at his club."

I don't ever remember seeing her so anxious.

She said, "Things are going so well. It'd be just too awful if he went and ruined everything now. He refuses to come on vacation and he's practically forbidding me to go without him. What am I supposed to do? Sit in London all summer? Trail after him to New York? I need a break, Maybell. And anyway, David's depending on me."

I said, "What will you do? If Ernest asks you to choose?"

She was quiet for the longest time.

She said, "Well, there's nothing to be gained by dramas and divorce, if that's what you mean. Ernest *wants* to be married to me. David *can't* be married to me. So it's idiotic even to talk of choosing. Everyone just needs to keep their head."

I said, "But you have taken a lover. Some husbands don't like that. They fear they're being made a laughingstock. And Ernest may be finding it bad for business."

She said, "I'd hardly call David 'a lover.' And Ernest didn't mind at the beginning. He can't expect me to turn these things on and off like a tap."

She says she's helping HRH to write an important speech he has to make to British war veterans next month. No wonder she needs a vacation. I thought he had a little man who did all that.

28th May 1935

Pips says Ernest is being talked about at his club. I said, "Well, she told me David isn't really her lover."

She said, "It doesn't matter if they play checkers all night. She sleeps over, and Ernest's a laughingstock."

3rd June 1935

To the Scottish Office to watch Trooping the Color. Melhuish had organized a window for us. Also came: Elspeth Laird, the Otto Bismarcks, Ena Spain, and George Lightfoot. More horses, more bands, then the King rode out on the very stroke of eleven. I suppose, if you're the King, you can arrange for a clock to strike when you're ready and not before.

Doopie wearing lip rouge and the little necklace I bought for her. Flora looked quite presentable in a blue dress with a white sailor collar, but she's in disgrace for trying to make skyrockets out of sugar and pickling salt.

As Doopie said, "Lide a madge. Boom!"

8th June 1935

Mr. Stanley Baldwin is the new Prime Minister.

George Lightfoot calls him The Dormouse. Mr. Atlee, the Socialist, he calls The Slug.

As our lovely cruise has been vetoed, HRH is taking Rock Cholmondeley's new villa instead. It's not absolutely finished, but we can have it for the month of August, because Rock will be in America, playing polo.

I can't believe Sybil Cholmondeley knows anything about this. She'd never have agreed to David bringing Wally there, using it as a love nest. Hattie says it's more Rock's house than Syb's, and anyway, whatever Syb's opinion, Rock will have been in no position to refuse a favor for the Prince of Wales. Rather like Ernest's situation, really.

12th June 1935

With Wally to Asprey to buy HRH silver hairbrushes for his birthday. I got him a propelling pencil. She has her eye on a gilt fur-clasp. A little more than I'd planned on spending for her birthday, but perhaps I'll treat her. She doesn't look well these days.

17th June 1935

Ernest has fabricated an urgent business trip to Antwerp and refused all Ascot invitations. Our revised summer plans are taking shape. After the Cholmondeley villa, we'll be traveling on to

Budapest. More worker housing for poor HRH to study, I suppose. Difficult to know what kind of clothes to take.

To the Crokers for a pre-Ascot dinner.

18th June 1935, Sunninghills

Boss Croker says Budapest definitely doesn't have a beach, so I'm going to need a whole other wardrobe. He and Ethel believe Ernest may be cracking up.

Ethel said, "The best thing that could happen now is for him to meet a nice girl."

Best for whom, though?

19th June 1935

Wally's birthday. She's thrilled with her fur-clasp. HRH has given her emeralds to match her Christmas pin. He kissed her in the drawing room.

Ladies' Day. Prince Harry's bride-to-be was in today's landau parade. Another little mouse. Elizabeth York wore buttercup, Marina Kent was in café au lait, Violet in the fourth carriage was unusually elegant in delphinium.

HRH drove straight to town after the big race. Tonight is his big speech to the men of the Royal British Legion, as composed by Wally.

20th June 1935

HRH's speech received a standing ovation, apparently. The gist of it was that it's time to put old enmities behind us and embrace the new Germany. He proposed that the British Legion set an example by sending a friendly delegation to break bread with German veterans.

Poots Butler said, "Sir! You'll be known as the Prince of Peace."

Jack Aird stony-faced.

22nd June 1935, Fort Belvedere

HRH has been summoned to the Castle. Jack Aird has gone with him. Poots thinks he'll be getting a rocket about inviting Mrs. Simpson without her Mr., yet again.

23rd June 1935

HRH did get a telling off from the King, but not about Wally. It was about the British Legion speech. Poots got it blow by blow from Humphrey, who got it from Jack Aird.

The King told him he had no business making speeches that contain anything of substance, and most particularly not sentiments that are likely to offend Mr. Mussolini. He told him his job is to cut ribbons, keep his mouth shut, and find himself a wife.

Well, HM King may not have approved of the speech, but Hitler's Mr. Goering did. I saw his telegram of congratulations. Fruity Metcalfe says anyway it isn't HRH who's likely to offend Mussolini but Anthony Eden, who campaigns against Italy's ambitions in Africa whilst conveniently turning a blind eye to Hitler's ambitions in Austria. Just thinking of it makes one tired.

Still, what a birthday present for poor David, rapped over the knuckles and in front of Jack Aird, too.

4th July 1935, Wilton Place

To the Compound. The Benny Thaws have gone back to Washington, so that chapter has closed. What a relief. Connie never forgave any of us who stayed loyal to Wally. Understandably. Her first loyalty was bound to be to Thelma. I hope Violet would be as staunch for me.

Randolph Putnam telephoned to wish me a Happy Fourth and tell me what he's going to do with my gardens. I said, "Not *my* gardens, Randolph. They're yours now."

He never gives up.

6th July 1935

Bumped into Philip Sassoon in Curzon Street.

I said, "I suppose Sybil's ordered you not to speak to me?"

He said, "My dear Maybell, Syb's far too busy to interest herself in Wales's sordid affairs, and so am I. I hope you're well?"

He didn't know about us using Rock's villa.

He said, "Le Rrroc, by rrroyal command! How very generous of him. I wonder if it will come up to Mrs. Simpson's exacting standards."

He pecked me on the cheek. Lime cologne.

Dinner at the Prosper Friths. Prosper reckons Anthony Eden is going to push Mussolini into the arms of Adolf Hitler. Well, I hope he waits until we've all taken our vacations.

7th July 1935

To Carlton Gardens. Flora and Ulick were fighting, because she'd twisted the head off one of his tin grenadiers.

He said, "The sooner you're sent to Suffolk and kept under lock and key the safer for all our property."

She wasn't supposed to know about Suffolk.

Doopie was just on her way out to visit with Marina Kent, all smiles. They've become great friends, apparently. I believe Doopie may have started wearing a girdle.

12th July 1935

Took Rory to Rules for sirloin of beef and Yorkshire pudding. Fourteen years old! A little down on his top lip, his voice no longer what it was but not quite what it will be. He has a new trick with two pieces of string, which he performed for me and then for the table next to ours, by popular request.

He said, "Flora doesn't want to go to her new school. She says she'll run away."

I said, "Well, she might take to it. I remember when you didn't like school so much."

He said, "Yes. But Flora's different. I thought I might hide a ten-shilling note in her manicure case, so that if she does run away, she won't be without funds."

I said, "Do you have a ten-shilling note?" He said, "Yes. Well, I did have. Uncle George Kent gave it to me, and I've got nine shillings and fourpence left. Do you think that would be enough?"

I said, "I think it's very generous. The trouble is, I very much doubt whether Flora ever opens her manicure case."

He said, "Aunt Maybell, can people get married even when they're old?"

I said, "Even when they're ninety-nine, so you've plenty of time."

He said, "I'll probably marry Moo Anstruther-Brodie. Lady Anstruther-Brodie thinks it would be a good idea."

I said, "I thought you were sweet on Ellen MacNab?"

He said, "That was when I was young. But her father's only a gillie, you see."

He says Ulick will go to Sandhurst in two years and eventually marry Lilibet York.

22nd July 1935

Freddie Crosbie is having dinner with Ernest this evening, at Ernest's request.

23rd July 1935

Lunch with Pips, Ethel, and Hattie. The top and bottom of Freddie's dinner with Ernest was that Ernest is coming to the end of his patience and is giving Wally till the New Year to decide.

I said, "To decide what?"

Pips said, "To tinkle in the pot or get off it."

Ethel said, "To decide whether she's going to get a divorce and marry the Prince."

Ethel's only a visitor here. She doesn't understand how these things work.

I said, "She can't marry him. David has to marry someone who can be Queen. She has to have the right blood and no previous husbands."

Hattie said, "Anyway, what's Ernest doing telling Freddie this? He should be telling Wally."

Pips says Freddie was there as a sounding board. She said, "Ernest doesn't really know what he's doing anymore. He was such a fan of the Royalties. Like a dog with two tails, to have Wales dropping by. He wants to make a stand, tell Wales to back off, but he can't bring himself to do it. It's against everything Ernest ever believed in, poor sap."

Hattie said, "Of course, there is another possibility for Wally. If David gave up the succession, he could marry her."

The silliest idea I ever heard.

I said, "What would he do?"

Hattie said, "I don't know. Putter around his garden. Take Wally shopping. It's just an idea. He's got three brothers, so there'll always be someone who can be King."

I don't agree. If you took Bertie York and Kent and Harry and put them all together, you still couldn't make a king out of them.

I said, "What I want to know is, why now? Ernest's known about everything for months, but he was grateful enough to go to the Jubilee Ball."

Pips says it's a lot of little things. The sapphires, the emeralds, the phone calls at all hours, Mr. Loo destroying his Aristophanes.

25th July 1935

To Bond Street with Wally for last-minute shoes. Ernest left for New York this morning. I said, "Everything all right?" She said, "Perfectly."

So much for the issuing of deadlines.

I said, "What would you do if David asked you to marry him?"

She laughed. She said, "Remind him he's the next King. Remind him things like that only happen in fairy stories."

I said, "And what would you do if he turned down the job of King so he could marry you?"

"Run!" she said.

28th July 1935

Lunch with George Lightfoot, who hardly spoke a word and allowed his turbot to go cold. I said, "Are you sick?"

"No," he said, "I'm in the pink. I just wanted to say, I'm very fond of you, Maybell."

I believe he's in love with me. Such a dear. He's far too boyish for me, of course, too virginal. It will take a man of the world to interest me in *that* way. Poor George. I just laughed gaily and told him I regard him as the brother I never had. He took it very well. Perhaps by the time I get back from Cannes, he'll be over it.

Tonight the train to Nice. Judson and Hattie, Whitlow and Gladys, Boss and Ethel. Oxer Bettenbrooke is equerrying.

4th August 1935, Villa Le Roc

Rock Cholmondeley's villa is well equipped but not luxurious. It has tennis courts, a swimming pool, sail boats, two Bugattis. A man's home.

5th August 1935

Judson and Whitlow have found bicycles and gone off exploring. Boss is swimming laps. HRH is doing needlepoint on the terrace, and leaping up and down to adjust Wally's sunshade. Winston and Clemmie Churchill are staying at the next villa and dropped by with their youngest girl. Clemmie looked a picture of elegance in vanilla silk and a big straw hat. Winston's plug ugly. HRH tried to engage him on the subject of what's to be done about the working man, but he seemed not to be in the mood for political debate. In fact, I rather thought he was quietly studying Wally.

7th August 1935

The Westminsters' yacht put in last night. We're invited to dinner. HRH is for it, but Wally never likes to be too much in the company of Loelia. So young, so beautiful, so rich.

8th August 1935

The Westminsters are setting off toward Sardinia and wanted us to join them, but Gladys says there's a very real danger of getting boarded and raped and plundered by Communist brigands, so we're all quite off the idea.

The Rogerses have invited us to dinner. Wally said, "Now Ethel, I don't want you and Herman dragging everyone down your Chinese memory lane. It was all a long time ago and it's very boring."

Ethel said, "Nothing much along *my* memory lane, Wally, apart from one dead husband."

14th August 1935

Kath Rogers says she sees a great difference in Wally. "More poise," she said. "For one crazy moment, I almost curtsied to her."

19th August 1935

Daisy Fellowes has arrived with the Bajavidas. There's talk of taking a trip to San Remo to see Lily and the Cavetts. We were supposed to have drinks with the Winston Churchills, but they've gone back to London because of the crisis over Abyssinia.

Wally's strapped for funds. With things as they are, she found it hard to ask Ernest for more.

23rd August 1935

A thunderbolt from Drumcanna. A call came through from Lightfoot.

He said, "I have something to tell you. Doopie and I are going to be married."

It was a very bad line.

I said, "She's mentally deficient."

He said, "She is not. She's adorable."

I said, "Don't do a thing until I get back. You have no idea."

He said, "I knew you'd be beastly. We're getting married tomorrow. Before she changes her mind."

I said, "Promise me there'll be no children."

The line went dead. French telephones. Now I don't possibly have time to get to Drumcanna to stop things. Violet is so incompetent.

Hattie says I'm overreacting. She said, "Doopie's thirty-two and she *is* adorable."

I said, "She can't hear."

Ethel said, "Well, she seems to have managed to hear a proposal."

I doubt it. Lightfoot probably got Flora to mime it.

24th August 1935

Finally got through to Violet. I said, "Are you going to allow this madness to go ahead?"

She said, "It's not madness, Maybell. They make a very fine couple."

They're being married at Crathie this afternoon. Melhuish is giving her away. Then they're going to Skye for the honeymoon. Honeymoon! I'm sure Violet won't have told her what to expect.

Whitlow says probably not a bad thing for one half of a couple to be deaf.

25th August 1935

To the Rogerses for dinner, though I was in no mood for a party. Bob Boothby was there, also on his way back to London because of the Abyssinian situation. He says if there is a war, it will only be a small one. He says the government has done the right thing in demanding sanctions against Italy, because there won't actually be any sanctions but Britain has been seen to make a stand, and the only damage sustained is to our friendship with the Italians, which, knowing the Italians, will soon be regained.

26th August 1935

Hattie insisted on motoring into Nice to buy a wedding gift for Doopie and Lightfoot. A Russian tea urn. I'm not sure I'll give them anything. Sneaking off like that.

Ethel said, "I think you were a bit in love with George Lightfoot yourself."

What silliness! He's too young for me and without a lick of sense, as he's just proved.

29th August 1935

Wally and HRH are back from San Remo, with a wonderful new dance called the rhumba. They've proposed themselves to the Bajavidas in Palm Beach for January. Ethel and Boss are going to come with us to Budapest, Hattie and Judson are heading back to London.

31st August 1935, Hotel Beau Rivage, Geneva

Tension. HRH and Wally had already left for the train station when Oxer realized nothing had been done about gratuities for Cholmondeley's staff. We raked up enough between us, but there was a very frosty moment when we caught up to the advance party and he pointed out the omission.

Wally said, "Why should we leave them anything? They get wages from Cholmondeley."

Ethel said, "But it is usual. They've looked after us very well, and it is usual."

Wally said, "Not for Royalties, it isn't. Don't you know the Prince of Wales doesn't carry money?"

He does sometimes, though. He bought Wally another wrist-watch today.

Bettenbrooke says he won't be sorry to get to Budapest. Jack Aird will be taking over once we get there.

3rd September 1935, The Danube Palace, Budapest

We are very comfortable. HRH has already had a very warm meeting with the Hungarian Regent—proof, if proof were needed, that his British Legion speech has caused no hard feelings at all among Mr. Mussolini's friends.

Gorgeous things on sale here. I'm considering a filigree pin with tiny enameled flowerheads that shake as one moves.

Ethel and Boss have found a wonderful place for coffee and walnut cake.

The Hungarians are a handsome people, although the standard of dentistry could be higher.

4th September 1935

An amusing little spat between Jack Aird and Oxer Bettenbrooke. Oxer had his valise packed ready to leave, when HRH sent down word he wanted to drive to the St. Gellert for a steam bath.

Aird said, "You go. Consider it your final duty."

Oxer said, "Not bloody likely. I'm off."

Aird said, "Well, I'm not wandering naked amongst crazy Magyars."

And he left immediately, with some cockamamie story about having to get a prescription filled. HRH ended up going with Boss Croker and two detectives.

Wally says she'd fire Aird in a heartbeat. I really don't see why we need all these equerries anyway. HRH was only going for a steam and a rubdown, and as Boss says, the visibility was too poor for an assassination attempt.

Charlie Bedaux is here, but not Fern. He's traveling with a scarfaced Frenchman. Ethel believes there are actually several Charlie Bedaux, ready to materialize with a fistful of cigars, anywhere, at any propitious moment.

6th September 1935

To a cellar bar. Dancing to gypsy violins. Wally and HRH are indefatigable. By three a.m., I was ready for bed, but David said, "You mustn't leave. I'm going to ask for some more czardas."

Personally, I couldn't have eaten another thing. In the end, Ethel and I retired and left Boss and Charlie and his friend to see the night through.

9th September 1935

With Wally and Ethel for a sulfur cure. Then to Lukacs for cherry pancakes, to take the nasty taste away.

I've bought the pin with the little flowers. Perhaps I'll give it to Doopie as a wedding gift. Then again, perhaps I won't.

Charlie Bedaux says Hitler is going to purge Germany of Jewish Marxists. Boss says Hitler appears to be spending money he doesn't have, so he'd better be careful not to purge any obliging Jewish bankers.

12th September 1935

To the KrisKros Club. A wonderful floor show. A little pony that can count, tumbling monkeys in romper suits, and a tame black jaguar. Charlie and the scar-faced Mr. Gregoire joined us. Wally says he got his scar in a duel years ago, and he's now a brilliant lawyer. I think she's rather smitten. Jack Aird says, with a shaving shadow like that, Gregoire wouldn't even get past the gate porter in Lincoln's Inn.

15th September 1935

Mr. Mussolini has refused to be cowed by the threat of sanctions. Boss thinks there really may be a war, and we should all go home. Wally says whatever Mussolini does, she's going to Paris first and so is HRH. She says I can please myself.

16th September 1935

To the Pussy Cat Club. Wore my rainbow voile and my new rhinestone fascinator. The floor show consisted of girls wearing nothing but spangles. HRH giggled helplessly.

Tomorrow my first flight. Ethel says there's nothing to it.

19th September 1935, Wilton Place

The joy of traveling the modern way! We had touched down at Croydon, and I was on my way home when I might still have been lurching and bumping across Germany in a railroad car. Wally really has to overcome her fears.

22nd September 1935

Took the little Hungarian brooch to South Audley Street, but Lightfoot and Doopie are apparently still honeymooning on the

Isle of Skye. On to Carlton Gardens, where Violet was in a black mood. Flora has already been expelled from the school in Suffolkshire for setting fires, and was dispatched this morning to Rathgussie to stay with her Aunt Jinty and receive a dose of sharp Scottish discipline. Also, Their Majesties are in low spirits, and Violet seems incapable of enjoying life if the King and Queen are out of sorts. But low spirits are only to be expected. All this rain, all this gloom about Mussolini, after a summer of sunshine and gay balls and cheering crowds. They're experiencing a natural sense of letdown.

Violet said, "They allowed Wales to go to Cannes on the understanding that Wally Simpson's husband would be in the party, which I'm sure was never going to be the case. And now he's taken her to Paris, interfering in government business and dragging her everywhere he goes."

I said, "I think Wally's only there to order clothes."

She said, "Well, Wales isn't ordering clothes. He's meeting high-level people, and Wally is a liability of the first order. She's a liar and an impostor."

Apparently, investigations have been made into the back of the Warfield closet.

It's come to light that her mother was unmarried when she was born, *and* Wally was never christened.

I said, "Well, that can hardly matter now. She's nearly forty."

Violet said, "It certainly does matter. It means she had that wedding in Christ Church, Baltimore, under false pretenses. It sums up everything about her."

I said, "But if that's the case, and her marriage to Win Spencer was irregular, then Ernest is actually her *first* husband, not her second, and there's therefore no reason not to allow her into the Royal Enclosure at Ascot next year."

That silenced her.

25th September 1935

Lunch with Penelope Blythe. She was in the next chair at Monsieur Jules and seemed at a loose end. She and Fergus have had a reconciliation. Boring, but necessary, she said. It had been a question of jingle. She lamented George Lightfoot's disappearance into the maw of marriage. She said, "I know she's your sister, but really! That puts him *hors de combat* for at least two years."

She says Ralph Habberley isn't in Bolivia at all but in Egypt with Ida Coote. He has a cousin there, who's in cotton. Jane Habberley apparently believes his behavior was all brought on by a fall he had riding out with the Quorn Fox Hounds. She wants him to see a brain man in Wigmore Street.

30th September 1935

Dinner with Pips and Freddie. Freddie says Violet is right about one thing: HRH had no business going to Paris and discussing British foreign policy.

He said, "I don't understand the man. He tells people all he wants is Wally at his side and more time for golf, and then he steams off to Paris and starts playing the statesman. Eden is at his wits' end, and so, apparently, is the King. Strictly between these four walls, it might not be a bad thing if David and Wally were to take the plunge, go away somewhere. Give Bertie York a year or two to limber up, I believe he could do the job as well if not better."

2nd October 1935

George and Doopie are back from their honeymoon. Doopie bashful with me, as well she should be. She liked her Hungarian pin. She's very upset about Flora.

"Boor Vora," she kept saying. "Boor Vora. See sood gum live wid us."

George said, "Darling, we have to respect Violet and Melhuish's decision. But I'm sure they'll let her visit. I can't believe Jinty will be anxious to hold on to her for long."

They asked me to stay to dinner, but I see enough kissing and hand-holding at the table when I'm with Wally and her Prince.

4th October 1935

Mr. Mussolini has invaded Abyssinia.

7th October 1935

Wally is back from Paris. Main Bocher is making her five wool suits and three evening gowns, one in balboa, two in charmeuse. She says it was the best part of the vacation, because HRH was kept busy all day brokering peace and she had lots of time for shopping with Elsie Mendl and her useful antique-sleuth, Kenny Opdyke.

Lady Mendl gave a dinner, and the lawyer Gregoire introduced Wally to everyone worth knowing.

I said, "And how's Ernest?"

She said, "I haven't seen him yet. This little Italian war is creating extra work."

I said, "And are you going to Prince Harry's wedding?"

She said, "Prince Harry? Who cares about a minor royal wedding? I'm beyond that."

11th October 1935

Marina Kent has given birth to a son.

15th October 1935

Dinner at the Belchesters. Came: the Westminsters, the Boddie-Fultons, Violet and Melhuish, Oxer Bettenbrooke. Much talk of the situation in Abyssinia. Percy Boddie-Fulton says there's a killing to be made in mining rights. If Danforth Brumby were still alive, he'd be in there already. Anne Belchester has a bee in her bonnet that the League of Nations should be doing something.

Melhuish said, "You're wrong, Anne. In these little African situations, it's almost always best to do nothing. It's no use baying for sanctions and then finding them left on one's hands, like yesterday's herrings."

Fiona Boddie-Fulton said, "What I'd like to know is, what does Wales think he's up to, sticking in his silly oar? Is he trying to send the King to an early grave?"

Violet tried to hush her, but the Belchesters' hock was talking.

She said, "No, Violet, Oxer is a member of the Inner Circle. I think he should explain."

Oxer said, "Nothing to do with me. Ask Aird. All I did was pay the bills and oil the wheels from Cannes to Budapest."

I said, "That's funny. I thought Boss Croker paid most of the bills and Ladbroke oiled the wheels."

Much laughter. Belchester said, "*Henry VI*, Part II. And that's my only word on the subject."

I said, "And what does that mean?"

He said, "York is the worthier. That's what it means. Mark my words."

26th October 1935

To Carlton Gardens. Flora is still at Rathgussie.

Ulick said, "Best place for her. One can't go around setting fires. It's completely not done."

I said, "Well, I just hope she doesn't climb out onto any more roofs."

Ulick said, "I can't agree. A cold night on the tiles might do her a world of good."

Took Rory to the Golden Egg.

I said, "Why didn't you tell me Doopie and Lightfoot were planning to get married?"

Sheepish grin.

He said, "Well, I only sort of knew. It wasn't definite until Aunt Doopie said it was. Daddy says it's a lady's privilege to change her mind."

He has a new trick with steel rings.

7th November 1935

Prince Harry has married Alice Montagu-Douglas-whatever her name was, and they've been made the Duke and Duchess of Gloucester. Lightfoot says now the pressure is really on HRH. The one they're looking to for an heir, and he's the only one not married.

I said, "Just because you rushed into things. David has plenty of time. He's young for his age."

16th November 1935

Wally and Ernest seem to be over their difficulties. Wally's stayed home every evening this week, and now they've gone to the Perry Brownlows for the weekend.

I, on the other hand, am invited to Fort Belvedere!

17th November 1935, Fort Belvedere

Dickie and Edwina Mountbatten are here with their two little girls. HRH seems to dote on them. Dickie's such a fusspot, always checking his timepiece and squaring things away. He must be the bane of his sailors' lives. Edwina is much more relaxed. She's quite willing to stretch her long legs on a couch and leaf through a magazine. Also here, Bernie and Zita Cavett and the Erlangers. Hattie says the reason Edwina Mountbatten acts the tiniest bit *grand* is a sense of inferiority, because Dickie's a royal and all she brought to the marriage was pots of money.

I said, "Dickie's only a minor royal. And there's nothing wrong with money. I'm sure you've been glad of Judson's."

"Well," she said, "at least Judson's isn't *Jewish* money."

Took morning tea with HRH after our calisthenics.

He said, "Do you know what I'd really like to do, Maybell? I'd like to take Wally and run away to my place in Canada. Leave the world behind."

I don't really see Wally as a rancher's wife. Alberta would be a terribly long way to come for fittings, but I didn't have the heart to say so. I think I'd better warn Wally. Just when things seemed to be settling down.

20th November 1935, Wilton Place

Lunch with Pips. She, too, thinks the worst of the storm has now passed. She said, "All credit to Ernest. He's sweated it out and now he may well get his wife back. If he really wants her. Talk about used goods!"

Hattie thinks the Palace are about to rustle up a princess and get a ring on her finger immediately.

I said, "David didn't say anything when I talked to him."

She said, "It'll probably be in the bag before he realizes what's going on. Like giving a dog a worm powder."

25th November 1935

If Flora continues to keep her slate clean, she's to be allowed back to London for Christmas. The Cavetts want me for Christmas night, so that all works out rather well. Wally and Ernest have accepted, too.

I said, "All quiet on the home front?"

"Yes," she said. "Almost too quiet."

9th December 1935

Ernest is in Stockholm. HRH came to Bryanston Court for drinks but couldn't stay to dinner. His Aunt Toria died today, so he had to go and condole with Their Majesties. He says she was a hypochondriac and an old shrew but she cheered the King up with her complaining so he's bound to feel her loss greatly, which fore-shadows an even gloomier Christmas than usual.

12th December 1935

My Christmas plans have fallen into place. On Christmas Eve, dinner at the Erlangers. On Christmas afternoon, tea at Carlton Gardens, then Kettle will drive me to the Cavetts in Surrey. Wally's joyful at the prospect of my company there. She says my job will be to engage Ernest in gay chitchat if HRH's telephone calls become too frequent. As she says, *she* doesn't particularly welcome all those calls, either. They go on forever and never amount to anything. But she's determined to see it out now and hopes Ernest can be soothed into doing the same. Well, if anyone can pull it off it's Wally. Still, I do feel for Ernest. He's not a bad husband by any stretch.

21st December 1935, Fort Belvedere

Our last royal weekend for a while. Ernest has made himself busy in town. HRH leaves for Sandringham tomorrow afternoon, so he and Wally have exchanged Christmas jewels. From her to him, a set of onyx dress links. From him to her, a gold clasp bracelet set with three rubies. I gave him a red Japanese maple. I said, "To save you going away to Canada, sir." He laughed. Almost the only time I've heard laughter today.

Poots Butler says Humphrey and Fruity keep trying to have a man-to-man chat with the Prince, but so far they haven't managed to separate him from Wally.

She said, "You and I have to take her away for an hour or two tomorrow morning. It has to be done."

I said, "Wally's not the problem. I'm sure she'd love to go into town. The problem is getting David to let her out of his sight. He's not going to see her for three weeks."

She said, "Well, Humphrey's determined to have this out with him. The King won't stand for any more half-truths and gossip about Wally. He's in an absolutely thundering mood. David has to be made to understand. The party's over."

22nd December 1935

Wally came to church with me, Poots, and Baba. It was quite charming and took only forty-five minutes. HRH tried to talk her out of it, but she insisted that he see Fruity and Humphrey. She said, "They're only courtiers, darling. Don't be scared of them. You're the Prince of Wales."

When we got back, Humphrey and Fruity were fuming over very early whiskies, and HRH was bubbling away, talking about taking Wally to Palm Beach in the New Year.

Baba said, "No joy?"

Fruity said, "It went in one ear and out the other."

Baba said, "Not surprising. There's very little in between to stop it."

27th December 1935, chez Cavett, Teddington

Flora was back from Rathgussie in time for Christmas. A little thinner. She sat between me and Doopie at Carlton Gardens and hardly said a word. Violet was very much on edge, checking all the time that the help hadn't left matches lying around, whispering to Lightfoot not to flaunt his cigarette lighter. He said, "I think you're worrying unnecessarily, Vee. She's tried her hand at fires and all it bought her was a long stretch at Rathgussie. I don't believe it'll happen again. She may try other types of mayhem, but I think we're safe from being roasted."

Rory thinks it might be better if they didn't send her to any more schools for a while. He said, "She just likes playing with her dolls. My friend Massingham's sister only likes riding her pony. Girls can get away with that kind of thing, because they'll never have to go into Parliament or the Colonial Service or anything."

Lightfoot said, "I don't know. Lady Astor's in the Commons, never forget."

Ulick said, "And that surely strengthens the argument against educating girls."

Much talk, too, about the divinely handsome Mr. Eden who is the new Foreign Secretary. Melhuish doesn't care for him. He says Eden seems determined to make an example of Mussolini.

He said, "Why not let him have Abyssinia? No one else wants it, except a few spear carriers and that strange cove Selassie."

Rory put on a little display of conjuring for us after tea and asked Flora to be his assistant. He said it was safer than allowing her to sit in the audience shouting out all his magic secrets.

I gave her a compendium of board games. It will give her an interest, wherever she ends up. She said, "I expect I'll be going to live with Doopie and Uncle Lightfoot."

The poor deluded child.

Bernie and Zita have the Milwaukee Gunters staying, which is a further diversion for Ernest. The Gunters are Ernest's kind of people, and Bernie and Zita are very gay hosts. There's never a quiet moment. HRH called three times, and then Wally went out for a drive with Zita, leaving me to speak to him if he called again, which, of course, he did.

He sounded so disappointed. He said, "Ask her to call me the moment she returns, no matter how late. You can't imagine how time drags without her."

I said, "What have you been doing, sir?"

"Oh, just helping Her Majesty with a jigsaw puzzle," he said. "I expect Wally's been dancing everyone off their feet?"

2nd January 1936, Wilton Place

We toasted the New Year at the Embassy Club, then went on to the Berkeley in the hope that a change of scene would make us feel peppier, but somehow the evening never took off. Came: the Erlangers, the Cavetts, Daisy Fellowes, Wally, and her friend Kenny Opdyke who's in town from Paris. I don't very much like Kenny, he has sly eyes. The Crosbies didn't show. Pips says Freddie's in a depression because there'll probably be another war. Judson says it's more likely he's depressed because he's going to be forty.

Hattie was scandalized by the way Wally was flirting with Kenny Opdyke, but I'm certain there can't be anything in it. He flaps his hands around like a great big fairy, so I'm sure there's nothing like *that* between them.

3rd January 1936

Lunch with Pips and Hattie. Hattie still talking about Kenny Opdyke.

She said, "I think she's trying to hurry David along. Make him a little insecure, so he settles some serious money on her."

Pips said, "More likely she's just plain bored. I never thought I'd feel sorry for Wally, but just look at her. She's trapped between Boy David and Deadly Ernest, and neither of them will give her an inch to move. It must be a nightmare."

6th January 1936

Shopping for Palm Beach. A pretty pleated chiffon dance gown and a cotton print playsuit. Wally got two skirted bathing suits and a pair of grosgrain sandals. She says the Bajavidas keep an indoor staff of thirty. She says Kenny Opdyke is an old, old friend and a fruit. I knew it!

9th January 1936

Violet and Melhuish have agreed Flora can stay with Doopie and Lightfoot instead of returning to Rathgussie, but only on condition that she behaves nicely to the tutor they're going to find her, and works hard at her lessons. Violet says she seems very happy and already has her dolls packed and ready for the move.

She said, "Now, this jaunt to Florida, Maybell? Can't you talk Wally out of it? Their Majesties are so distressed about it."

I said, "It's a private vacation, Violet, which a prince is certainly entitled to. And as for Wally, this situation is hardly of her creation. If anything, she's the one who tries to get him to spend more time with his family. But he won't be thrown off. Even if we don't go to Palm Beach, he won't be thrown off."

10th January 1936

HRH has had to cancel our weekend at the Fort. The King has a heavy cold and has deputed him to take over his appointments for the next week. I'm not sorry. I still have a million and one things to do before we sail. How much easier it is for men. A good valet will see to everything.

Wally says the Bajavidas eat everything off gold plates, even hamburger!

13th January 1936

The King's cold is worse. He should take Dr. Collis Browne's linctus.

14th January 1936

Called briefly at South Audley Street. Doopie and Lightfoot have engaged a young woman as a day governess for Flora, and they're getting along very well. She allows the dolls into the schoolroom, including Damned Wales, who, I notice, is back dressed in her flamenco gown. I never saw Flora so happy. Lightfoot says she's fairly ripping through geography and history. Doopie is quite the chatelaine these days. She still sits with her needlework basket close to hand and pretends to defer to Lightfoot, but I believe he actually does whatever she tells him. She calls him "Dordie darlin."

15th January 1936

Drinks at Bryanston Court. The Prince left before Ernest arrived home, and so did I. HRH has two engagements to perform for the King tomorrow morning. If he's still too sick to go out after that, Bertie York and George Kent will have to manage things while we're away.

He wants Wally to go with him to the Fort for the weekend, but I saw her hesitate. She's already had a scene from Ernest about our trip, and the very least he expects is for her to stay at home for a few days and do wifely things. How difficult. A prince who behaves like a husband and a husband who's starting to behave like a prince. No wonder she has ulcers.

16th January 1936

Wally called just before five. We have a crisis on our hands. The King's condition has suddenly worsened, and HRH has hurried back to Sandringham. I wonder how bad he really is. It could just be a ploy to prevent him taking a vacation in Florida. I suppose the rest of us could still go. The Bajavidas will be so disappointed if we cancel.

17th January 1936

Snow overnight. A scratch lunch with Wally, who was pensive. HRH telephoned twice. The King is comfortable but very weak. I said, "What will happen if he dies?"

She said, "He's not going to die. He has a cold."

I said, "But he's an old man. Just say he did die, where would that leave you?"

She said, "It would leave me very nicely, thank you. If David were King, he could see who the hell he liked and do whatever he damn well pleased, and he'd be kept a lot busier."

I think she is just a little bit anxious though. All the newspaper placards say is **THE KING**.

18th January 1936

The King's condition has worsened. The George Kents and the Princess Royal have gone to Sandringham, but HRH told Wally his father is so confused he hardly knows any of them. He and Bertie York are driving down to see the Prime Minister, but this is not to be generally broadcast. Hattie Erlanger says this undoubtedly means that the King is dying and funeral plans have to be discussed.

Padmore is certainly wearing a funereal face, and my breakfast tray was late because everyone below stairs keeps stopping to listen to the wireless bulletins.

Another heavy fall of snow.

19th January 1936

Wally has invited herself to luncheon. David has been calling her at least once an hour and she feels it would be tactful to leave Ernest to enjoy his Sunday nap in peace. She says HRH is desperate over his father's condition. Panic-stricken, in fact. She said, "I don't understand it, Maybell. He's had forty years to get used to the idea of being King, so why the flap now?"

20th January 1936

This evening we should have sailed away to a month of sunshine, but the King is dead, and everything is changed.

Wally and I were in a movie theater, in retreat from the jangling telephone, when things started to happen last night. They broke into the Fredric March feature to post a news bulletin on the screen. *The King's life is drawing peacefully to a close.*

Wally was on her feet immediately. I said, "We may as well see the end of the movie. David will be at the bedside. He won't be calling you."

She said, "Possibly. But if anything happens and he can't get me, he'll go to pieces." We went back to Bryanston Court. Ernest was listening to the wireless, very affectionate with Wally, his usual old self with me. Perhaps he feels he'll soon have Wally to himself again.

The call came almost on the stroke of midnight. I suppose we were among the first people to know. All we heard Wally say was, "Your mother must need consoling, sir. And I'm sure you must have a lot of people waiting to speak to you. But I'll sleep by the telephone. I'll be here."

They played "God Save the King" on the wireless, and Ernest stood to attention throughout. Then he went to bed.

Wally said HRH was almost hysterical. He told her they'd all been at the bedside when the end came. He's not HRH anymore though. He's HM the King.

She was talking to him again as I left, soothing him like he was a fretful baby. "There's nothing to fear," I heard her say. "*Einums Deinums* will still take care of her boy."

She was very tender with him.

Everything today has seemed muffled by fatigue and snow and a dead king. They fired cannons before it was daylight. Pips says Freddie was in the Commons by seven, ready to swear his oath to the new monarch. He's to be King Edward VIII, but I shall never be able to think of him as any such thing. To me, he'll always be yellow-haired David.

21st January 1936

Dinner with Pips and Freddie. Freddie said, "What's Wally up to? Melting down the Crown Jewels?" I don't know about that, but she's certainly at St. James's Palace taking care of her King.

HRH—except now I must get into the habit of calling him HM—HM and Bertie York flew down this afternoon, ready for tomorrow's proclamation, which is not the same thing as a coronation, apparently. That will come later, perhaps not till next year. He's the first King of England ever to travel by airplane. Advance warning to all those wheezing old courtiers that a new era has dawned.

Violet called to see if I wanted to go with her to hear him proclamated. I said, "I've already made arrangements. I'll be watching with Wally and His Majesty."

She said, "I think you've been misinformed, Maybell. A king doesn't watch his own proclamation. And as for Wally, she might take her cue and fade into oblivion."

Violet never misses an opportunity.

22nd January 1936

I always thought St. James's was rather a toy-town-looking palace, and Friary Court made a very dull setting for a proclamation. Oxer Bettenbrooke found us a window to watch from just as the heralds' carriages began arriving. The trumpeters came out onto a balcony, all scarlet-and-gold, and played a fanfare, and then a twenty-five-gun salute began on Horse Guards' Parade, so we couldn't hear the words that were being read.

Anyway, Violet was wrong, because HM *did* watch with us, the first sovereign ever to do so. Another sign that he's going to do things in his own, modern way.

Edward Albert Christian George Andrew Patrick David, King of the United Kingdom of Great Britain and Ireland and Emperor of India.

He had Ladbroke drop us off at Bryanston Court on his way back to Sandringham. The King of England dropped us off! We laughed and laughed about that.

I said, "Now what?"

She said, "Well, I can hardly leave him at a time like this."

23rd January 1936

HM has been dealt a terrible blow. His father's will was read last evening, and he's been left nothing. Wally called me first thing.

I said, "Well, he can't be penniless. He's the King."

She said, "He has income from his duchies, but that's not the point. The brothers and sister get all that money when David's the one who'll have the much greater expenses. It's sheer vindictiveness. He's always said his father preferred all the others, and there it is."

Dinner with Lightfoot and Doopie. Lightfoot said, "But he ought to be able to live perfectly well on what he has, provided he eases up on the purchase of sparklers for Wally."

I said, "I'd have thought the need for the woman in his life to outsparkle all others is greater than ever."

He said, "That depends on what one means by 'the woman in his life.' When he chooses his Queen, she'll have all the *richesse* of the family jewels at her disposal, not to mention the Crown regalia. But that won't be Wally. So, Wally's sparkle will have to be bought out of income."

Doopie said, "He good sell Buggingham Balass."

They brought the old King back to London today for the lying in state. They say there are already long lines to view the coffin, but Wally says we won't have to queue. The funeral is at Windsor on Tuesday.

24th January 1936

Penelope Blythe forced herself on me for lunch. She says when the gun carriage was bringing the coffin to Westminster Hall, the jeweled cross on the top of the Imperial Crown fell off and rolled along the street. She says it's an omen. Penelope is one of the silliest people I know.

To Selfridges for black stockings.

25th January 1936

To Westminster Hall with Wally and Pips. We were ushered in through the Private Members' entrance. The coffin is covered with a purple cloth. There's the crown, back in one piece, and one small family wreath. There's an officer of one of the Household brigades guarding each corner of the catafalque. I never felt such cold. When we came out, there was a car waiting to take Wally to St. James's Palace.

Pips said, "She's going to find it very hard to give up the Waiting Car treatment."

I don't know that she is going to give it up.

Tea at Carlton Gardens. Anne Belchester was there, and Ena Spain, come for the funeral. According to Melhuish, it was a Grenadier sergeant major who saw the cross fall off the crown and scooped it out of the gutter, without even breaking step.

Anne Belchester asked after Wally. She said, "I suppose she'll retire to the country now?"

Ena Spain said, "I don't see why? As long as she behaves in a seemly way. Kings always have mistresses."

Anne said, "But one would expect her to withdraw, at least while he's choosing a Queen."

Violet said, "And anyway, Ena, you're wrong. Kings don't always have mistresses. His father never did."

Ena said, "Then he was the exception. I should know."

Poor Ena.

26th January 1936

Ernest has had to go to Hamburg on business. Freddie saw him at his club and he told him that he believes everything will now be resolved. He said, "A King is a very different person than a Prince, Freddie. His Majesty will now move far away from our humble orbit."

Loelia Westminster's mother is making one of her windows available to me and Wally for the funeral procession. They have to take the coffin from Westminster Hall to Paddington Station for the journey to Windsor. Imagine having to go to a railroad station even in death!

28th January 1936

Another gray, bitter morning, and Pall Mall was lined with gray, silent people. The only sounds were the muffled drums and the boots of the Foot Guards. The coffin was borne on a gun carriage, with HM walking behind. He looked up at our window. He knew exactly where Wally would be. I thought how small he seemed in his greatcoat and that funny old bicorn hat. Bertie York, George Kent, and Harry Gloucester walked behind him. Then, as they turned into St. James's Street, the Queen's carriage came into view. She sat very stately, in a black cloth coat and a fox capelet.

All the shops were closed for the day, so we rustled up Pips and Hattie and went to the Savoy for an early lunch. Wally says she's going to get Elsie Mendl's decorator boys in to redo Buckingham Palace. She says it needs a clean sweep and not only the décor. There are courtiers who are practically mummified they've been around so long. Perry Brownlow's going to be Lord-in-Waiting, which will be a very good thing. But Rock Cholmondeley is the new Lord Great Chamberlain, which may not be such good news, with Sybil thick as thieves with the Bertie Yorks and the old Queen.

Hattie said, "Well, you can't sack the Lord Great Chamberlain, Wally. It's hereditary."

Wally said, "*Has* been hereditary. Don't forget, Hattie, you're under new management now."

I don't think the Lord Great Chamberlain is likely to give Wally much trouble, whoever's in the job. From what I've gleaned, he's only a kind of stage manager. Once the Coronation's been held, he doesn't seem to have a whole lot to do.

Alex Hardinge is to stay on as Private Secretary. Wally said, "We'll see about that."

She won't even consider rebooking our passage and going to the Bajavidas. She says the King can't go, and if he can't, she can't.

1st February 1936

With Pips to buy a christening gift for some distant Crosbie infant. When we got back to Halkin Street, we found Freddie in the drawing room, struggling to find the right thing to say to a clearly overwrought Ernest. Freddie must have been praying for our return. As soon as Ernest saw me, he erupted. He said, "She's at Windsor, Maybell. Did you know she was going? Windsor! And the old King barely cold in his grave."

I can honestly say I didn't know. I'd rather assumed our week-ends would go the same way as Palm Beach house parties, for a while. Violet gives the impression that we're all supposed to sit around dabbing our eyes with black-edged handkerchieves for six months. We're even excused from going to the opera.

Ernest said, "I may not have as much pep as His Majesty, but I think I know how to behave. Well, the King obviously takes Court Mourning rather lightly, so I see no reason to hold back. I'm going to speak to him. The time has come."

Pips said, "Better not to go to the Castle, Ernest. You could get arrested."

He said, "Don't worry. I shall simply wait for him to turn up for cocktails. I'm sure I shan't have long to wait. He seems so very attached to my drinks' cart."

He went off very pink and puffed up, his good-byes rather formal.

He said, "I bear you no ill will, Maybell. I know Wally inspires great loyalty, and I'm glad she has yours. She's sailing into uncharted waters. She's going to need her friends more than ever."

Pips said, "Poor sap. The sooner he leaves London the better."

Freddie says the straw that finally broke poor Ernest's back was the blocking of his application to become a Freemason. Freddie said, "It's because his wife is known to 'associate' with another member of the Lodge. In short, HM the King. But I promised I'd have a word with Prosper Frith. He might be willing to propose Ernest for his Lodge."

2nd February 1936

Ernest has moved out to his club. Wally's looking very strained.

6th February 1936

A chilling scene at Bryanston Court this afternoon. We'd just sat down to tea when Ernest arrived to collect more of his things. I made to leave, but he asked me to stay. He said, "As well you hear this, Maybell, in case Wally fails to understand me. Our marriage is at an end. I'll have my books collected later in the week."

Wally said, "You can see I'm not well. Why are you making a scene now?"

He said, "Because an hour ago, His Majesty informed me he intends to marry you and be crowned with you at his side."

Wally said, "This is sheer fantasy. You know it can't happen. Tell him, Maybell. We all know it's out of the question."

Ernest said, "So we're all told, but I've begun to see that nothing's impossible for a king. He tells me he's already settled £300,000 on you, as a token of his sincerity. I wonder, Wally, you never thought to mention it to me."

I wonder she never thought to mention it to me.

She said, "I didn't say anything because the papers haven't been signed, and as I recall, it's only £100,000. It's in recognition of the expense we've been put to by our friendship with him."

Ernest said, "I never counted the cost of having the Prince of Wales at my table. Not till now."

Well, that's not strictly true. He's always gone through the housekeeping books, querying every little item of expenditure. But still, it was too awful a moment. A man should never walk out on his wife while they have company.

She cried after he left, but I think they were tears of exasperation, not sorrow.

Later on, she said, "He'll change his mind when he realizes what a vulnerable position he's putting me in. Once he's calmed down."

But I think he was horribly calm throughout. I think between them, Ernest and HM King have outmaneuvered her.

9th February 1936, Fort Belvedere

No change of heart from Ernest. He's having his books packed while Wally's out of the house.

Went up to the Castle to watch *King Kong*. The place is an unmanageable pile. If HM has any sense, he'll keep the Fort on for weekends and only use the Castle for big State affairs. Wally had some fun with those poker-faced footmen. She made them serve refreshments on their knees so as not to cast shadows on the screen and ruin the movie.

10th February 1936, Wilton Place

Wally stayed on at the Fort this morning, to talk to HM about "The Situation."

A message from Ernest when I returned home. Would I be kind enough to see him? He came at four, very composed, dapper as ever.

He said, "I owe you an apology. My behavior last week was unpardonable. I allowed passion to overrule good manners."

I said, "The most important thing is, you mustn't leave Wally. She's devastated."

He said, "Only devastated that things haven't gone according to her plan. I don't think anyone can accuse me of being hotheaded. I've been more patient than most. She's made her bed, Maybell, and now she must lie in it."

I said, "It's just that all those times when David used to send for her you never seemed to mind."

He said, "I did mind, but there was the honor of a royal friendship to consider. I minded very much more when all of London began laughing behind my back. And now, with money settled on her, and talk of marriage, well, there's nothing left for me but to go."

I said, "So, are you divorcing her?"

He said, "I believe the procedure is for her to divorce me. Don't worry. I'm not going to make a fuss. I'll cooperate."

He kissed me on both cheeks when he left. He said, "Take care of her for me, Maybell."

I called Pips and we went directly to Wally's. She was sitting in her coat and hat, drinking brandy. She'd just come from York House.

She said, "David has lost his mind. He doesn't seem to realize, we can't allow Ernest to leave me. It's going to ruin everything and achieve nothing."

Pips said, "Well, what about if *you* leave David? Wouldn't that settle it, if you want to keep Ernest?"

Wally said, "One doesn't just *leave* the King. Especially not David. Anything might happen. God, I'm so tired."

Red carnations everywhere. I said, "And what about von Ribbentrop? I see he's still pursuing you. No wonder you're tired."

She said, "Those flowers aren't for me. They're for *us*. Me and David. And they're not from Ribbentrop. They're from Adolf Hitler. He's invited us to visit with him in the summer."

Pips said, "Well, then. I won't waste any more time commiserating with you. Seems to me you have everything under control."

14th February 1936

HM has given Wally a gold sweetheart locket set with aquamarines. He also seems to have persuaded her that becoming Queen isn't impossible, after all. Apparently, he's gone into it with a brilliant lawyer, and there's a very simple way out of this muddle. Wally can have both her marriages annulled on the grounds that, to all intents and purposes, she's a virgin.

I said, "Are you?"

She said, "To all intents and purposes, yes."

Extraordinary.

I said, "But if you become Queen, won't you have to have a baby?"

"Not at all," she said. "The Yorks are in line after David, and they have those two girls. One of them can succeed."

Judson Erlanger says if Wally's a virgin he's the King of Siam, but Freddie says HM's lawyer is Walter Monckton, and if anyone can achieve miracles, Monckton can.

Penelope Blythe says Wally might want to think twice about seeking annulments. She says doctors could be brought in to give evidence, not to mention two discarded husbands.

19th February 1936

A little lunch party at Bryanston Court for Lily Drax-Pfaffenhof. She's encouraging Wally to explore every possible way for HM to marry her, and Wally certainly seems to be changing her tune. Yesterday, she said, "There's no such thing as the impossible. Read the history books."

Today, she said, "I have my detractors, of course, but all I need is a little time. The public just needs to get to know me. I could be very popular. I'm hardworking. I've pulled myself up by my own boot straps. And they'll love my clothes."

Lily said, "And when you're Queen, I wonder who you'll choose as your Lady-of-the-Bedchamber?"

"Yes," she said. "I wonder who!"

The Socialists got elected in Spain. I don't imagine poor Ena would want to go back now even if they asked her.

20th February 1936

Wally is looking into having her family tree tidied up. She's tired of HM's old courtiers looking down their noses at her. As she says, it's no fault of hers that her parents weren't married until after her birth. Her father was a consumptive and forbidden to marry. And the only reason her mother sometimes had to charge her guests rent was the sheer meanness of the Warfields. Her uncle Sol Warfield had plenty of money. He just never missed an opportunity to remind Wally's mother she was a charity case.

24th February 1936

Tea at Carlton Gardens. Violet says HM is making a fool of himself talking about a throne for Wally. She said, "All the annulments in the world won't make her suitable to be Queen, so she may as well hang on to the husband she has."

Doopie looked in with Flora very nicely dressed in a tartan skirt and a cardigan set. I was just thinking there was hope yet of making a lady of her, when she said, "Aunt Bayba, does Damned Wales still give The Wally lots of gisses? Ulick says he's asking for a bloody thrashing."

Violet busied herself with the teacups.

Sunday, to Paris. Wally has a very long shopping list. Now HM is free of his killjoy father, he intends taking a villa near Cannes and vacationing with whomsoever he pleases.

3rd March 1936, Meurice Hotel, Paris

To Elsie Mendl's pied-à-terre for a working luncheon. Every one of HM's homes is going to require complete refurbishment, and Wally's going to make sure Johnnie MacMullen does everything.

To the Eugene Rothschilds for drinks. Tomorrow, to Paquin for light woolen wraps and to Hermès for clutch purses.

5th March 1936

Wally has ordered Chinese side-buttoned evening sheaths in coral, lime, and hyacinth. Tomorrow, daywear, shoes, lingerie.

7th March 1936

We've decided on candy-colored ginghams from Schiaparelli, to be worn with canvas pumps and flowered barrettes. A very youthful, carefree look.

Mr. Hitler has entered the Rhineland.

8th March 1936

Not a good day. One sales clerk wouldn't allow Wally to take a little musical box on approval, and another, at Genevieve, was very offhand about the delay with Wally's camisoles. I don't think these people realize quite who she is. Then, at Chez Raphael, they served her omelette too *baveuse*.

She told them, "I don't know about the Rhineland. I hope Hitler invades you, and soon."

13th March 1936, Wilton Place

HM's brother-in-law Earl Harewood has made a speech to the British Legion condemning Hitler and entirely contradicting everything HM said in his speech about the avoidance of future wars. Wally's dictated a note for HM to send to Harewood, telling him to keep his warmongering opinions to himself.

14th March 1936

Dinner at the Belchesters. Came: the Crosbies, the Metcalfes, and the Humphrey Butlers. Belchester said Wally might as well be crowned next week, because she's obviously running everything already.

Fruity says the amazing thing is, HM now seems to be enjoying his new role, after all that talk of not being cut out to be King. He said, "Say what you like, I think it has to be down to Wally. She invigorates him."

Anne Belchester said, "But come on, Fruity, she can never be a serious contender as a wife."

Fruity said, "If you'd asked me a month ago, I'd have agreed, but I'm beginning to think she's essential. If Monckton can fix it for her, the country will get a much more effective King."

Belchester said, "Never heard anything like it in my life. Invigorates him! He needs a dose of salts."

21st March 1936, Fort Belvedere

Just me, Wally, and the Erlangers. Ernest has gone to a country hotel to have breakfast in bed with a floozie and get his moral turpitude certified.

I said, "How long till you'll be free to marry David?"

She said, "Don't say that. Don't ever say that. You never know who may be listening. I'm not divorcing Ernest so I can marry David. I'm divorcing him because he abandoned me and he's about to become an adulterer. Be clear about that, Maybell. I am the innocent party."

Such a charade.

25th March 1936, Wilton Place

To the Westminsters. A dinner for the von Ribbentrops. Came: Violet and Melhuish, Jimmy Graham, Ava Ribblesdale, Jack Aird, and the Crosbies. Everyone is agreed that it was only a matter of time till the Germans were permitted back into the Rhineland, so all Hitler has done is to anticipate the inevitable, and there won't be any retaliation from the French, who are shivering in their shoes. So we can all carry on as before. Aird says HM is making economies right and left, and the staff at Sandringham fear for their positions.

Melhuish said, "That's Wales all over. Sack a few gardeners so he can buy another bangle for his tootsie. And I hear he's had the clocks changed, too, so there goes another tradition. Sandringham Time has always been half an hour ahead, and Balmoral Time, for as long as I remember, and my father before me. I suppose the next thing, he'll decide he's going to be crowned wearing a check suit. We'll be seeing our monarch reviewing his troops in golf knickers. Mark my words."

Violet darting anxious looks in my direction, trying to hush him with light remarks about their new terrier, but he was enjoying the sound of his own voice. It's finally dawning on her. They're going to live the rest of their days under a King who doesn't like them any more than they like him. The old Queen's going to be retired to a little palace somewhere, Wally will be declared a virgin, and Violet and Melhuish will be outcasts forevermore.

Pips says Ribbentrop makes her think of a commercial salesman.

29th March 1936, Fort Belvedere

HM in good spirits this morning in spite of a telling-off from Wally last evening because he stood his nightcap glass on top of some official papers and left a ring mark. Wally says Hardinge is a complete martinet over Cabinet papers and has a fit if he thinks HM has been perusing them in the drawing room. It's about confidentiality. But our weekend parties are small while Court mourning prevails, just the Inner Circle, and I'm sure we're all to be trusted with any Government secrets we happen upon. And Wally sees absolutely everything anyway. Otherwise, how could she advise the King?

3rd April 1936, Sunninghills

At the Crokers, for their first weekend party of the season. They've taken their usual house. Ethel says all their American friends are lining up to come to Merrie England and meet the King.

She's wondering whether they'll be invited to the Coronation. I was able to put her mind at rest. All HM's *true* friends will be invited. It's people like the Devonshires and the Melhuishes, who so blithely take for granted that they're the crème de la crème, *they* may as well put their Court costumes in mothballs.

The postage-stamp people have gone ahead without permission and made a design showing HM in right profile. Wally says it'll have to be changed. He looks so much more kingly from the left. Alex Hardinge says King George was pictured from the left, and it's the tradition to alternate, but he has to understand, David isn't going to be that kind of King. If something needs changing, he won't be afraid to change it. As Lightfoot says, Wally is throwing wide the windows, and HM is enjoying the breeze that's blowing between his ears.

8th April 1936, Wilton Place

With Violet to a charitable sale of work. Bought raffia bread baskets but omitted to bring them home. The person selling them was worryingly vague as to whether they had been made *by* lepers or in *aid* of lepers. Jane Habberley was manning the tea urn. Marina Greece looked in and bought a sponge cake. Ettie Desborough won a bottle of sherry wine. I must say, the lepers seem to know everyone.

Friday is Good Friday, and I've promised to go to Fergus and Penelope Blythe's for Easter weekend. Pips says we all have our crosses to bear. She and Freddie are also invited and have begged a ride with me.

13th April 1936

The Halifaxes were at Leake Priory for Easter. Halifax says HM is receiving bad advice from Walter Monckton if it's persuading him he can ever marry Wally. He said, "The kindest thing would be for their friends to deprive the idea of oxygen and allow it to die."

Pips said, "That's you, Maybell. Can't you take Wally away somewhere?"

I said, "Wally's hardly the problem. It isn't her fault if they can't come up with a single tempting princess. Marriage wasn't her idea."

Halifax said, "Indeed. From what I hear of Mrs. Simpson, she doesn't seem terribly suited to the condition."

He has the perfect face for running a funeral parlor.

Wally got diamond-and-filigree earclips from David for Easter.

15th April 1936

Ambassador von Hoesch is dead. I only saw him on Monday.

He waved to me as Kettle turned into Carlton Terrace. Fifty-five. They say it was a heart attack.

Wally said, "It doesn't make a lot of difference. He was about to be recalled anyway." She gets to hear everything now she helps HM go through all those official papers every day.

She says Leo was shaky on a number of key points. She never did like him. I suppose she'll be rooting for Ribbensnob as his replacement.

Pips says the papers HM receives in his Despatch Boxes are confidential government papers and not intended for Wally's eyes. I don't see what difference it makes. HM practically asks her advice before he blows his nose, so I'm sure he wouldn't sign anything important without checking with her.

17th April 1936

With Violet and Melhuish to pay our last respects to Leo von Hoesch. The Grenadier Guards provided an escort for his coffin as far as Victoria railroad station.

He gave such wonderful parties.

20th April 1936

HM is taking Wally to Royal Lodge to have tea with the Yorks. She's going to wear a polka dot silk and matinee pearls.

21st April 1936

Wally says yesterday was an ordeal not to be repeated. Bertie York hardly spoke a word, and the wife didn't have a serious thought in her head. Apparently, she just twittered to HM about his bagpipe compositions and didn't ask Wally anything about herself. But then, what could she have asked? There's so much about Wally one no longer dare mention, and anyway, I'm sure Elizabeth York has it all unabridged from Violet.

Wally said, "I suppose I daunted her. She's like a little pink marshmallow."

26th April 1936

Luncheon at South Audley Street. Lightfoot believes Leo von Hoesch was bumped off on orders from Berlin. Doopie shaking her head and saying, "Dordie, nod in vront a Vora."

Flora's reading is coming on very well with this new tutor, and they do singing, too. She couldn't carry a tune in a bucket, but she's very enthusiastic.

4th May 1936

To the Crosbies. Freddie says HM and Wally went together to Walter Monckton's chambers this morning. He said, "What can David have been thinking? If he insists on Wally using his lawyer, which is a bad idea, he certainly mustn't be seen to attend their conferences. It makes it look as though he's a party to the case."

Pips said, "Oh please! It's only the difference between a bare-faced lie and a polite pretense."

Freddie says that's a very important difference. He's suggested I have a word with Wally. He says when the case is called, if the judge has any doubts about Wally being an innocent party, she just won't get her divorce, King's lawyer or no.

5th May 1936

Wally says HM went with her to see Monckton purely as a friend.

I said, "If you needed support, surely I was the one to ask?"

She said, "Well, yes, but David insisted. Frankly, I'd rather have had you there, Maybell. You don't fuss."

I told her what Freddie said. She said, "Oh, but I'm not using Monckton. I just went to him for a recommendation. I'm using a man called Goddard. He's supposed to be very good."

7th May 1936

Marina Kent is expecting again. Wally has hired Theodore Goddard.

10th May 1936

I'm invited to a little reception at the compound on Tuesday, to meet the Charles Lindberghs. They've come to Europe to get over that sad business with their baby.

Wally ruffled not to have been invited. I called Judson immediately and pointed out the oversight. This is no time to be making an enemy of the future Queen of England.

11th May 1936

The date for HM's Coronation has been announced. It will take place one year from tomorrow. Violet says a coronation is a day of enormous import, and ancient ceremonial, and can't be put on at the drop of a hat. Well, I'm sure it wouldn't take me and Wally a year to organize it. Heavens, we've worked out whole complicated dinner *placements* while having our toenails painted.

Freddie says if he's determined to marry Wally, it would make sense to wait until after he's been crowned, but we all know he wants Wally crowned beside him.

Wally's pretending to be bored with the subject and refuses to comment. Her ulcers have flared up again. Her invitation to the Lindbergh reception arrived by special messenger.

12th May 1936

Colonel Lindbergh is very good-looking. "Just plain gorgeous," was Wally's appraisal. She didn't rate the wife, but she's going to have them to dinner at York House anyway.

Hattie Erlanger has heard a whisper about HM and a Danish princess.

14th May 1936

Violet says Princess Alexandrine of Denmark is indeed a strong possibility. She's only twenty-one, but I guess he's missed the boat with the older ones.

So, perhaps everything can be resolved, after all. Wally will get to keep the money HM has settled on her, and she'll be free of Ernest. She could do what Elsie Mendl did and marry a titled pansy. Leave Princess Alexandrine to supply the nation with royal babies. It sounds perfect to me, but I thought Wally reacted rather sourly.

She said, "Alexandrine! Not that silly story! I don't suppose Violet mentioned that they tried to marry him off to her mother twenty-five years ago. That's how desperate they are. Well, I'd say he's given them chance enough to find someone acceptable. Now they'll just have to let him please himself."

15th May 1936, Fort Belvedere

The Stanley Baldwins are dining tomorrow evening. HM wants them to see Wally in action and understand what a wonderful Queen she'd make. Meanwhile, there's been a ruckus because HM has to receive some Arabs on Monday and, quite naturally, wants Wally to assist him, but the Foreign Office say they won't allow it. The Foreign Office, dictating to the King! How can they prevent it, that's what I'd like to know? If HM wants a chimpanzee to assist him, what business is it of pen-pushers in Whitehall? Apart from any other consideration, HM is a better man with Wally at his side. Everyone says so.

17th May 1936

The Baldwins were so lacking in fire and sparkle. Quite out of their depth. I heard Mrs. Baldwin talking to HM about the folk dances of Worcestershire!

Alice Gloucester has been rustled up to help meet the Arabs tomorrow. Wally says she couldn't care less.

20th May 1936, Wilton Place

To the *Pearl Fishers* with the Crosbies, the Belchesters, Lightfoot, and Doopie.

Philip Sassoon was in Lady Cunard's box. Blew me a kiss but he didn't come round in the intermission.

HM has taken a villa for August. Chateau de l'Horizon. He's stayed there before and says it's a wonderful place, with a marble chute one can slide down, straight from the sun terrace into the sea. He wants Wally to get complete rest before she faces the divorce ordeal. How his eyes shine when he talks about her! I don't think Princess Alexandrine ever stood a chance.

28th May 1936

Wally's dinner for the Lindberghs was stunning. Artichokes with a mousse of foie gras, tarragon chicken, blueberry ice cream. Edwina Mountbatten tried to draw out Mrs. L. with questions about her flying adventures, but Wally was determined to keep the Colonel in the spotlight. "What a waste," she keeps saying. "A great man like that puttering around in exile, and all because of a baby-crazy wife."

I hope she isn't planning another seduction. Freddie Crosbie says he hopes she is. He thinks that may be the kind of cold shower to wake up HM to realities.

5th June 1936

The Communists have been voted in in France. Boss Croker thinks we should cancel the villa, but HM says the Reds have no quarrel with him. He's always been for the working man. Wally says look what happened in Russia. We could be murdered in our beds. HM said, "Darling, we'll see how things develop. I'd never take you anywhere you'd be in danger."

7th June 1936

Our villa has been canceled. HM spoke with Herman Rogers, who said the Red Flag flies over the Cote d'Azur, and he and Kath are away for the summer. They're thinking of Portofino. HM has instructed Jack Aird to find us a yacht.

Lunch with Penelope Blythe. She said she's bored to distraction and needs a summer affair. Just something to get her through August. She says Templemore talks about salmon rods in bed.

8th June 1936

Wally has asked me to help her out on Friday. They have the King of Egypt coming to call, and he's only a boy. She said, "You're used to children, Maybell."

12th June 1936

To York House. Wally has done wonders already. Masses of white flowers, needlepoint cushions, well-placed mirrors. There was far too much furniture in there before, and no light. King Farouk is a very jolly boy. He arrived laden with shopping bags and unpacked all the toy cars he'd bought at Hamley's. He loved the angel food cake.

13th June 1936

Wally says a silver snuffbox has disappeared from a side table since little King Farouk's visit. She says it's not at all the way things are done. She says if a Royalty sees something they'd like to have, they simply let it be known that it would make an acceptable gift. Queen Mary got half her stuff that way.

15th June 1936, Fort Belvedere

With Wally to Garrard to collect engraved claret jugs for HM's birthday, then Kettle drove us here. HM was in Hampshire all day, visiting army camps and inaugurating a new fire house, but he was back in time for dinner. The Erlangers and the Crokers are here. Humphrey and Poots Butler are driving down tomorrow. In time for lunch, before the racing. Oxer Bettenbrooke is equerrying.

17th June 1936

Another Ladies' Day. Now we'll start to see a few changes. Already Melhuish has been relegated to the fourth carriage with Ena Spain and the Gloucesters, and Violet only made it to the fifth. By next year, she'll be watching from the sidelines and *I'll* be the one riding in the parade. Elizabeth York was in azure, Marina Kent in pigeon, Alice Gloucester in peach.

HM escaped at the first opportunity, and we had a gay evening, with Wally's fried chicken and dancing to gramophone records.

19th June 1936

Wally's birthday. I gave her a snakeskin roll for her costume jewelry. HM has given her a Buick, an exact replica of his own. It comes with an advanced driver, approved by Scotland Yard, in case anyone tries to attack her. Though who would? Outside of fashionable London, no one knows who she is.

21st June 1936

Poots Butler says I'd be surprised at how many people know exactly who Wally is and would love to see her Buick run off the road. Lady Astor, for one, who had always understood that Royalties only mixed with Americans from good families.

HM is in great form. He said, "Things are going awfully well, you know, Maybell? I never thought I'd enjoy king-ing but I've really rather taken to it. Wally makes all the difference, of course. I don't think I'd enjoy it one little bit without Wally to come home to."

Jack Aird may have found us a yacht for August. We'll be able to keep clear water between us and the Communists.

1st July 1936

Our yacht is chartered. She has eight staterooms and a crew of fifty, and Jack Aird promises there'll be no mad cooks and no monkeys running wild. We'll travel to Venice by train and then sail to Greece. Lily Drax-Pfaffenhof has confirmed. Herman and Kath Rogers may join us, too.

4th July 1936, Wilton Place

A call from Randolph Putnam. He said, "I'm amazed to find you at home. I thought maybe you'd moved to Buckingham Palace."

I said, "By this time next year, I may well have done. Wally is getting a divorce from Ernest and His Majesty is set on marrying her."

He said, "I know. We see her picture in the papers all the time."

Very odd. She's not in the papers here.

He said, "I'll see you for the Coronation, if not before."

I said, "You won't be able to get a seat, you know? It's not like a ball game. It's strictly by invitation."

He said, "Won't bother me. I'll stand in the street, like everyone else. Can't miss a historic moment like that though. An American Queen! And from Baltimore."

12th July 1936

Rory's fifteenth. Gave him a set of magic nesting glasses and a trick cigarette pack. For his treat, he chose *Rise and Shine* at the Theatre Royal, with Fred Astaire. Lightfoot, Flora, and Doopie came, too. Afterwards, to the Cosy Corner for a mixed grill. Flora had memorized all the tunes in the show. She has no natural shyness about her and sang away all through high tea.

She said, "Let's talk about The Wally. She's going to be the Queen."

Rory said, "No she's not, Flora. Absolutely not."

Lightfoot said, "She'd have to change her name, for one thing. 'Wally' isn't a very queenly name."

I said, "Well, her real name is Bessie Wallis, and Bessie is certainly a queenly name. Good Queen Bess!"

Rory said, "But she's the wrong kind of person. It's obvious."

Doopie said, "Bud Ging loves her, Roar."

Rory said, "But it's not suitable. Daddy says so."

Doopie said, "Ging loves her a lod. Vunny. See loogs lige a nudgragger."

She did a very good impersonation of Wally, with that hard jaw of hers snapping open and closed and her eyes never still.

13th July 1936

Dinner at Carlton Gardens. Family only. Ulick and Rory were allowed to join us for drinks. Melhuish said, "Maybell, I heard the King may be going to Italy. Is it true?"

I said, "Yes, it's all arranged."

Ulick said, "One would have thought he'd go quietly to Balmoral, this year of all years."

Violet said, "He never liked Deeside. I don't suppose we'll ever see him up there now. It'll be all cruises on floating gin palaces."

Melhuish said, "Perhaps he'll bugger off on a permanent cruise, Vee. Leave the Yorks to take over."

Lightfoot said, "Take care now, old boy. If Maybell repeats this over their morning calisthenics, you could find yourself in the Tower."

Doopie said, "You'll be vor the chob, Melsh. You'll have your head tugged udderneath your arb."

Ulick asked if I still keep my diary. He said, "What kind of things do you record in it? Appointments at the beauty salon?"

I said, "No. I jot down the things people say to me."

He said, "I hope you ask their permission first."

17th July 1936

A madman has tried to murder the King. HM and Bertie York were on horseback on their way from a military parade in

Hyde Park yesterday, when a Communist pulled out a gun and would have shot him had a police horse not frisked into him and knocked the gun from his hand. Jack Aird was a few paces behind and saw the whole thing.

I must say, Wally seems very unconcerned about it. A heat wave is forecast for the weekend.

19th July 1936, Fort Belvedere

Wally threw an impromptu poolside party this afternoon. The Kents and the Louis Mountbattens looked in but kept their distance from the Inner Circle. I remember when George Kent was more than happy to eat Wally's crab claws and dance a tango. I think marriage to Marina Greece has made him very stuffy. HM and Jack Aird retold Thursday's drama. HM says he saw something go flying through the air and found himself wondering very calmly if it was a bomb. Aird says he would have dismounted and kicked the gun into the middle of Constitution Hill but his uniform is so tight these days he was worried about getting back on his horse.

20th July 1936, Wilton Place

It looks like all out-war in Spain. Lightfoot says he'd like to go and fight. I can't think why, unless marriage is palling already.

24th July 1936

To the Shim-Sham with the Erlangers, the Crokers, Kenny Opdyke, and Wally. Home just ahead of the milk cart.

HM had to dine with his mother. Judson may be posted to the Low Countries. Hattie says they speak English there.

28th July 1936

We're having to make fresh arrangements for our cruise. The Foreign Office found out our plans to start from Italy and have told HM it will cause the country great embarrassment if he sets foot there, given the current international situation. Wally says Anthony Eden is full of bluster and we should go anyway, but HM doesn't want to make unnecessary trouble when he'll need the government's cooperation if he's to marry Wally. Our boat will now pick us up somewhere on the coast of Yugoslavia, which means HM will have to make a courtesy call on the Crown Prince Pauls. Bolsheviks in Cannes. Situations in Italy. War in Spain. Travel is becoming impossible.

31st July 1936, Sunninghills

Boss and Ethel's final English party for this year. A clambake in Surrey! They had sand laid around their pool and a top chef brought in to cook the lobsters. We had great fun in spite of the rain. Boss told me he saw Ernest last week, in the Aldwych, and he seemed very well. He said, "Between you and me, Maybell, I don't know that he's so heartbroken over Wally. I think he's decided it's all worked out for the best."

Monday, to Paris, to await HM, who's king-ing till Friday. Just the Erlangers, the Humphrey Butlers, and the Crokers for the first leg. Jack Aird to equerry.

6th August 1936, Meurice Hotel, Paris

Shopping for peignoirs with Ethel, Poots, and Hattie. Wally has hardly left the side of Kenny Opdyke. She says he knows everything there is to know about Paris. Poots says he's completely harmless, but I don't think HM would at all like the way he whispers in Wally's ear and makes her laugh. HM never makes her laugh.

10th August 1936, somewhere in Austria

We finally got away on Saturday evening. HM finished his duties and just hopped across the Channel in a little airplane. I do wish Wally could be persuaded to fly. It may be frightening, but the ordeal is over faster. Our railcar is well-appointed but still a railcar. Pips says she feels carefree and adventurous when she travels by train. I find the swaying doubles the time for my toilette.

Lily Drax-Pfaffenhof joined us at Salzburg. They say we should reach Yugoslavia by this evening.

11th August 1936, somewhere in Yugoslavia

The landscape grows wilder. Jack Aird says these mountains are full of cutthroats. Wally is already a nervous wreck. She and HM had to go to tea with the Crown Prince Pauls yesterday afternoon, and she says their driver fairly threw the car around blind bends, in case any brigands lay in wait. The wife wasn't at all friendly toward her, either. Well, she's Marina Kent's sister. Ice maidens both, I'm sure.

13th August 1936, the *Nahlin,* off Sibenik

At last, the sea and our spandy white yacht. She's called the *Nahlin*. There were crowds of well-wishers lining our route from the railroad station to the harbor, all dressed in their gay peasant costumes. HM said, "Come along, darling. Give them a wave. You're going to have to get used to this."

I caught Humphrey and Aird exchanging looks.

We have two dear little destroyers escorting us, so I now feel completely safe.

14th August 1936

The staterooms are rather smaller than they first appear, and completely airless. HM and Wally have nabbed the best suite in the bow. The only thing to do is stay on the sundeck as much as possible. HM and Boss and Hattie have been larking around in the sea. They say the water is warm. I'll take their word for it. Humphrey sits all day with an atlas on his lap, trying to identify islands. A fool's errand. They're just white rocks. Why would they have names?

Tomorrow Dubrovnik. Lily says it's an enchanting town with lots of inexpensive little things to buy.

16th August 1936, at sea

The press were waiting for us when we moored yesterday. Jack Aird suggested we leave immediately, without going ashore. HM said, "Why?"

Jack said, "Might we have a word in private, sir?" I never saw HM angry before. He said, "Absolutely not. Explain yourself here."

Humphrey said, "Jack's worried about photographs, sir, and so am I. With Wally as the innocent party in a divorce case, one needs to be cautious. About her being seen in the company of a man, if you see what I mean?"

Wally said nothing. She'd be desperate if anything scuppered her divorce. But HM said, "Nonsense. The British press promised me complete privacy during my vacation. These johnnies are all foreigners, and English judges don't read foreign newspapers."

Wally made all the girls wear sunglasses and headscarves for going ashore, to confuse any mischievous hacks. "HM's harem," Hattie called us.

Aird stayed on board and stewed. He's not much of a shopper anyway.

19th August 1936, still at sea

Wally's being a very strict taskmaster with HM. He'd asked for the dinghy to be put out this morning so he and Judson could fish for octopus, but Wally countermanded his order and said he had to do his Despatch Boxes first. Even on vacation, a king has official papers to read and sign. Humphrey said, "You know, Wally is starting to look like a very promising Queen. She takes it all jolly seriously."

Aird said, "Perhaps I should just get her to do the Boxes and leave His Majesty to play in peace."

HM did his duty in record time, and then was allowed the dinghy. As Hattie said, from a distance, paddling around in his bathing trunks, he looks like a boy. A very happy boy.

20th August 1936

Humphrey and Poots are going to leave us when we get to Athens. Bernie and Zita Cavett will take over their stateroom. First we have to call on another royal cousin. George of the Hellenes. HM wants to make an excuse and get out of it, but Wally says it would be unpardonable. Actually, she's rather keen to meet him, because he's a king *and* divorced *and* he has a divorced sweetheart. She's interested to find out how the Greeks manage these things.

21st August 1936, Corfu

HM and Wally have gone ashore to have dinner with King George. HM dragged his feet, and they were very late setting off. Jack Aird says Greece will be the next place to have a revolution. I can quite see that by next year, the only place left for us will be Palm Beach.

22nd August 1936

Having tried to wriggle out of dining with George Greece last evening, HM has now invited him to come aboard for luncheon before we sail. He said, "To tell you the truth, Maybell, it's not that I especially like him, but I do feel sorry for him. They've brought him back here to be King, but he really has nothing to do. He's just hanging around waiting for them to put a bomb under his car or send him back to London. He's quite miserable."

Wally says the girlfriend has good bone structure but no pizzazz. She's also furious with HM for talking to her too avidly and omitting to turn between courses.

Poots said, "That's pretty rich, Wally, considering you and Kenny Opdyke are always sniggering at private jokes and neglecting the rest of us."

24th August 1936, Athens

Bernie and Zita Cavett have come aboard. Zita isn't happy with their accommodation, but she might spare a thought for those of us who've sweated and suffered thus far. Big crowds waiting for us as we nosed into Piraeus. Jack Aird got a tongue-lashing from Wally for suggesting HM might want to put on a shirt before getting within range of the press cameras. She said, "If His Majesty needs your advice, he'll tell you."

Aird is returning to his regiment after the cruise and not before time. With Wally in charge, his days must be numbered anyway.

Humphrey said, "Poor Jack. Cruising isn't his kind of thing at all. I think he's worried he'll be required to wear espadrilles to the next Investiture."

Tonight we dine on dry land in a picturesque tavern. I pray the revolution Jack Aird is predicting holds off till tomorrow at least.

Lovely cloisonné belt buckles to be had here, and all kinds of darling amulets and crosses for knockdown prices.

1st September 1936

A heavy swell. Next summer I shall vacation on dry land.

2nd September 1936

Smaller seas, but I've returned to my room. Wally is snapping at everything HM says, and it makes for such a tense atmosphere.

Tomorrow we're to visit the Dardanelles. Jack Aird speaks of them as though I should know them, but I really don't recall them. One meets so many people.

3rd September 1936

HM went ashore with Bernie, Boss, and Aird. We girls stayed aboard and had massages and pedicures while they visited a battle-field. Padmore and Wally's *lingère* went, too. They both lost brothers there.

Tonight we sail for the fabled city of Istanbul, but there is a terrible row brewing. The British Ambassador says HM absolutely must meet the President of Turkey. HM says he's on vacation and has no intention of meeting any more people. We're only going to Istanbul so he can play a round of golf. Now the ever-interfering Foreign Office has entered the affair, and Wally is adding her two cents. She says it would be rude to call in and not at least say hello to Mr. Ataturk. Jack Aird agrees. He says in the event of any future troubles, we want the Turks firmly on our side, not running off to the League of Nations, and there's no better person to convey the message than the King of England.

4th September 1936, Istanbul

The diplomats had their way. HM went ashore to be received, and he got along so well with President Ataturk that he brought him back for drinks. *Very* good-looking and quite charming. He brought Wally a choker of hammered gold and turquoise, a very pretty rug, and an invitation to dinner.

5th September 1936

It was midnight before HM and Wally came back from being feted, and they had an escort of thousands. Little boats strung with lanterns milling around them. Jack Aird says it was a nightmare for the detectives. This morning, HM is in a black mood. It turns out there's nowhere for him to play golf, and Wally has done nothing but talk about Mr. Ataturk's lovely eyes. She says he's the kind of man who could make a girl melt.

To the bazaar with Ethel, Zita, and Lily. Bought bangles and sheepskin rugs. Our last night on the *Nahlin*.

6th September 1936, another train

Mr. Ataturk put on a wonderful farewell firework display for us and has loaned us his train for the first part of our homeward journey. When we get to Bulgaria, King Boris is going to meet us with *his* train, which he actually drives himself. What hard times some of these little kings have fallen upon.

HM seems very depressed. When we get back, he has to go to Balmoral. He doesn't like it, but it's expected of him. Also, just as Aird and Butler warned him, his lawyer has told him that if he doesn't behave more discreetly, there's a real risk that he'll endanger Wally's divorce. Monckton recommends that he simply not see her at all until the case has been heard, but he'll never agree to that.

8th September 1936

The air is crackling between HM and Wally. The Pauls of Yugoslavia have sent their train for the next leg of our journey, so Wally says the very least we must do is have them to dinner. HM says he's tired of all these relations who litter his path wherever he goes.

9th September 1936

Wally won the day and the Yugoslavias came to dinner. HM said, "Well, don't expect me to talk to them. It's only a month since I had tea with them. I've done my whack."

And he was as good as his word. He sat right through dinner and hardly spoke. After the Yugoslav suite had left, we could all hear Wally telling him what a naughty king he'd been. Hattie said, "Lord, listen to her! If they ever crown her, she should carry a cane instead of a scepter."

12th September 1936, approaching Paris

HM left us at Zurich. There was a plane waiting to take him to London. He has a dinner engagement with his mother. Wally gave him a most affectionate send-off. A great relief, because nerves have been frayed this last week. I'd begun to wonder whether the shine hasn't gone off the affair, but this morning they were as devoted as ever.

Wally says she believes HM has the makings of a great King, if only these so-called advisers would stop interfering and leave her to handle him when he becomes difficult. She says he's just not accustomed to applying himself, but she has a knack with him, a little discipline, a little reward, like training a dog. Funny, that's pretty much what Kitty Rothschild said when she saw them together.

As soon as we get back to London, she's going to resume house-hunting. She says it's not only a question of security but also fittingness. She said, "It was one thing for the Prince of Wales to come to Bryanston Court. But not the King."

Lily said, "So, are you going to marry him?"

She said, "I'm not free to marry him. But if I get my divorce, and if it can be managed, yes, I'll marry him."

Ethel said, "But can it be managed? That's the point."

Wally said, "If His Majesty says it can, it can."

If it comes off, her title will be Queen Consort. And I'll be the Queen Consort's Best Friend. Let Nora Sedley Cordle put *that* in her teapot and brew it.

15th September 1936, Wilton Place

To South Audley Street to give Flora her sheepskin rug and Doopie her bangles. Lightfoot says HM dropped an enormous clanger by not inviting the Prime Minister to Balmoral. He says it's something that's written in stone. The Prime Minister always goes, and the Archbishop of Canterbury, who hasn't received his usual invitation, either. I'd have thought they'd both be grateful for the change.

16th September 1936

House-viewing with Wally. We've seen properties in Mount Street, St. James's Square, and Beauchamp Place. More tomorrow.

To Carlton Gardens with Violet's Turkish jam spoons. She said, "Ah, so you're back. Well, I hope you realize you people are breaking Her Majesty's heart."

A fine greeting.

I said, "What people?"

She said, "You know. Truck tycoons. Johnny-come-latelies. Swanning around the Mediterranean. Don't imagine we didn't get to hear about it at Drumcanna."

I said, "David is a grown man. He can surely choose how to spend his vacations."

She said, "He is a grown man, and a king, too, though you'd never think it to see pictures of him cavorting half-naked with gangsters."

Boss Croker is no gangster, and they weren't cavorting. They were shrimping.

She never mentioned Wally, and neither did I. Let her hear it from the Yugoslavias next time they come to call.

18th September 1936

Penelope Blythe says she saw newspaper photographs of HM on his cruise, but Wally wasn't in any of them. Very strange, because he was never more than two inches from her side. They must have removed her. I wonder how one does that.

Wally is taking a house in Cumberland Terrace. Its furnishings are rather overbearing, but it has good views across Regent's Park and anyway, she's not likely to be there for long. I have a feeling she'll have yet another address by the time the year turns. The lawyer Goddard says she'll need an advocate to represent her in court. He's recommended someone called Birkett.

To the Crosbies for dinner.

19th September 1936

Freddie says Penelope Blythe is absolutely right. Wally was scrubbed from the photographs before they appeared in the British newspapers, to spare the feelings of the Royalties and shield all concerned from the tittle-tattling of the man in the street. He also said Wally's divorce is being discussed in Whitehall, the principal question being, can HM be allowed to marry a divorced commoner?

Pips said, "Cut to the chase, darling. We already know the answer to that. The real question is, when Parliament tells him he can't marry her, what will he do?"

No one has any answers. As far as we know, there are no more princesses in prospect, not even from the bargain basement.

21st September 1936

The lawyer Goddard says there are so many divorces waiting to be heard in London this fall Wally might have to wait as long as a year for her case to be called. HM says the delay is completely unacceptable. He wants Wally free to marry him before the Coronation on May 12th. Supper with Wally at Bryanston Court, just we two. HM telephoned three times. She's as jumpy as a flea. She said, "It's all too hurried, Maybell. There's too much to be worked out, and if we rush things, it could all go wrong."

If only they'd nursed the old King more carefully. He might have had another year or two in him.

22nd September 1936

Mr. Goddard has come up with a suggestion: Wally's divorce could be heard in a little country court, where there aren't such long lists. It would have the dual advantage of speeding things along and removing the case from the spotlight of London. HM and Wally are both in favor.

24th September 1936

Wally's divorce has been transferred to a town called Ipswich. We have to go there. She has to be in residence for three weeks before the case is called.

She said, "Please come with me, Maybell. I can't face it without you."

She isn't sure where Ipswich is, but HM has Oxer Bettenbrooke finding us a house.

She's gone off to the Perry Brownlows for the weekend.

25th September 1936

To Ciro's with the Crosbies, the Erlangers, and the Cavetts. Hattie says Ipswich is no distance from London. She's offered to drive out and keep us company from time to time. Pips says she'll do the same.

Zita said, "I'm muddled. Everyone says David can't marry Wally, but what will they do if he just goes ahead and does it? They can't fire the King. And who are 'they,' anyhow?"

Freddie says the marrying couldn't take place because there'd be no one willing to perform it. Well, I'm sure someone could be persuaded. A crisp banknote left between the pages of a prayer book to whet the appetite. There's always *someone*.

Freddie said, "The greater danger is that David will do something hot-headed. Run away to Canada, for instance. I know he's spoken of it. You may be crucial in this, Maybell. Remind Wally what the risks are. Ask her to think of stopping her divorce until after the Coronation at least. I think he may be less likely to bolt after he's been anointed."

Zita said, "Yeah. I guess those ermine robes'd slow him down some."

Zita may have famous legs, but she's not terribly bright.

29th September 1936

Wally couldn't be clearer. She absolutely will not marry HM if the throne is at risk. She said, "Of course not. You know as well as I do what happens to those exes, trailing around the world, hocking their jewels to pay their hotel bills. That's not for me, Maybell. I've tried poor, remember? It just doesn't suit my constitution. So, if they make things impossible for us, it's me he'll have to give up."

I said, "But where will that leave you?"

She said, "I'll be just fine. I'll look around and find someone else. I'll have the pick of London."

She seemed pretty breezy for a person who's already tried the throne for size. Then there's HM. I can't imagine him letting her go, and they'll get no proper king-ing out of him if he doesn't have Wally cracking her whip. It would be a disaster.

Von Ribbentrop is the new German Ambassador.

"See?" she said. "Didn't I tell you?"

1st October 1936

Wally has her going-away-to-get-divorced gifts from HM. A black fox capelet to keep her warm while they're apart, and a river-pearl sautoir to remind her she's his Queen. Bettenbrooke has found us a house in a town called Felixstowe. He says it's quiet and handy for Ipswich. Wally's things will be moved into Cumberland Terrace while we're gone. I have drunk my last martini at Bryanston Court.

2nd October 1936

To Harrold's for candy. Saw Philip Sassoon.

He said, "Maybell! What a very large box. Have you left any fondant crrrèmes for the rest of us?"

I said, "I'm going to Felixstowe for three weeks, and I'm sure they never heard of Charbonnel and Walker there."

He said, "Give me your address. I shall have crrrystalized quince sent to you from Lympne. But why Felixstowe? Why, why?"

I felt him cool as soon as I spoke of Wally's divorce.

"Oh dear," he said. "The tigress's cage is about to be opened wide. Do take care, Maybell."

Lightfoot says London is quietly assembling into two camps. Those who are for HM, Wally, and True Love, and those who don't want anything to upset the old Queen.

I said, "I know where Violet and Melhuish stand, but what about you and Doopie?"

He said, "You know we're both romantics at heart, but frankly, I think there are more important battles on the horizon."

He's still talking about going to Spain and fighting the Fascists. Crazy. George Lightfoot couldn't fight his way out of a paper bag.

5th October 1936

Penelope Blythe says Ernest is seeing someone. No names. All she's heard is that it's an old acquaintance he looked up when he was in the States, and he's very smitten. If Wally knows, she's not letting on.

7th October 1936, Felixstowe

We are installed in a cold, cramped house at the ends of the earth. I don't believe Bettenbrooke even looked the place over before he took it. HM will be furious when he finds out Wally's living in such grim conditions. The sea is gray, the sky is gray, Wally's mood is black. Pips is coming down on Friday, thank heavens.

A pause in the rain this afternoon, but our detective has warned us against venturing into town. He said the place is crawling with American press. So much for getting out of the spotlight of London. Wally says there's nothing worth seeing in Felixstowe anyway.

10th October 1936

Pips arrived with extra blankets, more vermouth, and a checker board. She also confirmed the story about Ernest. Not only is he seeing someone, the "someone" is none other than Mary Kirk. He met up with her in New York in August, cried on her shoulder, no doubt, and now she's planning to leave her husband and follow him to London. All this delivered in whispers after Wally had retired. I think she should be told. Wally hates not knowing things. And little Mary Kirk! Who'd have thought she'd keep popping up in Wally's life like this? Bridesmaid when she married Win Spencer, matchmaker between Wally and Ernest, and now "the other woman." What a busy bee. Perhaps I'll wait till after the weekend before I bring it up with Wally.

Pips also says Walter Monckton just came back from overseas and is letting it be known that he thinks the divorce case is being badly handled. He says Goddard shouldn't have had it moved out of London and he shouldn't have hired a big-gun advocate like Birkett.

I said, "Well, Monckton recommended Goddard."

Pips said, "I know, but you can see his reasoning. Instead of treating it like any ordinary little divorce, it's drawing attention to the fact that there's something big at stake. It could look like a put-up job."

But it *is* a put-up job. And it's too late to change everything now. We just have to stay in the house with the drapes closed and hope for the best.

13th October 1936

Wally says she already knew about Ernest and Mary.

I said, "Then why did he have to go to a hotel with a floozie?"

She said, "Because he doesn't want her name dragged in. You know Ernest. Ever the gentleman. But it's only happened because he's on the rebound. If I called off the divorce, he'd drop her like that."

We risked a brisk walk along the beach and met no one. I guess the press are very sensibly holed up in a cozy bar in town.

16th October 1936

Hattie and Judson are visiting. They brought magazines and smoked salmon and new rumba records. One week to go.

17th October 1936

An unexpected guest. HM drove through the dark and arrived in time to take in Wally's breakfast tray. Cries of surprise and joy. Judson said, "Is this advisable, sir? Isn't Wally supposed to be in purdah until after the divorce?"

HM said (a) no one need ever know he was here, and (b) if they do, what could be more natural than one friend visiting another when they're in the throes of a divorce.

He's given Wally a bracelet of channel-set rubies. It has "Hold Tight" engraved on the clasp. He's staying the night. Bernie and Zita are going to motor down for the day tomorrow.

18th October 1936

A telephone call just as we were finishing luncheon. Fort Belvedere trying to track down HM. The Prime Minister wants a meeting at his earliest convenience and is willing to go to Sandringham if necessary, where he'd been given to understand HM was hosting a shooting party. But Sandringham were under the impression HM was already back at the Fort.

Hattie said, "Alex Hardinge must be having kittens. He's mislaid the King!"

HM was very relaxed. He said, "It's Sunday. Let the buggers wait."

Wally was beside herself. She said, "Sir, please don't antagonize Baldwin. And please don't risk being discovered here. I haven't endured two weeks in this hellhole to have my divorce thrown out of court."

HM made a leisurely departure after dark. Kings don't jump for the likes of Mr. Baldwin.

19th October 1936

Wally on the telephone for hours with HM. I ate dinner alone. He granted the Prime Minister an audience. Baldwin asked a number of personal questions relating to Wally, and HM put him firmly in his place. Reduced Baldwin to tears, effectively. She seemed reassured but went to bed without eating. She's looking as thin as a pencil.

Not a light to be seen outside, and all I can hear is the boom of the sea. The ends of the earth.

20th October 1936

A different version of the Baldwin meeting from Pips, courtesy of Freddie who had it from Fruity Metcalfe who had it from Alex Hardinge.

Baldwin wants Wally's divorce case dropped and for her to leave the country, so there can be an end to speculation that HM intends to marry her as soon as she's free. Well, if Stanley Baldwin wants to get to the heart of the matter, he should apply to me. I could tell him everything he needs to know. Wally won't leave the country. She's made London her home and she likes it there. And as for the marrying, it will only happen if there are no obstacles to her becoming Queen Consort. Wally has always been firm on that point. If there's opposition to her being crowned, she'll retire quietly to Cumberland Terrace with her nest egg. If they won't have Wally as Queen, they'll just have to dig deeper and find HM another candle-end princess.

Wind rattling the windows. More rain. Three days to go.

21st October 1936

Ernest telephoned. He isn't coming to Ipswich for the hearing. His lawyer will represent him. Wally seemed unsettled by his call. She said, "We weren't unhappy, you know? If David hadn't come along, I suppose we'd still be getting along perfectly well."

23rd October 1936

Tomorrow is Wally's hearing. She's decided on a navy wool coat and a felt hat. No jewels, except for a platinum bangle. She said, "My one and only appearance as a Baptist missionary." The first laugh we've had in weeks.

24th October 1936

The worst thing. This morning we were told Wally's case had been postponed because the judge's calendar was too full. The earliest it can now be heard is Tuesday, and we are prisoners here for the weekend. The town is full of American newspapermen, so we daren't even peek outside, and the lawyers have absolutely forbidden any further contact with HM. Easier said than done. His telephone messages are so tearful and anxious, I wouldn't put it past him to turn up here tonight. I feel like a switchboard girl, and Wally is like a caged animal.

25th October 1936

I made warm milk for Wally last night, and it seemed to help her to sleep. This morning, she was in a much brighter mood. She said, "David isn't worrying, so why should I? He says everything will fall into place once I'm divorced, so let's look on the bright side. Let's make plans."

I said, "You mean wedding plans?"

She said, "Wedding plans. Honeymoon plans. Coronation plans. We should go to Paris as soon as this is over, to start choosing my trousseau."

She says they'll keep on the Fort even after she's had Windsor refurbished, because it's a place where they've been happy. She intends getting rid of Sandringham House, and I agree with her. Let someone who enjoys freezing flatlands have it. Then there's his ranch in Calgary. All very well when he was an adventurous young man, but he's King now, and not so young. He needs homes appropriate to his position, in sunny climes where she can help him relax after his kingly duties. Wally favors Majorca.

She's thinking of Brussels lace over ice-blue satin for her wedding gown. It will probably be an April wedding. And for the Coronation, she's thinking of using the coronet David had for his investiture as Prince of Wales. It's an adorable little circlet set with pearls and amethysts and, as she says, will be far less ruinous to the hair than one of those dreadful old crowns. She's full of modern ideas.

I feel very excited. We've been jogging along at a steady pace, but suddenly we're on a runaway train. Little Minnehaha is going to be Queen of England, and I'm her right-hand woman.

26th October 1936

Rain again, and Wally is sitting on thorns. She says the old King's dying has plunged her life into unsought chaos. I said, "Are you telling me you don't really want to be Queen?"

"No," she said, "I don't mind being Queen, but they're all going to make it so tricky for us. His mother's against me, the Yorks are against me, that little pig-farmer Baldwin is against me. What if David caves in to them now? He's quite easy to push around, you know? Where will that leave me?"

I said, "But David adores you. He'll always take care of you."

She said, "I imagine Thelma Furness believed that."

I said, "It's just the waiting that's getting on your nerves. But it's almost over. Why throw it all away now?"

She said, "I don't know. My head's spinning. Half of London has been waiting for me to fail. I'd hate them to think they'd scored some kind of victory over me. It might all be easier if Ernest and I just go away together. South Africa sounds interesting."

I think Mary Kirk might have something to say about that. She's left her husband to be with Ernest, after all. Fortunately, just at the moment of Wally's greatest wobble, a courier arrived with a diamond pin and a note from HM. He says he cannot and will not live without her.

Pips has often said she doesn't think HM is very bright, but he seems to me to have an astute understanding of Wally. Tomorrow is the big day.

27th October 1936, Wilton Place

Our exile is over. Mr. Birkett met us at court and told Wally to breathe deeply, speak up, and simply answer any questions the judge put to her. I'm told he's one of the highest-paid advocates in the country. If that's so, I wonder he doesn't smarten up. He was wearing the most moth-eaten old rug on his head. The judge was extremely disagreeable, interrupting Wally when she was speaking, sneezing and coughing into a handkerchief, and there was one awful moment when he just sat in silence, glowering at Birkett. I thought he might be going to throw the case out. And then, all of a sudden, it was over. He awarded her a divorce decree *nisi*, which means she will be free to marry David in April. We were in and out in twenty minutes, and the press were prevented from leaving the courtroom until we were all safely out of the building and into our cars.

We went directly to Cumberland Terrace. It's in a messy state, half of Wally's things not unpacked and more boxes have arrived from Buckingham Palace, things David wants her to have. It all seems rather silly to me. In six months time, it will have to be packed up and sent back there. Wally said, "I don't live my life that way, Maybell. Making do. I pay attention to every detail every moment of every day. Why would I use a creamer from Heal's when I can have one that's been used by monarchs?"

She'd told her cook we'd have Spanish omelettes at eight, but at seven HM appeared with chilled champagne and pheasant sandwiches and an enormous emerald on a platinum band.

Wally said, "Maybell was just leaving."

Pips gave me dinner. Freddie was at a January Club dinner. Pips says Wally had better not start flashing a royal engagement ring around, the day after her divorce hearing, or she could find herself hauled back before the judge.

31st October 1936

To Carlton Gardens for tea. The boys are home on Long Leave.

Violet said, "You can wipe that silly smile off your face. It doesn't matter what sordid lengths she goes to, Wally Warfield will never be Queen."

Violet was a bad loser when we used to play Crazy Eights, and she's never grown up.

I said, "So far you've been wrong in everything you've predicted. You said she'd never get as far as Royal circles. She did it within months. You said she'd never go to the Kents' wedding ball or the Jubilee Ball, and she went to both."

She said, "It's a pity you clutter your mind with such trivia."

I said, "There's nothing cluttered about my mind. I have it all written down in my diaries. Every step in Wally's climb to the throne, and the names of all those swankpots and sneerers who've scoffed at her."

Rory said, "Gosh. I'd like to read those." Violet sent him out to walk the spaniels.

Ulick said, "I hope none of *our* names appear."

Violet said, "Do our names appear, Maybell?"

I said, "Yes, they do. You'll be comforted to know that every objection you've raised has been carefully recorded. No one will ever be able to accuse the Melhuishes of sitting on the fence."

Ulick said, "This is insufferable. I shall speak to Father."

That boy is old before his time.

Friday to the Fort. Pips and Freddie are coming. Also the Crokers and the Erlangers. "Little America," Violet calls it. Sour grapes, of course.

1st November 1936, Fort Belvedere

The men played golf yesterday afternoon. Freddie says he's never seen HM play so well, nor be in such good spirits, and I had the same impression at breakfast this morning. HM said, "Things are going our way at last, Maybell."

Oxer Bettenbrooke says the British people are one hundred percent behind him.

Ethel said, "I thought the British people didn't know about Wally."

He said, "It's not widely reported, true. But if they knew, they'd support him. All those factory workers he's taken the time to visit, all those Tommies who remember how gallantly he fought in the Great War, if it comes to a confrontation over the Wally Issue, *theirs* are the voices that will be heard."

HM said, "Oxer's right. A little thing like this isn't going to bother them."

Ethel said, "I know Wally keeps a slim line, sir, but I'd never call her 'a little thing.'"

He laughed.

2nd November 1936, Wilton Place

Dinner at South Audley Street. Lightfoot says big tables are hard on Doopie. Figs and ham, oxtail ragout, pear tart, all very well done. If Doopie can produce a decent dinner, why can't Violet? She was wearing a sweet pin-tucked gown, burgundy with a little ivory lace. Lightfoot holding her hand at every opportunity.

I was there to be pumped for information. Melhuish said, "What's your pal up to this week, Maybell? It sounds like the Great Terror at Buck House. Wigram's out as Private Secretary. Halsey's out as Comptroller. Even Trotter's out as Groom-in-Waiting, after all the years he's served. It's a bloody disgrace."

I happen to know that Brigadier Trotter had continued to fraternize with Thelma Furness, so the man has only himself to blame. He was as old as the hills, anyway.

Flora said, "Skinner says they have gartoon shows now at Uncle King David's house. And bath salts."

This is the kind of thing kitchen help chatters about. Violet tutting.

I said, "Bath salts! Well, that's a capital offense!"

She said, "And heaven only knows what he's spending on coal. Marina Kent says he has the furnaces roaring."

Lightfoot said, "We mustn't criticize that, Vee. Think of the Welsh coal miners. I'm sure he's doing it for the sake of the Principality."

Doopie said, "Or burnin old wood. Drow anudder gortier onna vire, Wally! Wades nod, wand nod!"

Thank goodness someone in the family has kept their sense of humor.

3rd November 1936

Today HM opened Parliament, and Wally and I watched him from the Distinguished Strangers' Gallery. The next time he does it, Wally will be beside him in that gilded coach. She watched everything very closely and made notes.

5th November 1936

Randolph Putnam telephoned to tell me Roosevelt has been reelected. I can't say he ever did a damned thing for me except steal my gold. Randolph said he'd seen Junior and his awful wife at Nora Sedley Cordle's museum gala, and they were very curious to know how close I am to Wally Simpson. *Le tout* Baltimore is talking about her, apparently. They should be talking about me, too. Last night I wore my chocolate silk and danced across a glass floor with the King of England.

6th November 1936

To the opera. The Cunard box for *Götterdammerung*. Wally, Emerald C., Lily Drax-Pfaffenhof, and the Erlangers. Philip Sassoon sought me out during the intermission. He said, "Maybell, I note there are two dazzling emeralds in your box this evening, and one of them is on Brrrunnhilde's finger. Is she betrrrothed? I think we should be told."

It's too late for him to try and humor me now. He never invites me to Trent anymore, for fear of Sybil. Sunday, to Paris.

9th November 1936, Meurice Hotel, Paris

Bought nightgowns at Cadolle and ordered day dresses from Patou, simple crepes. Wally's not short these days, but she doesn't seem in any hurry to settle her bills. We've gone our separate ways for the evening. I'm dining with Ena Spain, Wally's going dancing with Kenny Opdyke.

11th November 1936

Ena is very troubled about HM and Wally. She says the old Queen is desperate and the Yorks are furious. She said, "It's the unseemliness of it, Maybell. The weekends, the niteries. That cruise. He's tarnishing the crown before it's even properly on his head."

I said, "Well, David's his own man."

She said, "Oh, I don't think he is. I think we both know that's not the case."

Ena should have someone ease the seams on her bodices. I'm sure she wouldn't perspire so if she accepted that we all grow a little rounder with the passing years. It's our glands.

To Schiaparelli for evening gowns, then the boat train to London. HM is inspecting the Fleet. We rendezvous at the Fort for the weekend. The Brownlows and the Erlangers are joining us.

13th November 1936, Fort Belvedere

An unsettling evening. We were at drinks, when a letter arrived for HM. He read it, then asked Perry B. to go with him to his study. He didn't even show the letter to Wally. He and Perry were closeted for the longest time, then Alex Hardinge arrived. Raised voices. Dinner was delayed until ten-thirty, and was then hurried through without any attempt at gaiety, even on Wally's part. HM was drained of all color. Wally went straight to bed after the savory. Hattie's gone up to see whether Kitsie B. knows what's going on, and Judson's downstairs playing solitaire, hoping to glean some information.

14th November 1936

Four a.m. and Wally just went back to her room. The letter that blighted our evening was from Hardinge, warning HM that the British newspapers are about to reveal all about the love affair. I said, "But isn't that good? If you're getting married in April, surely you need to reveal all before too long?"

She said, "Not by newspaper reports. They'll get everything wrong, and anyway, there are procedures to be observed. The Government has to give its agreement, and so far it hasn't even been asked. And apart from anything else, this might cost me my divorce. If this is splashed all over the papers, that old beak might refuse to make my decree final. Birkett said there was a very sticky moment in court when he thought the judge was going to throw out the chambermaid evidence against Ernest. Something like this could finish it. David's been too damned impetuous. I told him to be more careful."

She said the letter was signed by Alex Hardinge, but she's sure the old Queen and the Yorks had a hand in the composing of it, threatening him with the government resigning, trying to spook HM into giving her up.

She feels the only thing to do is to go away until it's all blown over. Paris, probably. She said, "We'll go today. Have your maid start packing now. Leave early, before David is up. I'll make your excuses. Then meet me at Cumberland Terrace."

I said, "I have commitments. I'm running the tombola at Anne Belchester's epileptics' benefit on Wednesday. I can't just run away."

She said, "We're not running away. *I'm* defusing a delicate situation, and *you're* keeping me company."

15th November 1936, Wilton Place

Padmore is unpacking. We're not going to Paris, after all. I waited for Wally at Cumberland Terrace all afternoon yesterday, and heard nothing till six p.m. Then she telephoned to say HM had persuaded her to stay at least while various avenues are explored. She said, "I'm sorry, Maybell. He won't hear of my going away at present."

All very well, but Anne Belchester has now given the tombola to Daphne Frith.

Pips and Freddie gave me dinner. Freddie said Wally's name has been mentioned in Parliament. She'll be thrilled. He thinks HM is hoping to talk his mother round to accepting Wally. If the old Queen relents, something might be managed. Pips thinks he's already decided to give up the throne. He'll be wasting his time if he does. Wally's not interested in ex-kings.

16th November 1936

Violet was shown into my morning room at the ungodly hour of nine-thirty. I received her in my wrap. She said, "I can't be long. I have my Pit Ponies at ten. Is it true you're going away with Wally Warfield?"

If you want news spread in London, just allow a boot boy to overhear it. It'll travel from Belgravia to St. James's via Mayfair faster than a hackney cab.

I said, "We'd thought of going to Paris for a while, but now we may not."

She said, "I very much hope she does go to Paris, or somewhere more distant. It may be the only way to shock His Majesty into sanity. But you mustn't go with her, Maybell. She's going to be remembered evermore as the hussy who almost ruined a king, and you'll be remembered as her friend."

I remarked that even a hussy is entitled to a friend. Violet said, "Well, let it not be you. Let it be that silly Hattie Erlanger, or one of those gangsters' wives, but not you. You'll be ruined."

I said, "Well, we're not going. David won't allow it. He's talking to the Prime Minister and the old Queen. It's all going to be worked out."

She said, "Worked out? Worked out! This isn't a quarrel over a grouse moor. There isn't anything to work out except how far away that woman can be sent and how fast. David Wales is going to be anointed and crowned six months from now, and he has to start behaving correctly. Wally must go. There is no place for her in the Royal Family."

I said, "Don't you feel sorry for him? All he wants is to marry her."

She said, "Yes, I do. But sympathy doesn't come into it. Kings have to put duty first."

I said, "Pips thinks if he can't have Wally, he'll walk away from the job."

She said, "A very good example of the silliness surrounding His Majesty. Anyone who understands anything about this country knows that kings don't walk away. He needs stiffening, Maybell, not tempting with idiotic fantasies. Well, until you come to your senses and distance yourself from the affair, please stay away from Carlton Gardens. I have Melhuish to think of, and my boys."

And out she blazed.

Treated Ida Coote to the Dorch. She now eats only vegetables and nuts. Daphne Frith cut me.

17th November 1936

Freddie Crosbie has come up with an idea and has asked to see HM tomorrow. He thinks the answer is simply to take a more leisurely approach. To silence all talk of marrying until after the Coronation, giving Wally time to set out her stall. Do some volunteer work. Make carefully selected public appearances. Let the British public get to know her and take her into their hearts.

HM is dining with his mother this evening, then leaving first thing tomorrow morning on a tour of shipyards.

18th November 1936, Cumberland Terrace

Wally has asked me to move in for a few nights. Her ulcers have flared up, and she's finding it hard to sleep. We're supposed to have an armed guard outside the house around the clock, but all we seem to have is two dopes in a car and a bobby who bicycles past once an hour.

HM's dinner with the old Queen didn't go well. All he got was a sermon on the subject of duty. When he gets back from Wales, he's going to see George Kent and Harry Gloucester to try and get them on his side. Also Mr. Beaverbrook. If he were to come out in favor of Wally in his newspapers, it would make an enormous difference.

Freddie's proposal fell on deaf ears. HM says he doesn't want Wally laboring away at charity galas and consigned to the tail-end landau. He wants her at his side.

19th November 1936

The newspaperman Harmsworth has asked Wally to have lunch on Thursday. He says he'd like to help.

To the Rialto with Lightfoot and Doopie to see *Show Boat*. The newsreels showed HM surrounded by cheerful welders. I'm sure simple folk like that would be perfectly happy for him to marry Wally. It's all so silly.

It turns out that Mr. Beaverbrook is on his way to Arizona for his asthma, but he's been told to sail right back. His King needs him.

20th November 1936

Wally went to Claridge's to meet with Esmond Harmsworth and hear his rescue plan. I lunched with Penelope Blythe. Fergus dined with Humphrey Butler last night, and Humphrey told him the latest from the Royalties. Apparently, the Kents and the Gloucesters are lukewarm about Wally, but if it comes to it, they'd prefer accommodating her to losing HM. For one thing, if HM goes, Bertie York will have to be King, and the rest of them will all have to do a whole lot more prince-ing. The Yorks absolutely won't accept her, but they don't want the throne, either. They seem to want everything their own way. And poor HM is caught in the middle.

21st November 1936

Wally is in much better spirits. Esmond Harmsworth has come up with a very clever idea and has offered to take it to Mr. Baldwin on Monday morning. It's called a morganatic, or "left-handed," marriage, and they were apparently once popular with the Prussians. Even the old Queen's grandfather did it that way.

It would mean Wally agreeing not to receive and never to seek the title "Queen." She says she'd be quite contented to settle for Royal Duchess. Also, any children of the marriage wouldn't be eligible to succeed, but as Wally says, there aren't going to be any children. The simple beauty of it is that HM could marry her and still remain King. I don't see how anyone could object to it. Not even Violet.

To the Fort.

21st November 1936, Fort Belvedere

HM doesn't like Harmsworth's left-handed idea. He said, "Darling, I won't have you shortchanged. I want you to be my Queen, not the Duchess of Lancaster. And anyway, Baldwin and the whole bally lot of them would still have to approve it. I don't see why we should make all these concessions. It smacks of groveling."

Wally's asking Fruity Metcalfe to try and make HM see the beauty of the morganatic solution.

The Crokers and the Cavetts are coming to dinner, and Wally's ordered a gypsy band from the Hungaria. We have to do something to lighten the mood.

HM said, "I've had the most marvelous welcome in the Rhondda this week, Maybell. They sang *Men of Harlech* for me. Everywhere I went, they lit their Davy lamps and cheered me. I'm still their Prince of Wales, you see, even though I'm King."

22nd November 1936

Fruity played golf with HM and persuaded him to look again at Esmond Harmsworth's proposal. They took beer and sandwiches into the study and came out an hour later with HM all in favor and wanting it put to the Prime Minister immediately. Walter Monckton's been sent for.

Wally said, "David's so alone with all this. If only he had a few wise heads to advise him."

Fruity said, "He had plenty of wise heads. Somebody sacked them."

Dinner with the Crosbies. Freddie said, "The morganatic idea will never succeed, but it may buy us some time. At least while Baldwin's looking at it, HM isn't likely to do anything rash. Between us three, things are far worse than he understands. It's not just the divorce. There's a whole dossier on Wally. Family, husbands, various goings-on in China. And then there's the von Ribbentrop business. Did you know she gave him a signed photograph for Hitler?"

I thought Mr. Hitler preferred blondes.

23rd November 1936

To South Audley Street. I may be banished from Violet's hearth, but at least I'm still welcome there.

Lightfoot says there's a growing body of opinion that HM should go, even though the Bertie Yorks are reluctant to be King. Melhuish told him confidentially the old King always hoped HM would neglect to marry, so the succession would pass to Bertie York and then his girls.

I told him about the morganatic idea. He said, "It might have worked if Wally was a pious, virginal Citizen Jane, but as things stand, there's too much against her. Two husbands too many. Not to mention her gate-crashing the Kents' wedding ball, and all those courtiers she trampled over to get to the bridge of the *Edward VIII*. No, I really don't see the Archbishop of Canterbury buying it."

He agrees with Freddie that whatever else happens, the Coronation should come first. Doopie busy with some item she's crocheting for Marina Kent's baby. Flora reading *The Fortunes of Philippa*, following the words with her finger.

Lightfoot said, "Of course, Archduke Franz Ferdinand made a morganatic marriage, and we all know what happened to him."

Flora asked what I dared not. Apparently, the Franz Ferdinands were shot. What an unhappy thought.

25th November 1936

HM has sent for Mr. Baldwin. The man has had Esmond Harmsworth's proposal on his desk for almost two days and seems to lack any sense of urgency. Wally afraid we're all being spied on by Alex Hardinge. She wishes she'd gotten rid of him while she had the chance. She has gowns waiting to be fitted in Paris, but HM won't let her go. He's afraid she won't come back.

26th November 1936

Mr. Baldwin is not being helpful. He told HM the morganatic idea would have to be put to Parliament, where he had every reason to believe it would be rejected, and that it would also have to be put to the Dominions, whoever they are, and they would certainly reject it.

Boss and Ethel are getting up a crowd to go to the Paradise Club, but neither Wally nor I are in the mood. Freddie Crosbie talked to the lawyer Monckton. Monckton says HM isn't willing to wait to get married till after his Coronation, because it would mean swearing the Oath with a lie in his heart.

Wally thinks David should go on the wireless and speak to the nation. She says if the ordinary people knew how unfairly he was being treated, there'd be riots in the streets and Stanley Baldwin's head on a pike.

Beaverbrook's boat docks in the morning. He's going straight to the Fort to meet with HM.

27th November 1936

Beaverbrook's advice is to withdraw the morganatic proposal immediately. He says Baldwin is holding a very strong hand, and the most sensible course is for Wally to go away, for the Coronation to take place, and then, in the fullness of time, for the nation and Commonwealth to become properly acquainted with Wally through her charitable works and occasional, decorous appearances. He says if it's put to the Dominions, Eire will vote against anything involving a divorcée, and so, in all likelihood, will Australia and New Zealand, because they have Roman Catholic Prime Ministers.

I often think politics would be more agreeable in the hands of women. What could be a more sensible arrangement than a happy King and a Wally satisfied to be a Royal Duchess? Pips says Wally's satisfaction may be one of the problems.

She said, "She might agree to 'Duchess of Lancaster' now, but she'd soon start wheedling for more. You know Wally."

Hattie said, "And what if a baby were to come along? It's not out of the question. Jane Habberley's sister had a child when she was forty-six."

What a very unsettling piece of information.

Wally is now cooling on the morganatic option herself. At dinner, she said, "Have your bags packed, Maybell. I'm reconsidering plan A."

28th November 1936

Cross words between Wally and HM this morning. I heard her say, "It's a goddamned fiasco! What does Monckton say? Why don't you listen to him?"

She was blazing when she came off the telephone. It transpires it's actually too late to withdraw the morganatic idea, because it's already been put before the Dominions. That little man Baldwin certainly moves fast when it suits him.

She sat for a minute, then she said, "There's nothing left but to disappear."

I said, "But Sir will never allow it."

She said, "He should have thought of that before he bungled this business with Baldwin. Well, now he'll have to manage without me. We'll go tomorrow, early. But whatever you do don't tell anyone. Not Pips, not Ethel, not anyone."

She had a headache, so went back to bed. I took a stroll toward the new rose gardens but soon turned back. There's no place more chilling than a London park in November.

My luncheon soup had just been served when HM arrived. He ran straight up to Wally's bedroom and didn't say a word to me. It was almost two when they came down together, Wally still pale but sporting a new star sapphire pin on her lapel, HM fussing about whether the coast was clear out in the street. He might have thought of that before he left his Daimler standing there for an hour. All Wally said was, "Maybell, I'm going to the Fort. I'll send for you."

I said, "Is it still plan A?" From the way she hushed me, I think it is.

David said, "Hurry along, darling. I want to get you to a place of safety."

The maids went in Wally's car. Now there's nothing to do but wait.

29th November 1936

I was woken just after midnight by the sound of breaking glass. The footman found a brick end thrown through the dining-room window. The kitchen maid had hysterics and went home to her people in Hackney, still in her nightdress.

Lightfoot drove over immediately to collect me. He believes there's a plot to murder Wally and that I may get blown up by mistake.

30th November 1936, Wilton Place

The news from the Fort is that Wally is prostrate with sickness of the nerves and is not to be disturbed. HM has had three doctors to see her, and they all agree the only thing is for her to rest in a darkened room, so it seems unlikely we'll be traveling for a while. I've given in to Pips's pleading and am moving to Halkin Street this evening before *I* need three doctors.

Freddie thinks it's all up for Wally, even though Mr. Beaverbrook appears to be championing HM and trying to find a solution. He said, "Beaverbrook's only in it to bait Baldwin. He doesn't give a damn about the King. Well, only in the way one might feel a pang for a cat squashed on the roadside. What Beaverbrook wants is for Baldwin to bungle this and have to resign."

It's all such a horrid muddle, and I must say, some of the blame must rest with Ernest. If he'd kept the situation under control and not allowed Wally to get in too deep, we'd all be able to sleep safe in our beds.

1st December 1936, Halkin Street

Great excitement last night. The Crystal Palace Pleasure Gardens burned to the ground. The sky was quite red as we went to dinner. They say every Hook and Ladder was called out, so just as well I hadn't stayed on at Cumberland Terrace waiting to be fire-bombed on behalf of Wally.

I mentioned to Freddie Wally's idea that HM should speak to the nation by wireless. President Roosevelt's fireside chats have proved very popular, and something similar would remind the British public that the King is a man just like themselves. However, Freddie says the King can't just sit in front of a microphone when the urge seizes him. He'd need the Prime Minister's agreement, and the Cabinet would want to check in advance that they approved of what he intended saying. Very puzzling. What's the point of the King having a government if he has to go to it, cap in hand, every time he wishes to open his mouth? And I suppose the same would apply to Wally, which leads me to think she might not be so suited to be Queen, after all. She'd just come right out with it.

2nd December 1936

Further alarms. Beaverbrook says the British press is about to break their silence on the Wally situation. He says it's already started in the provinces. A North Country cleric made a speech yesterday, questioning whether HM is approaching the Coronation with the correct sense of duty, and the local papers reported it. This morning, the *Manchester Guardian* has picked up on it and asked if the British public are really willing to accept a divorced American as their Queen? Well, it had to come out before long, and now is as good a time as any. HM has never been more popular. I'm sure all those dusty little miners will scrape together their farthings to send him a wedding gift. King Edward VIII and the Duchess of Lancaster will be loved and remembered when Stanley Baldwin and the Bishop of Bradford are long forgotten.

Tried to do a little Christmas shopping, but it was hard to concentrate, and then I found myself having a dizzy spell among the neckties. Wally isn't the only one feeling the strain. One can't be braced for action day after day without the body eventually breaking down. And as sweet as Pips is, I think I need to go home, unpack my bags, and sleep in my own bed. We'll look back on this in a few years and laugh at all the fuss and drama.

4th December 1936, somewhere in France

Yesterday was the longest, most extraordinary day.

Hattie Erlanger woke me early to tell me every newspaper had front page photographs of our cruise on the *Nahlin,* photographs in which Wally had magically reappeared. Then Lightfoot called to tell me the Bertie Yorks had cut short their visit to Scotland and were on their way back to London in an absolute fury with HM. He said, "The fat's well and truly in the fire now, Maybell. It's decision time for HM."

I no sooner got him off the line when Wally called.

She said, "It's all over. We'll leave after dark this evening. Bring no more than two valises. A car will collect you at four."

I said, "Where are we going?"

"Abroad," she said. "You're not to tell anyone, particularly not Violet. This morning, I need you to go to Cartier and collect everything of mine they've had for cleaning or remounting, ready or not. Ask for Phillips. He's expecting you."

Pips was very sweet. She promised not to tell anyone else, at least until we were clear away. She said, "Ignore what Wally said about luggage. Two valises sounds pretty mean to me. She's sure to have at least forty."

I dropped by the Grosvenor Chapel on my way to see Lightfoot and Doopie. Just sat there awhile. I don't know why. They had all the newspapers at South Audley Street. Lightfoot said Beaverbrook and Harmsworth had written up HM in a very complimentary vein, but Wally is going to be harder to sell. He thinks she looks too angular and polished. He said, "We British like our royalties to have womanly hair and a generous prow, to carry off the regalia. While you're away, see if you can't fatten her up a little."

I said, "Do you think she'll be coming back to wear the regalia?"

He said, "Actually, no, I don't."

Doopie said, "Where you going, Bayba? Wan Dordie da gum with you?"

Flora was allowed down from her schoolroom, but we didn't tell her I was going away. She said, "Hurrah! Are we going to a Gorner House?"

Doopie said, "Negs dime, Vora. Negs dime."

I wish I could have seen Rory, too. If we have to stay away until after Wally's divorce, we'll miss our pantomime. Passed Gladys Trilling as we turned out of Curzon Street, but she didn't see me. All the newspaper placards said the same thing: **THE KING AND MRS SIMPSON.**

The fog was rolling in by the time I got to the Fort. Wally was very pale and quiet and hardly greeted me. HM was bustling about, full of light chitchat. Perry Brownlow was there. The plan is to catch a ferry boat to France and then drive south to stay with Herman and Kath Rogers. They expect us by Sunday or Monday. Two cars. One for me, the luggage, and Wally's maid. The other for Wally with Perry Brownlow and a Scotland Yard detective named Jimmie. Tea was brought in at five, but no one touched it. Wally had her sable on already, anxious to be gone. It was HM who was reluctant to let us leave.

When she went out to the car, he said, "She's everything to me, Maybell. Take care of her. Make sure she eats properly."

We left the dog behind. HM lifted it up and waved its paw as we pulled away. He looked so lost. He reminded me of how Rory used to look when it was time to go back to school.

I didn't get another opportunity to speak with Wally till we reached our cabin. We were on the ten o'clock, sailing from Newhaven. She said all she felt was relief. She's felt in constant danger these past few weeks, from the Palace plotters, from any crazy who got it into his head to remove her from the scene. Even from David.

She said, "He's a weak man ordinarily, but he's had such a strong grip lately. They say that about drowning men, don't they? That they can pull a stronger person under."

Just as well the maid wasn't there to hear that unfortunate comparison. She told me in the car that she's a nervous sailor. She lost a brother at Jutland, and her stomach has never been right since Walter Guinness sailed us through that hurricane off Biarritz.

We docked just after midnight and drove to this hotel, God knows where.

Perry B. decreed that the drivers had to get a few hours sleep, and Wally seemed happy for him to take charge. She's tired, I suppose. We all are.

Perry says my job is to paint a bright picture of the future and not allow her to dwell on thoughts of HM. But I don't think she is. I think she's completely resigned. HM is the one who's obsessed.

Perry says HM told Wally he'd soon be at her side, but he won't be going anywhere. He's going to be kept busy in England, safe from acts of romantic folly, until he's safely crowned. He said, "If Wally understands that, good. But she may waver, especially if he sends her letters full of wild promises. So you must help me keep her steady. Plan trips. Chat to her about gowns. Encourage her to notice eligible men."

The sheets are coarse, and the pillows are like rocks, but Wally is fast asleep.

6th December 1936, Villa Lou Viei, Cannes

Arrived at the Rogerses last night after battling with snowstorms, and roads without signposts, and uncooperative French peasantry. Where Wally and Brownlow are, we have no idea. The decision to travel separately instead of in convoy was made by Perry when he realized the press were on to us.

That was Wally's fault. She's grown so accustomed to giving orders she's lost all idea of how to be a discreet presence. If she hadn't started complaining the minute she walked through the door, I don't suppose the *patron* would have paid us any attention. I don't like to see stale flowers in a hotel lobby myself, but we were only there for the briefest stay *and* we were trying to travel incognito. But Wally started up, a phone call was made, and reporters began. They set up camp in the car park to prevent our slipping away, so Perry decided we had to create a diversion. Wally's maid and I were to leave by the front door and take the Buick, while he and Wally slipped out through the kitchens and into our station wagon. I said, "No one's going to mistake me for Wally, you realize."

He said, "Paint on a beauty spot. Wear a headscarf. We have darkness on our side."

How little men understand of what it is that makes every woman uniquely herself. No cosmetician in the world could turn me into Wally, I'm glad to say. But the press, being simple-minded men, saw me dash for Wally's car and fell for the ruse. They gave chase, and it was only when we had to stop for gas and they saw me with my hair prettily ruffled and the beauty spot wiped away that they realized their error. It was a rather amusing moment.

The weather worsened the farther south we drove. Ladbroke telephoned to the Rogerses that we shouldn't arrive here before midnight, and Herman told him the reporters were here, too, watching for Wally, so someone has blabbed. It's a pity Wally made enemies of so many of HM's staff. People like that are quick to turn.

What Herman had described as "a small press presence" was at least a hundred, and more have arrived since. I can see them from my window. There are gendarmes down there, too, keeping the photographers from mobbing every vehicle that tries to get through to the house.

Herman and Kath have made me as comfortable as they're able, considering they're in the middle of refurbishments. Herman says it was the most astonishing phone call he's ever received, HM begging him to take in Wally on short notice.

Kath keeps saying, "It won't suit her. I know Wally. There's brick dust everywhere."

Herman says they had no choice. It was tantamount to a Royal Command.

HM has been telephoning at all hours, checking to see if Wally has arrived. Herman said, "The next thing will be *he'll* be on his way here."

I said, "That's not the plan. They're going to keep him in London until he's gotten over her."

He said, "Well, I suppose if there's anyone resolute enough to deliver the death blow it's Wally, but I can't imagine anything she could say to him at the moment that would do the trick. The man seems to be out of his mind."

I hope we're not going to spend the rest of our lives on the run from HM King.

7th December 1936

Wally and Brownlow arrived last night. By the time they got here, there were so many reporters and police outside the gates it looked like an army camp down there, but they didn't get the photograph they'd been waiting for. When the car pulled up outside the house, there was no sign of Wally. She was on the floor beside Brownlow's feet, covered in a tartan rug. She thought the whole thing was a great lark and was in very good spirits, until Herman told her HM had been telephoning all day and was likely to call again at any minute.

She said, "I'm not speaking to him. This craziness has to stop. Put Maybell on. Maybell, tell him I'm not here yet. Tell him spies are listening in."

I refused. Kath and I have discussed this and are agreed, Wally is far too free with her orders, and now that she's withdrawn from Royal circles, she'd better accustom herself to behaving like a mere mortal again. So, she was left with no choice but to speak with HM, and I believe there were tears, at both ends of the line, especially when he put the dog on to say good-night.

Kath had given me a bed in the dressing room adjoining Wally's room. She thought Wally would be glad of my company after the terrors of the journey, but Wally has insisted that Brownlow have the dressing room *and* that he keep the door open. She said, "I'll sleep better with a man nearby."

Her last words before she retired were, "Tell Herman to turn up the furnace. Kath keeps this house so damned cold. And has she got my special soap?"

Herman joked that someone had better warn Kitsie Brownlow about the sleeping arrangements, because if Wally's back on the loose, Perry's virtue may not be safe. But Wally's not going to be interested in a minor courtier. As a matter of fact, I think she's altogether bored with love.

The news from London is unsettling. Before he turned in, Brownlow spoke to Fruity Metcalfe. The Stock Exchange is jittery, and public sympathy seems to be moving away from HM. Fruity says the Socialists are certainly against him. Well, that's no surprise. They're always against everything. Then the Conservatives are against him, because of the way he keeps visiting paupers and raising their hopes, and the Court wives have let it be known they have no intention of curtsying to a woman who grew up in a boardinghouse. Which, as Perry says, leaves only the true romantics and perhaps those chafed by the chains of their own imprudent marriage who may be hoping Wally is going to make divorce the latest thing.

8th December 1936

Wally emerged just before luncheon. She slept through all the ringing of telephones. HM, desperate to talk to her. Fruity, desperate for her *not* to talk to HM, in case she weakens. The secretary of the lawyer Goddard, to say he's on his way here. Freddie Crosbie, with bulletins. Also, Daisy Fellowes sent a wire. She'll be arriving off Cannes tomorrow and has offered to keep her yacht steamed up and ready to whisk Wally away at a moment's notice. I'll bet Hattie put her up to that.

Perry said, "Let's keep that one up our sleeve. It might provide a useful emergency exit, but we don't want Wally going anywhere else until she's made it clear to the King that they're finished. She has to deliver the death blow."

The puzzle is why is Goddard coming? Wally can offer no explanation.

Herman said, "You didn't slip any Crown Jewels in your bag, did you, Wally? We don't want to get arrested as accessories."

HM telephoned throughout the afternoon. Wally says she wishes they'd find some extra Despatch Boxes to keep him occupied.

At dinner, Perry floated a new suggestion. He said, "Wally, if you were to withdraw your divorce action now, wouldn't it send the clearest possible signal to HM that marriage is out of the question?"

She said, "It should. But it's David. I don't think he'd take any notice. I don't think anything is going to stop him now."

It seems to me it's worth a try, if she really wants to disengage herself. That's the crux of it. I'm not sure she does want to. I never saw her dither like this before.

She's said she'll sleep on it. She went to bed as soon as dinner was over, with orders that she wasn't to be disturbed, but she heard the telephone when Fruity called just before midnight and came out in her wrap to find out if there was any news, which there certainly was. HM has begun negotiating for a title and an income in the event of his abdication.

Kath gave her a brandy and soda, but she didn't drink it. She just sat twisting the glass around and around.

She said, "You see? This is what I was afraid of. He's only saying these things because I've gone away and left him. Talk to him, Perry. Tell him to stay calm. Tell him I'll wait quietly until after the Coronation, and so must he."

She started to go back to bed, then she stopped again. "Tell him I have no interest in being the Queen of Nowhere."

I stayed down and had a nightcap with Kath. She said, "She has an escape route staring her in the face. All she has to do is stop the divorce. Why is she hesitating, Maybell? Can it be she actually loves him?"

I think perhaps she does, just a little. And she could still be the Duchess of Lancaster. It surely has to be better than being Mrs. Simpson.

9th December 1936

The lawyer Goddard has arrived, and not alone. He's brought a physician with him, because HM is worried Wally's health is breaking down under all this strain. Perry B. is livid. He said, "Just what we need! Five hundred hacks outside the gate, watching every move we make, and we get a house call from a Royal doctor. You realize what everyone's going to think?"

He delegated me and Kath to find out from Wally if she's carrying HM's child.

She shrieked with laughter. She said, "I've got ulcers and palpitations and my hair's falling out, but not that, thankfully. Never that. David isn't heir-conditioned."

The doctor has prescribed rest and plain food. I think I could have been a doctor.

The purpose of Goddard's visit is rather serious. On Monday afternoon, a person in London swore an affidavit that he can show good cause why Wally and Ernest's divorce shouldn't be finalized. He's called a Common Informer, with the emphasis on "common," I'm sure. It's just some elderly clerk who has obviously been paid to do it, but Goddard says it places HM in a very dangerous position, the allegation being that Ernest's infidelity was a charade performed to oblige the King.

Herman said, "Of course, this Common Informer is only saying what everyone has known all along."

Goddard said, "He most certainly is not. When His Majesty asked me to advise Mrs. Simpson in the matter of a divorce, I had absolutely no idea he had in mind to marry her."

Herman said, "I see. And would you be uncovering your legal ass too much to advise Mrs. Simpson what she should do now?"

Goddard said, "She could withdraw her application. Or not."

Wally said, "It's obvious. I have to call the whole thing off. If I stop the divorce, Mr. Common Informer can go to hell, and they can keep their King. Ernest will understand. I'll call David now."

Perry went with her to the dining room to wait for her call to be put through, and we all sat in nerve-stretching tension, but it turned out HM wasn't available, and he still wasn't available by the time dinner was over. Wally said, "I'll do it in the morning. If I tell him at this time of night, he'll get drunk."

Kath said, "I don't believe I've ever seen David drunk."

Perry said, "There was a time when we all drank too much. When we were young."

Goddard is leaving in the morning with Wally's new instructions. The question now is, how Ernest will take the news. I don't imagine he'll want Wally back when he has Mary Kirk waiting in the wings. In fact, he may absolutely insist on being discovered in adultery and divorced.

Wally said, "In the morning, Maybell, I want you to go into Nice and buy us tickets to somewhere. China. Anywhere."

Herman said, "Do you want to go to China, Maybell?"

I'm not at all sure I do.

Wally was very sharp with him. She said, "China was the first place that came into my head. We can go anywhere. Maybell knows what to do. And the detective can go with her. He's supposed to have a brain."

Rain lashing against the windows. I haven't been outside for two whole days.

Letters have begun to arrive. How puzzling people are, to take out their pens and write pages of abuse to a total stranger. We read a few, and when the tone of them became clear, Herman told his head gardener to take all mail addressed to Wally directly to the incinerator.

10th December 1936

Everything is falling apart. When Wally finally got through to HM and told him she was stopping her divorce, he said it would make no difference, because the papers for his abdication have been drawn up and he intends to follow her to the ends of the earth.

"To the moon!" she said. "I don't know whether to laugh or cry. He says he'll follow me to the moon, if necessary. He's really quite lost his mind."

Herman and I drove in to Nice and purchased tickets for the overnight train to Brindisi on Saturday. There are plenty of sailings to faraway places from there. There's a boat sailing for Ceylon on Sunday, which Herman thinks may fit the bill.

Wally took a pill after lunch and slept. News came from London in fits and starts.

Sometimes the telephone rang, but the line was so bad we couldn't hear anything. It seems the lawyers are arranging the transfer of Balmoral and Sandringham to the Yorks.

HM has agreed to leave Britain for at least two years, and in exchange may be allowed to keep Fort Belvedere, except for the lawn-mowing machine, which Bertie York always coveted. Kath said it sounds more like a fire sale than the end of a reign.

HM's new title will be His Royal Highness Prince Edward Duke of Windsor.

Herman said, "So, Wally still has a chance to become a Royal Highness. I say, Maybell, if I were you, I'd hold off ordering your tropical gear. Ceylon may be off."

As far as I'm concerned, it was never really on. Wherever Ceylon is, I'm sure it's inconvenient.

Ernest called, but Wally was still in a drugged sleep, so Herman asked me to speak to him. He was very civil.

He said, "I heard from my lawyer. Will you please tell Wally, I'll do whatever seems best, but in the long run, I'd still like a divorce. I'm with Mary Kirk now, you know, and I want to be free to marry her. But if it helps Wally to delay things a little, till all this has calmed down, she has my word."

I said, "There's talk of going to Ceylon."

"Is there?" he said. "Well, I'm sure she'll be a great hit wherever she goes."

Then Fruity got through to say that the abdication papers had been signed and Baldwin was making a statement to Parliament. Perry sat with his head in his hands after taking that call. He said, "His Majesty is to make a farewell broadcast to the nation tomorrow evening."

Except I suppose he won't be HM anymore.

Apparently, he's giving a little dinner tonight. The Erlangers, the Crokers, Fruity and Baba. The old faithfuls. "The Last Supper," Perry said.

Wally came down, still groggy from her pill, and took a call from HM. We heard her say, "But where will you go? You can't come here."

She put Perry on. She said, "You talk to him. He says he's going to a hotel in Zurich. He can't go to a hotel. The man is clueless."

She paced around while Perry was on the phone. He suggested the Westminsters' place in Normandy, or Schloss Pfaffenhof. I heard him say, "Sir, a private house would be much more suitable."

It was Herman who thought of the Eugene Rothschilds.

Wally was shouting, "Tell him the Rothschilds'll have him. Tell him Herman's going to wire them and arrange it. Tell him he absolutely must not come here. And tell him I've gone back to bed."

Perry looks quite gray. Kath said, "Does anyone else have the feeling they've slipped through the looking glass? Is this really happening?"

I said, "It's a pity a sweet little King like David can't be allowed to marry the woman he loves."

Kath said, "If you ask me, the real pity is that he doesn't love a better woman."

Herman spoke with Kitty Rothschild. Eugene is away in Paris, but she's happy to put Schloss Enzesfeld at HM's disposal, if he doesn't mind sharing it with her. More calls to and from the Fort. It seems there's nothing left to be done. David has given up his throne so he can have Wally, but Wally doesn't really want him without his throne.

Herman answered a final call just as I was preparing to come upstairs. He said, "If you look in on Wally, please tell her Rex Quondam says 'sweet dreams.' "

I found her on the bed, still in her clothes and sobbing quite pitifully. Such tears. I've never, never known Wally to go to bed without putting on a fresh nightgown and having Burke take everything away for brushing and hanging.

"He's ruined everything" was all she'd say. "The goddamned fool has ruined everything."

She was so distressed. I didn't even mention Mr. Quondam. Perhaps he'd be willing to go with her to Ceylon. Whoever he is.

11th December 1936

This has been the saddest day. HM, or HRH, as we must now revert to calling him, left Fort Belvedere this afternoon. He went up to Windsor Castle to dine with his mother and his brothers and then made his wireless broadcast from a room in the Augusta Tower. We heard it in Herman's library, relayed by French radio. He said that he had felt unable to do the job of King without the help and support of the woman he loved, and so he had been succeeded by his brother, the Duke of York. He didn't actually say Wally's name. He called her "the other person most nearly concerned." He said the decision to abdicate was his and his alone, and that she had tried to dissuade him from it. Then they played "God Save the King." It was all over in five minutes.

I cried, and so did Perry and Kath. Wally remained very composed, but I guess she's already done her crying.

Pips called us later. She said everything seemed muffled in London, like after a fall snowfall. She said there were crowds outside Buckingham Palace, but all very orderly, just standing there, trying to take in the news. Freddie thinks once everyone is over the shock, they'll take quite happily to the new management, especially with them having those two little girls. They'll be able to trot them out in pretty little dresses, and the newspapers will adore them. This could be a big opportunity for Flora, if only she'd stop wearing Rory's old sweaters and learn to get along nicely with the York girls. There must be great excitement at Carlton Gardens today. Violet will be getting her coronet out of storage.

Bertie York is going to be known as King George VI. I wonder what they'll do with all those Coronation items they've already had manufactured? They'll have to start over now, with new pictures.

The telephone has now fallen silent. I guess HRH must be on his way to the Rothschilds.

12th December 1936

The Brindisi train, for which we held tickets, left without us. All the pep seems to have gone out of Wally. She said, "Maybe I'll go to Argentina. I know people there. I think I'll talk to David. See what provision has been made for him. I think he'd rather like it there. He likes ranches, and they have good golf there, too."

Herman says she's been doing her math. Wally minus David equals middle-aged outcast living off her capital. Wally plus David equals a title and an income for life. He said, "I think, Maybell, you may soon be off the hook, Kath and I will be left in peace, and Perry will be able to go home."

I don't know that it's going to be so simple.

Walter Monckton called this afternoon with a progress report on HRH. He drove with him as far as Portsmouth, saw him aboard the destroyer that was taking him to France, then said good-bye. David is traveling with just one valet, a detective, Joey Legh as equerry, and Wally's dog. Monckton said the final moments were quite heartbreaking. The royal party, such as it is, should be at Enzesfeld sometime tomorrow.

"Twenty-four hours without pointless phone calls," was Wally's only comment.

I still can't believe it's over. We all know about revolutions and the havoc Communists can wreak, but I'd never realized a king can just stop being king.

14th December 1936

HRH—just when I'd grown accustomed to calling him HM—HRH is now installed at the Rothschilds, but there's already a problem, because neither Joey Legh nor the detective nor the valet speak German, and Kitty R. hasn't trained her servants to understand English. If I married a Rothschild, even a minor one, like Eugene, the first thing I'd do is import a smart American staff.

Wally is in a softer mood. Now the throne is well and truly gone, I think she's preparing herself to become the Duchess of Windsor. She's certainly told Goddard to go ahead with the application for her divorce to be finalized.

She said, "I'll take my chances with this Common Informer. I didn't go through the hell of Felixstowe to have some hired monkey deprive me of my divorce. I want it, Ernest wants it, and anyway, what can they do to David now? Send a constable to Austria to arrest him?"

Perry B. is leaving for Enzesfeld in the morning. Herman drove me and Wally into town to shop for Christmas gifts for him to take for David. Cigars from me, cashmere sweaters and a possum leather coat with a fur lining from Wally.

More rain. The press are packing up and leaving.

18th December 1936

A difficult day. Wally is down in the dumps. She says she's committed no crime and yet she's been sentenced to life. She says she felt in constant danger yesterday while we were in town, as though at any moment some mad person might shoot her or throw acid in her face. Of course, if she'd just dress "down" a little, no one would even notice her. So many jewels before luncheon is guaranteed to draw attention.

I said, "People will soon forget." Even that was the wrong thing to say.

She said, "I'm not the kind of woman people forget. Those Yorks are probably planning to have me assassinated."

Herman said, "Wally, dearest, if that's what they wanted, they'd have had it done while you were handy. I don't think the Yorks would go to the expense of sending an assassin to Cannes."

She said, "None of you has any idea. I'm stuck here in this freezing house, weeks and weeks of it stretching before me, and at the end of it, nothing but uncertainty. It's all very well for you. You can come and go as you please. You can go back to your old lives. But I've given up everything. I'm a prisoner here, and I'm going through absolute hell."

She slammed the door and went to lie down. Herman slammed another door and went to burn some more of her hate letters. As Kath says, we seem doomed to pay for each of Wally's gayer moments with ten of Lady Macbeth's.

She said, "I don't know how you put up with her, Maybell."

Well, we go back a long way. I'm the sister she never had, and she appreciates me a good deal more than Violet Melhuish does. And Wally may be going to be the Duchess of Windsor, but I still see that desperate little girl from Biddle Street.

Kath says she should look for a house in the New Year. She said, "She needs her own establishment. She's driving all our help to distraction, and it's going to be months before she can join David, if that's her plan."

I said, "I know. I'll suggest it. Are you worried about a repetition of what happened in Peking?"

She said, "Nothing happened in Peking. Not that it wasn't offered and not that Herman mightn't have been tempted by a beautiful woman, but Wally had far too much mileage on the clock even then. She was really known as quite an old drab, you know? And that voice! Of course, she's toned it down since she moved to England, but it still reminds me of a buzz saw."

20th December 1936

Perry Brownlow is in Enzesfeld and reports that HRH is very happy and optimistic. "Demob fever" Perry called it. That nice young attaché, Forwood, has agreed to act as German-speaking equerry. Wally's happy about the appointment.

Perry was supposed to go home directly from Enzesfeld, but he's agreed to make a detour to come back here and deliver Wally's Christmas gifts. Wally tried to wheedle out of him what he's bringing, but he wouldn't even give her a hint.

23rd December 1936

Perry B. got here late last night with a mink cape and a choker of baroque pearls. Wally says the cape is of a rather old-fashioned cut, but she'll probably be able to have it remodeled once she gets to Paris.

She gave Perry quite a grilling on the state of negotiations over HRH's money and was far from satisfied with his answers. He said, "These are complicated affairs, and without precedent, so we must just be patient. His Royal Highness is hardly on the breadline, Wally."

She said, "Don't you Wally me. You'll call me 'ma'am' from now on."

We were all speechless. He left for the aerodrome immediately, anxious about getting home for Christmas.

Kath gave her a piece of her mind. She said, "How could you speak to him like that? Perry's been a tireless friend to you and the loyalest of servants to David."

Wally said, "I know that, and he knows I know. But he still better get used to calling me ma'am."

Kath said, "Don't you think that's a bit premature? Don't you think you ought to count your friends and your blessings while you're still Wally Simpson?"

Herman said, "And Perry's borne heaven knows what expenses out of his own pocket."

She said, "He can afford it. It's only for the time being. David will take care of things when his money comes through."

I don't know. David doesn't usually take care of anyone except himself and *Einum Meinum.*

I hope they'll have patched things up by dinnertime. We're supposed to be going to the Palm Beach Casino. Daisy Fellowes is giving a party, and the Cavetts will be there.

25th December 1936

All the church bells were ringing as we drove to the casino last night. It was wonderfully picturesque. I gave Wally a set of silk lingerie bags, which are going to be embroidered with her monogram. As she says, whether she becomes the Duchess of Windsor or reverts to Wally Warfield, a W will see her through the rest of her life. She gave me Vetiver cologne and the Rogerses a little silver card tray. I think I remember it from Fort Belvedere, but Herman and Kath don't need to know that. Perhaps they'd be thrilled though.

I put a call through to South Audley Street and spoke to Lightfoot. He said things are so calm in London you would never believe how people felt only two weeks ago. He said, "It's all going to turn out for the best. Bertie York didn't want the job, but now he's got it he'll settle down to it."

He and Flora were about to leave for luncheon at Carlton Gardens. Doopie was with Marina Kent, who is expected to give birth today.

He's still talking about volunteering for Spain. I said, "What about Doopie? You can't get married and then go off fighting other people's wars."

He said, "Perhaps she'll volunteer, too. I think she'd make rather an angelic nurse, don't you?"

Wally was on the telephone with HRH for more than an hour. The tone seemed to be intimate. Herman says a pearl choker is a well-known aphrodisiac. Tonight to Cap Ferrat, for dinner with a neighbor of the Rogerses, who writes books. A Mr. Maugham. Wally insists that I've heard of him. Apparently, he used to be married to Syrie Maugham, but now lives in an unnatural alliance with a secretary from California. Poor Syrie. She was the one who did

Pips and Freddie's sitting room in bone and buttermilk. It was considered the height of fashion for about five minutes.

26th December 1936

Wally says she enjoyed last evening, but I found Willie Maugham rather rude. I asked him all the questions one knows to ask a writer. Are they at work on their next tome? Where do they find their inspiration? I even offered him some of my own ideas, but he didn't thank me for them. And Wally may think he found her very witty, but I think his tone was rather mocking. Also, the secretary kept interrupting dinner with abrupt entrances and exits and silly remarks to no one in particular. I believe he may have been tight. Not surprising, because the martinis were stiff ones, but still, a secretary should be kept busy at his typewriter. He should have no occasion to go anywhere near the drinks' tray.

31st December 1936

The sun tried its best to break through this morning, but Wally's mood is somber. I suppose whether she looks back or ahead, she sees nothing but regrets. When I wrote my first entry for this year, how little I suspected.

Kath has invited people in for this evening. Her idea is to nip in the bud any talk of going to a casino.

1st January 1937

Herman and Kath did their very best to keep things gay last evening. Came: Daisy Fellowes, the Bajavidas, the Cavetts, and the Genoas, who'd motored in from Menton. But the telephone was brought to Wally during dinner, and one couldn't help but hear poor HRH sobbing in faraway Enzesfeld. It was a tricky moment, but Wally remained very calm. "Tomorrow's a new year, darling," she said, "and we can attack all these problems with new vigor."

When the call ended, she said, "He's had too much brandy. No one will have thought to warn Forwood about solitary drinking. I seem to be the only person who takes proper care of him."

Pips and Freddie are proposing to visit on their way to Chamonix. Kath and Herman say they may take advantage of Wally having new distractions and go away for a few days themselves.

4th January 1937

Dudley Forwood reports that HRH is suffering from earache. Wally told him to get a doctor sent out from Harley Street, but Forwood says that a very good ear doctor from Vienna had made a house call, and Kitty Rothschild is personally supervising the treatment he recommended.

Wally said, "Is she indeed. Well, she'd better not be getting any ideas."

Kath said, "What can you mean? Kitty is a happily married woman."

Wally said, "Happily married for the *third* time. Who's to say she's not on the lookout for number four? Especially a king."

Kath said, "Wally! Aren't you planning to marry for the third time? Anyhow, David's not King anymore, and Kitty must be fifty-five if she's a day."

"All the more dangerous then," Wally snapped right back. "The desperate age."

5th January 1937

Every time Wally speaks to HRH, she questions him about Kitty Rothschild. I had no idea she could be so jealous. She denies it, of course.

She said, "I'm not jealous. But David's hopelessly weak. Look how he allowed Baldwin to bully him. Look how he allows the Bertie Yorks to dictate to him. Keeping him out of his money. Forbidding the brothers to visit. If Kitty Rothschild decided to seduce him, he'd just cave in."

HRH had been hoping that George Kent or Harry Gloucester might fly over for a weekend, to keep him company, but apparently this has been vetoed from above.

8th January 1937

Pips and Freddie have arrived like a breath of fresh air. Pips says anyone known still to be a friend of HRH or Wally has been dropped. Daphne Frith cut her in the Army & Navy. Melhuish walked into the Guards' Club, saw Freddie, and walked right out again. And the Perry Brownlows sound to be absolutely finished. I feel so sorry for them, especially her. She didn't do anything. She didn't even know Perry was escorting Wally to France until after we'd set off, but his actions have damned them both. Pips says they may just as well pack up and go to the South Pole.

Wally's been pumping for stories about Elizabeth York. Who's going to be her couturier now she's Queen? Does she still talk about fishing? Will she get her teeth fixed before the Coronation?

Pips says she doesn't like to disappoint Wally, but all the signs are that the Yorks are going to be very popular. She said, "All that talk about David modernizing things. I think the country's relieved. The British don't like modernity. They like squashy old armchairs covered in the same style of chintz their mothers had, and that's exactly the kind of monarchy they're going to get with Elizabeth and Bertie York."

9th January 1937

The Rogerses have left for a short holiday at Schloss Pfaffenhof. Kath said, "Wally's talking about taking a house till her divorce is final. Will you go back to London?"

I said, "I will if someone spells me as her companion. I promised David I'd look after her."

Pips said, "Don't look at me. And I wouldn't oversell yourself as *companion,* Maybell. Frankly, I think she uses you."

Once upon a time, maybe, but not anymore. She may have HRH, but I'm her closest friend. People talk about her vivacity, but she's lonely, too. She needs someone to confide in. And we do have some laughs. Not recently, perhaps, but we will again.

10th January 1937

Instead of going to Chamonix, Pips is going to stay on here a little longer, and Freddie's going to join Fruity Metcalfe's skiing party at Kitzbuhel. We girls are going to shop and have a jolly time together. We're going to put this shocking last month behind us.

Dudley Forwood says Kitty Rothschild is going to Paris at the beginning of February and then on to New York, leaving them with sole occupancy of Enzesfeld. Wally won't have to worry about guarding HRH's honor for much longer.

Freddie says he's not surprised to hear the Rothschilds intend to spend more time in Paris, because Eugene R. is a Jew, and if Adolf Hitler takes over Austria, people of that persuasion can expect the same treatment as their German cousins.

Apparently, they're not allowed to sit on park benches, and can have their *schloss*es taken from them at the drop of a hat. I had no idea.

13th January 1937

Wally is being disagreeable to the Rogerses' staff. She says she's just attempting to bring them up to standard mark, and it's true they are not as efficient as the staff she's been accustomed to in London, but France is a backward country, and I'm sure Kath has done the best she can. Anyway, I don't think it's at all right that Wally's having furniture moved and *objets* stored away. It's not as though we've taken a lease here.

Pips said, "Wally, you have no class. How would you feel if I came for the weekend and started bundling all your horrible embroidered cushions into a closet?"

Wally said, "*I'd* never ask anyone to live with all this oak and pewter, and my cushions aren't horrible, they're witty."

Pips said, "Oh well, let's change Kath's drapes while we're about it. And how about knocking down a few walls?"

Wally said, "Don't think I wouldn't if I had to stay here much longer."

The main butt of her crossness is HRH. She goes through lists of complaints whenever they talk, and she never seems satisfied with the answers. She's made several marks on the dining-room table where she keeps banging with her gold pencil.

This morning, we could hear her blessing him out, "Tell them you'll go back if they don't pay you every cent you're owed. Go anyway. Take the damned crown back. You're such a milksop. Why did you let them push you out? Why didn't you go to the people? Those little miners would have defended you. They still would."

She was white with fury when she came off the telephone.

Pips said, "You're not serious about David going back? That would amount to a revolution."

Wally said, "What if it did? We Americans had one and it didn't do us any harm."

But she isn't truly serious about it, because she's going to marry him and she already told me she has no intention of living in England again.

She said, "They could have had me as Queen. They could have had me as the King's special friend. But nobody gets a second chance with me."

Pips said, "Then be careful what you say to him, or he may just go and do it."

Wally said, "No he won't. He can't organize a tea party without me, let alone a coup. I only say these things to try and put a little fire in his belly. He's up there in that goddamned *schloss,* practicing his putting while the Yorks are taking the bread from his mouth. And he doesn't have anyone there to keep him on track. Legh's a yes-man, and Forwood doesn't have the confidence. Brownlow might have been more useful, but he's gone scurrying back to wifey at the first opportunity. So it falls to me. If I don't nag, he's going to end up with nothing."

As Pips says, "Oh boy!"

Only a few newspaper stragglers left outside the gates now. The world has forgotten about Wally already, just as I predicted.

15th January 1937

Drove into Monaco to meet Hattie Erlanger, who's in town with Daisy Fellowes. Also came: the Genoas and a little Maharaja they have staying with them. Modest losses at roulette. Wally and the Maharaja played chemin de fer. She says she made enough to buy herself a little something. Hattie says the Belchesters have dropped her and Judson, and are now sucking up to the New Bunch.

18th January 1937

Wally spent her casino winnings on a python purse. The Crokers may come for a few days next week. Every little bit helps.

We drove up into the hills this afternoon and bought honeysuckle scent for a song.

20th January 1937

Fruity Metcalfe has offered to go up to Enzesfeld when his ski party leaves Kitzbuhel and relieve Joey Legh as equerry. HRH is thrilled, which has put Wally's nose out of joint, for some odd reason. I heard her say, "Day after day I try to comfort you, and all I hear is what a wretched time you're having of it, but as soon as Metcalfe deigns to pay you a visit, you become bright and cheerful. It's pretty insulting."

25th January 1937

Pips left this morning just as Boss and Ethel were arriving. As Ethel says, it's like relay race and Wally is the baton that must not be dropped.

To the Ladybird Club. The Bajavidas are giving a party.

26th January 1937

Who should turn up with the Bajavidas last night but Fern and Charlie Bedaux.

Charlie says his money is still on David for King. He said, "He'll make a comeback. You'll see."

Wally said, "He doesn't want to. He's glad to be out of it. And the New Bunch don't even like him telephoning to offer advice, so to hell with them. He can be the King across the water and have more time for his golf."

27th January 1937

Fern Bedaux telephoned this morning. She said, "I know there are rules about the way these things are broached, but I'm not even sure if David's 'royal' anymore. Charlie and I would like to offer Chateau Candé. Wally can stay there till her divorce is through, and then, if they want to, she and David can be married there. Kath and Herman are sweeties, but I really don't think you can perch there for months. Will you put it to Wally, or David, or whomever? I can have Candé ready in two weeks."

Wally accepted immediately. Once she's settled at Candé, I think I'll go back to London for a while. See whether there's anything left of my life to pick up.

28th January 1937

Dudley Forwood has warned HRH against accepting offer from Charlie Bedaux. He says certain adverse reports exist, in which Charlie's name appears. Adverse reports! The British hate a self-made man, of course. They don't want to know you unless you have a bed King Charles slept in and a family tree that goes back to 1066. Anyhow, Wally has already accepted, and I don't see it's anyone else's business.

29th January 1937

Shopping. Wally bought a silver-fox coat and a gray crepe day dress with little mirror buttons. Blue skies and sunshine. We sat out on the quay, had champagne and shrimp, and talked about the great turnaround of the past year.

I said, "You know there was a time when I thought you didn't want to marry David."

She said, "I never looked for it. I never meant for all this to happen, but then the King went and died on us. I blame myself in many ways. I should have realized David's judgment wasn't to be relied on. But what's done is done. Now I'm going to make lovely homes for him and take care of him. He's not difficult to manage, after all, and quite presentable. I think we'll do very well."

I said, "I thought I might go back to London. See a few people."

"What people?" she said. She forgets I have a family.

I said, "You'll have Fern for company. Three can be a crowd."

She said, "But I don't know if Fern will be available for shopping. How long did you want to take off?"

I said, "I'm not the hired help, Wally. I dropped everything to dash down here with you when things went bad, and I do have a life of my own."

She said, "Very well. But you know you are practically part of the firm now, so please don't be gone for long. We're going to have a royal wedding to organize and lots and lots of shopping to do!"

2nd February 1937

A call from Dudley Forwood, who asked for me. He said, "It's rather delicate, Mrs. Brumby. Baroness Rothschild left for Paris yesterday, and I'm afraid His Royal Highness has caused her great offense. First of all, he didn't get out of bed to say good-bye to her. But what concerns me more, he didn't tip any of her departing staff, and they'd looked after him exceptionally well. I wondered if Mrs. Simpson could bring her influence to bear? Perhaps get His Royal Highness to write the Baroness a little note? I wondered if you could mention it? Also, there's the question of ongoing expenses. The Baron and Baroness have been very generous, but they're not *that* kind of Rothschild, you understand? The telephone bills alone are terrifying. I think a word from the right quarter might encourage more consideration."

I said, "Why don't you speak to Mrs. Simpson yourself?"

He said, "I very much doubt she'd listen as patiently as you have."

Wally said, "How petty. Telephone bills! Well, I'm not bothering David with a thing like that. He has quite enough to do, battling with the New Bunch for his dues. Let Metcalfe deal with it, and the tipping. Let him earn his keep."

Hattie has arrived.

4th February 1937

HRH's sister, the Princess Royal, is going to Enzesfeld to visit him this weekend. Wally says this may be a positive sign. It may mean that Baldwin has at last loosened the purse strings and agreed an allowance. She says Bertie York is too stiff-necked to let

George Kent or Harry Gloucester bring David the good news but probably feels it's all right to allow the sister.

Hattie said, "David must be so happy. He adores his sister."

I said, "I met her once, at Violet's."

Wally said, "Well, I never met her and never wanted to."

6th February 1937

HRH is in the doghouse. He went into Vienna to meet his sister and her husband, and discovered that instead of bringing good news they brought bad. He's to receive no monies from the Civil List. Not a dime. This means that all he'll have is a pittance from the sale of Sandringham and Balmoral, out of which he'll have to pay pensions to old retainers who will, as Wally says, all live to be a hundred. So, effectively, he's going to be living on his meager capital. Poor HRH, literally. And poor Wally. This is not at all what she'd been led to expect.

She said, "He's taking it lying down, of course. No spine. And as if that's not bad enough, he's offered to give them a day of his time and show them around the Schonbrunn while they're in town. I told him, he'd better charge them. He'd better tell them that's what he has to do for a living now those ingrates have cut him off without a penny. A King giving guided tours! What a shabby outfit England has become. *And* he treated them to lunch at the Bristol."

Hattie says she doubts HRH ever treated anyone to lunch in his life. She predicts that Fruity will have had to put his hand in his pocket.

It's all a gruesome mess. At this rate, I can quite see the wedding not coming off.

9th February 1937

Georgie Kent is now going to visit Enzesfeld, after all, but without his wife. She's only just out of childbed. Wally's hoping it means Baldwin has had second thoughts about HRH's money. Hattie says there's been a rumor circulating ever since the abdication that HRH walked off with some very particular emeralds, formerly the property of his grandmother, so it could be Kent is being sent to retrieve them.

Wally said, "David took no jewels. He left in the clothes he stood up in. I wish he had taken them. They'd look a damned sight better on me than on that little Scotch dumpling they have for a Queen now."

12th February 1937, Chateau Candé, Tours

Fern and Charlie's chateau is exquisite. We arrived just after a shower of rain, and the pines along the driveway smelled wonderfully refreshing. There is a first-rate American furnace keeping the place warm, and an army of properly trained staff. The crystal and plate are all of the highest quality, the flowers are perfectly arranged, and Fern Bedaux has even given up her own room, so Wally is happy at last.

Hattie and I can leave her without a backward glance.

16th February 1937, Wilton Place

It feels unreal to be here. Every pillow and powder bowl exactly as I left it, when so much else has changed. Two letters from Randolph Putnam, the first written while HM was still HM, the second wondering whether "the strawberry blonde companion of the exiled King's moll" could possibly be me!

No one at home at South Audley Street or at Carlton Gardens. Bumped into Penelope Blythe in Piccadilly, and she suggested lunch, but at some little hole-in-the-wall in Chelsea. She said she had a portrait sitting at two, so it would be more convenient, but I guess she didn't want to risk anyone connected with the New Bunch seeing us together. She even insisted on going Dutch for lunch, drawing a certain line between us, I suppose.

She said, "I do feel sorry for you, Maybell. After all, anyone can back the wrong horse."

I said, "It all depends whether you think it was a fairly run race, and I don't. I feel HRH is being treated very badly."

She said, "But he was the one who started it. This is England, you know. In this country, when a king takes on Parliament, Parliament wins, thank God. Well, now he's ruined. Wally Simpson's best plan would be to go to Australia and hope to meet someone with money."

I was never especially fond of Penelope.

17th February 1937

Violet appeared just as I was about to go up for my bath. She said, "So? Back with your tail between your legs?"

I said, "No. I'm here to see my London friends, but not for long. I'll be going back to France, to help Wally plan her wedding."

"Ah," she said, "the blushing bride. Again. Just as well you're not staying long. I must ask you not to come to the house. Melhuish has been rocked by recent events. I won't have him upset."

I said, "But he always reckoned Bertie York would make a better King. Surely he's happy the way things have turned out?"

She said, "You misremember, Maybell. He never reckoned any such thing. Melhuish was always loyalty itself to Wales. He'll never forgive him for what he's done. Queen Mary is heartbroken. And the poor Yorks. Their lives will never be the same."

I said, "Well, HRH isn't having such a wonderful time of it. He's stuck on a mountainside in Austria and having to count every cent."

She said, "He gets no sympathy from me. Nothing has happened to him that he didn't bring on himself. I've come only to tell you that Doopie and Flora are at Carlton Gardens. You'll find no one at South Audley Street. Lightfoot has gone to Paris to volunteer."

We must have passed each other in transit.

I said, "So, how am I supposed to see my sister and my niece if I'm not allowed across your threshold?"

She said, "You should have thought of that before you threw in your lot with that woman. I rue the day you ever brought her home from school."

17th February 1937

Intercepted Doopie and Flora at Duck Island. Flora was so excited to see me. She said, "Aunt Bayba! You've been even badder than me! Ulick says we're not obliged to know you anymore, but me and Rory still love you."

Doopie smiled. She said, "Done worry. Zoon be vagodden."

I said, "And what does Lightfoot think he's doing, volunteering for wars? Why did you let him go?"

Flora said, "But it's exciting. I wish we could go."

Doopie said, "Baps we will, iv it's a log war."

If Violet heard that kind of talk, Flora would be back at St. Audrey's under lock and key. But she won't hear it from me.

To the Crosbies for dinner. I said, "Shall I wear a wig and come to the tradesman's entrance? I don't want to ruin your standing in London."

Pips said, "You can come in a grass skirt, for all the difference it'd make to us. We don't have any standing. Never did have."

18th February 1937

Pips has started wearing pants. Très chic. Of course, she has no BTM.

Freddie says Fort Belvedere is closed up, and HRH's things have been taken to Frogmore for storing. All he took with him to Enzesfeld were twenty-six suits and his photographs of Wally. Perry Brownlow continues to be treated disgracefully. He's been sacked as Lord-in-Waiting to the new King, for no reason except he was loyal and obedient to the last one. Damned if he did, damned if he didn't.

Lunch today with Ida Coote. She, at least, is willing to be seen with me at the Dorch, if there's a free meal on offer. She says London is changed. She went to Ciro's the other night and didn't see anyone she knew. She's thinking of volunteering for Spain, like Lightfoot. She has no nursing experience but believes there may be a need for concert parties. Everyone seems to have Spain fever.

I've decided to pay a visit to Eton College on Sunday. Violet may have banned me from Carlton Gardens, but I don't believe she said anything about visiting Rory at his school.

19th February 1937

Rory's House Master was charming when I telephoned. He said Melhuish Minor would be delighted to see me after Chapel on Sunday.

He said, "Unfortunately, Melhuish Major will be in Snowdonia for Cadet Force exercises."

Good. I didn't want to see him anyway. To a wonderful little shop behind the Strand for a ghost tube and a selection of magician's silks.

21st February 1937

The familiar road to Windsor, and yet it seemed like a lifetime ago. I had Kettle drive me up to the Fort before we continued on to Eton. It was as Freddie said. Everything closed up, and the gardens looked so sad and wintery. There'll be no more gay chicken-fries here I'm sure.

Rory tells me he is now five feet eight and a half inches tall. He said, "It was pretty plucky your coming here. Ulick says we should have nothing more to do with you. Ulick thinks kings who abdicate should be strapped across a gun carriage and flogged, and their friends should be sent to Coventry."

I said, "And what do you think?"

He said, "I don't agree. Not if it's an aunt, because family is family. And not if it's a lady, because ladies should never be blamed for their errors."

We went to the Nook Tea Rooms for cream buns, and he tried out the ghost tube. He said it was highly excellent. He asked in a whisper about Wally.

I said, "She's going to marry the King."

He said, "You mean the Duke of Windsor. We've got a new King now."

He said he likes school, except for the canings. I said, "But why do they cane you? Have you been a naughty boy?"

He said, "Not naughty exactly. I forgot to light Cooper-Grenfell's fire. I forgot twice, actually, but he let me off for my first offense, which was pretty decent of him."

I said, "But why should you have to light this person's fire?"

"Because I'm his fag," he said. "Don't worry, Aunt Maybell. You see, Cooper-Grenfell's a Senior, and when I'm a Senior, I'll have a fag to light my fire, too. So it's all perfectly fair."

I said, "Does your mother know you're being beaten?"

"Of course," he said. "Melhuishes have always taken their beatings. And I expect in the future I'll be grateful for it."

He tried his trick cigarette pack on the people at the next table. People fall for it every time.

22nd February 1937

Such a horrid day. First, Elspeth Laird accosted me as I was leaving Derry and Toms. "People like you," she said, "are a stain on decent society. That woman has as good as killed Queen Mary, and you, you! You're shortening my brother's life with your scandalous associations."

Completely unfair. If anything is shortening Melhuish's life it's all the Stilton cheese he eats.

Then Gladys Trilling was ushered to the chair next to me at Monsieur Jules while I was being curled, and asked very loudly to be seated elsewhere. When I think of the hospitality HRH lavished on them, I hope Whitlow Trilling gets posted to Mumbo Jumbo Land and Gladys's one and only evening gown grows mildew.

Then, when I got home, Violet was waiting here, pacing the

floor. She didn't even wait for me to take off my hat. How dare I sneak off to see Rory expressly against Melhuish's wishes, how dare I discuss That Woman with an innocent boy, how dare I taint the Melhuish name with my infamous connection.

I said, "You only forbade me to come to your house. You never mentioned school. And Rory was delighted to see me."

She said, "Rory isn't there to be delighted. He's there to make the right kind of friends, although heaven knows what harm your turning up has done him. And the consequences are even worse for Ulick."

I said, "I didn't even see Ulick."

She said, "That's not the point. One of the Belchester boys saw you. It's all over the school that Mrs. Simpson's best friend visited Rory Melhuish. Ulick's hoping for Sandhurst next year, and this is the kind of thing that will follow him around. You're so selfish, Maybell. You expect to swan around with Wales and his crowd without paying a price. You and Wally thought it great fun to run away and topple a crown and leave others to pick it up and try to repair the damage. And now you walk back into our lives as though nothing happened. Well, no more. I forbid you to have any contact with any of my children anywhere. And don't get tricky with me. I'm having Duck Island watched."

So. Penelope Blythe will only meet me incognito in Chelsea, Gladys Trilling refuses to be dried in the chair next to mine, Elspeth Laird believes I'm killing the Queen, and I'm cut off from my kith and kin. Pips says I should think of it as liberation.

She said, "Melhuish and Violet will mellow. In the meanwhile, think of the gains. No more of Gladys's baby pictures to admire. No more of Violet's poached salmon."

But it's easy for her to say. She has Freddie. They're very jolly together in their own impecunious way. I'm alone. I think I may return to France. There's not much reason to stay in London.

28th February 1937

Spoke with Randolph Putnam. He said, "Why don't you give that place up? Seems to me it's a waste of good money. I've called you every week since Thanksgiving and you're never there."

He said someone has bought the house the Warfields had on Biddle Street, planning to open it as a museum and charge people to see Wally's old bedroom.

He rather wishes he'd thought of it himself.

2nd March 1937

An excited phone call from Wally. The Common Informer has withdrawn his allegations. She has no more idea why he stopped his action than she does why he started it, except that he was obviously put up to it.

She said, "It doesn't matter. I'm in a forgiving mood. In six weeks, I'll be a free woman, and then David and I are going to be married. I need you here, Maybell. There are a thousand and one things to do."

Pips very caustic at lunch. She said, "A thousand and one things to pay for, more likely."

I said, "Well, call me a softie, but when I hear the sound of wedding bells . . ."

"Wedding bells!" she said. "I hear the ringing of cash registers. Be careful you don't end up paying for the whole bang shoot, Maybell. You're such a softie."

I don't care. What am I supposed to do? Go back to Baltimore to be gloated over by Nora Sedley Cordle? Stay in London to be pilloried outside Derry and Toms? I may as well go where my money and I are appreciated. Besides, I'm not rushing back the instant Wally snaps her fingers. First I'm going to Paris to visit with Ena Spain. I leave on tomorrow's lunchtime sailing from Newhaven.

6th March 1937, Meurice Hotel, Paris

Ena Spain is good company. Unlike Wally, she doesn't race from shop to shop and skip lunch. Of course, she was raised the old-fashioned way. In the morning, she writes letters, in the afternoon, we go out for a little fresh air, whatever the weather, then take tea. Ena thinks the positions people are taking up in London are so much hypocrisy. She says the old King used to tell anyone who'd listen that he hoped Bertie York would get the throne. She says he never liked David. She says actually he didn't really like any of his children except the girl, who could do no wrong.

The Yorks' Coronation is somewhat on her mind at present. She'll have to be in her seat by nine o'clock, and then have to sit for hours without being able to powder her nose. It's all right for the men. They can secrete comfort bottles under their robes, but the women just have to suffer. It's amazing to think that an establishment like Westminster Abbey doesn't have restrooms. That's something Wally would have had corrected before any coronation of hers.

9th March 1937

Ena and I have had an adventure. We rode on the Metropolitan underground railway from Rue de Rivoli to the Tuileries Gardens and back again. You purchase a ticket and climb aboard, and you have no way of knowing who you may find sitting next to you. Rattling along beneath the streets in the company of total strangers! Ena has done it several times before. She says once you have lost a child, nothing holds any fears for you.

Tea in the Winter Garden. I sometimes think I could happily give up luncheons and dinners and live on tea and cake.

Friday, to Candé.

13th March 1937, Chateau Candé

The chateau is an absolute spring picture. Miniature jonquils, crocuses, the last of the snowdrops. Wally is looking much more relaxed. I believe she's gained a few pounds. She's decided she doesn't want a May wedding, because May is unlucky and also the attention of the world will be on the Coronation. It looks like June 3rd.

Fern's worried she's tempting fate by making plans before the divorce is definite, but Wally says it's a risk she has to take, otherwise there isn't a hope of her trousseau being ready in time. She's already talked to Main Bocher about her gown. On Tuesday, a *vendeuse* is coming from Schiaparelli, and on Wednesday, a little woman from Reboux to talk about hats.

Wally's already filled several notebooks with lists. She says she's going to make a perfect wedding for David.

Dudley Forwood is leaving the diplomatic corps to become a full-time equerry to HRH. Wally says he'll do nicely once she's trained him.

We now have one of the doggies here. Slipper. HRH thought he'd be company for Wally, so sent him by train with a footman. I wonder how many of Kitty Rothschild's rugs he's ruined.

16th March 1937

A most productive day. Wally is never more decisive than when she's buying clothes. She's ordered five of the nip-waisted wool day dresses, one in each color; some good basic knitwear, edge-to-edge cardigans, evening sweaters decorated with fringing and *marquises;* and then some wittier outfits. A sealskin suit with a matching Tyrolean hat, a Rhodophane evening coat, and a wonderful scarlet cocktail gown with tiny buttons like little holly berries. Main Bocher is bringing his wedding dress drawings on Friday and staying overnight.

There's a panic on though, because Wally has mislaid her birth certificate. She's sent a wire to her aunt Bessie Merryman in Baltimore, but I don't suppose there's anything she can do about it.

17th March 1937

Pips called. She said, "Lost her birth certificate my eye. I'll bet she's lied to HRH about her age."

21st March 1937

Wally has chosen gray-blue for her wedding outfit, ankle-length bias-cut satin crepe with a little box-shouldered jacket, pin-tucked to show off her tiny waist. Main Bocher is delirious about being chosen to make the wedding gown of the year. He flitted around with fabric samples, lavishing compliments on Wally's bony line. For me, he's proposed orchid silk with butterfly wing sleeves. Perfect for a chateau garden in June.

HRH is leaving Enzesfeld at the end of the week. Without the Rothschild staff, the *schloss* has become very inconvenient to manage, so Forwood has found a secluded guesthouse in St. Wolfgang. I suggested Wally arrange a little gift for Kitty R., to say thank you and good-bye, but she didn't respond.

Perhaps Fruity will think to do something.

22nd March 1937

Wally now has a very positive attitude toward the future. She said, "I know I'm not beautiful, and David's not the sharpest item in the knife box, but we make a good team. The world had better watch out. Especially those Yorks. They may have the throne, but once David and I are established, we'll give them a run for their money. *We'll* be the ones people talk about."

She's bought some colored pencils and begun sketching designs for their servants' livery. They'll have a house in Paris and then a place in the country or maybe something near Cannes, a place to relax away from the pressures of being the Windsors. Fern Bedaux has her people looking out for suitable properties.

Wally says HRH is like a lost puppy without her. Wally always had a strange fondness for little dogs. She's so fastidious in every other respect, but it amuses her when they tinkle on the rugs and leave their teeth marks on the chair legs.

A courier just arrived from Enzesfeld with this week's love token. A corsage of knotted gold chains. The note says, *Darling, this is a double half-hitch. A knot that holds fast, however great the storm.*

26th March 1937

A miracle. Wally's Aunt Bessie has managed to track down the doctor who attended at Wally's birth, and he's agreed to swear an affidavit. It should serve in place of the lost birth certificate. HRH is now installed at St. Wolfgang, and Dickie Mountbatten is traveling there tomorrow to pay him a visit. We're hoping he's taking with him better news about money.

28th March 1937

Mountbatten arrived at St. Wolfgang empty-handed. A social call, he said. He wanted to offer himself to be HRH's best man, but apparently a royal bridegroom doesn't have a best man. Wally said, "Princes have supporters, as Dickie Mountbatten well knows, and David intends to follow tradition."

We don't expect the Yorks to attend. They'd only sour the happy occasion, so let them stand on their dignity and stay away. But we do hope George Kent and Harry Gloucester will come, and perhaps the sister. There's even room here for them to land their airplane.

Dudley Forwood is still nagging about us using Candé for the wedding. He says Charlie Bedaux has dubious friends and fingers in suspicious pies. He's only been a proper equerry for five minutes, but he's already getting above himself. Anyway, the wedding has to be here now. Wally's chosen the color of her gown to tone with the silk on the walls in the salon. She's blooming. Like a true bride.

Sunday to the Rogerses for two nights. We have houses to view. Possible future residences for the Duke and Duchess of Windsor!

5th April 1937, Villa Lou Viei

We've looked at properties from Théoule all the way to Nice and my head is spinning. The favorite so far is Chateau La Croe in

Cap d'Antibes. Herman thinks it looks like a beached ocean liner. Wally said if she takes it, it'll not only *look* like a liner, it'll be run like one, with constant hot water and staff who know how to mix martinis. Herman said, "Ah! You mean unlike our poor, leaking ship of fools."

La Croe's situation is very lovely, though I'm not sure I'd want Willy Maugham as a neighbor. He's rude and difficult and as he's had to turn to scribbling, one presumes he wasn't a good doctor. Lost his license, probably.

8th April 1937, Château Candé

Mr. Loo, Wally's little terrier, is dead. We got back here this afternoon, he went gamboling into long grass, and was bitten by a snake. She's inconsolable.

I feel badly now that I complained about him so.

9th April 1937

A letter from Pips. Freddie says HRH is in for an almighty shock if he thinks he can have a royal wedding. He predicts the only royal thing about it will be the frosting on the cake. *What cleric is going to be willing to do the marrying for them?* she writes.

Well, we haven't gotten around to things like that, but the one thing the world will never be short of is priests. Anyway, now is certainly not the time to bring this up with Wally. She's visited Mr. Loo's grave three times today.

12th April 1937

Wally has picked up her wedding lists again, even though, as she says, her heart isn't really in it now one of the principal little guests is dead. She says they don't need a clergyman. She says the local mayor will do everything.

13th April 1937

HRH says he very much wishes to have a church wedding. He's getting Forwood to arrange the English vicar from Vienna. Wally says if it makes HRH happy, she has no objections. The only question is, if there are to be two ceremonies, should there be two wedding gowns? Fern has a pretty little painted cabinet in the drawing room, which turns out to contain a harmonium, so we'll even be able to have the "Wedding March"!

Wally is hesitating about leasing La Croe. It does need improvements, and HRH's budget is still far from clear.

14th April 1937

Wally has *two* new doggies. HRH bought one in St. Wolfgang, and Fern went out and brought one home. It's been named Pookie. Poopie, more like. Wally hasn't let it out of her sight all day and screams at anyone who leaves an outer door open.

Some good news. The New Bunch have at last agreed to pay HRH a pension. I should think so, too, after everything he's done for that country. Fighting in its army. Smiling and nodding his way around those endless factories. Wally says she can now get to work creating a suitably royal ambience for their life together.

Only a week to go, and her divorce should get its rubber stamp. What a long wait it has seemed. She'd have had time to go to Reno, get married again, and be filing for another divorce.

18th April 1937

The Archbishop of Canterbury has forbidden the vicar of Vienna to marry any divorced person. I question why the Archbishop was even consulted on the matter. Everyone knows he's an avowed enemy of Wally and David. Well, it's the Vienna man's loss, not theirs. There must be plenty of vicars in England who'd give anything for a free jaunt to France and the honor of marrying the former King.

HRH has toothache. Gown fittings on Tuesday.

Particulars keep arriving of Paris houses, but so far, nothing seems suitable. Wally says she has to consider appropriateness as well as security. She said, "Royal Highnesses can't live in a walk-up. They can't have an address on any grubby little street."

They can always keep a suite at the Meurice until the right house turns up. There's a lot to be said for a good hotel. I'm thinking I may take Randolph Putnam's advice and let Wilton Place go. Claridge's has always taken good care of me.

20th April 1937

My gown is looking wonderful. Still undecided between raspberry straw or moss green for my pillbox.

Wally said, "Don't fuss so. The cameras are going to be on me, not you."

Perhaps so, but that doesn't mean I should attend her wedding dressed in an unflattering hat.

Herman and Kath have invited me to go with them to Italy after the wedding. I'd been thinking of going back to London, packing up Wilton Place, but Kath has persuaded me. She said, "Italy first, then chores. We all need to remind ourselves there's such a thing as Life After Wally's Wedding."

27th April 1937

We are almost through our ordeal. Wally's lawyer expects her case to be considered on either Friday or Monday. In anticipation, HRH has chosen the first stop on their honeymoon, an Austrian *schloss*. It's called Wasserleonburg and is owned by Count Munster. He used to be a friend of Melhuish and the Yorks, but he now seems to be nailing Windsor colors very prominently to his mast. The *schloss* has a swimming pool and a golf course nearby, and Munster has even offered to have the tennis courts resurfaced.

30th April 1937

Lily Drax-Pfaffenhof knows Wasserleonburg.

She said, "Wally, it's on the top of a mountain. You'll never get down to do any shopping. Tell him you want to go to Capri."

Wally says it wouldn't have been her destination of choice, but she's going to let David have his way. It's his first honeymoon, after all.

1st May 1937

Charlie Bedaux is home. He said, "Can't have His Highness arriving without a proper welcome from his host."

Wally slightly miffed. I believe she's grown to consider Chateau Candé as her own. She was looking forward to playing the grand chatelaine, with Fern discreetly in the background, but Charlie doesn't know the meaning of background.

2nd May 1937

Charlie gave me a golfing lesson. He says my style is "wristy," which sounds like a very desirable quality.

Charlie says the New Bunch at Buckingham Palace show no interest in using HRH's talents and experience, so he intends stepping into the breach.

"Like a Dad," he said. "Or a big brother. That's what the kid needs."

I said, "Hardly a kid. He's forty-two."

He said, "Maybe so, but he still seems like a kid to me. And I'm going to give him a bit of fatherly direction. Foreign visits. I'm gonna send him to Germany. Sweden. The States. People love a royal visit. I tell you something, Maybell. He may be an ex-king, but he's far from finished. And Wally's a real asset. She's got the right instincts, and I've got the useful contacts. Between us, we're going to get him back into the swing."

3rd May 1937

Wally's divorce was made final this morning, and HRH is already on his way here. Fruity is returning to London till the wedding, so there'll just be Forwood, a valet, and a detective. Their train should get to Verneuil by early tomorrow. Wally's sending the Buick and a station wagon to meet him.

I said, "You're sending a car? Don't you want to meet him yourself?"

She said, "No. After all we've been through, I don't want to meet him at some hayseed railroad station."

She is nervous, I think. After all, in a separation of five months, all kinds of changes can occur. I'd say Wally is certainly more in love than she was in December. I just hope HRH is as ardent as ever.

5th May 1937

HRH *is* as ardent as ever. I watched from an upstairs window as he emerged from the car. He fairly sprinted up the steps to embrace Wally. It was rather a shy embrace, considering he gave up a throne for it, but I like to see physical reticence in a man. Philip Sassoon may be a turncoat, but I will say this much for him: he never pressed for anything more than a kiss on the hand, and even then was restrained enough not to make contact.

Quite a crowd had gathered outside the gates to see HRH arrive, and several of the maids were watching from a landing window, till the majordomo hauled them back downstairs to be on parade.

Charlie greeted David American-style, Fern curtsied, and by the time they all trooped through the front hall, Wally had already gained a bouquet of edelweiss and a gold bangle. HRH was delighted to see me. He's thinner.

6th May 1937

The wedding date is now firmly fixed for June 3rd, and Planning Headquarters have been set up in Charlie's den. Fern and I expected to spend the day sending out invitations, but only Wally's Aunt Bessie is to get anything in writing. HRH says we can circulate the date by word of mouth, and then it's up to people to propose themselves as guests. I suppose this is another of those royal wedding customs.

Wally has a new engagement ring and is radiant. She always felt the emerald had been selected with undue haste and is much better pleased with this sapphire. HRH has asked to see me privately tomorrow morning. I expect he's eager to settle Wally's expenses over these many months. I think, too, I may be offered an official position in the new household. Lady-in-waiting, perhaps.

He's presented the Bedaux with a cuckoo clock, as thanks for the use of the chateau. I wonder whether Kitty R. ever got anything for her trouble.

A new wireless was delivered today, to ensure good reception of a certain event in London next Wednesday, an event I'd have thought we'd all be happy to ignore.

7th May 1937

I was fully an hour with HRH, who is completely recovered from his long journey and bouncing with energy. He said he was fully cognizant of the debt of gratitude he owed me, for remaining staunchly at Wally's side while others ratted on her, right and left. He presented me with a set of painted wooden spoons, which are apparently a very popular item in Tyrolean kitchens. He wanted to know whether London is still talking about him.

I said, "Sir, London will never forget you."

He said, "I'm jolly glad to hear it. Not that I miss it one iota. Now on to business. I notice you're not yet in the habit of curtsying to Wally. Well, in less than a month, she will be a Royal Duchess, so I must insist that you accustom yourself to correct behavior without delay. Others who aren't certain of protocol will be watching you and following your lead. You have an important role to play."

It's going to feel very odd, curtsying to a girl from Biddle Street. I shall have to ease myself into it. Heavens, even Ena Spain doesn't expect curtsies from me anymore.

I asked whether I'd have any other role. He said, "Yes. I want you to continue as before, doing those little things that relieve *Einum Meinum* of at least some of her worries. And you know, Maybell, you will always be welcome in our homes."

So, effectively, lady-in-waiting!

It seemed an opportune moment to bring up the subject of some accounts that are overdue.

He said, "These dressmakers won't expect to be paid. They only send in their bills to satisfy their accountants. Don't give it another thought. Dressing Wally is a huge honor for these johnnies, and of course, in the long run, they're going to benefit enormously from the connection. In fact, it seems to me that if any money is to change hands it should be them paying us."

He said he had planned to wear his Welch Guards uniform on his wedding day, but it transpires he's no longer their colonel-in-chief. The small print of abdications!

11th May 1937

The wedding date has been announced to the press. Tomorrow is Coronation Day. How far away London seems. Tried to put a call through for news of Lightfoot, but couldn't get a connection.

12th May 1937

The Yorks were crowned this morning. King George VI and Queen Elizabeth. We listened to Bertie York's Coronation broadcast on Charlie's new wireless. A very labored affair. He isn't a natural speaker. Heavy rain here and in London, too, according to Pips, who called this evening. She said everyone at the Abbey sparkled, even Violet, whom she'd spotted sitting between Ettie Desborough and Anne Belchester, but Loelia Westminster had stolen the show with her rubies. She said everything ran like clockwork until after the Royalties had processed out. Then it developed into a robed free-for-all, and Tommy Minskip complained that Baron Hulver had pushed his way out to the conveniences ahead of all the viscounts. I expect he was in a hurry to get back to Yorkshire for the Battle of Waterloo.

She said Freddie hopes to be offered a peerage before the next Coronation, because you get a better seat.

HRH is knitting a sweater for Wally, "to match her beautiful eyes," he says.

14th May 1937

I was worried that the arrival of the British newspapers might cast a pall, but Wally has greatly enjoyed the Coronation photographs. She's gone over them and over them. She describes Bertie York as looking like a rabbit caught in someone's headlights, and his wife like a little roly-poly cook. Bunny and Cook!

She said, "I'm glad it's done. Now all that's out of the way, *we're* going to show the world how these things should really be done."

Only three weeks to go, and Forwood still hasn't managed to find a clergyman. They all seem to be yes-men to the Archbishop of Canterbury, all too frightened of hazarding future preferments.

17th May 1937

A letter from Ernest in today's post, wishing Wally all the very best in her new life and informing her that he and Mary Kirk hope to marry before the end of the year, too. Funny the way things turn out. We all made our debut the same year—me, Wally, Pips, Violet, Mary. Now Wally's going to be a Royal Highness, and Mary gets Ernest as a consolation prize.

He wrote that he deplored the way she'd been made the target of so much ill feeling in Britain, and hoped she'd found the happiness she deserved with "her princely Peter Pan." I thought it was rather sweet, but HRH was fuming when he read it. I think it was the Peter Pan bit he didn't like. He's asked me to retrieve the letter from Wally's room and destroy it. Wally says she's torn it up already, but I'm not sure I believe her.

The Dickie Mountbattens will not be coming to the wedding. Neither will the Princess Royal.

19th May 1937

Not a single member of HRH's family will be at the wedding. At the very least, they might have sent Harry Gloucester. Wally says she couldn't care less.

"Bunny and Cook got at them," she said. "And there's not one of them with enough spunk to defy them."

Then we heard that the mayor expects Wally and David to go down to the Town Hall, like ordinary people. HRH got on to the British Ambassador immediately. He's insisting on a house call. They can't possibly be expected to trail down there and get jostled and gawked at and photographed by all and sundry. Mr. Cecil Beaton is coming to do the wedding portraits, and absolutely no one else.

20th May 1937

A breakthrough. A vicar has written, offering to officiate at the wedding, for the usual fee plus travel expenses. Dudley Forwood is investigating his bona fides.

The Crosbies and Lily Drax-Pfaffenhof have proposed themselves, but the Perry Brownlows find themselves already engaged for June 3rd. Pips says it isn't to be wondered. They've taken such punishment from the coterie around the New Bunch. All the more reason, I'd have thought, to remain firmly in HRH's camp. Fruity Metcalfe will be HRH's supporter. I'm to be the matron of honor.

24th May 1937

The plucky Reverend Jardine has been hired to perform the wedding ceremony. He told Forwood he thinks it's a scandal the way HRH has been treated and he doesn't care a damn about the Archbishop of Canterbury; in fact, he's been thinking of emigrating to America anyway. The wife is insisting on coming, too. Wally objected, but soon gave in. It's too late in the day to start quibbling over extra little expenses.

Wally and HRH in such high spirits, opening wedding gifts, throwing sticks for the dogs, dancing to gramophone records till long after midnight last night.

30th May 1937

The Crosbies have arrived, and the Erlangers and Walter Monckton, who, as lawyers so often do, brought with him a black cloud. The King has issued a decree that Wally will not become a Royal Highness. She's to be styled Her Grace, the Duchess of Windsor. It's to be gazetted in London tomorrow, so it will be general knowledge and a great triumph for Wally's enemies. A charming wedding present.

There was the most blistering row between Wally and HRH after Monckton broke the news. We could hear her throwing things. Then we heard David crying outside her door, begging to be let in. It was pitiful.

Freddie says either HRH didn't pay proper attention to the terms that he agreed or the lawyers have dropped a tremendous clanger. Monckton says there was nothing in the abdication settlement about Wally's future title. This is an afterthought, and one that can be challenged. He says Elizabeth York was a commoner, but there was never any question of denying her an HRH.

Pips thinks Wally will call off the wedding. She said, "I can't see Wally settling for this. As well ask her to be called Mrs. Windsor."

Neither Wally nor HRH came down to dinner.

I went in to her late, and she was wide awake, wearing eye shades. She said, "Another insult from Bunny and Cook. And not the last, I'm sure. They're little people with little minds."

Hattie says Emerald Cunard cut her in the Ritz Grill. Of course, it's possible Emerald simply didn't remember her. Hattie has one of those faces.

She says the news from Spain isn't good. There's been fierce fighting, and someone Penelope Blythe knows has arrived home without any legs. I do hope Lightfoot has come to his senses and returned to London.

31st May 1937

HRH summoned us all to the apricot drawing room and told us that yesterday's announcement is to be ignored. He said, "My wife will be addressed as Her Royal Highness and will be curtsied to. Kindly inform your staffs."

Wally is calm after yesterday's storm. She said, "They'll be shamed into giving it to me someday, and in the meanwhile, the world is going to find out I'm a thousand times more regal than Queen Cotton Candy."

Main Bocher and his people have arrived, and so has the *chapelier*, and clothes always cheer her up. Tomorrow Mr. Beaton arrives to take the official photographs. Dudley Forwood has set off for Cherbourg to meet Wally's Aunt Bessie and bring her here. The secretaries can hardly keep pace with the gifts. Mr. Mussolini has sent a clock. Mr. Hitler a gold candy box.

1st June 1937

Baba and Fruity Metcalfe are here, and the Rogerses are driving up today. All we need now is the vicar, and the party is complete. Aunt Bessie is a game old bird, dashing around the chateau with her sleeves rolled up, looking for things to do. Plain-spoken, too. She said, "Wally had better make this one work. Three husbands is enough for anyone. And why aren't there more guests? Where are their friends? I disapprove of hole-in-the-wall weddings. It's not a good way to start."

I think everyone found this "propose yourself" idea very confusing.

Mrs. Spry has arrived to do the flowers. I'm giving her a wide berth. In spite of there being a Mr. Spry, she is apparently of the same persuasion as Nada Milford Haven, and I'm in no mood to find myself cornered in some turret of the chateau by an invert with a pair of secateurs.

Mr. Cecil Beaton is buzzing around downstairs, making all kinds of demands. Aunt Bessie doesn't approve of the wedding clothes being worn before the event. She says it brings bad luck. Worse luck to have Mr. Beaton here on the wedding day, moving vases.

2nd June 1937

As Mr. Beaton left, the Reverend Jardine arrived. A blustering, red-faced man, but he wears a dog collar and seems to be the genuine article. He and Charlie are ordering people around, trying to create a more chapel-like ambience. I came upon them, sleeves rolled up, huffing and puffing, ransacking a linen press for something suitable as an altar cloth. They're like a pair of removal men from Maples.

Telegrams have come from the old Queen and from the Yorks, but no eleventh-hour appearance by any family member. George Kent could have hopped over in an airplane in no time. It would mean everything to HRH. The Erlangers have just arrived. The Crokers are expected any minute.

Burke has everything laid out ready in Wally's dressing room, and it all looks magnificent, except for the hat, which I always did think was a mistake. To me, it looks like something one might use to decorate a cake stand. I much prefer my own little confection. HRH's wedding gift to her is a tiara of diamonds. I just hope she's going to find opportunities to wear it.

No sign of nerves in Wally. Well, it is the third time. She said, "Thank you for everything, Maybell. I couldn't have got this far without you."

I said, "All the years I've known you, I finally get to your wedding."

She said, "And this is the wedding that matters."

I said, "Did you know, the first time you met David? Did it cross your mind?"

"No," she said. "It didn't. To tell you the truth, he didn't impress me. But it all seems perfectly obvious now. We're a good fit."

We took one last turn around the house before dinner, checking that everything is in order. Mrs. Spry has really done a very fine job. There can't be a peony left standing in France tonight. Wally had the help move a gilt mirror behind the altar, to give an even more sparkling effect when the candles are lit. The weather forecast is good.

3rd June 1937

The deed is done. Little Bessie Wallis Warfield is now the Duchess of Windsor, and whatever Buckingham Palace may have said about it, *everyone* here curtsied to her when we went in to lunch. The convoy with the honeymoon luggage left at breakfast time, then Herman went down to the gates to brief the newspaper people. They've promised to leave Wally and David in peace at Wasserleonburg.

Lily says that's because they've seen where it is!

The mayor came just before noon, swathed in an enormous red-white-and-blue ribbon—in honor of the British groom and the American bride, I suppose. A nice gesture, although the red argued a little with the pink of some of the flowers. He did the French part of the marrying in the drawing room. It was over in no time at all, then we processed to the salon for the Reverend Jardine to do his part. Herman gave Wally away.

David actually wept a little, which led to a slight fluffing of his lines, but Wally was word-perfect, and she was so right about having that mirror placed where it could reflect the candlelight, too. Her sapphires and diamonds were dazzling. More tears from HRH when they were pronounced man and wife, so Wally postponed the traditional kiss rather than muss up her makeup. I saw a look pass between Baba Metcalfe and Walter Monckton. I don't think they'll ever forgive Wally her American polish.

I've also heard a few sniggers about the statue Fern and Charlie have given as a wedding present, because it's *new*. The British hate anything new. I suppose, certain parties think one of Mr. Elgar's armless old marbles would have been more appropriate.

Lunch was lobster, strawberries, and champagne. The newlyweds plus dogs left at three, with motorcycle outriders and cars full of detectives and staff fore and aft. David all smiles, Wally looking a little tense, I thought.

Tonight, dinner for the survivors, as Herman calls us.

4th June 1937

I had Fruity on my right last evening. He's *very* charming. I can't imagine why Wally doesn't like him. He said it was the most melancholy wedding he'd ever attended. "All perfectly staged," he said, "and pretty as a picture, but not fitting for a man born to be king."

I said, "Well, that's all over. Now he's starting a new life."

He said, "He was greatly loved, you know, till this? There were men who would have laid down their lives for him. I still would. But we're a diminishing band."

I believe it was the champagne talking.

He said, "Wally had better be good to him. He's sacrificed everything to be with her."

I said, "He's not the only one who'd made sacrifices."

Aunt Bessie said, "Yes, let's not forget poor Ernest."

Fern said, "And Wally. Her life is never going to be the same again. She's setting out with David into the unknown. That's love for you."

Baba Metcalfe said, "Well, she doesn't behave as though she loves him. I didn't see a single loving gesture from her today. Not one."

Of course, Baba is famously generous with *her* loving gestures.

Herman told Freddie that some of the press photographers down at the gate described Wally as "having a tang of the dockyard" about her.

I said, "What can they mean?"

Pips said, "Darned if I know. Apart from her big beefy hands and that hyena laugh, she's a picture of femininity."

Dudley Forwood has asked to see me before we leave for Italy. He has something for me from His Royal Highness and Her Grace, the Duchess. I think I can guess what it is. HRH knows I've always admired the silver rose bowl that used to stand in the Octagon Room at Fort Belvedere, and now Daisy Fellowes has sent an almost identical one as a wedding gift, so I believe I may be the lucky beneficiary of the original.

5th June 1937

Forwood handed me a bundle, an *absolute bundle* of accounts this morning. I told him, now the royal monies have been agreed, Wally has no need of me to keep her creditors happy. He said, "I see. Her Grace gave me the impression . . ."

I said, "I never mind picking up a few things here and there. I was raised to be open-handed. But these are major expenses."

He said, "Yes. Of course, if it's a question of timing, I'm sure some of these people would be prepared to wait."

Freddie says Forwood is about to discover the real cost of being David's equerry.

Pips said, "And what about the honeymoon expenses? I wonder what they're doing for jingle up on that mountaintop?"

I said, "Wally told me the blockage in the tube had been cleared, and David's funds are now flowing freely."

Hattie said, "Dribbling, Maybell. Not flowing. Dribbling. David doesn't have enough a year to cover Wally's gowns, let alone anything else."

No rose bowl, either. But Forwood has put the bills back in the letter tray. He's off to Austria, as Honeymoon Equerry. And I refuse to be in a bad mood. Tomorrow, Italy!

10th June 1937, Portofino

We are at the Splendido Mare. Wally would be so jealous if she knew. Dozens of people are in town. Tonight, the Genoas are giving a party.

15th June 1937

Walked as far as the lighthouse with Kath and Herman. Portofino is such a pretty town. I could settle here in a moment. Rent one of these adorable pink houses and hire a handsome Italian driver. The Gandolfis are throwing a cocktail by the saltwater pool. Afterwards, to the Regina di Liguria, for dinner with friends of Lily Drax-Pfaffenhof.

17th June 1937

Boss and Ethel's yacht put in this morning. They have the Bajavidas on board and two other couples from Palm Beach, the Dekuypers and the Orly-Guzmans. They saw Bernie and Zita Cavett in Monaco. Ethel says Zita's still in a huff about missing the wedding. They sent a very good tea service, apparently.

I think a lot of people sat around shyly waiting for an invitation, but if Boss and Ethel understood that they had to invite themselves, I don't see why Bernie and Zita couldn't have done the same.

Betty Dekuyper wears so many gold bangles she can barely lift her cigarette to her lips. The Orly-Guzmans made their money in sisal and have a Degas in their gymnasium.

20th June 1937

Boss Croker says HRH may live to regret allowing Charlie Bedaux to arrange his foreign tours, especially to America. He says Charlie may be known over here for his generosity, but in the States he's known for taking on the trade unions and squeezing the life blood out of the working man. Lily says she doesn't know anything about that, but Charlie's the perfect man to arrange something in Germany. He knows everyone worth knowing, and with HRH speaking German so well, it's bound to be a profitable partnership.

On Thursday, we move on to Como, and on Tuesday, to Sirmione. Bought some smart new luggage and a selection of lace dressing table mats. The Crokers and their party are continuing on to Capri.

25th June 1937, Mistral Blu, Sirmione

Everything is going to seem second-rate after the Villa D'Este. Our rooms here are meant to have lake views, but the rain has so far prevented us from judging them. There doesn't seem to be anyone of consequence in town. Lily may be taking us to meet her friend Prince D'Annunzio of Montenevoso, who has a place nearby. She says he's a poet, a war hero, and a general all-round scalawag. I believe he's an old beau of hers.

2nd July 1937

The visit with Prince D'Annunzio finally took place. He said, "I had ten thousand centurions at Fiume. I was a Duce before Mussolini." He's a pint pot, but small talk seemed not to be his forte. He was in leather, in spite of the heat, and his coat dragged on the ground.

The gardens were beautiful, but his interiors were very dark and cluttered. Masks, elephants, crystal buddhas, Lalique statues, tapestries, daggers, silver tortoises, saddles, vestments, clocks, telescopes, bowls of glass fruit. He showed us his amphitheater, where he does recitations of his poetry. Seats for more than a thousand people!

Pips whispered, "Wow! I'll bet they go like hot cakes."

She says he reminded her of a crazy old rooster. Lily said, "They don't make them like him anymore."

She leaves us tomorrow to prepare for houseguests, and we'll probably head down to Venice on Tuesday or Wednesday. Pips is already thumbing through her Baedeker, earmarking paintings she wants to gaze at yet again.

4th July 1937

No celebrations. The Italians appear not to know about the Fourth. This is the first year since I became a cosmopolite that I've evaded a sentimental phone call from Randolph Putnam. One of the bonuses of keeping on the move.

8th July 1937, The Excelsior, Venice Lido

Received such a warm welcome. *All* the staff remember me.

Kath has heard that Wally's old Peking flame, Ciano, is in town. We're going to try and see him. He's now married to Mr. Mussolini's daughter, apparently.

10th July 1937

With Pips and Herman to a tiny, mosquito-ridden island to see mosaics. No shops.

This evening, to Freddie's old college friend, Bobo Farinacci. He has a palazzo but not an important one.

12th July 1937

It's a small world. At Bobo Farinacci's, we met Ludo and Fancie Fannulloni. Behind these difficult foreign names one often finds an American. Fancie is from Savannah and, it turns out, was at school with Breeze Bajavida. Also came little Barbara Hutton, no longer married to that Russian and minus her new husband. She was being squired by a Woolworth cousin.

Rory's sixteenth birthday.

13th July 1937

To lunch with the Fannullonis. They're sending their boat.

18th July 1937

I have met Wally's Count Gian Galeazzo Ciano! Devilishly handsome. I can see why she fell for him. He and his wife were lunching at Herman's favorite fish restaurant, and we invited ourselves to join them. I felt Herman was rather showing off his Italian, ordering platters of this and vats of that, most of it ugly little creatures that ought to have been thrown back into the ocean. How hard it is to find a good broiled steak in this town.

Ciano believes democracy will soon be a thing of the past.

23rd July 1937

Pips and Freddie are leaving on August 1st. I may go with them. So many things to do, and there'll be no one left in London to snub me.

27th July 1937

The honeymooners are here.

We realized something was about to happen this morning, because the lobby was suddenly buzzing with pressmen. Then a concierge told Pips that the Duke and Duchess of Windsor were on their way from the railroad station in a motor launch. Wally pretended to be surprised when she saw us, but I'll bet she's had every hotel in Italy telephoned, trying to track us down.

Herman said, "What's this, Wally? Is the honeymoon over?"

"No," she said, "this is part two. The *schloss* was all right, but once I'd reorganized the furniture, there wasn't really anything to do up there. There comes a time when a girl needs to see civilization."

We're all having dinner tonight. I grabbed a moment with her when she went up to bathe.

I said, "Well? How has it been?"

She said, "Maybell! I'm hardly a child bride. It's been fine. Boring, but fine."

I said, "You'll never guess. Count Ciano's here."

Not a flicker.

She said, "Is he? Well, I suppose a lot of people are. Venice is that kind of town."

28th July 1937

HRH has gone to Alberoni to play golf with Judson. Wally joined us by the pool. She's desperately looking for volunteers to tag along when she and David move on to their next destination, another of Charlie Bedaux's residences. Borsodivanka. She thinks it's in Czechoslovakia, but it may possibly be in Hungary.

Kath said, "I always thought honeymooners wanted to get away from people."

Wally said, "We've already had six weeks of *that* kind of honeymooning. Now David needs diversions, otherwise he just pads around behind me. I can't even go to the bathroom without him missing me. So far, the only time he's left my side was when I got Forwood to suggest a hike, and even then he kept signaling me with a damned pocket mirror so I'd know how far they'd progressed."

Complaints already, as Kath says, but all very lighthearted. I think she loves being a duchess. The staff here are meticulous about bows and curtsies.

We took a launch into town after lunch.

Pips said, "Hold on to your purse, Maybell."

But those days are over. Wally picked out dozens of table linens at Asta's and she signed her own chits without hesitation. I knew Forwood was mistaken about those wedding bills.

Babs Hutton is giving a party tomorrow night at the Grand.

30th July 1937

The Hutton party was well attended. Came, among many: Ludo and Fancie Fannulloni, Bobo Farinacci, Tori and Paola Nasibruni, Clarice Sfogginomi, and the Count Galeazzo Cianos.

Kath and I waited with baited breath to see how Wally handled meeting the Count again, but she was as cool as a cucumber. He might have been no more than a nodding acquaintance from long, long ago. HRH chatted with him, too. There was apparently one sticky moment, when Ciano demanded to know why Mr. Selassie, the sacked Emperor of Abyssinia, had been invited to the Coronation. He said it was an insult to Italy. HRH said, "Nothing to do with me. It wasn't *my* Coronation."

Peals of laughter.

With Wally to Nardi to help her pick out a pair of blackamoor earclips. Venice is the most inconvenient of cities. One trudges over bridge after bridge, and none of the streets is wide enough for a limousine, so it's impossible to have a driver waiting. If they only filled in the waterways, the locals would notice an immediate improvement in efficiency. They should send someone to Baltimore, to see how a modern city should be run.

2nd August 1937

The Crosbies left this morning, but not before Pips brought up the subject of money with Wally. She said, "You know, Forwood gave Maybell a load of your bills to settle, and she would have done, too, if the rest of us hadn't stopped her. She won't bring it up herself, but I think it's time you were clear about money. Tell her you don't need her picking up your checks anymore."

Wally said, "It was a misunderstanding, Maybell knows that. Fortunately, she doesn't worry about such things, but for *your* peace of mind, Pips, I can promise you Borsodivanka isn't going to cost her a cent. Charlie Bedaux is paying for everything."

I do wish Pips wouldn't interfere. Now I feel cheap.

9th August 1937, Borsodivanka Castle

Like Candé but smaller and wilder. Lots of dark wood and boars' heads. The footmen wear baggy trousers tucked into high leather boots and are rather fiercely good-looking. Fern is in Paris,

Charlie comes and goes, always busy, busy, busy, sending wires, making calls. Lily Drax-Pfaffenhof has driven over with the Cavetts and some jolly Austrians in national costume.

14th August 1937

Wally has been so disagreeable, picking on HRH all through dinner. She's bored and seems to have spent the afternoon brooding over the events of last December, especially Esmond Harmsworth's morganatic proposal, which she now regards as a major mistake.

She said, "You should never have given Baldwin an excuse to go to the Dominions for an opinion. It was obvious they'd raise objections. You never stop to think."

He said, "But darling, you seemed so keen on the idea."

She said, "Don't blame me. All those advisers you had on the payroll. What were they thinking of? You as good as handed the Yorks your crown on a plate. You should just have gone ahead with the Coronation, to hell with the goddamned Dominions, to hell with marrying. We could still have seen each other. We could have worked out something. But no. You're such a fool."

It was a very unhappy moment. Herman tried to change the topic, and so did I, but she wouldn't be stopped, and poor HRH just chewed the inside of his cheek.

15th August 1937

Kath says it's time to go home. She says the whole thing is too gothic, sitting here with the rain lashing against the glass, playing checkers and listening to Wally lambasting David. Today's bugbear is Walter Monckton. She wants to know what he'd been doing allowing Bunny and Cook to cheat her out of her rightful title. She said, "He knew the New Bunch would be looking for ways to spite me. It was a fundamental point, and he should have been watching out for their dirty tricks. Calls himself a lawyer! Well, I hope he hasn't been paid, because he doesn't deserve a penny."

Forwood said Monckton quite definitely hasn't been paid.

It's all very well to talk of leaving, but we're not even sure what country we're in.

Zita says it doesn't matter, as long as our drivers know where we are. I suppose.

20th August 1937

The Rogerses left this morning. Herman said, fond as he is of Fern, he, too, is beginning to have second thoughts about Charlie's German connections. He says Mr. Ley, who Charlie talks of all the time and who features so prominently in plans for our tour of Germany, is nothing but a thug in a suit. Forwood agrees.

He said, "His Royal Highness has had a year of bad press. He should be thinking about ways to repair his reputation, not make matters worse. In my opinion, he needs to be very careful about where he goes and who he's seen with."

Of course, scratch Forwood and you'll find a Foreign Office clerk. A belt-and-suspenders man. He doesn't at all understand Charlie's grand plan. Or Wally's flair for putting on a good show.

22nd August 1937

Calisthenics with HRH this morning. Quite like the good old days at the Fort.

HRH asked me how I think Wally seems. Very irritable is how she seems, but I didn't really feel I could say so.

I said, "She's a little strained. It's been a big year."

He said, "It has. She's suffered terribly. And she's being so unfairly treated by certain parties. That's why the German trip is so very important. She'll receive a very warm welcome from the Germans. Bedaux's doing a marvelous job. It'll be as good as a State visit, and that's what Wally deserves. She's going to be so awfully good at this."

Charlie has left for New York. He's going to prepare the way for a November tour of the United States. Oliver Templemore and Oxer Bettenbrooke are coming here for the chamois hunting. Also the Humphrey Butlers.

It seems a very social time, considering it's a honeymoon. Brumby and I had a few days at Marshalls Creek, just the two of us and a stock market tickertape machine, but Wally and David seem to thrive on company.

27th August 1937

We hear that the Reverend Jardine has surfaced in America. He's announced his intention of writing his memoirs and opening a wedding chapel, something exclusive, suitable for Hollywood stars.

Wally said, "Bumptious little chancer. He'd better not include us in any memoirs."

Hardly fair. After all, he did travel a long way at short notice and defied his bishop and destroyed his chances of preferment. No one else volunteered, and if he hadn't come along when he did, Wally and David would have had to make do with being married by a Frenchman draped in a flag.

Zita said, "If you don't want to get memoired, you'd better have a word with Maybell. She writes us all up in her diary."

Wally said, "Do you still do that, Maybell? Did you ask His Royal Highness's permission?"

I said, "Hardly. They're just my own little musings. Current affairs. Family things."

"Oh," she said. "How dreary. If people must keep diaries, they should make them worth rereading."

Zita said, "Yes. When I went into show business, my Ma said, 'Keep a diary, Zita. Some day it may keep you.' But I never did."

2nd September 1937

The Humphrey Butlers have arrived. Walter Monckton has also asked to make a flying visit. Wally said, "He'd better come with an apology from the Yorks and my rightful title."

I made noises about returning to London, but Wally won't hear of it. She said, "We have to go to Paris, Maybell. I don't have a thing to wear. And then I'm going to need you in Germany. You're my lady-in-waiting."

Poots Butler says only Royalties have Ladies-in-Waiting.

4th September 1937

Monckton has brought neither an apology nor a title for Wally. He's come to try and talk HRH out of going to Germany. He says Charlie Bedaux's German friends are all Nazis, and the trip will be a great embarrassment to the British government. Wally said, "He's been sent by the New Bunch, I'll bet you dollars to doughnuts. They're nervous about David getting back in the public eye. Serves them right. It's their own damned fault for sending him to the scrap heap. Well, we're going to Germany, whatever anyone says."

We head for Paris next weekend. Poots says she discerns a pattern with Wally. Two happy days followed by twenty-four hours of snapping and paranoia.

I don't think she's paranoid at all. I think she's being treated very unkindly indeed.

5th September 1937

Today's subject has been HRH's banishment. Wally says much as she adores Paris, England is where they really belong. She said, "It's a terrible waste of a king. David knows everything there is to know about running the country. He was trained for it, unlike Bertie York. He should be asked back and given something useful to do."

Humphrey Butler said, "The problem with that, Wally, is that no new king wants to have an ex-king watching over his shoulder."

Wally said, "Well, he'll have to be given something to do. I can't have him under my feet for the next thirty years."

6th September 1937

HRH says he won't go back to England until and unless Wally gets her due rank and is properly received by the two Queens. Walter Monckton told him he sees no reason why this can't be achieved, given time, patience, and tact.

Wally said, "Patience and tact, fiddlesticks! Go and phone your brother and tell him you have to have a job. And this time, don't allow him to fob you off."

7th September 1937

So far, the King hasn't been available to come to the telephone and speak to David. Wally said, "Of course he's available. He just daren't contradict orders from the Scotch Cook. She's the one who wears the pants. You wouldn't think it, to look at those dimpled cheeks, but she does. And she's the one who has it in for me."

We sensed another rant coming on, but Poots headed it off by asking Wally's advice on hemlines.

HRH is acting so forlorn about us going to Paris. He keeps saying, "Must you go, darling? After what we went through last winter, I don't ever want us to be separated again."

It's so silly, because Wally's organized a lovely shooting party to see him through her absence. And his night table is covered with photographs of her.

10th September 1937

Charlie now has everything in place for our first two tours. Forwood is preparing a bulletin for the press. We go to Germany on October 11th, for two weeks, then back to Paris, just long enough for the maids to turn everything around and repack before we sail for New York on the *Bremen* on November 6th.

12th September 1937, Meurice Hotel, Paris

Wally is lunching with Elsie Mendl and has left me with lists to go through with her *lingère*. I'm sure I'm efficient enough to manage lingerie lists *and* go to Trianon for lunch. Ena Spain is still in Scotland.

Bought stockings.

13th September 1937

No sign yet of Wally. Her maid says she didn't come in till two a.m. If HRH was trying to get through to her for his good-night kiss, he'll be frantic.

Appointments at Chanel and Main Bocher. Tomorrow, lunch with Kitty Rothschild.

Instead of Prunier, we're going to go to a real Parisian market, buy ingredients, bring them to the house, and cook them ourselves. What unusual lives people lead in Paris!

14th September 1937

Wally was at the Bricktop last night with Kenny Opdyke and his crowd. She says there were naked black girls in the floor show.

She's having new buttons put on her dark blue coatdress. She evidently plans to meet Mr. Hitler dressed like a Bible class teacher, to impress upon him her seriousness of mind.

The Rothschilds have a very modest apartment. They are staying liquid until they see what Germany's intentions are. Kitty says if Hitler takes Austria, they stand to lose Enzesfeld. It's the Jewish question. She says we're going to be very shocked by what we see on our trip. Thuggery in the streets. Shops that are barred to Jews. She made it plain she doesn't approve of HRH's visit, but he's only going to study labor conditions and housing and all those things he's keen on. I see no harm in it. And what can we do if German shopkeepers choose not to serve Jews?

Anyway, it's all arranged.

She said, "I only hope Charlie Bedaux doesn't turn the Windsors into a pair of performing pooches. That man never does anything for nothing."

Lunch was exhausting. First, we went all the way to St. Germain with Kitty's friend Winnie Gulliver, battling through the crowds to buy mushrooms and salad greens and cheeses, then we carried them home by taxi cab and made our own omelettes. Thank goodness, she had the help clear away. Playing house is good fun, but it takes up so much time.

Winnie Gulliver says she cooks for herself all the time, but she's English and quite down on her luck, by all accounts. Rather like Ida Coote, except Winnie does afford a daily.

18th September 1937

Called Pips but got Freddie. He said, "This German jaunt is a wholly bad idea. It's going to send completely the wrong message to Hitler."

I said, "It's a private visit. A few folkloric pageants and luncheons with dignitaries. It's going to have no more significance than if we motored down to Menton for a weekend."

He said, "Private visit! That's not how it's going to look, and David knows it."

Lightfoot has been heard from, apparently, and is alive and well, or, at least, alive. Doopie volunteered, too, for nursing duties, but is still at Carlton Gardens. Well, I'm sure they won't take her. She can't even say "bandage" properly.

A valet has arrived with the dogs. HRH will be here tomorrow. That will put a stop to late nights at the Bricktop.

21st September 1937

HRH says he received a letter from Prosper Frith, asking him, for the sake of Great Britain, not to break bread with Adolf Hitler. Prosper Frith! He's got some nerve, after the way that wife of his switched camps. Anyway, we're not *breaking bread* with Mr. Hitler. We're having afternoon tea.

Ena Spain is back.

25th September 1937

Fruity Metcalfe has now joined the throng telling us to cancel our trip. Wally says he's just disappointed not to have been asked to equerry. Well, Forwood suits us better. He has the language and he doesn't presume upon an old friendship.

Ena Spain is terribly depressed about the war. She says the Godless are fighting the Godless, and it's the poor little people who are being squeezed between the two.

I wonder if Lightfoot realizes he's in the ranks of the Godless. He was always pretty keen on churchgoing at Easter and lowly mangers on his Christmas cards.

We have received our program for the United States. Charlie Bedaux has been very busy. HRH will start by visiting industrialists in Rochester, Schenectady, Wilmington, and Bayonne. Wally and I will have our own activities in New York. We'll all then make a brief stop in Washington to see Wally's Aunt Bessie, and Baltimore, for old times' sake. This is going to give Nora Sedley Cordle and Brumby Junior something to think about. If they make any approach, hoping to use me as a conduit to the Royalties, I shall snub them. As far as I'm concerned, the only friend I have in Baltimore is Randolph Putnam.

The tour will then resume, with HRH going to Detroit, but Wally and I may go directly to San Diego and then meet up with him again in Honolulu.

Charlie says he can arrange further fact-finding tours for next spring, too. There's interest from Sweden and Argentina. What wayfarers we're becoming!

3rd October 1937

It seems that no one wants us to go to Germany except the Germans. The newspaperman Beaverbrook is trying to dissuade us. He says it's too controversial a thing to do so soon after the abdication, and that having clashed head-on with Stanley Baldwin, the last thing HRH should do is set a collision course with the new Prime Minister. He says if HRH and Wally hope for an early end to their exile, they must make a friend of Neville Chamberlain.

Now Forwood tells us that the British Embassy in Berlin has been instructed to offer us nothing more than powder rooms and a cup of tea. Wally says it'll be the doing of Bunny and Cook.

She said, "They know we're going to be a big success. They're terrified David's going to stage a comeback."

I said, "Is he going to?"

"That," she said, "remains to be seen."

I wish they'd make up their minds. The last I heard, she had Elsie Mendl's people combing Paris for a suitable townhouse.

The maids and valets start off with the luggage in the morning.

8th October 1937

A little farewell dinner at the Tour D'Argent. Came: the Ambassador Bullitts, the Marquess of Graham, Fern Bedaux, and Elsie Mendl. The Eugene Rothschilds sent regrets. Jimmy Graham says Adolf Hitler doesn't have any policies as such, only random thoughts, some of which are followed through but many of which are not. According to Elsie, the man to watch is Dr. Goebbels.

11th October 1937, Kaiserhof Hotel, Berlin

Charlie Bedaux has been as good as his word. Everything got off to a wonderful start. We were met at the railroad station by a very smart contingent of top Germans. By contrast, the British Embassy sent only a Third Secretary—the Ambassador and most of his suite having chosen today of all days to leave town. So mean-spirited. But Charlie's friend Mr. Ley had organized sparkling Mercedes limousines to take us to our hotel, with brass bands and an escort of storm troopers and hundreds of smiling Germans lining the route. I can't say I noticed any of those anti-Jewish shop signs Kitty Rothschild talked about.

Tonight, dinner with the Otto Bismarcks at the Eden.

12th October 1937

Wally and I shopped while HRH visited a ball-bearing plant. He was most impressed by what he saw. He says the workers are given a free meal that provides them with all their daily nourishment, and they have glee clubs and inoculations and beautiful flower beds all around the factory. I wonder what Brumby would have thought of that! We had mines and smelters all over the world, and they were perfectly productive without us going to the trouble of flower beds.

Wally bought two dozen Meissen plates and three pairs of branched candlesticks. Wally says she finds Mr. Ley overfamiliar, but he'd arranged private visits to the most exclusive shops and really nothing seems to be too much trouble for him.

Tomorrow HRH has to go to Potsdam to inspect a flap-valve factory. He was keen for us to go with him, but we have hair appointments, and Mr. Ley has more shopkeepers expecting us. We can hardly disappoint them.

13th October 1937

To the Kranzler coffee house for ice cream. Wally has let it be known she's seen two pieces of Biedermeier that would be very acceptable as late wedding gifts, should anyone ask: a walnut secretary, and a four-drawer dresser with some very pretty marquetry. Tonight, to Mr. Ley's home for drinks. It's a pity he picks his teeth.

14th October 1937

Everyone who's anyone in Germany was at Mr. Ley's last evening. Very few of the wives though, which suited Wally. She always prefers a room full of men. She quite monopolized Mr. Speer, but I made a great hit with Colonel Jodl, who offered me the use of his hunting lodge. What I'd do there I can't imagine.

Champagne in abundance, mountains of caviar and pretzels, and a Tyrolean band playing HRH's favorite music. A gay evening, which ended with scowling faces and HRH pulling out of the luncheon he was supposed to attend tomorrow.

Dudley Forwood says it's to do with a newspaperman called Streicher, who's on the guest list for a luncheon. Apparently, Mr. Streicher just published a story stating that Wally has Jewish blood. Too ridiculous for words. We didn't have Jews at Oldfields. Hattie Erlanger once hinted that Ernest was slightly Jewish, but even that's nothing to do with anything anymore. Ernest Simpson is history, and Mr. Streicher should check his facts.

Tonight to the opera.

15th October 1937

A difficult evening. HRH still simmering about Mr. Streicher's slur and dragging his feet over *Lohengrin,* and then, when we arrived at the Opera House, Mrs. Goebbels was wearing a white taffeta identical to Wally's. Wally carried hers better, and her diamonds outshone all the Germans put together, but still, it quite ruined our entrance and was an unforgivable gaffe on the part of the *vendeuse.* HRH felt that Mrs. Goebbels should have with-drawn, but, of course, she didn't have the wit to do it. She's just a *milch* cow with her head full of feeding schedules and baby ail-ments. They say Dr. Goebbels can send for any movie actress who takes his fancy. Extraordinary. To me, he looks like a little goblin in a surgical boot, but Wally talked to him and she says he has a bril-liant mind and a voice like black velvet. She'd better not share that observation with HRH.

The opera went on for hours, and as Guests of Honor, we felt obliged to stay to the end, though one act is surely enough for anyone.

Today, we visited with the Air Marshal Hermann Goerings. They say he used to cut a dashing figure, but now he wears his trousers hoisted far too high. Emmy Goering is very vivacious and a former movie star. I wonder whether Dr. Goebbels had her? She'd just learned that she's expecting a child, and so Hermann was like a dog with two tails. He said, "When my son is born, one thousand planes will fly overhead in salute."

A German tradition, I suppose, but I wonder people don't just send flowers. So much quieter.

Hermann and HRH played with a magnificent electric train set while Emmy gave us tea and a tour of the garden.

17th October 1937

While HRH has been descending into coal mines and inspecting new highways, Wally and I have visited two kinder-gartens, three hospitals, and an institute for old soldiers with no legs. It's so hard to know what to say to such people. We were also subjected to an overly detailed demonstration of the manufacture of synthetic rubber, which made us so late returning to the hotel the manicurist had to rush, and I went to the Saxe-Coburg dinner with a smudged left hand. If this relentless busyness is a taste of what Wally has let herself in for, I pity her. At least I can get Hattie or someone to take over as Lady-in-Waiting, but for Wally, there'll be no such escape. No one can stand in for the Duchess of Windsor. I begin to understand her flashes of bitterness.

If David had hung on to his throne and kept her quietly in the wings, she would have had none of these tiresome duties—smiling at cripples, admiring fat babies, showing an interest in welding processes. That side of the business could have been left to

Elizabeth York and Marina Kent. I'm sure it's the kind of thing they enjoy.

18th October 1937

A display of flag-twirling by the League of German Maidens. Tomorrow, dinner with dear Prince Louis Ferdinand and his mother, then, on Friday, we visit with President Hitler. Wally is still set on wearing the dark blue coatdress and a little felt hat. I can't think why. If all these cheerful flags and banners flying along Unter den Linden are any indication, Mr. Hitler is rather fond of red. I'm going to wear my scarlet twill.

We went a different route to avoid traffic and saw some of those shops with Jewish star placards in the window. Mr. Ley says they are public information notices, to save Jewish people wandering into stores that sell things like blood sausage, forbidden to them by their religion. Not at all the impression Kitty Rothschild gave.

19th October 1937, Cecilienhof, Potsdam

Crown Princess Cecilie may be a Romanov and a Mecklenberg and a great many other unpronounceable things, but her house is of a comfortably manageable size and quite reminded me of houses I've seen in Surrey.

Louis Ferdinand as adorable as ever. He thinks he's found a wife, one of his Russian cousins. He says she's not only extremely suitable but also good and beautiful. Still, I always rather hoped he'd marry a nice American girl. He's working in an airplane factory now and quite enjoying it. Hudson's choice, I suppose. There's no work for Royalties in Germany at present.

While Wally was freshening up, Cecilie told me that Hitler is rumored to have moving pictures of her, taken when we were on the *Nahlin*. She said, "They say he plays them all the time. He must have quite a crush on her!"

I'm afraid the Fuehrer may be in for a disappointment. Emaciated women may photograph well, but in the flesh, they lack the bloom of natural good health. There's a happy medium between the stoutness of German women and Wally's sharp angles, and there's no better example than myself.

Louis F. says von Ribbentrop is on the outs, and Mr. Hess and Mr. Speer are the darlings of the moment.

Tomorrow, Munich. A demonstration of butter-churning and a youth concert.

20th October 1937, Bayerischer Hof, Munich

Forwood says Friday's meeting will be strictly between HRH and the Fuehrer, and that Wally and I will just be shown around the gardens. Forwood obviously hasn't heard what Crown Princess Cecilie has!

22nd October 1937, Goldene Ente, Salzburg

Today we visited with President Hitler. We were given a trout luncheon at a wayside hostelry, then driven up to the Berghof in time for tea. As our car approached the house, Forwood let out a great whoop of laughter.

He said, "Good grief, it looks like something a builder just put up in Middlesex."

Forwood has a certain side to him. I thought it was a charming house, and with matchless mountain views. Also, it's in a very select neighborhood. The Albert Speers have built nearby, and the Martin Bormanns are just a little farther up the road, so everyone knows everyone, rather like West Palm Beach.

As Wally got out of the car, Mr. Hitler came trotting down the steps to greet her. He has a pasty face and is rather short in the leg. He was wearing patent leather evening shoes and an ugly brown jacket, but was all smiles and not at all overwrought as he always appears to be in the newsreels. He and HRH spoke in German, and then the three of them set off up the steps. Forwood and I were rounded up by two aides and taken in by a different door to meet his fiancée. Miss Eva Brown.

Well, Eva may *style* herself "fiancée," but she wears no ring. She's a natural blonde, average figure, very young. She calls the President "Uncle Fuehrer." We went to her sad little sitting room. Cheap chintzes, animal pictures torn from magazines, a small shelf of novelettes. Tea and éclairs were served, and she showed us her collection of glass animals. She'd been kept strictly off-stage during our arrival and so was eager for information about Wally's clothes. She chattered away so inanely Forwood had difficulty keeping up as our interpreter.

Does the Duchess wear a foundation garment? What's her favorite scent? Had Uncle Fuehrer presented her with flowers?

What are her dogs' names? Has she seen the new Nelson Eddy and Jeanette MacDonald movie?

There's no date fixed for a wedding. She said the Fuehrer is too busy at present. She said she'd so wanted to meet Wally and His Royal Highness, but protocol prevents it until she becomes Mrs. Hitler. I don't see why. HRH always presented Wally to everyone, even when she was still married to Ernest. The Germans are such sticklers.

She clung to my arm when we got the word that HRH and Wally were ready to leave, doing everything she could think of to delay our departure, but she didn't come out with us to our car. Not allowed, I suppose.

Once Wally and HRH had climbed into their motor, I seized my opportunity. I caught the Fuehrer's eye. I told Forwood to tell him how glorious his zinnia beds were and that I hoped he and Eva would have a lovely wedding. Soon.

I received a very cordial bow. I wish I could have had more time to talk with him though. For one thing, I should have liked to recommend Dr. Prilstein's Tonic Iron Pastilles. I'm sure he'd benefit from them.

Forwood said, "Don't be disappointed. I don't think Ladies-in-Waiting usually get to speak. You and I are just spear carriers, after all."

Spear carriers! I said, "Speak for yourself. If it weren't for me, the Duchess of Windsor would still be having her gowns made by a little seamstress in Cromwell Road."

HRH is full of their visit. He said, "We hit it off immediately. He's a thoroughly agreeable sort and only wants a fair deal for his country. Who can fault a man for that? All this scaremongering by men like Eden is so much nonsense. I told him, as far as I'm concerned, there must be no more wars between Britain and Germany, and he agreed with me. We're all of the same blood, after all. Go back far enough, and we're all Huns."

Well, *I'm* not. Father's people were from Richmond, Virginia, and Mother was one of the Washington Woodhams.

Wally also very smitten. The Fuehrer told her she'd have made a very fine Queen and that her day will yet come. He'd showed her the view from his panoramic window, clear across into Austria. She says he has artistic hands and eyes as blue as a mountain lake. I must say, he put me in mind of a ventriloquist's doll.

Tomorrow, we turn for home.

28th October 1937, Meurice Hotel, Paris

Two more secretaries started today, but we're still working against the clock, to finish the letters of thanks for the wedding gifts *and* finalize our U.S. engagements. I'd have thought it was enough to have a letter that says *Thank you for the gift* and just run off however many copies, but Wally insists that we personalize each one by filling in the blank. Thank you for the most useful shooting stick. Thank you for the thoughtful lobster hammers. So tiresome.

Tea with Ena Spain.

2nd November 1937

Our luggage was dispatched to Cherbourg this morning, but there is a small cloud on the horizon. Since the newspapers reported Wally and David's tea party with Mr. Hitler, the Jewish lobby in America has been putting people under pressure to cancel our engagements. They say no one who is a friend of Germany can be a friend of Jews, which is not at all fair. The Eugene Rothschilds are Jews, and HRH stayed with them for months. Also, it's not Germans in general who dislike Jews, nor even the Fuehrer. It's Mr. Streicher who's the problem and, as Wally says, he's of minor importance in the coming Germany. She laughed off his slurs, and the Anti-Defamation League might learn to do the same.

4th November 1937

Our trip to America now hangs in the balance. The New York longshoremen have said they won't unload the *Bremen* if it has bedfellows of the German National Socialists on board. Hardly *bedfellows*. All we did was pay a few visits, exchange gifts and pleasantries, and oil the wheels of international goodwill, something these Communists don't understand. I think we should just quietly change to a different sailing, but Freddie Crosbie says it makes no difference. Whether HRH deliberately climbed into bed with Hitler or got there by sleepwalking, the damage is done. He says David and Wally are now labeled as Nazi sympathizers and don't have a snowball-in-hell's chance of slipping unnoticed into the United States.

HRH is going to speak to the press tomorrow morning, to clear up the whole misunderstanding.

5th November 1937

America is off. Charlie Bedaux wired this afternoon that he could no longer guarantee the success of the tour, because of adverse union propaganda. Also, that at the request of the British Ambassador, the State Department would not be according Wally royal status. That was what decided HRH. He canceled immediately.

It's such a waste. All our wonderful new gowns, all those people who are going to be disappointed. Pips was on the telephone the very moment she heard. She said, "Well, Freddie did try to warn you."

I said, "Freddie didn't see what a huge success Germany was. We had no problems there with trade unions and people refusing to curtsy."

She said, "Maybell, you're spending too much time with that pair. You're losing touch with reality."

I think Pips may be envious of my position.

Wally's blaming the New Bunch for our predicament.

She said, "Bunny and his Cook again! They have wall-to-wall advisers on foreign affairs and could easily have spared one to pop over here and explain the political nuances to HRH, instead of allowing him to go ahead and get into this scrape."

I don't know. I'm not sure he's disposed to listen to people from Westminster anymore. Still, let's hope sanity prevails and I shall get my chance to spurn Nora Sedley Cordle.

7th November 1937

The *Bremen* sailed without us, our luggage is sitting in some quayside shed, and Charlie Bedaux has checked out of the New York Plaza, destination unknown. The whole business has been a disaster.

Elsie Mendl is giving us a consolatory dinner.

13th November 1937

A wonderful evening at Elsie Mendl's. Her help all wore stars and stripes, and she had hired an all-girl saxophone band to play for us after dinner. Came: the old Queen of Egypt, the Dimitri Shapaleffs, Henri and Alix Piston-LeRupin, Lucky Patrice, and Count Maximilian Finto. Nazli Egypt wore a Molyneux gown and a rivière of brilliants and cognac diamonds. I'd rather expected her to be shrouded in black.

15th November 1937

Flowers from Maxi Finto. I think I have an admirer.

17th November 1937

Ernest Simpson and Mary Kirk are to be married tomorrow in Fairfield, Connecticut. Wally says he still carries an enormous torch for her, but I think she was just having a bad day. This damned rain has kept David off the golf course for a week now.

More flowers from the Count. He wants dinner. Elsie Mendl says he has a spread somewhere in South America. When he's in Europe, he just stays with people.

20th November 1937

Herman and Kath Rogers are going to the States for Christmas and have offered Wally and David their house. Tonight, I dine with my Count Maxi! He sent an orchid.

21st November 1937

Confined to bed with the repercussions of sauerkraut *garni*. Maxi said he thought a brasserie would be more fun than going to Grand Vefour yet again. He's a fascinating man. Mother was Irish, father Italian, born in Argentina. He used to raise cattle until he had a bad polo accident. Now he does this and that. Green eyes and still a fine head of black hair. My wrap still smells of his bay rum hair dressing. It made me quite nostalgic for Brumby.

He calls me "May-*belle*" and is very attentive. He wanted to know *everything* about me and hardly told me anything about himself, but he does seem to be unattached. He's avid to see me again before he leaves for Paraguay on Tuesday. A business trip of some kind, and quite unavoidable.

Wally's invited Lily Drax-Pfaffenhof and the Bernie Cavetts to Cannes for Christmas.

I said, "Does that mean you can spare me?"

She said, "As long as you're back by the middle of January. We have to get down to house-hunting."

She's going to show La Croe to David while they're down there at Christmas, and then decide on a Paris house in the New Year. The Meurice is delightful, but with a hotel, there's always the problem of security. She says she lies awake listening for assassins.

HRH has no idea where he wants to live. "Whatever you think, my darling," he says. She could propose moving to Greenland, and he'd go along with it.

22nd November 1937

Count Maximilian Finto says I'm never out of his mind. A single rosebud arrived with my breakfast tray, a signed book of love poems was delivered while I was out to lunch, and Maxi himself appeared at seven to whisk me away to Boulevard St.-Germain for grilled pigs' feet.

If Nora Sedley Cordle could only see me now!

23rd November 1937

Maxi has left me his opera scarf as a memento, until he returns in the New Year. He says his life turned a corner the day he met me. I think Maybell, Countess Finto would sound very well. But one can't rush into these things. To have a man in my life again would change so much. Wally would have to manage without me, for one thing. And then, there can be an irksome side to husbands. Brumby was rarely any trouble to me, but I know what others go through. I may see what Harrold's Lending Library has on Paraguay.

Pips wants me for Christmas. She's promised there'll be no lectures from Freddie about the German situation. Actually, *I* may give Freddie a lecture. *I've* met the Fuehrer, after all. And I have this feeling that someday people like Freddie are going to view Adolf Hitler in a very different light.

I fly—*fly*—to Croydon Aerodrome on November 30th. Wally thinks I'm crazy.

25th November 1937

Dear Ena Spain has taken up my cause with Violet. She told her, it made no sense to keep the drawbridge raised when the battle is over and the troops have all gone home. David and Wally are leading a new life far from Carlton Gardens, and the New Bunch are apparently making a decent job of things, so there's no longer any reason for a family to be divided. Violet told Ena that if I choose to call when I'm next in London, I won't find the door barred.

I said, "Hardly a warm invitation."

Ena said, "Now, Maybell, Violet always *means* well. Just go and see her. Life is short."

29th November 1937

A last doggie walk with HRH.

He said, "Remember me to dear old London, Maybell. I do miss it all."

I said, "Well, sir, you've already served nearly a year of your time. Time flies."

He said, "It does, but sometimes I think we'll never be able to go back. I want you to take soundings while you're there. When you come back, I shall want to hear about the mood of my nation."

We reminisced about that gay weekend we had at the Fort, when Wally cooked campfire sausages and Bernie Cavett played the accordion. Then, for one awful moment, I thought he might cry. He's plagued with toothache, and smoking far too much.

Freezing fog. I wonder how my airplane pilot will know which way to go.

1st December 1937, Claridge's Hotel, London

A corsage waiting for me at Le Bourget, from Count Maxi. Pips looks well. They have a new crimson dining room.

3rd December 1937

A year ago this night, Wally and I were hurtling through the dark to Newhaven.

Perhaps I'll call Perry Brownlow.

Doopie is back at South Audley Street, hoping to be sent to Spain.

She said, "Dordie wone gum home dill a jobs done."

Flora is growing a bosom, but she still carts around that Spanish doll given to Wally at Corunna.

She said, "Are we speaking to you? Are you allowed to take us to Lyons for gake?"

I guess I am. Tea with Violet tomorrow.

4th December 1937

Violet's first words were, "Are you back to stay?"

I said, "No. Just for Christmas. I'm letting Wilton Place go."

She said, "Are you going back to Baltimore? Is it Randolph?"

I said, "No. I have a suite at the Meurice. I'm a European now."

"Oh dear," she said.

Rory will be home on the 10th.

She said, "Of course, he may not want to see you. I make no promises. He's all too aware of recent events."

Her hair is whiter, Melhuish's gout is apparently worse, and there's a scorch mark on the stairhall runner where Flora set a fire while she and Doopie were back in residence. It seems to have been brought on by Elspeth Laird suggesting it was time they tried her at another school.

We embraced. Violet's still rather stiff with me, but at least the ice has been broken. I believe I smelled poached salmon as I was leaving.

Spoke with Perry Brownlow.

I said, "I hear you've been well and truly pilloried."

"Ah," he said, "an anniversary call! One veteran to another."

He said, "It can only be a matter of time till we're back in fashion. The silliness of London will always outweigh its viciousness."

He asked after Wally and HRH. He said he never hears *from* them, only *about* them.

He said, "I did everything I could to keep him from abdicating, you know? But now the dust has settled, I think it's all turned out for the best, don't you?"

I do.

6th December 1937

To the Erlangers. Hattie says no one's talking about Wally anymore. Freddie says that's because they know they may soon have a war to worry about.

10th December 1937

Rory and Flora are very impressed to have an aunt who flies in airplanes. Flora kept asking, "But how do they stay in the sky?" A very good question.

Rory says it's due to aerodynamics.

We went to Madame Tussaud's Museum to see a wax likeness of

Wally. Rory was spellbound but, of course, he's never actually seen her in the flesh. In my opinion, they don't quite have her. She's in a red gown, glaring across at the Archbishop of Canterbury, so they're on the right track, but they haven't quite captured her. Afterwards, to the Marble Arch Lyon's. Flora announcing very loudly that she now wears a bust bodice. "Thirty-four inches," she bellowed. She forgets we're not all like Doopie.

How grown up they both are all of a sudden. I'd so love them to visit with me in Paris.

Flora said, "Let's go now."

Rory said, "You have to learn French first, you noodle."

Such nonsense. I live there and I don't speak a word.

They chose their own presents: a nest of wands and a rather alarming set of magic handcuffs for Rory. Next year, I shall go to Truefitt and Hill and get him a shaving brush. Flora got *The Secret of the Border Castle* and a flashlight. She picked out a woolen scarf for Ulick. Harrold's will always change it if he finds it too colorful.

13th December 1937

Anne Belchester called to invite me to her Spanish field hospital benefit. Doopie will be selling prize-draw tickets and is sure to be glad of help. I believe I'm in the process of being rehabilitated. If I'm not very careful, Gladys Trilling will start speaking to me again.

17th December 1937

Lunch with Penelope Blythe, and at the Dorch! I must truly be on my way back.

And so much news. Ralph Habberley has sunk without a trace, Jane Habberley has turned to God, Percy Boddie-Fulton was arrested for drunken driving—in Battersea, inexplicably—Ida Coote is working on a telephone switchboard, and Tommy Minskip has taken to shooting at people who approach his front door. Not that there can be many of those. Penelope says if Maxi Finto played polo, Fergus may remember him, and if he doesn't, Rock Cholmondeley certainly will.

She says the new Queen is blossoming, the old Queen is nesting at Marlborough House, and Fergus predicts HRH will eventually be asked to go to Australia as Governor General. I don't think Australia is what Wally has in mind.

19th December 1937

Spoke with Zita Cavett. They have rain in Cannes. Wally was resting, and HRH was in town, picking up her Christmas necklace. Zita says they've received Christmas greetings from President Hitler, Mr. Mussolini, and the New Bunch.

To the Legation for Christmas carols.

23rd December 1937

Penelope telephoned all the way from Leake Priory to say Fergus has never heard of Maxi Finto. And a merry Christmas to you, too, Penelope.

2nd January 1938

To the Savoy with the Erlangers and the Crosbies. We learned a riotous new dance called the Lambeth Walk.

5th January 1938

Encountered Daphne Frith in Church's trying on ankle boots. She said, "I hope we can let bygones be bygones, Maybell. I do hope we'll see you at Hoxney Court this year."

I should be so desperate.

I said, "I live in Paris now, Daphne."

"Yes," she said, "I heard. No distance from Kent at all. I should so love to see Paris again sometime."

7th January 1938

Gladys Trilling made straight for the seat next to mine at Monsieur Jules.

She said, "It's too bloody, everything that's happened. How are poor Wally and David?"

I said, "Never better. They adore living in France. We all do."

"Still," she said. "It must be small comfort after everything they've lost. Stripped of rank. Reduced to penury. Although, of course, Wally was always terribly clever about making a little go a long way."

Damned cheek from a woman who takes soap from hotel powder rooms.

Judson says Whitlow is being posted to Jakarta. There is a God.

9th January 1938

To tea at Kensington Palace with Ena Spain. She's visiting her mother. Ena is convinced Anthony Eden is going to drag us into a war. She said, "I'm going to move to Switzerland, Maybell, and you should think of doing the same. When it comes, as it will, I don't want to see or hear anything about it. I'm too old for more heartache."

Poor Ena lost a brother in the Somme. Old Princess Baby didn't come down. She's in a bad way with rheumatics but doesn't seem to know how to die.

Wally wants me back posthaste. She's found a house near Versailles.

I said, "I thought you wanted to be in town."

She said, "I do. But if we take this, David can garden."

There's a flight on Thursday.

15th January 1938, Meurice Hotel, Paris

Wally signed a six-month lease in a fit of frustration, but now she's having second thoughts. She said, "It's not quite right for us. I'm going to get us out of it. I don't see why we should make do with the first thing that comes along, like a pair of refugees."

HRH roamed in and out till she told him off. There's been too much weather for him to be able to play golf. His face fell when he saw her gathering up her things to go out. He said, "I rather hoped we'd have lunch."

She was running out to meet Kenny Opdyke. He said, "Shall I come with you?"

"No," she said. "Kenny's found me a nice little console table, but I'm going to have to beat the dealer down. I don't want you there, confusing things."

I stayed behind and shared his plate of sandwiches. He said, "I don't believe Hitler wants a war, but if it should come to it, I shall go back into uniform. I know war is a terrible, terrible thing, but I must say, I remember it as the happiest time of my life. Except for now, of course."

He asked a thousand questions about London. I think he pictures it just as it was when he left it—frozen, waiting for him to return. It would break his heart to know no one talks about him anymore.

Charlie Bedaux is back in town. He and Fern are dining with us next week. The America fiasco is not to be mentioned. Wally says what happened was completely beyond Charlie's control, and anyway, he's still a very useful and understanding friend.

No word from Maxi.

25th January 1938

Came last evening: Charlie and Fern, Princess Grimaldi, the Lazslo Melchiors, and a movie star called Maurice Chevalier. Charlie says we should all be in armaments. I must talk to Randolph Putnam.

Walter Monckton has proposed himself for next weekend. HRH is very buoyed up. He thinks it signals that the New Bunch are ready to welcome him back.

26th January 1938

Randolph Putnam says I'm already in armaments.

Walter Monckton brought no news at all. He says he came simply to see how HRH was faring. Wally says he came for a jaunt, more like. She's now talking about going back to the States instead of settling in France, but Monckton advises against it. He says if they go to America, they'll get squeezed for taxes, whereas the French are proving to be very considerate about David's particular financial circumstances.

Monckton's also concerned that HRH doesn't get political briefings anymore.

I said, "He gets lectures from Freddie Crosbie."

He said, "Well, it's not enough. It's no wonder he seems so lost. The man needs to be kept au courant."

I said, "Wally sees to that."

He said, "I don't mean au courant with hat fashions and Paris niteries."

He underestimates Wally. She reads the newspapers cover to cover every day. Anyway, Monckton says he's going to try and impress upon London the importance of HRH continuing to receive little notes and visits, to help keep him informed of British policies.

"Otherwise," he said, "I very much fear the Germans will gain his ear and he may go off at dangerous tangents."

3rd February 1938

Wally is busy with fittings. HRH is in a depression. I walked the dogs with him this morning. He said, "My brother Bertie used to do whatever I told him, but since he's been King, he gets quite testy if I telephone him with advice."

I've suggested watercolors. When time hung heavy at Drumcanna, I found it a very useful way of getting through the day.

Hattie Erlanger is coming for the weekend. Alix Piston-LeRupin says she heard Maxi is back in town, but no one has actually seen him.

6th February 1938

With Wally, Hattie, and Kenny Opdyke to a flea market. Hattie says Wally looked like an old rag-and-bone man, the way she picked over everything. Hattie can be very cruel.

HRH has decided to write his memoirs. Wally said he should find out how much a publisher is willing to pay for them before he wastes any time on them, but he's already filled five and a half pages.

She's going down to Cannes with Kenny Opdyke and Johnnie MacMullen to make a final appraisal of La Croe. I think she's already decided to take it.

12th February 1938

Wally has signed a ten-year lease on La Croe and is on her way back to claim her Valentine. There have been heavy hints about an unset canary diamond.

14th February 1938

Wally got a bracelet of cat's eye rubies and a suite full of long-stemmed roses. HRH was pipped at the post in the bidding for the canary diamond by Mrs. Standard Oil. Such a disappointment Maxi couldn't be back in time for Valentine's Day. I believe he's a great romantic.

16th February 1938

Maxi is back. We were at La Huchette with the Lazslo Melchiors and the Piston-LeRupins when in he walked, with that awful Princess Didi Grimaldi. He came over the instant he saw me. He's just back from his travels, literally. By the time he called, I'd already left for the evening. Two foxtrots. It was such a pleasure to be back in the arms of a natural dancer. I believe I feel the sap rising.

The Crosbies are going to try and come down to Cannes at Easter, international tensions permitting. Pips says there's a big row brewing in Parliament over the Italy question. The general feeling is that some kind of accommodation should be reached with Mr. Mussolini, but Anthony Eden is digging in his heels. Freddie is behind Eden. He would be.

17th February 1938

Luncheon with Maxi. A private booth at Bofinger. He says Didi Grimaldi is absolutely nothing to him, but she's rather dug in her claws and expects him to squire her around. He says he's going to make his feelings very clear before he leaves on his next business trip. Only just back and already planning to leave! But, as he says, money can't sit idle in bank accounts, it has to be made to work. How like Brumby he sounds.

18th February 1938

A lost afternoon. Darling, darling Maxi!

Sent for an atlas of the world. Paraguay is a very long way from Paris, or from anywhere really.

22nd February 1938

Wrecked. Went with Maxi to a *caveau* near St.-Lazare to hear a rough little chanteuse he's discovered. Edna Piaf. The show didn't finish till three. Wally barked at me, said she doesn't want a yawner-in-waiting, but she's keen to come along next time we go. She likes to keep up with trends.

Anthony Eden has resigned, so perhaps we'll be spared from going to war with Italy.

26th February 1938

A red-letter day! *Look!* magazine has named Wally as one of the ten best-dressed women in the world. She's deliriously happy and says now she's on the list she intends not only to remain on it but to achieve Number One position. Designers are going to be queuing up to dress her now. There'll be no more overdue accounts hanging around like last week's fish.

Maxi gave me a sweet decoupage trinket box and a pair of gypsy earrings.

Wally sneered. She said, "If that's the best he can manage when he's courting you, I'd send him on his way."

I said, "I don't judge a man by the price of his gifts."

"Then more fool you," she said. "And whatever you do, don't try wearing those earrings. They'll stain your earlobes green."

1st March 1938

Sunshine at last. HRH has laid aside his memoirs and gone to play golf with Ambassador Bullitt. Maxi gave me lunch in a droll little bistro near St. Severin. He's desolate about having to go back to Paraguay so soon, but he's been able to put a very interesting investment opportunity my way. Oilseed. It's top secret at present, to prevent too many people getting in early and ruining our prospects.

He hopes to be back by May. He said, "It's impossible to be sure of dates. Business takes as long as it takes. Think of it this way, *chou-chou.* It's the future I'm investing in. Both our futures."

Chou-chou is French for "sweetest darling."

4th March 1938

To Elsie Mendl's, where we heard that Lily's friend Prince D'Annunzio passed away. I wonder who'll get his house. The German Ambassador von Welczeks were there, also Henri and Alix Piston-LeRupin, Sylvie Vieille-Soiffarde, and Lucien Ecornifleur. I taught them the Lambeth Walk. They very much regard me as their eyes and ears in London. A sort of cultural attaché.

I noticed Sylvie cut Maxi and was pretty cool toward me. Perhaps she nursed hopes herself.

Wally's in a whirl of color charts and fabric samples for La Croe. Everything from the Fort is being fetched out of storage, ready for shipping. She said, "They may have taken away his palaces, Maybell, but he's still a prince of the blood, and I intend to give him what he's due. I'm going to give him a truly royal home."

They're very affectionate at present. Lots of golf seems to be beneficial.

Pips says now Anthony Eden's gone, homburgs are absolutely out. She's making Freddie get a bowler.

8th March 1938

My last evening with Maxi for a while. To Crocodil, where we tangoed and drank far too much champagne, and then to Les Halles for onion soup, while the gay market traders bustled around us with their trays of meat. The sky was turning mauve as we kissed good-bye.

Wally on the telephone at ten, urgently needing my opinion on water carafes.

9th March 1938

It's been announced that King Bertie York and his Queen will make a State visit to France in July. The whole world at their disposal, and they have to choose France! Wally says we're not going to wait around to be ignored while Bunny and Cook get the red-carpet treatment. We shall leave the country. HRH has Forwood looking into yachts.

Johnnie MacMullen has made a brisk start on La Croe. Blue and white for the drawing rooms, with accents of yellow; peach for Wally's suite; royal scarlet for HRH; Toile de Jouy for the guest rooms; Wedgwood blue for mine.

12th March 1938

Hitler has sent his troops into Austria. Everyone is walking around with shocked expressions, but Kitty Rothschild has been predicting it for weeks. They all speak the same language, so it simply amounts to a revision of frontiers and, as HRH says, there were many who argued for this very arrangement at the end of the war, and the case may be stronger now, because the Fuehrer is himself Austrian and so has a natural care and affection for the place.

Tomorrow to Cannes. We're staying at the Cap Argent until La Croe is habitable.

15th March 1938, Cap Argent, Cannes

The Crosbies are still dithering. Freddie says now Austria has fallen, Czechoslovakia will be next. I don't see that that need upset our plans. Adolf Hitler is hardly going to send his tanks to the Cote d'Azur.

Boss and Ethel are going to motor over from Menton with Lily and the Bajavidas, so things may liven up. Herman and Kath are sweet, but they don't keep late hours, and they have Monckton and his wife staying. Hardly the life and soul of the party. The Moncktons are the kind of people who sit for hours studying books with no illustrations.

22nd March 1938

Motored to Monaco to meet the Crokers. Played a little roulette, but Lady Luck deserted me. The Moncktons stayed home with the Rogerses and played bridge.

Lily says Eugene Rothschild's brother has been arrested in Vienna. HRH wants to propose himself to go and parlay with the Nazis, but Wally won't hear of it. She says he could easily be taken hostage, and the New Bunch wouldn't lift a finger to rescue him. Also, his furniture from Fort Belvedere arrives next week and she needs him here to decide which pieces he wants in his rooms. Still, what a worry for Eugene and Kitty.

29th March 1938

The King of Albania is to marry a stenographer called Geraldine. Her mother was a Stewart from Richmond, Virginia. Married a Hungarian who ran through her money, and there's not much left, by all accounts. As suitable royal brides go, this girl makes Wally look like a Crown Princess.

The first of the furniture wagons are expected tomorrow. Wally is praying the good weather holds. She's going to have everything unloaded onto the lawns and inspected, so as not to waste time carrying into the house pieces that have no place there. The carpenters are on standby with their chisels. The housemaids are at the ready with beeswax and cloths.

3rd April 1938

HRH has spent the day running around in golfing knickers, reclaiming forgotten treasures. "Oh look, my drum table!" I heard him cry. "And remember this, darling? My tapestry footstool!"

Wally's creating a special room for him on the top floor. She's in great form.

I think she's quietly rather pleased with what she's found in the crates. None of the silver is missing, the linens have survived the trip, and there are lots of decent paintings HRH had in storage, things she's never seen before. There's going to be enough for here and for Paris.

Fruity and Baba are going to come for Easter.

10th April 1938, Chateau La Croe

Our first night in residence. Wally and David seem more like honeymooners today than ever they did last June. I wish Maxi were here.

HRH waylaid me as I was going up for my bath. He said, "Maybell, I haven't shown you my new realm. Come up and visit the Admiral of the Fleet."

This is Wally's special gift to him. You go through his dressing room and then up in a tiny elevator to the penthouse. MacMullen has fitted it out like a boy's dream. It has a desk for his typewriter and baize on the floor so he can practice his putting. He has his bagpipes up there, and his ukulele, and a telescope on the little terrace, so when he goes out for a cigarette, he can survey the horizon for battleships. He's named it The Bridge.

I said, "Sir, you'll be able to alert us when Daisy Fellowes hoves into view."

He said, "I will, indeed. Isn't it all wonderful? Wally's so, so clever. I've never had a room like this before."

Tomorrow, a lunch party for the Erlangers, the Metcalfes, and the Rogerses, to celebrate the completion of Wally and David's first home.

12th April 1938

La Croe made a glorious debut. Wally had the terrace doors thrown open so that when people arrived, they had an uninterrupted view through the hall, across the lawns, and down to the sea. Herman murmured, "Good old Wally, ever the stage manager. Even the sun remembered its cue."

The entrance hall was filled with sprays of white lilac. No paintings. Just a scarlet-and-gold flag hanging from the stair gallery. Very dramatic. It's David's old Knight of the Garter banner. Apparently, when he abdicated, the New Bunch had to remake him a Garter

Knight, with a new emblem and everything, so Wally snapped up the old one and told Johnnie MacMullen to do something with it.

Wally kept trying to herd us out to the terrace for drinks, but HRH was bounding around, overexcited like the dogs, pointing out little features and *objets*. It was such a good-humored lunch. Piquant chicken livers, eggplant baked with tomatoes, custard ice with crème de cassis.

Fruity says he's relieved to find HRH looking so well. From what Monckton had reported after his last visit, he'd expected to find David smoking like a chimney and generally going to pieces.

I said, "Wally won't allow that. She finds little chores for him, but it's all a strain on her. It'd be far better if someone else were to give him things to do. Papers to sign or something light like that, just for the mornings."

He said, "I know. Chamberlain will bring it up again with His Majesty. It's a question of timing. What about his memoirs? Monckton had high hopes of that, but he doesn't appear to have made much progress."

I'm not sure. I think his pen ran out of ink one morning, and then Dimitri Shapaleff called up and suggested golf, and somehow he just didn't get back to it.

I said, "All I know is, it seems crazy that he's hanging around, opening and shutting snuffboxes and checking the time every few minutes when Wally and I are up to our necks in menus. Surely there's something the New Bunch would be grateful to offload?"

He said, "It's a problem, Maybell. It's a family thing. Tricky. Her Majesty's worried that if David becomes active again, the country might rally to him, that there might be some kind of attempted return. Of course, she's remembering him when he was full of vim. If she'd seen him after those months at Enzesfeld, she'd know that much of the fire has gone out of him. Actually, I'd say he's entirely harmless and could be a useful extra pair of hands, but Her Majesty's very protective of the King, you see? Every bit as fierce as Wally, when it comes to looking after her husband."

18th April 1938

Fruity and HRH have been up and down to The Bridge all day. Roars of laughter and the reek of tobacco. Wally's all gaiety and confidence. She even volunteered to keep Baba company when she drove over to see the Rogerses this afternoon, and she's never really been fond of Baba.

Hattie is trying to persuade me to go back to London. She says the monarchy has been saved, HRH has his Treasury elves cranking out ready money, and Wally is in her element, so there'll be no further excitement. She says I should leave them to live happily ever after.

I said, "I'm Lady-in-Waiting."

She said, "Wally doesn't need anyone in-waiting. She doesn't have State occasions to attend."

Hattie didn't see us in Germany. Besides, what would I do in England? Put up bottled plums? Weekend at Leake Priory and play whist in gloves? How can I return to that after Paris? I need a colorful arena. I need food for my lively mind.

19th April 1938

HRH wore his Lord of the Isles kilt at dinner and played one of his own bagpipe compositions, *The Belle of Baltimore*. Afterwards, to the casino. Saw Nazli Egypt and Lucien Ecornifleur at the chemin de fer tables. No news of Maxi.

Lucien said, "You know Maxi. I bet he's busy investing someone's money in a surefire scheme."

I said nothing. I'm sure he was trying to trick me into divulging things. Maxi warned me there'd be a stampede to get into oilseed once people got wind of it.

Back to Paris on Friday. Fern Bedaux's people have found a house that sounds promising. Boulevard Suchet.

26th April 1938, Meurice Hotel, Paris

Wally has snapped up the house. It's on a very busy street, but once you're inside, the noise doesn't penetrate, and the interior has great potential. There's an important staircase, an enfilade of salons, and a pretty view over the Bois de Boulogne. It needs bringing up to scratch from A to Z, but Johnnie MacMullen says he can make a start on it as soon as he's finished the Lazslo Melchiors' house at Le Touquet.

Randolph Putnam says I shouldn't have put anything into Maxi Finto's oilseed factory until I'd had him look into it. He treats me like a child. I only wish I could hear from Maxi. Paraguay even *sounds* dangerous.

To the Piston-LeRupins. Just carafe wine and saltines, and far too many people. Wally says it was their way of discharging a whole year's worth of social debts.

Afterwards, to the ABC to hear Johnny Hess. Kenny Opdyke said Sylvie Vieille-Soiffarde had been planning to oust me as Lady-in-Waiting until she discovered all the job paid was a dress allowance and accommodations. Dress allowance! If only!

I said, "Excuse me, Kenny! All it pays is a suite at La Croe and an interesting life."

10th May 1938

News at last of Maxi, and not from a welcome source. Didi Grimaldi.

It turns out, she's gone into oilseed, too. So much for it being hush-hush. She said, "He's been seen in Rio and he's been seen in Montevideo, but he'll be back here sometime. I have every confidence."

I thought last night's Scavenger Hunt was rather a put-up job, because Winnie Gulliver must be the only woman in Paris with access to a size 13 evening sandal. Still, *I* was the only one who managed to produce a four-leaf clover. Cloisonné, admittedly, but I was still the only one.

Lord Halifax is coming to tea today. Part of Walter Monckton's campaign to keep HRH in the swim vis-à-vis British foreign policy.

Dudley Forwood has found us a yacht for July. She's called the *Gulzar*. We're going to take her down to Portofino, pick up the Venetian contingent—Tori and Paola Nasibruni and Clarice Sfogginomi—and continue on to Capri. As Wally says, best to give the Bertie Yorks a wide berth while they're king-ing in Paris, and with Queen Dumpling, that means a very wide berth indeed.

Tomorrow, back to La Croe. Boss and Ethel are coming for Wally and David's anniversary. Possibly Bernie and Zita Cavett, too.

1st June 1938, La Croe

The Hermann Goerings have a baby girl. What a blessing. Only five hundred airplanes in the fly-past. Anniversary cards and letters and presents are arriving by the dozen, many of them addressed simply to "The Duke and Duchess of Windsor, France." All offering affectionate good wishes. The difference a year makes.

We're going to mark Friday with a small lunch party.

3rd June 1938

HRH and Wally posed for photos on the lawn before lunch. Fern came without Charlie, who is away on some secret mission. Lily believes it's not unconnected with the bailing out of that poor Rothschild, who's still incarcerated in Vienna.

Great hilarity over the quantity of baby booties among the anniversary gifts. Boss said, "Well, Wally, what about it? It'd be cute to see a little David gamboling on the lawn."

Ethel said, "She already has a little David who gambols on the lawn."

Wally said, "I have an even better idea. Let's pack up the booties and send them to Emmy Goering."

David gave her a platinum eternity band.

Ethel said, "I take my hat off to her. She's taken a disaster and turned it into a happy ending."

Well, Wally was never deterred by unpromising material. Even at Biddle Street, she made her mother use their few bits of good china every day.

Lily has offered a little birthday dinner for Wally in Nice.

20th June 1938

We took over Le Cirque last night. Lily had offered to pay for twelve, but, to my certain knowledge, Wally invited twenty, and then people like Lucky Patrice, whom we actually hardly know, brought extras with them. Wally says Lily can afford it.

HRH gave her a jet-and-diamond leopard pin.

30th June 1938

Judson and Hattie have arrived, and Bernie and Zita Cavett are expected any minute. We board the *Gulzar* tomorrow in time for dinner. First stop, Rapallo.

1st July 1938

I've bagged an upper-deck cabin. Let the latecomers sweat and suffocate.

Frette bed linens, a walk-in closet, chairs and vanity stool covered in dark raspberry ostrich hide. I'm *very* comfortable.

5th July 1938, off Rapallo

Wally and HRH have gone ashore to see the King Victor Emmanuels, so we are at leisure. Tori and Paola Nasibruni came aboard last night and are sleeping in. Hattie is wearing bobby socks and the most extraordinary gingham playsuit bunched up between her legs like a diaper. What can she be thinking! Judson and Bernie are playing at quoits.

12th July 1938, off Anzio

All day being dragged around Roman ruins by Hattie. Tomorrow, Judson can go with her. I'm going to the Tiberio spa to relax and put aside all busyness. Wally says the facials alone make the whole trip worthwhile.

Rory is seventeen today. How he'd love the *Gulzar*. Better than any of those little canoes he gets to sail with old Salty Laird. He'd be beating to windward and splicing the yardarm and having such fun. Perhaps next year. And Flora, too. Violet can't expect them to spend every summer of their lives at Drumcanna, persecuted by insects, playing Chutes and Ladders while the rain patters against the windows.

19th July 1938, Pensione Bon Sol

The most wonderful surprise. We put in to Sestri Levante for our last few days, and who should I find sitting on the veranda of our pensione but Maxi. He'd been chasing up and down the coast of Italy for the past three weeks, trying to find me. Tonight, dinner *à deux*. Zita says she can smell love in the air!

20th July 1938

Wore my orange china silk and my amethyst dragonfly pin. Maxi hardly let go my hand all evening. He said, "You know, May-*belle*, I adore you. But what do I have to offer? I have nothing in the world, only the head on my shoulders."

But it's a very handsome head and a very smart head, and that, after all, was all Brumby had. And it doesn't matter if he doesn't have money, because I do, and the oilseed business is about to take off in a very big way. This is a golden opportunity to increase the size of my investment. Wait till Randolph Putnam hears!

23rd July 1938

HRH offered Maxi a ride back with us to Cannes, but he's staying on in Italy to look into cork. Well, Brumby was also a great believer in diversification. Wally said, "What do you know about this man, Maybell? I hope you're not being silly."

I said, "I know he's looking out for my best interests, and there's nothing wrong in that. I know he dances like a dream."

She doesn't like anyone paying me attention.

She wanted to know how much I'd given him, but it's none of her business. And Randolph Putnam isn't going to hear about my oilseed prospects yet, either. Maxi says financial advisers are well known for scaring people off good things so they can mop them up for themselves.

1st August 1938, La Croe

We got back here late last evening, and the help were all lined up outside the front door, crisp summer liveries and nice straight backs. Wally's done such a good job on them.

Pips and Freddie were here ahead of us. Freddie says General Franco looks like winning in Spain, which will mean Lightfoot is on the wrong side. What a fool.

Pips says La Croe makes Fort Belvedere look like a flophouse.

11th August 1938

The Neville Chamberlains are at Balmoral. Monckton says HRH's future is definitely on the agenda.

15th August 1938

No news from Balmoral.

21st August 1938

We closed Boite Noire at five and went on to Chez Zazzi for pancakes and coffee. Still nothing from Balmoral.

24th August 1938

We're going back to Paris. Monckton wants to see HRH but is too pressed for time to come down to La Croe. Maybe this means good news. Wally says Monckton will never bring good news, from Balmoral or anywhere else. She says the man is a Jonah.

Freddie said, "Well, this is hardly the time to be pestering the King about David's future. I'm sure his mind is on the Sudetenland."

There's always something. One thing about the United States. There aren't all these little local disputes going on.

Wally said, "If they don't hurry up and do something for David, maybe we'll give him something else to worry about. We could, you know? We could go back and set up there and create a fearful row. They're completely outside the law, denying me my title."

She's always like this toward the end of a vacation. Nagging and picking and revisiting old wrongs. I hope Maxi's back in town.

3rd September 1938, Meurice Hotel, Paris

No word of Maxi.

Wally and Freddie were both right about Balmoral. Monckton says it simply wasn't the moment for Chamberlain to bring up HRH's future. He says there are worrying rumblings from the direction of Czechoslovakia, which monopolized everyone's thoughts.

Wally said, "Another opportunity missed. Another winter on the way with David unemployed."

Monckton said, "Strictly off the record, Halifax thinks the Czechs are bound to have to cede something to Hitler, so it may be settled pretty quickly."

Wally said, "And then there'll be something else. Everything gets settled except *our* affairs."

To Gerny's, to hear young Charles Trenet. They say he's going into movies, and no wonder, with those delicious golden curls and that angelic smile.

7th September 1938

The Ambassador von Welczeks to dinner. Also came: Bendor Westminster, the Lazslo Melchiors, and Elsie Mendl. I now understand all about the Sudetenland. Everyone who lives there is German anyway, so it makes no sense at all for the Czechs to hold on to it. Common sense must surely prevail.

12th September 1938

They say Germany troops are massing on the Czech frontier.

14th September 1938

Mr. Chamberlain is flying to Germany tomorrow to see President Hitler and ascertain his intentions. A perfect example of a job they could have given to HRH. As Wally says, Neville Chamberlain must have a hundred calls on his time, whereas HRH has spent the morning whistling through his teeth and watching the rain beat down.

15th September 1938

HRH's cousin Arthur Connaught has died, but as he still has three months of his exile to serve, he's not allowed to go to England for the funeral. It was cancer, apparently. I met the wife once, at Carlton Gardens. She's very keen on hospitals and sits on various committees with Violet.

Hitler told Chamberlain that the Sudetenland is a private German matter and nothing to do with the League of Nations. France says if so much as one German boot enters Czechoslovakia, it will take steps.

Forwood says what France means is, it will issue a statement deploring Germany's actions. He says they can't possibly think of going to war, because they'll find themselves marching alone. Britain is by no means ready for any military adventures, and America isn't interested. It's all so unsettling. Perhaps Ena Spain has the right idea. Move to Switzerland and stop listening to the wireless.

18th September 1938

Lunch with Kitty Rothschild and Winnie Gulliver. They think Hitler is playing with Neville Chamberlain as a cat plays with a mouse. Kitty says after Czechoslovakia it will be Poland, then Yugoslavia, then Romania, and so on, until the German flag flies all over Europe. Even France.

Eugene is in New York, overseeing work on their Long Island property, because they foresee it becoming their only safe haven.

Wally says the Rothschilds are one case, we're quite another. She says we'd have nothing to fear in the unlikely event of Germany invading France.

She said, "Don't forget, David's as much German as he is British, so it'd make no difference to us. In fact, it might be to our advantage. Adolf Hitler would certainly give him a job."

29th September 1938

Neville Chamberlain is flying to Germany again for more discussions with the Fuehrer, and this time, Mr. Mussolini will also attend. Everyone is very tense. After great difficulties, I got a call through to Carlton Gardens, but neither Violet nor Melhuish were home. Left a message.

Managed to speak to Pips, who says they're digging trenches in Hyde Park and the War Office is recruiting women for the Home Defences. Cooks, drivers, typists. She's going to volunteer.

I said, "You're too old." She said, "I'm not a bit too old."

I'll bet she is. She hasn't looked into it properly. She doesn't even know what the uniforms are like.

She was at the House of Commons yesterday to hear Chamberlain speak. She says there were extraordinary scenes, everyone very emotional and braced for the worst. She said the House was packed. Even the old Queen was there. Chamberlain was on his feet for more than an hour, recounting all his visits with Adolf Hitler and preparing everyone for gloomy news, but before he got to the point, a message was passed to him, and he went into a huddle with his advisers. Pips says the atmosphere was electric. Then he announced that Hitler and Mussolini had responded to his latest telegram and were willing to talk again. She said the place erupted, members of Parliament standing on their benches, cheering and throwing their order papers in the air. Freddie told her he cried. He said Chamberlain looked a little tired as he left the chamber, but gave everyone a smile.

Well, God bless Neville Chamberlain. If anyone can keep us from a silly war, he seems to be the man.

30th September 1938

Violet returned my call. They heard yesterday that Lightfoot has been injured in Spain, but not seriously, and is being sent home. No other information, except that it happened as long ago as August, so Doopie may find him on the doorstep at any moment. What a relief. I hope this has cured him of wars.

Fruity Metcalfe is here. He wants to discus war plans with HRH, but I don't think we have any.

1st October 1938

The warmongers have been routed! With the help of Mr. Mussolini's diplomatic efforts, Neville Chamberlain has achieved a concord with Hitler. He's to be allowed to have the Sudetenland, provided he promises to leave the rest of Czechoslovakia in peace. Exactly as Halifax predicted. It sounds to me as though Mr. Mussolini has earned that little piece of Africa that's been such a bone of contention.

Everyone is happy except Fruity. He says it's like telling a burglar you won't call the police if he puts back the diamonds and just steals the teaspoons. Of course, Fruity is itching to get back into uniform.

7th October 1938

Penelope Blythe has pitched up for a long weekend. She says she'd been looking forward to having Leake Priory requisitioned and being able to do some kind of daring war work, but everything has now gone off the boil. She's seeking new excitements.

Took her to lunch with Wally, who was at her most gruesome, nagging HRH to go to Boulevard Suchet and throw some Royal weight around with the laggard electricians. The suite was full of red carnations, never Wally's choice.

"Just cordial wishes from the Fuehrer," she said. "But no prizes for guessing the name of the delivery boy!"

Von Ribbentrop, of course. He and his *hausfrau* are in town. Wally and HRH are dining at the German Embassy tonight.

Penelope and I may go to Maxim's and then on to the Revue Negre. Sylvie Vieille-Soiffarde is getting up a table.

9th October 1938

Poor Ena Spain has lost another son. He was in a car accident in Miami. She's not in town, so I haven't been able to speak with her. Anyway, what can one say? Her life has been nothing but tragedy. And still old Princess Baby hangs on. The grandmother burying the grandchildren. That's not the way things are supposed to be.

Penelope swears Sylvie was wearing a wig last evening. She also swears Alix Piston-LeRupin offered her Benzedrine pills and Lucien Ecornifleur squeezed her thigh.

I said, "Start to worry when he squeezes your purse."

15th October 1938

Joey Legh is over to play some golf with HRH. Wally's relieved to have him entertained. He's become very peevish lately about her lunches with Kenny Opdyke. She said, "David, I married you for better or for worse, but not for lunch."

The Communists are threatening strikes.

17th October 1938

A letter from Pips. Lightfoot is home and in a much worse condition than they'd been led to expect, having lost an arm. He's in St. Thomas's hospital, being seen to.

20th October 1938

A brief conversation with Violet. George Lightfoot has lost his right forearm. It could have been worse. Just as well though that he had settled for Doopie, because his chances with anyone else would now be reduced. One saw a lot of it after the war, men with an empty sleeve pinned across their chest. I never found it in the least dashing.

Violet said, "I do wish you'd come home, Maybell."

I said, "I am home."

But I may visit. November is out of the question, because we have fittings for our spring gowns, and several important parties. Also, we're threatened with the Harry Gloucesters, who may call in on their way home from prince-ing in Africa. Perhaps I'll go in December, when Rory is home from school.

4th November 1938

Lily Drax-Pfaffenhof for the weekend. She says the Munich Accord was a simple case of common sense, because no one in Germany wants a war, not even Hitler. As for the way the Jewish folk are being bullied, she wonders whether the Fuehrer knows the half of what's going on.

Charlie Bedaux says I should buy francs while they're such good value.

7th November 1938

Maxi is back! He announced himself with a bouquet of miniature calla lilies. He says our oilseeds will be in profit by the summer, and he's found the very cork grove for me. He reminds me of Brumby in many ways. Always dreaming up business schemes, even on the threshold of the boudoir. Always alert to opportunities. Of course, Brumby never used brilliantine, and he was an early riser, whereas Maxi goes to bed with the lark.

Tonight to Pigalle.

9th November 1938

Bumped into Winnie Gulliver buying envelopes in Samaritaine.

She said, "Maybell, I hope you won't think me impertinent, but are you in deep with Maxi Finto?"

I very much like Winnie, but really!

She said, "I won't pry, but I think you should know there was a widow from Michigan who got rather badly burned. Something to do with trading in Peruvian bird poo."

10th November 1938

To the Bricktop Club with Maxi. There *is* a bird poo industry, apparently, so Winnie G. was half-right. But the Michigan woman got jittery and pulled out her money prematurely, always an unwise thing to do. As Maxi says, you need strong nerves to stay ahead of the crowd in business, and I have nerves of steel.

Wore my new magenta jacket. Two women at the next table were wearing tuxedos and smoking cheroots.

11th November 1938

The Harry Gloucesters to lunch with Wally and HRH. They toyed with their sweetbreads, she whispering to me that they prefer simple food. What a mixed bag these Royalties are. King Bertie York and Gloucester and the sister are so dull, and HRH and Kent are so vivacious, or at least they used to be. The only sign of animation in Gloucester came when HRH told him he'd sold off his Canadian livestock.

"Oh no!" he said. "Not the shorthorns! What a tragedy! Damned fine herd! How much did you get for them?"

I just hope he carries the story back to the New Bunch. It's high time they realized homes fit for a royal duke cost a great deal more money than they've allowed him, and sacrifices have had to be made.

After lunch, we showed them Boulevard Suchet, which smells of fresh paint but is almost ready for the drapes to be hung, then HRH went with them to the airfield to see them off.

12th November 1938

Mr. Ataturk died yesterday. We had such an agreeable time with him in Istanbul. Wally is wearing her Turkish choker in remembrance.

13th November 1938

Lunch at Brasserie Lipp and then to the bank with Maxi. I'm taking a rain check on cork groves but have plunged a little deeper into oilseeds.

He gave me a blue topaz pendant and a paperweight that contains earth from his ranch in Paraguay. As he says, now I'll have a little piece of him while he's gone. And he predicts that next year he won't need to travel quite so much. We'll have time to get to know one another, and time to enjoy all that money we'll have made. If things work out, I may let HRH in on it. Wally says he's far poorer than he thinks he is.

23rd November 1938

The Neville Chamberlains are dining here tomorrow. HRH hopes they're bringing news of a thaw at Buckingham Palace. Wally says as well look for a thaw at the North Pole.

25th November 1938

If Mrs. Chamberlain possesses any good jewelry, she elected not to wear it last evening, and her gown was *le dernier cri*. She was caught between the glitter of my diamonds and flash of Wally's sapphires, and looked like a dazed woodland creature. Still, at least she bobbed a curtsy.

Despite our best efforts, conversation was like a slow game of handball, and when the men joined us after their brandy, HRH looked ominously deflated. Apparently, Chamberlain's talk had been of nothing but international tensions, and his only word on the subject of David's exile had been that "now didn't seem quite the moment."

Wally said, "It'll never be 'quite the moment,' David. Why don't you face facts? We're never going back."

HRH says he found Chamberlain very sound on the important points. One, war against Germany is unthinkable, because the French are in no state of readiness and we can't start hostilities without them. And two, we should anyway be addressing the more urgent question of how best to deal with the Soviet bear.

We just heard that his Aunt Maud has died. They're taking her back to Norway, so, strictly speaking, he could attend the funeral without breaking any promises, but he's decided not to. He doesn't want to travel without Wally, and even if Wally could be persuaded to climb aboard an airplane, he knows when they got there none of the Royalties would speak to her.

He said, "I burn with shame, Maybell, every time I think of the wrong they're doing her. Her only offense has been to be loved by me."

Of course, there's more to it than that. They hate her because she's American. They hate her because she won't be fenced in by their silly old rules. But none of it matters anymore. Anyway, he wasn't close to Maud Norway.

Claridge's has reserved me a nice junior suite. Wally's shopping list grows longer. Marmalade, dog treats, ink, Mrs. Spry special flower-arrangement wire, magnesia tablets.

I'm going to try to coax Violet and Melhuish out of their rut and give them dinner. I'll bet they haven't been to a restaurant in years.

6th December 1938, Claridge's Hotel, London

Dear Lightfoot is in a very bad way. He's thinner than ever and racked with pain from the arm he no longer has. Still full of jocularity though, in spite of it. He said, "I suppose I should change my name to Light*hand*."

He's quite unrepentant about going to Spain. He said, "My only regret is that the British Battalion didn't stay until the job was done."

I said, "Well, please promise you'll stay at home from now on."

He said, "No choice. If it comes to another war, the army won't have any use for me now. Can't even push a bloody pen."

Doopie loved the scent I took her.

8th December 1938

Violet may still be a little starchy with me, but I seem to have reestablished full diplomatic relations with Melhuish. He actually kissed me as they were leaving. A roast partridge can work wonders.

He asked after HRH. I said, "He's fit and well but underoccupied. Why doesn't the King give him a job?"

He said, "I'm sure he will. As an opening arises."

Violet said, "Can't France use him? What about worker housing and pit head baths? Has he lost interest?"

As I reminded her, when he made a study of such things, he got nothing but criticism.

Melhuish is all for Chamberlain. He says British politics can always be relied upon to produce the right man for the moment.

He said, "Baldwin managed the Abdication satisfactorily, but only Chamberlain could have pulled off Munich."

Rory is home tomorrow. He has his heart set on going to Dartmouth next year as a cadet officer, and Melhuish is resigned to him choosing the Navy instead of the Army. He said, "Could be worse. At least he's not going to end up in the corps de bloody ballet!" A sly dig at the Belchesters' middle boy.

13th December 1938

Rory and Flora came to tea, looking quite the young lady and gentleman.

Flora said, "I wish Aunt Doopie and Uncle Lightfoot would have a baby. I like babies."

Rory said, "They can't have babies now, you noodlehead. Uncle Lightfoot only has one arm."

So adorable. He gave me a fake camellia that squirts water.

Tomorrow, home.

16th December 1938, Meurice Hotel, Paris

The station wagons leave for La Croe in the morning with the luggage. Johnnie MacMullen is going ahead, too, to supervise the dressing of the tree. The Crokers are coming and the Erlangers. Herman and Kath will motor over on Christmas Day.

22nd December 1938, La Croe

Arrived just before dark. MacMullen had had the shutters left open, and every window glowed with light. Pinecones dipped in colored wax burning in the drawing-room fireplace, the foyer tree dressed with snowberries and white velvet bows, glasses of eggnog waiting for us. Just as everything looked set for a perfect holiday,

Kath Rogers telephoned bearing the glad tidings that Thelma Furness and her sister Gloria are spending Christmas at La Belle Garoupe, not half a mile away.

Wally completely unperturbed. She said, "Half a mile *geographically,* Kath, but light-years in every other respect."

I think the news has slightly unsettled HRH though. He's asked me to go with him to Cartier tomorrow, to help him pick out a few extra little *douceurs* for Wally, just in case there are any "tricky encounters."

26th December 1938

Wally got a blue diamond pin. She gave HRH a pair of ship's decanters for The Bridge and me a set of ivory elephants that are supposed to bring good luck. I believe I remember them from Bryanston Court.

A strained moment after dinner last evening, when Hattie suggested a game of charades, and HRH clapped his hands for joy. He said, "Oh yes! I haven't done that in years."

Wally said, "We are *not* playing charades. This is La Croe, not Sandringham. We're going to the casino."

Fortunately, that little Maharaja friend of the Bajavidas was there and staked her very generously.

2nd January 1939

New Year's Eve at Willy Maugham's. A bad start, when a spiteful little cluster of guests stood in Wally's path and absolutely would not curtsy. HRH went right up to Isabel Carteret and asked her if she'd forgotten her manners. He was in a fury, and so was she. She said, "No, sir. In our family, we only curtsy to Royal Highnesses."

HRH is still simmering over it, but Wally hasn't said a word. Hattie says the Carterets don't give a damn. Their people have been around since 1066, so they don't feel the Windsors have anything to teach them.

6th January 1939

Johnnie MacMullen has gone back to Paris to make sure everything is perfect for the move to Boulevard Suchet. He says Wally's the most exacting person he's ever done a house for and he always feels he's only one misplaced pillow away from appearing in her Grumble Book. I'd say it's unavoidable. One needs four paws and an annoying little yippy bark to be spared that fate.

10th January 1939, Meurice Hotel, Paris

Boulevard Suchet is truly fit for a king. The livery looks especially magnificent. Black and scarlet for daywear, scarlet trimmed with gold for formals. The buttons have a coronet and a W intertwined with an E, which the valet seems to think stands for Edward Windsor but Wally says it stands for Wallis and Edward.

HRH insists it simply spells "we."

"*Einum Meinum* and her boy," he keeps saying, "against the rest of the world."

I do wish he wouldn't. And I wish he wouldn't kiss her in the drawing room. It's so juvenile, and I know Wally hates it, because of smudges.

12th January 1939

Wally and I now have a routine. We meet every morning in her little Louis Quinze sitting room, as soon as she's given the secretaries the letters for the day. We make telephone calls, find out who's doing what, decide on clothes, juggle guest lists. We lunch, usually with Didi Grimaldi or Fern Bedaux, or, if Wally's having a shopping lunch with Kenny Opdyke, I see Kitty Rothschild or Winnie Gulliver.

The hairdresser comes at five. If people are invited, I come back to the Meurice to change. Otherwise, I just have a sundowner with HRH while Wally's dressing, and then leave them to dine alone. If I'm not invited anywhere, I'm very happy to have a quiet night in with my magazines and something light served in my suite.

The Charles Lindberghs are going to be in town at the end of the month, and Wally's determined to get them for dinner. I believe she may still have a crush on him.

5th February 1939

Dinner at Boulevard Suchet last evening in honor of the Charles Lindberghs. Also came: the Ambassador Bullitts, Charlie and Fern, Lucien Ecornifleur, and the Lazslo Melchiors. I don't know what Wally sees in Lindbergh. All the man talks about is inventions. I don't believe he notices women at all. I had the impression he couldn't wait to escape from the table and go home and calculate velocities or whatever it is he does. Mrs. L. must welcome the opportunity to be in company. I find her rather sweet, but Wally doesn't see any point to her.

King Bertie York and his Queen are to visit the United States and Canada in the spring. I'll bet they're only going to rub David and Wally's noses in Charlie Bedaux's fiasco.

Freddie Crosbie has decided there isn't going to be a war, after all, so he and Pips are venturing to Paris for a weekend. They make it sound like trekking through darkest Africa. Pips has lost all her pluck. Whatever happened to the Pips who flew her drawers from the Oldfields flagpole on Founders' Day?

12th February 1939

Pips has a new short haircut. She got it in anticipation of wartime austerity and has decided to keep it. Freddie says a war grows less likely by the day, because Hitler is very unpopular with the German military and so can't depend on them at all. Meanwhile, Britain is rearming at such a clip Germany must think twice before embarking on any future adventures.

Wally told Pips off for slouching. Pips said, "Better a relaxed womanly posture than looking like someone put a broom handle up your gown."

Nervous laughter from HRH. Wally is fierce about deportment. Always has been.

Freddie thinks Maxi Finto sounds like a big fake. He says I should have gotten something on paper.

15th February 1939

Freddie went with HRH to the English church. Wally was cross. She says he'd meet a much better class of people at the Madeleine.

1st March 1939

I do wish Maxi would get in touch. It's not the money. I'd just like to know how things stand.

The Lazslo Melchiors are giving a costume party to welcome the spring. We all have to dress as rustics.

2nd March 1939

Wally says she's not dressing as a rustic for anyone. She may ask Main Bocher to make her a little cotton milkmaid gown and just add seed pearls. It's at times like this it would be so handy to have Doopie around the corner. I may just have my Bo-Peep revamped.

8th March 1939

I've written to Violet, suggesting Rory and Flora visit me as soon as Rory is released from school in July. That would give us three clear weeks for jaunts and much-needed shopping. Flora seems to own nothing but ragged woolens suitable for Drumcanna. She has practically nothing smart for town. What fun we'll have.

16th March 1939

After all those promises he made at Munich, Hitler has upped and marched into Czechoslovakia. People are saying Poland will be next. It's becoming very hard to keep a good opinion of Adolf Hitler. HRH says the average German is a jolly, sociable chap, and the last thing he wants is a war. He says the only conclusion he can reach is that Hitler now has a screw loose.

Tonight to the Lazslo Melchiors. Kenny Opdyke has it from a reliable source that Lucien Ecornifleur intends wearing nothing but a vine leaf.

18th March 1939

A fabulous party, and how we all needed it in these grim times. A Kentucky Jug Band and a strolling minstrel in thigh boots. Wore my Bo-Peep gown minus the muslin, with a silk lace fichu and a wreath of bay leaves in my hair. The Dimitri Shapaleffs came as vulgar boatmen, Sylvie Vieille-Soiffarde came as Circe with Johnnie MacMullen as an enchanted swine, and the Piston-LeRupins came as themselves, but the scene was stolen by the Esterhazys, who arrived on hired donkeys. Wally wore her Tyrolean dirndl and carried a wooden pail, and HRH wore his old gardening hat and carried a basket of nosegays. A cheap effort, I thought.

1st April 1939

Wally's ordering shorter skirts for the fall and big, square shoulders. In my opinion, her shoulders are already quite square enough.

Another month and nothing from Maxi. Sylvie Vieille-Soiffarde says he's one of those people who never write or telephone. He just materializes.

With my oilseed dividends, I hope.

2nd April 1939

Mr. Chamberlain has put his foot down. If Hitler makes the slightest move, Britain will go to Poland's aid. All very well, but if, as people like Winnie Gulliver believe, he has his eye on half a dozen other territories, too, then what? One can't rush around the world helping every little country out of difficulties.

Wally has had the idea of HRH making a broadcast to the American people. As she says, if Britain gets into another war, before too long she'll be looking to America for assistance, so the American public must be made to stop and think. They are the ones who'll be asked to pay the price, after all. And who better to make them think than a British Prince with an American wife. HRH is very keen and has Dudley Forwood looking into it.

8th April 1939

The world has gone mad. Italy has now invaded Albania, and poor Queen Geraldine has had to get out of her childbed and flee. If she has any sense, she'll get herself straight to a good American hospital.

Rory and Flora must visit me at the very first opportunity, before anyone else invades anywhere else.

9th April 1939

A letter from Violet. She says July is out of the question for Flora and Rory to come to Paris. She's convinced we'll be at war by then. Of course, what she doesn't know is HRH is going to broadcast to America and pull us all back from the brink.

Forwood is discovering great enthusiasm for the project. Replied by return. I said, then let them come sooner. Rory's Long Leave in June would be perfect. I know Elsie Mendl would adore to throw a little party for them.

I might make a start on jewelry for Flora, too. Another year or two, and she'll be out, and apart from a very dull tiara and an ugly cameo brooch, I don't believe she stands to inherit anything from the Melhuish side.

15th April 1939

HRH's peacekeeping message to America is to be broadcast in early May from the town of Verdun. Wally will accompany him.

17th April 1939

Freddie Crosbie got wind of HRH's broadcast. He said, "Tell him, Maybell, when you're out walking those bloody pooches, he's not going to help himself or world peace by asking America to wink at Germany's ambitions. He's going to come across as Hitler's friend, which, I may say, a lot of people already believe him to be."

I'm not going to tell him any such thing. He's so enjoying preparing his speech.

19th April 1939

Humphrey Butler wants to know if HRH has cleared his speech with the New Bunch. Wally told him to mind his own business. I agree with her. You can't throw someone out of house and home and then expect to be kept informed of their every movement.

Lunch with Winnie Gulliver. She said she hoped I didn't give Maxi Finto a lot of money. I wonder what she means by "a lot."

25th April 1939

Beaverbrook has now added his voice to the dissenters. He says he's concerned about the timing of the broadcast, because it will coincide with the New Bunch visiting with the Roosevelts and there may be confusion as to who speaks for Great Britain: the new and untested King or the seasoned older brother?

When one looks at it that way, perhaps he has a point. I think David should speak before Bertie York has time to open his mouth, but Forwood says the dates can't be changed.

7th May 1939

Walter Monckton called to try and persuade HRH to postpone his speech, but he and Wally had already left for Verdun. Anyway, their minds were quite made up. As Wally said, this could be a turning point, the moment when the world wakes up to David's value as a statesman. And it's a very fine speech. I've heard him practicing it.

I speak as a soldier who served in the Great War, all too conscious here in Verdun of the presence of that great company of the dead. It is my earnest prayer that such cruel and destructive madness shall never again overtake mankind. And so it goes on. Who could possibly object?

10th May 1939

Forwood says HRH's broadcast appears to have sunk without a trace in England. As does Maxi Finto. Winnie Gulliver saw the paperweight he gave me. She said, "Oh, you got one of those, too. He must have had dozens made. He must have dug up half of Uruguay."

I said, "Paraguay."

"Paraguay, Uruguay," she said. "I'm sure the stuff in our paperweights came from no farther away than the Bois de Vincennes."

I don't know what to think.

Elsie Mendl is going to give a birthday party for Wally at Villa Trianon. Wally has given me the job of pointing HRH in the direction of a diamond pendant she's seen at Cartier. It would do either for her birthday or for their anniversary.

12th May 1939

Violet continues to be obstructive. She claims Rory has to go to Felicity Massingham's ball during June Leave, and Flora has three teeth to be filled. Just because *she's* never been to Paris is really no reason to prevent her children broadening their horizons.

18th May 1939

Sacks of mail have started arriving for HRH, applauding his Verdun speech. Letter after letter makes the same point. No one wants another war. HRH has spoken to the ordinary little people of America and the Dominions and struck a chord, and if they're not prepared to fight, there can't be a war. QDE, as Danforth Brumby used to say.

23rd May 1939

Wally and HRH are going to Candé for their second anniversary. Returning, as Dudley Forwood puts it, to the scene of the crime.

4th June 1939

Such sad news from London. Philip Sassoon is dead. Violet telephoned to tell me. He had an infected throat, and instead of taking his doctor's advice and resting in bed, he went out in the rain and developed pneumonia. I can hardly believe it. Circumstances may have made us drift apart, but I shall always remember him as the most darling host. That tall glass of ice-cold mimosa that would appear at the very moment one's evening bath had been run. Those perfect chocolate truffles he'd have placed on one's night table. How he'd sit cross-legged in his cashmere socks and say, "Now! Whom shall we rrrip to shrrreds next?" The way he'd give you anything, *anything* you admired.

Violet says Sybil is devastated. Well, so am I, and Violet seemed in low spirits herself. They're calling up all twenty-year-olds for military training. She says Ulick is raring to go, but at times like these she begins to wish she'd had all daughters.

I said, "But Melhuish knows so many useful people in the Guards. If it should come to anything serious, I'm sure it could be arranged that the boy doesn't get sent into anything too dangerous."

She said, "Melhuish would never ask any such thing. Melhuishes do their duty."

I was only trying to cheer her up. Anyway, Ulick's very handy with a gun.

6th June 1939

Wally and HRH are back from Candé. She got a gold cobra bangle with sapphire eyes, so now she's fretting as to whether she'll get the desired diamond for her birthday. I said, "Well, I delivered the suggestion. I can do no more. I have more serious things on my mind."

"Such as?" she said.

I said, "Such as the death of an old friend and before his time."

She said, "I don't recall Sassoon being all that much of a friend. He dropped you soon enough. You should follow my rule, Maybell. Never forgive, never forget."

Well, *I* have some very happy memories of Philip.

7th June 1939

Kitty Rothschild says it's not done to send flowers to Jewish funerals. Too late. They're already sent.

10th June 1939

HRH says it doesn't seem appropriate to splash out on diamonds when the world is so full of uncertainty. He's bought Wally a pair of tourmaline earclips for her birthday. Very pretty, but a long, long way from a diamond.

Elsie Mendl wants to host Wally's birthday.

19th June 1939

Wally is forty-three again. Gave her an antique crystal scent spray filled with Joy.

She wasn't wearing her tourmaline earclips. She said, "Some messenger you turned out to be. Well, no matter. I'll buy that pendant myself."

Precisely. That's always the best way with husbands and jewels.

Tonight, to Villa Trianon.

20th June 1939

Elsie had boys with flaming brands standing at the iron gates to her estate, and that was only the start of it. She'd had the whole garden lit, and a sprung dance floor, and two champagne fountains. There were tumbling dwarves, and fire-eaters, and a darling baby elephant pulling a cart with Wally's birthday cake. Elsie's people seem to be able to get their hands on absolutely anything.

Wore my coral mousseline and a single strand of black pearls.

I can't say Wally was very grateful for Elsie's efforts. She seems more and more to regard all these entertainments as no more than her due.

Of course, Elsie loves giving parties anyway, and Charlie Mendl just smiles and coughs up.

24th June 1939

Fruity Metcalfe is going to come down to Cannes in August, but without Baba. She doesn't want to leave her family. He says London is all on edge about Germany and Italy and the Russians. He says the best thing would be if we make an alliance with the Russians while we can. He says that might cool Germany's Polish ambitions.

Wednesday, to La Croe. The Crokers are worried about remaining in Europe, and the Cavetts have canceled. Hattie may come, but without Judson. He can't get away. As for Adolf Hitler, I'll bet he's sitting up in the Berghof, eating cookies and laughing at all these nervous nellies. I'll bet *he's* taking a vacation.

1st July 1939, La Croe

So many villas seem to be empty. I think it's going to be a very dull summer. Daisy Fellowes is undeterred, however. Her yacht should be off Cannes in time for our July 4th chicken fry. She has Ludo and Fancie Fannulloni and Clarice Sfogginomi on board. Lily Drax-Pfaffenhof is motoring over with the Milwaukee Gunters, so at least there'll be a golf partner for HRH.

Kath Rogers is stockpiling canned goods.

6th July 1939

Maxi Finto has been back in France since April and never once called. We went to the casino after the chicken fry, and the first thing I saw was Mrs. Woolworth with Lucien Ecornifleur on one arm and Maxi on the other.

"May-*belle*!" he said. "It's been too long." Sweat on his top lip.

I said, "I'd expected a report on my investments by now."

He said, "I've had it in mind, but I was waiting, hoping for an upturn. Business is very flat just now, because of uncertainties, you understand? Because of the situation? But this isn't the time or the place. Lunch, tomorrow? No, tomorrow isn't good. I'll telephone."

He never looked me in the eye for one moment.

Wally said, "What's bitten you tonight? You look like you lost a dollar and found a dime."

She wouldn't understand even if I told her. It really isn't about the money.

Alix and Henri Piston-LeRupin are just down the road. They've managed to rent La Garoupe for a knockdown price, the season is so dead here.

12th July 1939

Rory's eighteenth birthday. Got a telephone connection with no trouble at all, but he wasn't at home. He was attending a tennis party at the Boddie-Fultons. Poor boy. He hates ball games. Violet says he can't wait to get started at Dartmouth. Of all the times to be joining the military!

Lightfoot is apparently still in a depression. Ulick is going to Drumcanna with him ahead of everyone else. They're going to try and rig up some way of him managing in the butts. I'm sure there's something safer than shooting he could do with only one arm. Netting butterflies, perhaps.

Boss and Ethel have braved it to La Croe. Ethel says if the world is going to end, let it happen while she's sunning herself beneath a blue Mediterranean sky. Hear, hear!

Alix Piston-LeRupin says she thought there was some kind of prohibition against Maxi Finto going into business again, after the cocoa-bean scandal.

I said, "What cocoa-bean scandal?"

She said, "I don't remember the details. I think it involved Costa Rica. But I do know there was an American woman who took quite a beating, and Maxi did a disappearing act for a while. Why? Have you sustained damage?"

I told her, it's pocket change to me. I'm not having this trumpeted around. For one thing, if it got back to Baltimore, I'd never hear the end of it from Randolph Putnam.

18th July 1939

Dudley Forwood has been told to report to his regiment. Wally said, "You can't leave until Fruity gets here to take over."

Forwood said, "I don't think you understand. I have to follow orders." She said, "You certainly do. *Our* orders. You're to stay here until His Royal Highness releases you."

I said, "Wally, you're putting Dudley in a very difficult position."

She said, "Do you think so? Then let me reconsider. Yes, on second thought, Forwood, pack your bags and go. You were never much use anyway."

I didn't mean to make things worse. Forwood says I didn't.

"Merely clarified things," he said. "Thank you, Maybell."

19th July 1939

Forwood was gone by the time we got up this morning. Faces like thunder, but neither HRH nor Wally has said a word.

25th July 1939

Fruity has arrived, and not a moment too soon, because now David's valet has been called for military service. Fruity says it's likely to get worse. He says von Ribbentrop is in Moscow, smooching with the Russians. Well, he is a very good dancer.

3rd August 1939

The Rogerses' gardeners have been called up. Kath says the same thing will happen to everyone, but Wally says we're a special case.

Wally and Hattie had words. One of the terriers chewed Hattie's tennis bat.

10th August 1939

Call-up papers for two of our footmen and three of our gardeners. Well, we'll just have to get staff from somewhere that isn't preparing for war. I always thought it most inconvenient anyhow, employing people who pretend not to speak English, and I'm sure there are plenty of American boys who'd jump at the chance to work for the Royal Windsors. Wally told HRH to make some telephone calls, but so far he doesn't seem to have made any headway.

She said, Charlie Bedaux has a Hawaiian nut plantation they may buy.

I said, "Does this mean we'll be moving to Hawaii?"

"Yes," she said, "if that's where we have to go for staff we can call our own."

Hattie said, "What nonsense. Come back to London with me, Maybell. Wally seems to be losing her grip on reality."

I don't know. They say Hawaii has a very agreeable climate. Hattie says she wouldn't buy a bicycle pump from Charlie Bedaux.

Herman says we should all keep locked canisters of gasoline in our garages, in case of shortages.

13th August 1939

Fruity says the Commons may be recalled early. If Germany moves against Poland, it's war.

18th August 1939

A letter from Violet. Ena Spain hasn't risked the trip to Drumcanna this year. Rory is crewing for his Uncle Salty off Dorsetshire. Lightfoot is crazed with pain and threw a bottle of scotch at Ulick. Well, there's been many an occasion when I've felt like doing the same. Ulick quite invites it. As long as Lightfoot hasn't turned on poor Doopie. They were such sweetness and light the last time I saw them together. And Flora has entered womanhood. So now her troubles begin. I do hope Violet has told her about boys. The child is still so natural and spontaneous.

23rd August 1939

The wily Russians have made an accord with Germany. Herman says this means Poland is done for. HRH has sent a wire to Hitler, reminding him of the lovely tea they enjoyed together and their agreement that there was only one enemy to be vanquished: Communism.

Boss and Ethel are leaving tomorrow. Also Fruity. He says the writing is on the wall.

24th August 1939

Fruity is gone. He leaves behind a large void. When Wally and I came back from shopping, HRH was in the morning room, trying to pluck a tune on his ukulele.

26th August 1939

HRH received a telegram of reply from Hitler. It said Germany had never wished to quarrel with England, but if, as it appears, England now chooses to pick a war with Germany, he'll have no choice but to respond. The housekeeper says there's already a run on blackout material.

1st September 1939

This morning, while Wally and I were having our nails done and HRH was up on The Bridge, scanning for battleships, Germany invaded Poland. Also, an anti-aircraft battery arrived and proceeded to dig latrines upwind of our bathing pavilion without so much as a by-your-leave. When war approaches, courtesy flies out the window.

3rd September 1939

War. It has finally come to it. Freddie got a call through to us last evening to say things were coming to a head and the House of Commons would be meeting this morning; the first time in all its history it has sat on a Sunday. He said the only question still being debated was how long Germany should be given to withdraw from Poland. The French are suggesting a week, Neville Chamberlain thought a day or two, but his Cabinet wanted an end to it. So, Hitler was given until eleven o'clock this morning, twelve noon here. We went up to HRH's Bridge to listen on his wireless.

Chamberlain said he'd asked Mr. Hitler to undertake to withdraw his forces from Polish territory, but no such assurances had been received, indeed German tanks had moved deeper into Poland, so, Great Britain was now at war with Germany.

HRH has been trying to get through to Bertie York all afternoon. He's going to offer to return to England immediately, at the service of King and country.

Wally says we can't leave until the best things have been wrapped and stored.

4th September 1939

We woke to the news that France has fallen into line with Britain, so, we're at war here, too. HRH is suddenly full of pep. He thinks it'll be a short war, but long enough for him to make his mark again. He spoke to King Bertie late last night and will be meeting with Walter Monckton in Paris, to discuss war jobs.

Tried to get through to Carlton Gardens, without success, but did speak with Flora at South Audley Street. She said, "We're at war, Aunt Bayba! Isn't it exciting! The sirens sounded yesterday, but we didn't get bobbed yet."

She said Lightfoot was having his Burgundy wines reorganized so as to make room for an air-raid shelter and that he'd gone to offer his services as a recruiting officer. Who knows, perhaps this new war will force him to buck up.

We got cut off before I could ask about Rory.

The silver and the smaller paintings have been taken down to a bank vault in town. Wally and I expect to be in Paris by Thursday at the latest.

5th September 1939

Kath and Herman came over to say good-bye. They may go back to the States, unless it's all over before they've had time to get a passage.

6th September 1939, Meurice Hotel, Paris

Paris doesn't look any different. The Pigalle is still open. The Communists are still picketing the factories up in Sentier. The front desk seems a little busier with people checking out, but that's about all.

To Samaritaine. Wally says we must stock up on face powder.

7th September 1939

We're all going to England. Monckton came to Boulevard Suchet this morning with the good news. There are several possible war jobs lined up for HRH, and they're sending a boat for us early next week.

Wally said, "Good. There are things I need to buy in London."

Monckton said, "Oh. I don't think they visualize this as an opportunity for shopping, ma'am."

She said, "They? Who are *they*?"

He said, "Well, the Navy, I suppose. And Their Majesties. If you were to accompany the Duke, I'm afraid you won't be received."

HRH said, "If that's the case, darling, you must stay here with Maybell. You know my feelings on this."

She said, "No, David, my place is at your side. This is war."

I'm not sure whether she meant the Germans or the New Bunch.

8th September 1939

Not only will Wally not be received, no provision has been made for accommodations while we're in England. We can't even use Fort Belvedere. But Freddie and Pips have offered us rooms at

Halkin Street, and the Metcalfes have offered us their place in the country. You find out who your friends are.

Dickie Mountbatten is picking us up from Cherbourg on Tuesday.

13th September 1939, Halkin Street

We docked just after eleven last night. Everything was blacked out, but HRH knew exactly where he was. He said, "This is where I said good-bye to England. This is the jetty I sailed from, on my way to Enzesfeld."

There was a small guard of honor, and a band played "God Save the King," but there was no welcome party. Just Baba Metcalfe with two cars. She'd made reservations at the best hotel Portsmouth can offer, but just before we disembarked, a signal had come through that Admiralty accommodation was being made available for HRH and Wally for one night. So, Baba and I were the beneficiaries. We took the pick of the rooms she'd booked, and poor Wally had to sleep in a Navy cot!

Baba grows on me. She's never concealed that HRH has been a disappointment to her, and she finds Wally common, but she's still doing everything she can to ease their homecoming, which is more than can be said for some. They didn't even bother to send them a car. She drove me up to town this morning and was fuming about the war work being offered HRH. There's something in civil defense, in Wales, or a desk job at GHQ in France. He's leaning toward Wales.

Baba said, "But he must get back into uniform. He got a Military Cross in the last lot, for heaven's sake."

Pips is glad to have me stay. Freddie's practically sleeping at the Commons. HRH is seeing the King today. Wally's been advised to stay down in Sussex and rock no boats.

14th September 1939

Freddie says HRH should take the civil defense job. He said, "They'll be able to live here, and Wally can be seen to take part in the war effort. By the time it's over, she'll have won the good opinion of even her greatest enemies."

Baba's been trying to rustle up people to go down to Sussex and keep Wally entertained. Hattie went down for lunch today, but a lot of people won't go anywhere, worried about gasoline shortages. We're supposed to carry gas masks, but they really don't look right with anything except a uniform.

Everything seems calm at Carlton Gardens. Dear Rory was home on twenty-four-hour furlough from Dartmouth, very smart in his midshipman's uniform. Melhuish is running an Air Raid Precaution post until such time as he's called from the Guards' Reserve, but he thinks the danger of raids by German bombers is greatly overrated. He says the Germans are far too busy with the Russians, dividing up Poland like a sponge cake, to bother flattening St. James's. I agree. Sounding those sirens unnecessarily only makes the servants hysterical.

Ulick is training artillery recruits, whereabouts undisclosed, and Violet has offered herself to the Navy. Her age is against her, but she has top brass like Sybil Cholmondeley and Salty Laird rooting for her, so she thinks she's bound to get something. I must say, it does have the best uniform. A good-quality doeskin skirt and a very stylish tricorn hat. I wonder if they'll make her cut her hair?

We parted more affectionately than I ever remember. War does so improve people.

Rory said, "Transport alongside, ma'am!" when my car came to pick me up. He almost caught me with his trick cigarette pack.

Tea at Fuller's the very moment this silly war is over!

15th September 1939

HRH is apparently not required to defend Wales, after all. He's to be attached to the British Military Mission at Vincennes with the rank of Major General. Fruity will be equerry. So it's back to France, as soon as a destroyer can be made available.

Lightfoot smelled of drink at eleven this morning. He said, "I'm a goddamned wreck. I wish they'd left me to rot on Hill 666."

His arm hurts him more now he doesn't have it than when he did. He said, "I've become the completest shit to live with, Maybell. What am I, Flora?"

"The completest shit," she said. I've noticed a lot of people are starting to use language.

Doopie smiled, as always, but she had tears in her eyes.

She said, "Bedda gum home, Bayba. Bedda gum live here."

I said, "Can't they give Lightfoot something for the pain?"

"Wizgy," she said. "Lodsa wizgy."

Flora came out with me to the car. She said, "Mummy says I have to go to Drumcanna, in case of an invasion. It's too beastly. I haven't even seen any bombs yet."

She's really getting to be quite pretty.

Freddie says passers-by cheered HRH when he went to Downing Street to call on Mr. Chamberlain.

Pips back late from Sussex. She says Wally's running the Metcalfes' elderly help ragged and compiling lists of things belonging to HRH that are still in storage and might usefully be taken to Paris. Pips predicts we'll be traveling back with a great deal more luggage than we brought.

19th September 1939

There'll be a boat available to take us back to France tomorrow night. Wally sent Fruity to York House to liberate some of the wines left behind, which are now ready for drinking. She said, "May as well get something worthwhile out of the trip." She's very upset, because the New Bunch won't even give HRH back his old honorary colonelcy.

21st September 1939, Meurice Hotel, Paris

Pitched and tossed all the way back to Cherbourg, and there was nowhere to lie down and die. If Adolf Hitler had sent a submarine to hunt us down, they would have met no resistance from me. I hope Rory understands what he's letting himself in for.

30th September 1939

We now have good supplies of stockings, soap, and hair color stored away. Wally says there's no point in stockpiling scent, because it evaporates. Anyway, we may still get an early peace. Three weeks of war, and we haven't heard a single shot fired.

3rd October 1939

Great excitement. Wally and I have volunteered for the Red Cross, and Main Bocher is going to make our costumes. I must say, war seems to suit HRH, too. He looks very well in his uniform, and Wally says he was up and gone by eight-thirty this morning, even though he doesn't really need to be in till ten.

5th October 1939

HRH has decided to put away his needlepoint for the duration and is knitting instead. Scarves for the troops. Next week, he'll be away, visiting fortifications. Fermont, Bois Karre, Thionville. It's all top secret.

Charlie and Fern to dinner. The Piston-LeRupins chucked. Winnie Gulliver thinks they've bolted for Switzerland. Winnie has signed up for the Red Cross, too, but at the moment, she goes every day to help with Elsie Mendl's comfort-kit drive. Wally and I may go with her tomorrow.

8th October 1939

Everyone was at Trianon with their sleeves rolled, even Sylvie Vieille-Soiffarde, and at an hour she's never normally conscious. Cigarettes, razor blades, socks, candy, all needing to be packed up for the soldier boys. It was the greatest fun.

18th October 1939

Harry Gloucester is being sent all the way to France to inspect British troops. Wally's steaming. As she says, HRH should have been asked to do it. He's on the spot and he's senior. HRH says he may go along anyway. He doesn't have anything else much on next week.

23rd October 1939

Fruity's getting it in the neck from all quarters. From the Commander-in-Chief's people for allowing HRH to turn up at Arras uninvited. From Harry Gloucester's people for allowing HRH to elbow in and take a salute intended for his brother. And from Wally for allowing him to wear suede oxfords with his uniform. But nothing seems to ruffle him.

30th October 1939

Our Red Cross uniforms are ready. Very fetching. Blue wool A-line skirt with a front pleat, belted jacket, white cotton shirt, and red necktie. We're going to be delivering supplies to hospitals, and Winnie Gulliver has been assigned as our driver.

Wally got a letter from Ernest. He and Mary Kirk have had a baby boy. They've named him Henry. He was born in London, but they're sending him to the States for safekeeping until the war has blown over. I hope they've chosen their baby-minder with care. I hope Ernest remembers what happened to Thelma Furness's sister Gloria.

3rd November 1939

Yesterday, we did our first hospital run. Winnie picked us up before first light, six hours driving, a two-hour break while the supplies were unloaded and we visited some French wounded, then six hours back. The roads are full of army convoys, so it's very slow going. More of the same next week.

10th November 1939

No sleep. We had two deliveries to make, one to a unit near Sedan, so even with Winnie's size 13 on the gas pedal, we didn't have a hope of getting back to Paris before morning. They put us up in nurses' quarters. The guns were going all night. I didn't feel frightened though. We talked in the dark, and Wally made us laugh with her impersonations of Queen Cotton Candy and King Bertie Bunny. It was rather like being back in the dormitory at Oldfields.

28th November 1939

Three runs to the Line this week. Invalid potties and Christmas candy. Nothing much happening. Winnie says Hitler intends to bore us into surrendering.

20th December 1939

The Lazslo Melchiors are giving a blackout party.

27th December 1939

Such a dreary Christmas. HRH decreed a period of austerity, so my gift from them was a book of Great Art, which I know was presented to them by the von Welzcecks, because they signed it. Wally's gift was to have her baguette-cut diamonds reset. They're going into a necklace with some Burmese rubies she's acquired. We managed to get oysters, but the girl Wally has cooking for her ruined the guinea fowl, so we had to fill up on cheese and almonds.

Apparently, they're going to start rationing butter and sugar in England. Poor Flora. She's going to miss her "gake." I shall try to send her an emergency parcel. I wonder if the Ladurée patisserie would ship macaroons.

Kenny Opdyke still has a rash from wearing black boot polish to the Lazslo Melchiors' party.

8th January 1940

Deep snow. We were supposed to do a Red Cross run, but it was only pajamas for hospitals up the line, so we're waiting for better conditions.

20th January 1940

Colder yet. Have worn my Red Cross greatcoat all day. Even Wally's having difficulty getting fuel delivered. She says she may close up Boulevard Suchet and move back into the Meurice. I'm sure they'll get a good rate. No one is traveling.

10th February 1940

The Army don't seem to have anything for HRH to do out at Vincennes anymore, and he's run out of yarn for his knitting. He says he may resume writing his memoirs. Wally says, if he wants to make himself useful, he can get the French Army to give us back our chef. Nothing much seems to be happening in this foolish war, so the man may as well be here, where he's appreciated.

Fruity is very frustrated. He said, "Frankly, Maybell, I'd like to be a good deal nearer to the Hun than a Paris drawing room."

27th February 1940

The French Army refuses to release our chef. Wally's told Fruity to resubmit the request at a higher level. Those Army boys must be eating well. Meanwhile, no one in Paris has the means of putting on a decent dinner.

Winnie Gulliver is organizing a Red Cross benefit. It'll be at the Bobino Club, and little Edna Piaf has promised to sing. Something to look forward to at last.

A letter from Violet mailed on December 29th to tell me she made First Officer and has a desk job at the Admiralty. Also that Flora and Doopie had just left for Drumcanna, to prepare it for use as a convalescent home. So, I don't suppose Flora ever received her macaroons. Lightfoot is helping at an NAAFI canteen at Victoria Station. Rory and Ulick both on active service, so we're not allowed to know where they are.

9th March 1940

Weak sunshine. HRH has been able to get in a little golf with Ambassador Bullitt.

We may go to La Croe for Easter. Fruity said, "If that's the case, I'd very much like to try and get to England, to see Baba."

Wally said, "Absolutely not. David needs you."

Fruity looked so disappointed.

I said, "Surely we can spare him?"

"We?" she said. "No, *we* can't spare him. Things could flare up at any moment, and the Duke of Windsor can't be caught without his ADC. Not that this is any of your business, Maybell."

15th March 1940

The Russians have taken Finland, and are expected to take Sweden, too. Fruity says Germany will probably take Norway and Denmark, Italy will take Greece, and civilization as we know it will be dead. At this rate, we'll all end up back in Baltimore.

The cherry blossom is out in the Bois de Boulogne.

17th March 1940

We're not going to La Croe, after all. Wally says she can't face seeing what the Army may have done to her lawns.

23rd March 1940

Easter Saturday, but you'd never know. We took a station wagon full of plasma up to a depot near the Line yesterday, and didn't get back till midnight. I nodded off after Epernay, and when I woke up, I heard Winnie saying, "Maybell's jolly game, Wally, sticking with you through all your ups and downs. She must miss her family."

Wally said, "She doesn't really have family. Just a pair of sisters. She's had much more fun with me. She's traveled, met important figures."

Winnie said, "She's such a willing pair of hands, and such a cheerful attitude. You'd be lost without her, I'm sure."

Wally said, "Dear old Maybell. She has her uses. And, of course, more money than she knows what to do with. I think of her as our little Paymaster General. She's always good for picking up the check."

Paymaster General, indeed! And I do, too, have family. *She's* the one who has no one in the world except HRH and me, and if she doesn't watch out, she won't even have me.

They say things aren't going so well for our sailor boys in the North Sea. I do hope Salty Laird is keeping my Rory out of it.

12th April 1940

Fruity was right. Germany has invaded Denmark. Winnie Gulliver predicts our Red Cross runs will liven up now.

To Maxim's. Came: Sylvie Vieille-Soiffarde, the Esterhazys, and the Dimitri Shapaleffs, who are apparently not the same kind of Russians as the ones who betrayed us. All we could get to eat was leek soup and horse steaks.

22nd April 1940

Everyone is closing up their houses. Didi Grimaldi's gone, the Piston-LeRupins have disappeared, the Lazslo Melchiors are heading for Switzerland, and Lucien Ecornifleur decamped without settling his hotel bill. We're doing an inventory of Wally's jewels.

11th May 1940

Germany has invaded Holland and Belgium. Fruity says, France will be next.

Kitty Rothschild's gone, heading for Spain. So is Kenny Opdyke, and without saying good-bye. Wally's been screeching all day. At HRH, for taking the first job he was offered instead of sticking out for something in London. At Fruity, for being Fruity. At me, for not having twenty pairs of hands. Go to the bank. Find a new manicurist. Get our furs out of storage. Call Maples about storing our furniture.

I said, "We should just close the shutters and leave."

She said, "And leave our good things lying around? There'll be nothing left when we come back."

I said, "The Germans are collecting countries, not furniture."

She said, "It's not the Germans I'm concerned about. It's the French. They're all resentful little revolutionaries under the skin. We'll go when I've made my property secure."

12th May 1940

Neville Chamberlain has resigned, and the new Prime Minister is Winston Churchill. That toothless old scowler who was our neighbor the summer we took Rock Cholmondeley's villa. Wally doesn't like him one bit.

According to the wireless, the south coast of England was bombed last night. Wally said, "Serves them right, after the way they've treated us."

I could see a vein throbbing in Fruity's temple. He left the room, and HRH trotted after him, flicking a cigarette lighter on and off.

I said, "That was an unforgivable thing to say. Fruity has family over there. I do. David does."

She said, "They have bomb shelters. Anyway, I've no time for sentimentality. If they hadn't forced David off the throne, they wouldn't be at war now. If he'd still been King, it would never have come to this. What goes around comes around, Maybell."

I always hated that expression.

She said, "Now, why don't you do something useful? Go and draw out lots of cash. Get everything they have."

I said, "Do you mean everything *I* have?"

She gave me a very long, cool look.

16th May 1940

Wally and I have parted company, and on very bitter terms. Fruity came with the news that the Germans had broken through the Line, which means that Paris is certain to fall. Wally was still in bed. HRH called an emergency meeting.

He said, "Maybell, you and Fruity must take Wally and the dogs to safety. Go to La Croe, help her secure the house, and then proceed to Biarritz, ready for a fast getaway."

Fruity studied his feet for a moment. He said, "I'm sorry, sir, but for the first time in all our years together, I'm unable to comply. I've decided to offer myself for active service."

HRH said, "What do you mean! You didn't ask me."

Fruity said, "No, sir. I decided on my way here. Things are hotting up, and the Army can surely find a better use for me than escorting Her Grace."

HRH left the room without speaking.

Fruity said, "I hope you understand, Maybell. I'll stay here with His Royal Highness until I get my orders, but I'm really not cut out for watering dogs and burying Wally's silver. You'll have your detective with you, and I'm sure your driver can handle himself. I don't think you'll be in any danger. I hope you get back to the States and have a decent war."

I might have gone with her, if she'd behaved halfway civilly to Fruity. If she hadn't screamed at the man from Maples after he'd been so obliging about storage, and if Pookie hadn't puddled against my favorite needlepoint purse. But everything just seemed to come to a head.

I said, "I'm not coming, Wally. I'm going home."

She said, "You simpleton, the whole country is on the run. You won't get anywhere without my name to open doors."

I said, "I'll take my chances. Nothing's certain for any of us, so I may as well go where I'm appreciated."

She said, "I've more than shown my appreciation. The places I've taken you. If it weren't for me, you'd still be sitting in Wilton Place."

I said, "And if it weren't for your little Paymaster General, you'd still be in Marylebone with a veneer sideboard."

HRH peered in to see what the shouting was about. He withdrew as soon as he saw her face.

She said, "Off you go then, Maybell. It's really no more than I expected. I've grown accustomed to betrayal."

I came back to the Meurice. Very strange to have no duties all of a sudden, no little errands to run. The place is almost empty, except for military. Winnie Gulliver is trying to get some gasoline. She thinks we can still make it to the coast.

20th May 1940

They say Rheims has fallen. Fruity says my best bet is to try and get transport west. He and HRH have patched things up, but he says the old warmth has gone and my name is now unmentionable.

Fruity said, "You know David. Wally's happiness is paramount. Make an enemy of her, and you're pretty much finished with him. But it's a loss I expect you can bear."

21st May 1940

Winnie still scouting for gas.

Fruity says Wally reached La Croe safely. Well, that's something. He'd quite expected a signal that the Navy were on their way to pick up HRH and take him to England, but his hopes are now fading.

He said, "He'd probably refuse to go without Wally anyway. I sometimes think all sense flew out the window the day he met her."

22nd May 1940

No gasoline, but Winnie may have found a bicycle.

23rd May 1940

Fern Bedaux has a van leaving tomorrow, carrying her linens across into Spain. There'll be room for me and Padmore, if we take no more than one small bag each.

Fruity says it's our best chance. The Germans are nearly at Abbeville, so if Fern's wagon doesn't turn up, we'll just have to put out German flags and hope for the best.

Fruity himself is in a state of bafflement. When he called HRH for the day's orders, the butler told him HRH had already left, for Biarritz.

He kept saying, "I must have misunderstood. He's still seconded to the British Mission, after all. David would never have abandoned his post."

Of course, he would. He gave up an empire to chase after Wally, so he'd certainly give up a little make-work Army job. GHQ has told Fruity to fall back to the nearest port. Ever the gentleman, he offered to wait and see me safely away, but there's really no need. I can look after myself. I'm the great survivor.

8th January 1946, Sweet Air, Baltimore

What a treat to crack open a nice, clean copybook and resume my diary with happy news. Susan Violet Melhuish Smith was born on New Year's Day. Melhuish says Flora is doing well and the baby looks like Violet, but men aren't good at judging these things. I hope for the child's sake she favors me a little. I've told Melhuish to make sure she's given cod liver oil and is kept to a routine. He says Doopie's back in her element with a baby in the house, but we can't allow another generation to grow up saying "gake" and "gustard," and I don't want Lightfoot cradling her with his game arm and dropping her on her head. The sooner I get there the better.

12th January 1946

Randolph has pulled every string he knows, but the earliest passage we can get is March 4th. That damned war. It's supposed to be over, but you'd never know it. Pips says the shortages are getting worse in England. Gasoline, clothing. Even bread's rationed now, and she hasn't seen an egg in months.

Good news for Wally though. I see the New York Dress Institute just named her as Best Dressed Woman of 1945. Well, now she's achieved that she'll stop at nothing to stay there. She and HRH have had a pretty good war of it from what one hears, sitting it out in the Bahamas while the Germans kept guard over their silver. They say their houses came through unscathed, apart from a few landmines in the lawns at La Croe. Well, they'll soon get some sappers in to clear those. Ethel Croker heard that Wenner-Gren, the Electrolux man, is their new best friend and he has billions. I'm sure he'll take care of everything.

28th January 1946

Judson Erlanger is in town to bury his father.

30th January 1946

Judson to tea. He says HRH has been in London, visiting his mother and angling for a new job, preferably Ambassador to Washington, but he's not going to get it.

3rd February 1946

Ethel Croker has written to Wally, hoping to rekindle the friendship when she and Boss resume their European vacations. She says I should do the same and let bygones be bygones. She said, "We all had a war, Maybell. Everyone's having to adjust to missing faces, even Wally. Charlie Bedaux's dead. Lily. Kenny Opdyke. Count Ciano."

Well, Charlie took an overdose, so that doesn't count, and I doubt Wally'll be grieving for Ciano. He took a great big piece of her Chinese history with him when he went to the wall. Anyway, they were just people she knew. They're nothing compared to our losses.

Dear Rory on the *Repulse* off Malaya. He'd be twenty-three by now, just starting out. Looking forward to demobilization and a nice tea at Lyon's Corner House with his Aunt Maybell. They say Violet never missed a day at her desk, not even the day the telegram came. She went right through to '44, till a rocket bomb hit the Air Ministry. It's all so unfair. She wasn't even working at the Air Ministry. She was just walking down the Aldwych, minding her own business, then gone. She didn't even live to hear that Ulick got a medal.

So, let Ethel pick up the threads, if she must. I can't imagine what Wally and I would find to say to each other.

10th February 1946

Pips says HRH was greeted by cheering crowds when he went to Marlborough House to see the old Queen. Probably all arranged by loyal old Fruity. Metcalfe's Rent-a-Throng!

1st March 1946

We sail on Monday, and now it comes to it, I feel quite apprehensive. Six years since I waved London good-bye. War seemed then like it might be rather an adventure. Pips says I'll hardly know the place. She says it's not just that London *looks* different, but the whole feeling of the place has changed, too. The bombs have stopped, but the gaiety hasn't returned. That will be because the Socialists are in. But as Randolph says, we're going because we're needed. Someone has to give some direction to Susan Violet's upbringing before the rot sets in.

10th March 1946, Carlton Gardens, London

Susan Violet is adorable and has my nose. She has signs of the Melhuish coloring, but we can hope for that to pass. Flora seems contented with motherhood after a pixilated fashion. She goes for hours on end without visiting the nursery, as though it slips her mind that she has a baby, but she'll get the hang of things eventually. At least she's not likely to turn into the kind of mother who keeps running out the door to Leper committees.

Her husband is in Lancashire, visiting with his people. As far as I'm concerned, it will be no loss to us if he stays there. A convalescent home is no place to choose a husband. Either he'll remain an invalid, which will soon become boresome, or he'll recover and start throwing his weight around in all kinds of unforeseen ways.

Melhuish says none of it matters if Flora's happy. He says the boy seems a decent type, although he doesn't have a penny to his name. Well, that's for me to worry about, not poor Violet. I believe Melhuish has gone soft in the head without her.

Pips was right about London. Buildings gone, people tired and pinched, nothing in the shops. She's very cheery, considering Freddie lost his seat. He has a few directorships and may try his hand at pig-farming. All in all, they got off rather lightly. Just a nephew of Freddie's killed at Arnhem, and they hardly knew him.

She and Freddie didn't try to see HRH when he was in town, and he made no effort to see them. Wally, apparently, had the wisdom not to show her face in London. I'm sure I never want to see her again. Too much has happened. Violet dead. Rory dead. And no matter which way I look at it, I can't help but think it all comes back to Wally.

If she hadn't been so anxious to escape from Baltimore and put her boardinghouse days behind her, she'd never have married Win Spencer, never have gone to Coronado, never met Benny Thaw, never happened upon him again in London.

No Benny, no Connie, no Thelma, no Prince of Wales, no Abdication. And that could have made all the difference. One thing about HRH, he got along well with Hitler. If he'd still been King, something could have been worked out, he'd have kept us out of that terrible war. But Bessie Wallis Warfield pulled one stick from the pile, and then everything came tumbling down.

We've all had to pay for it, but Wally and David always were slow to reach for the check. Still, as Randolph says, we have to look ahead. We have a new generation to think of now.

When Great Aunt Maybell left Paris on 24th May 1940, she joined the flood of refugees trying to stay ahead of the advancing German army. She rode in a laundry van as far as La Rochelle, and then reached Santander on the north coast of Spain by coal boat. In Santander, she was advised that her best chance was to make for Lisbon, where she arrived, almost penniless, on the last day of July. It was only thanks to the help of her friend Kitty Rothschild and a timely wire to Pan Am from Great Uncle Randolph that she was able to secure a seat on a Dixie Clipper bound for New York. As she learnt later, nearing the Azores, they passed directly overhead the steamship that was carrying the Duke and Duchess of Windsor to Bermuda, en route to his new job as Governor of the Bahamas. It was the closest she ever came to being in their company again.

When eventually she got back to Baltimore, Great Aunt Maybell rewarded Randolph Putnam for his patience and loyalty. She married him the day before Pearl Harbour. She once told me it had been no great love match, and she'd done it as much as anything to spite her stepson, Junior, but that with time she'd grown very fond of Randolph.

She said, "He wouldn't have suited me when I was younger, but after fifty, different things matter. And, of course, *he* got a very good deal. He couldn't run a place like Sweet Air without me. A man on his own, it was ridiculous. And if I hadn't taken charge after you were born, he'd never have known what it was to have a family."

I don't remember a single summer of my childhood when Great Aunt Maybell wasn't around from May to September, browbeating my mother and infuriating my Uncle Ulick. Wherever we were— London, Drumcanna, or, later, after we had to let Drumcanna go, at Canna Lodge—it was Great Aunt Maybell who had colour televisions installed, who ordered pork ribs when we had a larder full of grouse, who sent out to Harrold's, as she always insisted on calling it, for one bottle of Tabasco. Great Uncle Randolph, Grandpa Melhuish, Great Aunt Doopie, and Great Uncle Lightfoot would just hunker down somewhere with a bottle of whiskey and hope she'd forgotten them. Uncle Ulick always said it was a pity we couldn't choose our relations, and Great Aunt Maybell said it was the only point on which they had ever agreed.

She had just arrived for her annual visit, when we heard that the Duke of Windsor had died in Paris. That was 1972, the year I was expecting my first baby and Great Aunt Maybell was revving up for yet another attempt at raising the perfect child.

There was some difficulty over the date of the Duke's funeral, I remember, because it was coming up to the weekend of the Queen's Birthday Parade, and Trooping the Colour is one of those ceremonies that can't be postponed, not even for a man who once was king.

Grandpa Melhuish went to Windsor to pay his respects, one of the last outings he made, and Great Aunt Maybell gave him a letter of sympathy to deliver to the Duchess. She studied the photos in the next day's newspaper very closely and noted that the Duchess was wearing Givenchy and looked the very picture of grief.

"Poor Wally," I remember her saying. "She looks so lost. I suppose she did love him, after all."

Great Aunt Maybell herself died on 24th May 1986, one month to the day after the Duchess. She was in her eighty-ninth year. Her eyesight was poor, her heart was no longer strong, and she kept mainly to her rooms, but one of her greatest pleasures was to have a few choice obituaries read to her each evening, and news of the Duchess's death seemed to give her a new lease on life. In fact, she lost interest in any new deaths and preferred just to hear the Duchess's obituaries read over and over.

"Lies!" she said when the year of the Duchess's birth was given as 1896. "More lies!" she cried when it was said that the Duchess never gave a fig for titles. It was as though with each repetition she was hammering another nail in the coffin lid.

I read to her later than usual the evening of 23rd May, but she said she didn't feel ready for sleep. She wanted things brought to her from the drawers and dressers in her sitting room. Photographs she could no longer make out but knew by their different frames: she and two friends, all in feathered hats, taking a sleigh-ride in Garmisch; my Grandma Violet in her debutante gown; me on my first birthday. Then a crystal egg she'd shown me many times before, souvenir of some long-past house party.

She said, "Philip Sassoon gave me this. He hung it from an orange tree for me to find. Now *there* was a man who knew how to do Easter."

Silly things, too. A trick cigarette pack, once the property of my Uncle Rory; a threadbare, unidentifiable hand puppet—a pig, according to family legend, and one of my mother's childhood favourites; and finally, an assortment of exercise books filled with Great Aunt Maybell's loopy writing. They contained her diary begun in 1932 and kept faithfully until the war interrupted it. She had only taken it up again in 1946, to record my birth and make a few final entries.

"Susan," she said. "These are for you. These are history. But don't let your Uncle Ulick get his hands on them. He'll throw them on the fire."

I asked her if she wanted me to read to her from them.

"Oh no, honey," she said. "I already know how it goes. I was there."

Susan Melhuish Smith Erskine
CANNA LODGE
Aberdeenshire

LAURIE GRAHAM

The Unfortunates

What hope is there for Poppy Minkel? She has kinky hair, out-sticking ears, too yellow a neck and an appetite for fun, and her mother Dora despairs of ever finding her a husband, despite the Minkels' mustard fortune that seasons these dubious attractions. When Daddy disappears, Poppy's tendency to the unusual is quietly allowed to flourish. World War I opens new horizons. With never a moment of self-doubt, she invents her own extraordinary life in step with the unfolding century.

'A marvel. Graham's style is riveting; hilarious one-liners fall in quick succession'   *The Times*

'An irrepressible adventurer, Poppy is a comic combination of innocence and pluck, but although this is a brisk, breezy read, it's also a novel with serious bite'   *Daily Mail*

'Laurie Graham is a writer with a remarkably malleable comic voice'   *Guardian*

'Fresh, funny and smart, a novel that reels from the Titanic to jazz age'   *New York Observer*

'This wildly funny novel … is often on the brink of being a wildly tragic one'   *Sunday Times*

LAURIE GRAHAM

The Future Homemakers
of America

*Six women, their loves, laughter
and life-long friendship*

'Superlative. The writing sparkles from first to last'
DAVID ROBSON, *Sunday Telegraph*

'A wonderfully moving comedy' ALEX CLARK, *Red*

'My "leave-the-phone-off-the-hook" book of the year, in which we meet five American women with their husbands at a Norfolk airbase. While the guys patrol the skies, the gals cook chicken pot pie and sneak across the perimeter fence to meet up with Kath, who lives in the freezing fens. Together, they share love, laughter, triumphs and tragedies over forty years. One scene made me cry so hard I couldn't eat my lunch. Wonderful' VAL HENNESSY, *Daily Mail*

'Laugh-out-loud funny; intelligent; moving; has more delicious roll-off-the-tongue one-liners than Seinfield. One of those books you buy six copies of and send to all your old friends'
JULIE MORRICE, *Scotsman*

'Graham has wit and insight to match Nick Hornby, and the entertainment value of Helen Fielding'
NICOLETTE JONES, *Independent*

'Life-affirming. Pure pleasure' KATIE OWEN, *The Times*

ISBN: 0-00-723407-4

LAURIE GRAHAM

Mr Starlight

'What if Liberace had been born in Birmingham? As fresh as Graham's previous bestsellers ... so delicious'   *Guardian*

From the back streets of Birmingham and a tin bathtub to the glitter of America and gold-plated taps – that's the journey made by Selwyn 'Mr Starlight' Boff and his brother Cled. Cled tinkles the ivories while Sel slips on his gold lamé jacket and serenades the ladies. 'He could lift people out of themselves,' says Cled. 'That's why he got bookings while trained musicians went hungry.'

But times change. Everyone wants rock 'n' roll. Glamour is dead. And then there's family. You never know what skeletons they're going to start dragging out of your walk-in closets. Mr Starlight twinkles on, regardless.

'Touching, convincing and uplifting ... A wonderfully effervescent history of mid-20th-century show business'   *Daily Mail*

'Like Mr Starlight himself, this novel is pure entertainment'
                                                        Sunday Times